I0772351

# Kingdom of Masks and Mourning

## THE ONCE SEVEN KINGDOMS
### - BOOK ONE -

ABIGAIL EHRHARDT

# Content Warnings

This book contains subject matter that might be difficult for some readers, including death, violence, abusive relationships, domestic violence (one scene), sexual threat (one scene), a brief mentioning of stillbirth, and emotional manipulation.

For those who have learned the hard way how difficult it is to escape the cycle. I believe in you. Keep going.

# PART 1: SPARK

# Chapter 1

The gods-damned candle was mocking her. Again.

Analia sat on the edge of the turret's flat roof, glowering at the unlit candle before her.

"Nothing, huh?" she asked.

The candle did not respond. Analia, in turn, wondered when she'd started talking to it in the first place. Sighing, she leaned back on her elbows, taking in the rapidly lightening sky.

It was far from her first time on the turret roof. And clearly, it wasn't going to be her last.

"Your sole purpose is to burn," she said, prodding the wick with a finger. "You should want to be lit."

The white candle remained silent.

"You should know by now that we're not going anywhere until you do," she told it. "You might as well toughen up and burn."

Analia summoned all her concentration. She reached deep inside herself, calling the flames, touching her fingertip to the wick. And nothing happened.

"Crystal strike you down," she swore, nearly smacking the candle off the roof.

"Well, that is certainly no way to speak to a candle."

Analia looked up as her uncle pulled himself onto her turret. Dressed in his usual gray-and-black tunic, Accalon offered an amused smile, the early light turning his neat, deep red hair to flame.

"I think it will recover," she said dryly.

Accalon chuckled as he sat on the metal bench behind her. He'd had it made for her years ago, seeing as she spent more time on the roof than anywhere else. She still preferred to let her legs swing free—which would make the group of guards that had hauled the bench to its current resting spot livid. That, however, had less to do with the bench than it did her.

Analia scowled. She quickly tried to school her expression, but there was little her uncle's sharp gray eyes missed.

"Come," he said, patting the bench beside him. "Sit with me."

"Not until this candle is lit."

She turned back to the candle, reaching for heat, just to scrape the bottom of a dried-out well. A well that had never been filled in the first place.

Accalon cocked a brow. Raising his hand, he summoned a small blue spark to his fingertip and sent it zipping across the roof, the flame landing on the wick with a crackle.

"I meant not until I lit the candle," Analia complained.

"Did you now?" Accalon asked, feigning surprise. "My apologies, what a terrible misunderstanding."

"How funny that it keeps happening."

Accalon gave her an innocent look. Analia scoffed, but she couldn't suppress her smile. Rising, she moved to sit beside him, breathing in his familiar smoky smell.

"You know," he said, ruffling her hair, "you're allowed to take a break."

"Not when Royals from an enemy kingdom are arriving in a matter of hours."

Analia turned back to her candle. She mimicked Accalon's movements, willing a flame to appear; for the flame already there to grow.

Nothing.

"Still no spark?" Accalon asked, his thoughtful gaze on the candle.

"So it seems," Analia sighed. "I don't know what I'm doing wrong."

"Who says you're doing something wrong?"

"The candle, for one."

"Well," Accalon said, fighting a smile, "you did tell the Crystal to strike it down."

"That was after it refused to light."

Accalon chuckled, but Analia only dropped her gaze. Far below, she could see the Ash Kingdom beginning to stir, smoke already billowing from the forges to the west.

Her home was known for its creations: straight, concentric streets that formed innumerable hidden passageways and secret locations; buildings made from dark volcanic rock, decorated with fiery paints and obsidian glass. Every structure, from temples to statues to elevated walkways, was a work of art, perfectly coordinated with its surroundings to form a cohesive whole.

It was a kingdom forged from smoke and embers, heat and flame. And Analia couldn't even produce a spark.

"I just want to know why," she said, tracing the edge of the bench with her finger. "Why am I the only Ash Royal that can't summon a flame?"

Accalon's expression softened. "Anna—"

"I'm fine," she said, a bit harsher than she intended.

Accalon's face twitched. Guilt twisted in Analia's stomach, but he was only quiet for a moment.

"Little fledgling," he sighed, "don't give up on flying just yet. Every Royal has their magic. Sometimes, it just takes time."

"Twenty-two years?"

Accalon shrugged. "The Crystal works in mysterious ways. Perhaps it's not the right time."

Analia bit back a retort. It was true, no Royal developed their magic at a set time—although it was consistently early across all six kingdoms. Her younger brother Cadmus at three, their younger sister Lucilla at four. Accalon was apparently setting his swaddle blankets ablaze as an infant. Yet, after twenty-two years, Analia was still waiting.

"Come now," Accalon said, bumping her with his knee. "We both know phoenixes don't give up. We burn, yes, but what else do we do?"

Analia looked away, "Uncle—"

"Don't 'Uncle' me. What is our saying?"

"Rise again," Analia mumbled.

Accalon ignored her eye roll. "Precisely. And with every blaze, every pile of ash we rise from, we return stronger than we were before. In that regard, you are the strongest phoenix of all." He pulled her close. "Brush yourself off, little fledgling. You can try again next time."

Gods, how many times had she already done that? Failed, brushed herself off, tried again, just for nothing to change?

But how could anything change if she stopped?

Analia sighed. "Fine."

Accalon looked thoroughly pleased with himself.

"Even though your speech was horribly cliche."

His expression faltered. "Did you just call your king cliche?"

"Cliche and old." Analia shook her head. "Walking around, spouting lines like some ancient philosopher, hoping some sycophantic scribe will deem them worthy of transcription."

"I have much to say," Accalon said primly. "Kingly wisdom to impart upon my subjects. Some of it is bound to be insightful. I would even venture inspiring."

"It must come from all three hundred of those birthdays of yours."

"Two hundred and fifty-three," he corrected delicately.

Analia laughed, resting her head on his shoulder. "I must have forgotten."

When the Crystal Blessed those select humans millennia ago, it didn't just give them magic. They also received extended life spans, faster healing, heightened strength and reflexes—all of which Analia had. Everything but the flames.

This wasn't unheard of for the average Blessed. There were cases where the Crystal had withheld the magic aspect of its Blessing for reasons unknown, leading many to view the basic Blessing Analia had as the only guarantee. But not for Royals.

Accalon didn't catch her frown as he kissed the side of her head. "For now," he said, rising and heading for the edge of the turret, "it's about time you got dressed for the day."

"Why?" Analia asked, picking at her gray nightgown. "Do you think the Sun Royals would mind me meeting them like this?"

Accalon's smoky-gray eyes, twin to her own, sparkled with amusement. "Little fledgling, sometimes I worry what mischief you might get into when you do get your magic."

When, not if.

Accalon beckoned. Analia shot her candle one last indignant look. Then, she followed him off the turret, scrambling down the stone wall and landing lightly on the castle roof.

"Come along," Accalon said, pushing open the turret's watchtower door. "If we hurry, Lynette and Mardie may have mercy on you for making them wait."

Analia made a face as she stepped through the door. The castle was built from basalt, the volcanic rock's varying shades of gray and black swirling with lava flow lines. Echoes bounced off the rough texture, the darker tones allowing for shadows to collect around corners and in the spaces between windows.

"Come now," Accalon laughed. "You can face a perilous plunge to your death, but not a few servant girls?"

"I'm more concerned about their combs," Analia muttered. "I'm going to be bald within the month, and you'll just tell me 'Rise again, little fledgling, from the ashes of your yanked-out hair.'"

Accalon tugged on a lock of her hair. "Ask Lynette and Mardie questions," he suggested. "There's nothing people like more than talking about themselves."

"Nothing except one-word answers, it seems."

"Ask Lynette about her sister. She just won a contest in the local festival for her strawberry tarts."

Analia made a noncommittal noise, and Accalon poked her in the ribs.

For a few moments, they walked in silence, Accalon lighting sconces as he passed. Before his rule, they had been lit by the Everflame, a flickering torch flame left behind by the first Ash King. But Accalon always insisted on maintaining the castle's flames himself.

"Uncle, what do you think happened?" Analia asked.

Accalon sighed, running a hand down his long face. "Honestly, I'm unsure. Although I know it wasn't an accident."

"And if Sun's to blame?"

Accalon paused. Expression hardening, he said, "They killed one of our own. That requires retribution."

Analia shivered. Her uncle had always been a peaceful king, but he never forgot that peace had a price. And sometimes, that price was blood.

"But," he said, returning to his usual unruffled state and continuing down the hall, "we will just have to wait and see."

"But—"

"Well, here we are," Accalon said, stopping outside Analia's chambers.

"Uncle!"

"In you go now." Bowing, he ushered her inside. Analia spluttered, but he only waved as he continued down the hall, quickly disappearing around the corner.

Sometimes, Analia didn't know what to make of her uncle. Shrugging to herself, she turned and stepped through her door.

Despite having ample space, she preferred to keep her chambers sparse. The furniture she did have was made from muted woods and velvets, matching the tapestry of her kingdom's sigil on the far wall: a burnt-orange phoenix rising from a plume of smoke. The one pop of color came from her gilded harp, tucked away in a corner.

Unlike magic, music was something Analia was innately good at. When she was young, she and Ember had dreamed of running away from the Ash Kingdom and becoming traveling bards. But Analia was a princess, and Ember had been chosen by the Crystal to be a healer.

There was a part of her that always wondered if that shared cage of responsibility was the only reason she and Ember were... friends? Acquaintances? She could never tell. At least she was utterly certain where she stood with the two maids stiffly waiting for her at the end of her bed.

Even though the two women were dressed in the same gray-and-white uniform, it was easy to tell them apart. Lynette was tall, willowy, and young, whereas Mardie was shorter, her face creased with wrinkles and hair streaked with gray.

"Good morning," Analia said, forcing cheerfulness.

"Good morning, Your Highness."

Neither of them looked at her. Analia wasn't surprised.

Lynette gestured with her comb for her to sit at the dressing table, Mardie half disappearing into the massive armoire. Analia could feel herself shrinking back, curling inward like a piece of metal in a forge as she took her seat. But maybe one-on-one would be easier.

"How's your sister?" she asked tentatively.

"Fine."

Lynette's comb snagged in a tangle. Analia fought back a wince.

"What's her name again? Senna?"

"Yes, Your Highness."

Analia watched Lynette in the mirror, the maid refusing to look up. "I heard she won a baking contest recently. For her strawberry—"

"How do you know about that?" Lynette's eyes finally snapped to her face in the mirror.

Analia recoiled, "My uncle told me."

Lynette relaxed slightly. Accalon knowing made sense.

After the Blessed-Human Civil War centuries ago, the resulting treaty declared humans could no longer be slaves to the Blessed. Some still decided to work as servants in the six Royal castles, and Accalon made it a point to try and bridge the remaining gap: learning their names, remembering their families, hearing their stories. But with Analia?

Lynette pursed her lips, dropping her eyes without another word. Analia clenched her hands into fists to stop their trembling.

After the last fifteen years, she'd become accustomed to their blatant disrespect. But the sting of rejection somehow never faded.

She didn't try to engage Mardie as she reemerged from the armoire, gown in hand. She didn't meet either woman's gaze as they braided her hair and helped her dress. She only looked up once the door had closed behind them, both maids only offering a clipped farewell.

Most of her long, dark red hair was left down, with a small spiraling braid wrapping around her head like a crown. Kohl rimmed her smoky-gray eyes, which she had always thought were too large for her small mouth and sharper features. Scarlet, gold, and orange threads twined through the skirts like streaks of a dying flame.

Analia rested her forehead against her mirror. She couldn't even command the respect of a few servant girls. How in the name of the Crystal was she going to survive the day? Especially considering the reason Sun was coming in the first place.

# Chapter 2

## Two Weeks Prior

The sun was beginning to set as Analia and her companions stepped out of the shadows.

The Ash Castle had been just sitting down to dinner when Kuno, one of the Crystal Guards, slipped through the Great Hall doors. He quickly made his way to Accalon's side, leaning in to whisper something in his ear. After a few words, a grim Accalon took Analia by the hand, his other gripping Kuno's armor-clad shoulder as he stepped into the shadows.

For a moment, the world faded away around her, leaving her in a cold, dark emptiness outside her uncle's hand as he pulled her along. It was a power only the strongest of Royals possessed: the ability to enter a shadow and exit another—if the latter was in a location that the jumper had physically visited before.

Now, Analia blinked in the sudden light as they reemerged not far from the Sun Kingdom border. This far northeast, the land was a mass of hardened lava and black volcanic sand, originating from the string of volcanoes referred to as the Belt.

The smoky air stung Analia's nose as she followed Accalon down a steep decline, a knot of Ash soldiers wearing the same dark steel armor as Kuno waiting below. They parted to let Accalon through, but Analia paused as her father, Brenn, emerged from the shadows nearby, Cadmus in tow.

Both Brenn and Accalon had the deep red hair and smoky-gray eyes of the Ash Royals. But where his older brother was tall and lean, Brenn was shorter with broader shoulders. Shoulders he had once carried Analia around on.

Now, she faded back into the crowd, craning her neck to see—although there wasn't much to look at.

Baylen, one of the distant Royal cousins, lay in the center of the sandy hollow. It was as if he had been posed like a doll: body straight, arms to either side, glassy gray eyes fixed unseeingly on the bloody sunset above.

"We found him like this, Your Majesty," one of the guards said to Accalon. "We sent for you immediately."

Analia's heart squeezed as Accalon crouched beside Baylen, resting his fingers on his neck. They all already knew. But that didn't stop the collective shudder as Accalon sat back, giving a single nod.

"But how?" Brenn exclaimed, crouching across from Accalon and lifting Baylen's limp wrist. "He only jumped out this morning, and his body is already cold!"

"Whatever happened must have occurred as soon as he got here," Accalon said.

"You mean when he was murdered?" Brenn retorted.

"Well, that's an awfully bold claim," Accalon murmured.

"Bold? He's dead on the border of an enemy kingdom!"

Yes, he was certainly dead, but something bothered Analia about the body. She edged closer.

Brenn was still ranting, insisting they march on Sun immediately and demand answers. Accalon, however, merely cocked his head.

"Tell me," he said. "Do you notice anything... unusual about the body?"

"Besides the fact that he's dead?"

Accalon didn't reply. He simply allowed for a hush to spread, gazes redirecting to the dead Royal before them. Motionless, as if he were sleeping.

"There's no wound," Analia said to herself.

Slowly, malevolently, Brenn turned to look at her. Analia's stomach sank, past her feet, through the ground, into the Hell Realm itself. Crystal spare her from that look.

She immediately dropped her father's gaze, just to catch Accalon's eye. He smiled, beckoning her closer.

Analia wavered. But knowing there was no avoiding this burn, she reluctantly stepped out of the crowd and to her uncle's side.

"What do you see?" he asked as she crouched beside him.

Brenn, kneeling across from her. His face, smoothed into a lazy, indulgent smirk that had the icy fear in her stomach twisting into something hotter.

"There's no blood," she said, looking away from her father. "No sign of a stab wound, or a weapon that could have caused it.

"Even if he'd been struck from behind, the blood would be pooling beneath him. But if that were the case, the force from that blow would have sent him face down, not face up. I suppose he could have been struck in the back of the head and we can't see from this angle..."

Analia could feel the soldiers' eyes crawl over her skin. Assessing. Judging. Waiting.

"There's more," Accalon prodded.

Analia's gaze drifted across Baylen's neck, and her breath caught. "Uncle," she said. "What is that?"

She hadn't been able to see it before. Now, she traced her finger around the perfectly circular black mark on the side of Baylen's neck.

"I have no idea." Accalon looked to Brenn. "Are you aware of any Royal that is capable of leaving such a mark?"

Brenn did not respond.

"I believe," said Accalon, "this means the question is not who killed Baylen..."

"But what," Analia finished.

The guards shifted uneasily, Analia's stomach following suit.

Brenn sat back on his heels, his eyes momentarily meeting hers. "Well done, duckling."

The sting was reflexive at this point. Just a duckling, posing as a phoenix. Deemed unworthy by the Crystal. And he would never let her forget it; wouldn't let anyone forget that she was no more than a candle with a perpetually unlit wick. That it was her fault he could no longer love her.

Cadmus came to crouch beside her. At eighteen, he was more gangly than tall, with the same red hair as the other Ash Royals.

"Are you saying this could be a rogue monster?" he asked, solemn blue eyes trained on Accalon.

"It's certainly a possibility," Accalon said. "I don't think any of us could claim to know every creature that stalks the plains of Elefthia."

Rising, he dusted the black sand from his pants. "For now, we need to go about collecting more information."

"What else do you need?" Brenn demanded, also rising. "He's dead, on the border of an enemy kingdom!"

"And what if whatever killed Baylen was also aware of that?" Accalon asked.

"How do you know it isn't Sun gambling on your reluctance to act?" Brenn countered, stepping closer. "This is exactly what they want. The longer we wait, the more time they have to prepare."

"We can't accuse a foreign kingdom of assassination over a possible coincidence."

"Since when have coincidences lost all weight?"

"They haven't," Accalon said. "Hard evidence simply holds more."

Brenn's jaw worked, but he bit his tongue.

"I think Father's right," Cadmus chimed in, still crouched beside the body. "Even if it wasn't Sun, waiting makes us look weak. Shouldn't we strike before they have time to prepare?"

There came a murmur of agreement from a handful of guards, although none dared to directly insert themselves. Analia sifted her fingers through the sand. That wasn't the point.

"Analia?" Accalon asked. "What are your thoughts?"

Analia froze as all eyes shifted toward her. She didn't have to look up to see their contempt; Brenn's gaze mirrored in the others.

"I..." She dragged her eyes from the crowd, focusing on Accalon. "I think we should remember we're looking for retribution, not war. And they might be inter-laced, but we don't know that for certain yet."

Accalon nodded. "We wait," he declared.

No one dared to argue.

Analia forced herself not to sag as those eyes flitted away once more. Nothing had changed. On either side, apparently.

Brenn tugged on his cloak, obviously agitated. "Someday, brother, that nobility of yours is going to get you killed."

"Then you will get to be king," Accalon said, mild as ever. "And what a joyous time that will be. But until then, I'm afraid we are stuck with my noble, self-sacrificing ways."

Brenn snorted. He turned away, his exasperated mutter trailing behind him. "One daring adventure in a volcano thirty years ago and he thinks himself invincible."

Accalon's lips twitched. Turning to the guards, he swiftly delegated orders around tracking and body retrieval, the guards giving sharp salutes before dashing off.

Analia turned to Cadmus. "Give me your cloak."

Cadmus didn't need to ask why. He silently unfastened his orange-and-gray cloak, moving to drape it over Baylen's face.

"Wait." Analia reached out, gently closing Baylen's eyes. "Rise again, cousin," she whispered. Then, she nodded to Cadmus, and he covered Baylen's face.

For the briefest moment, his hand brushed hers as they adjusted the covering. He spared her a single, quiet look, then rose and moved away.

Her own brother didn't want to be seen getting too close. Analia was too tired to be fazed.

Rising as well, she flagged down Warack, whom Accalon had charged with watching the body. "Make sure you keep his face covered at all times," she told him.

"Why?" Warack asked, disinterested.

Out from under Brenn's gaze, Analia's temper finally flared. "You never know who could wander past. Would you want to unexpectedly see the face of your loved one on a corpse?"

Warack's face pinched as if tasting something bitter. "I only do as my Royals command."

Analia wanted to spit back that she was a Royal, magic or not. Instead, she waved over Cadmus and quickly filled him in.

"Do you agree?" she asked.

"Uh, yes."

Warack bowed to Cadmus. "It will be done, Your Highness."

More confused than anything, Cadmus departed. Analia turned to leave as well, her cheeks burning. Not because of flames, though. If that were the case, then Warack would have had to listen to her. Someday, she would get them to respect her again.

Analia couldn't stop her mind from spiraling back in time. Back to the faces, the stares, the jeers that slowly rose to a cacophony—no. She would not think about that, would not wonder how Brenn could do that to his own child.

Analia ascended the slope and found her uncle. He pulled her close, murmuring a "well done" in her ear. Analia sighed.

Just as she faded into the shadows, one of the guards, Rois, caught her eye. He tried to give her a sympathetic look, but she jerked her head to the side.

A year ago, Rois simply looking at her would have made her heart flutter against her rib cage, just like it had that first day in the back of the music hall. But apparently, Brenn had to take that, too.

# Chapter 3

## Present

Analia looked up at the massive Phoenix Gate, her hair fluttering in the breeze.

Composed of thin, twining golden rods, the gate loomed in the center of the wall surrounding the Ash Castle. A scarlet-and-gold phoenix marked its center, its wings spread wide.

Accalon had spent months laboring over it in the forges during the early years of his kingship. It was only one of his many unconventional ventures—his advisors having given up trying to dissuade him long ago. Yet, he always said the Phoenix Gate was his favorite.

"It's my fingerprint," he'd say. "A way for the kingdom to always have a piece of me."

By the time Analia arrived, everyone had already gathered to await the Sun Royals' arrival. A unit of Ash soldiers stood at attention, swords hanging from their belts. Cadmus and Lucilla stood off to one side, the latter showing Cadmus something in her palm.

At just eleven, Lucilla was a tiny replica of their mother: silky blonde hair, heart-shaped face, vivid blue eyes.

"Analia." And speak of the woman.

Her mother's voice wasn't raised, but it nevertheless cut through the throng like a blast of wintry air. She crooked her finger at Analia, who reluctantly crossed the twenty paces to where her mother stood beside Brenn, who was engrossed in conversation with the captain of their guard.

"You're late," Aeley informed her.

Analia smothered a sigh. If not late, she would be dirty, and if not dirty, just impertinent.

"I apologize, Mother."

Aeley gave her a once-over. She wrinkled her nose, but before she could comment, Balstaire gave a sharp salute and jogged off. Then, Brenn turned to Analia.

"Aeley, would you give us a moment?" he asked.

Aeley looked as though she wanted to protest, but she gave a single nod. Analia watched her go, wondering how a woman Blessed with frost managed to survive in a kingdom fueled by fire.

"So," Brenn said, slumping back against the gate. "You showed up after all."

"Father, I'm not late; Accalon hasn't even arrived yet."

"I'm not referring to your punctuality."

Analia felt her entire being go still. Blank. As easy as a reflex, trained by every time she was left alone with her father.

Brenn went on, "This meeting is between Royals, and you know that."

"I am a Royal," Analia said quietly.

"Maybe by blood, but not to your people. Not to the Crystal, that's for gods-damned sure."

Brenn pushed off the gate, advancing on her. Analia took a step back, but Brenn didn't stop.

"You are here on a technicality, and a technicality alone," he said, his voice a harsh whisper in her ear. "You will be invisible. You will not speak unless spoken to, and you will immediately extricate yourself if so. You will not embarrass me any more than you already have."

Brenn's hand snaked around her head, magically burning fingers pressing down behind her ear. "Do I make myself clear?"

Analia nodded, fighting the urge to shove him away.

"I said," Brenn pressed down, "do I make myself clear?"

"Yes." Analia didn't know which was hotter: Brenn's fingers, or her shame as her voice cracked.

She wanted to hate him in that moment. Wanted to let years of stored-up venomous words and burning touches finally erupt, make him know every single hurt she'd ever had—

"I'm doing this for your own good," he said, extinguishing his fingers and stepping back. "The more attention you get, the worse it will be for you."

Analia's heart twisted. She knew it was all lies—at least, a part of her did. But what if it wasn't? Which possibility hurt more?

Brenn didn't seem to notice her turmoil as he looked up at the sound of approaching footsteps.

"I see we're all here," Accalon said as he strode into their midst. Dressed in gray pants, shining black boots, and the kingdom's orange phoenix across his chest, Accalon looked every part the Ash King. Especially with the sleek obsidian crown shining atop his head, flickering with captured firelight.

Without a word, Brenn moved around Analia to greet his brother. She didn't miss the look in his eyes, the one that hissed with the echo of his voice from long ago. Worst decision I ever made.

Left alone, Analia released a long, shaky breath. Then, quickly composing herself, she followed her father.

"So," Brenn said, "you finally arrive, brother."

"You say that like I'm late."

"Everyone else is here."

"Ah, but not Sun. That means I'm remarkably early." Accalon stepped around an exasperated Brenn to face Analia. "Little fledgling, where is your Kingdom representation?"

Analia looked around, noting the phoenixes emblazoned across Cadmus's and Brenn's chests; the pins in Aeley's and Lucilla's hair.

Analia raised her chin. "I don't have anything," she said, knowing that was purposeful.

Accalon clicked his tongue. "Well, that certainly won't do."

He thought for a moment. Then, he detached the pin from his tunic. Analia took a hasty step back, her panicked gaze flashing to Brenn.

The pin—rimmed in dark gray steel with a soaring phoenix in the center—was very much Accalon's pin. She couldn't remember the last time she'd seen him without it; she doubted anyone had.

Accalon followed her gaze. "Come now, little fledgling, you can't be the only one without representation. That would simply look odd. Almost like an embarrassing oversight, wouldn't you say, brother?"

Brenn looked like he was trying to swallow a lemon whole. "If you insist."

"Excellent!"

Brenn's eyes momentarily rested on Analia with a look of pure loathing. Then, he turned, rejoining Aeley, Lucilla, and Cadmus beneath the gate.

Accalon's eyes sparkled with amusement as he carefully attached the pin to Analia's dress. "Your father has always had a spine of iron," he said confidentially. "It will break before it bends, and sometimes—"

Analia flinched. Accalon's gaze sharpened. He had been tucking her hair behind her ear, just for his fingers to brush the tiny set of burns Brenn had left behind.

"Anna—"

"I'm fine," she said, quickly stepping away.

She couldn't confirm his suspicions. It would only make it worse.

She hurried to rejoin the main group, but Accalon caught up with her easily. All he said was, "You don't have to be."

Yes, she did. Because she couldn't be anything else.

Analia gave a brief nod, and Accalon's brows furrowed. He didn't leave her side as they moved to stand beneath the Phoenix Gate, flames crackling in his eyes. She was almost certain he was about to ignore her request to drop it, but she was spared by a golden carriage soaring out from behind a bank of clouds.

Finally, the Sun Kingdom had arrived. And recent history was about to be made as a Royal stepped onto foreign soil by invitation for the first time in one hundred years.

After the seven Defiants released the Crystal's magic all those millennia ago, they each established their own kingdom: Ash, Wind, Sand, Mist, Sun, Moon, and Star. In the centuries that followed, there were a variety of political systems that were tested, destroyed, and redesigned. Eventually, the kingdoms became mostly autonomous, although the Star Kingdom—founded by Talitha, leader of the Defiants—maintained ultimate authority.

It was a system that supported peace—for the most part. A system of friendship—most of the time. Enough so that trade routes were well established and negotiations and alliances between kingdoms were commonplace. All until King Hester Stelingente took the Star throne.

In the seven-year war that followed, it wasn't just the target that was struck, but everything around it as well. For the hundred years since the eradication of the Star Kingdom, known as the Shattering, the remaining six kingdoms had snapped into a pervasive era of isolation, suspicion, and muted hostility.

It was this overarching distrust that had the guards snapping to attention. They fell into formation around the Ash Royals, the carriage rapidly drawing closer. But despite its glittering gold exterior, it was the twin sun dragons harnessed to the front that demanded all attention.

Their long, serpentine bodies were encased in scales that glinted in varying shades of gold. Two rows of short, stubby legs churned through the air, although it was their small, white wings that kept them aloft.

"Beautiful!" Lucilla breathed, somewhere to Analia's left. "Cadmus, look at their eyes! They're like tiny suns!"

The carriage thumped to the ground a few paces outside of the Phoenix Gate. Accalon flicked his wrist, deactivating the wards and opening the gate for the dragons to scurry through. For a few moments, the only sound was the roll of carriage wheels. But even that faded away as the dragons finally came to a halt.

The first to emerge from the carriage was a tall, olive-skinned guard with a hawkish nose. He adjusted his white cloak over his gold-and-white fighting leathers, his dark eyes taking in the assembly before him.

"Presenting," he said, "Queen Deardryn Oshar of the Sun—"

Deardryn gently brushed the guard aside, heading straight for Accalon. She wore a gown of swirling white and gold, her blonde hair pinned back and out of her oval face.

"Accalon!" Deardryn beamed, raising her hand to him, palm out. "It's been too long since our families met."

Accalon touched his palm to hers, the traditional greeting in the Sun Kingdom. "Indeed, it has. About ten months since the last Solstice Ceremony."

Behind Deardryn, King Othin and Prince Pryanth descended from the carriage. Both tall and tan, Othin sported a trimmed black beard and amber eyes, whereas Pryanth had the soft gold hair and honey eyes of his mother. The rest of their guard quickly followed.

The two families merged, slate into gold, power thrumming through the air like a plucked bowstring. Accalon drew Analia forward, preventing her from completely hiding behind him. But she kept quiet, only observing the exchange of pleasantries and noting the vague stiffness between groups.

Accalon hadn't disclosed what he wrote in the letter he sent after discovering Baylen's body. He only told everyone not to mention anything until he broached the topic himself.

Peeking at their faces from over Cadmus's shoulder, Analia could only read a mix of confusion and wariness across their expressions. What was Accalon up to?

After dispatching Rois and a Sun guard named Joshel to take care of the dragons—Lucilla delightedly joining them—Accalon led the way back up the winding path to the Ash Castle. Guards and Royals alike flowed around Analia like a current around a boulder, leaving her somewhere near the back. Behind her, she could just make out the voices of two Sun guards.

"So that's her, huh?"

"The Dud Princess of Ash."

Analia tried to pick up her pace, but there were no gaps in the crowd she could squeeze through.

"I'm surprised they let her keep the title. Honestly, what kind of help will she be with the Solstice Ceremony when she ascends the throne? You can't bless the land with magic if you don't have any."

Invisible. Even as they spoke her very fears aloud.

Originally, the Crystal maintained the magic flow across Elefthia. But after it disappeared sometime during Talitha's reign, the responsibility fell to the Royals. And with no flames, Analia would have no way to assist in the annual magic release at the foot of Mt. Raegyr. A fact so disgraceful that even those without magic had no pity for her.

"Would they even let her be queen?"

"They couldn't! The kingdom would die of embarrassment."

Fire. Coursing through her veins.

"There must be some legal clause that allows them to skip her. You can't have a magicless ruler."

"Dud princess, dud queen."

Analia whipped around, her voice shaking with fury. "Dud princess?"

The guards looked up, mildly surprised. The guard on the left—who had introduced the queen—turned to his olive-skinned friend. "That face isn't too striking, either."

"No, but she'd still have more luck pursuing more womanly duties."

"Yes, and those skills take practice to develop—"

"I'm sorry," Analia broke in. "The men I concern myself with wield swords, not daggers."

Well, that certainly put an end to Brenn's "invisible" plan.

The left guard's face flushed, hand drifting to his dagger hilt. His friend guffawed, "This one's got a temper!"

The left guard ignored him. He stepped forward, and Analia quickly backed up.

She had not thought this through. Even with her people's disdain, she knew they would never truly harm her. Not with Accalon around.

But clearly, these Sun guards played by different rules. And when her father found out—Crystal spare her, the one time she needed to keep her mouth shut.

The guard reached for her, "You little—"

"We meet at last," came a voice from behind her.

Not another one. Analia dared a glance over her shoulder as a third Sun guard approached.

Startlingly silver eyes met her own, sending a chill down her spine. Those eyes were too observant. He stepped up beside her, forcing his fellow guard to take a step back.

"I was starting to think I would never find you," he said. His voice had the faintest hint of texture to it; a sleek piece of glass stained with smoke.

Analia's eyes moved over him. Sharp, angular features. Messy dark brown hair. Sun Kingdom tan. "Who are—"

"Your father noticed you lagging behind and ordered me to retrieve you."

How did he already know?

"He'll just have to wait," the first guard interrupted, pushing forward once more.

The newcomer turned to face him, a faint smirk on his lips. Crystal spare her, every movement was pure, unconcerned predator.

"Will he?" The man rocked back on his heels. "I'd love to see what happens when you inform him of this."

"Lev and the princess are preoccupied," the right guard chimed in.

"Yes, Andrik, I heard. What a breath of fresh air it must be for Lev to ask before simply taking. Honestly, Lev, you've set the bar so low for yourself, and yet you still manage to crack your forehead on it with remarkable consistency."

Each guard made to speak, but the newcomer turned away dismissively.

"Shall we?" he asked. And before Analia could respond, he took her by the elbow and steered her away.

What in the name of the Crystal just happened? Analia struggled to keep up with her escort's swift pace, at a loss for words. He, however, seemed to have plenty.

"What in the name of the five gods was that?" he demanded once they were out of earshot.

"Excuse me?"

"You're the reigning Royal Princess, and you allowed those two idiot guards from a foreign kingdom to blatantly disrespect you."

"I don't need an 'idiot guard from a foreign kingdom' to save me."

"I wasn't saving, I was assisting—which, by the way, thanks for your help back there."

Analia dug in her heels, bringing them to a stop. Was he teasing now?

The man continued, "I did all that work. Coming up with a cover story, insulting Lev—although I'll admit that was more for selfish reasons than—"

"Cover story?" Analia interrupted. "You mean my father isn't looking for me?"

"What? No."

Analia's relief was cold and heavy.

"You couldn't have picked any other story?" she asked, heading off once more.

The man easily kept pace. "I thought that'd get you out fastest."

"But why bother getting me out in the first place?"

"Because you looked like you could use a hand," he said simply. "And mine has proven to be incredibly helpful."

Analia shot him an incredulous look. He grinned. A wicked, lazy grin that promised midnight sheets and whispers in her ear.

"How insolent are you?" Analia demanded. The man made to reply, but Analia went on, "You try to scold me for letting a guard harass me, and yet here you are, continuing the cycle. How are you any different from him?"

Something sparked in those silver eyes. He was silent for a few steps, fiddling with a silver chain that peeked out from his leathers.

"You are not what I was expecting," he finally murmured.

Analia's face twitched. "Sorry to disappoint," she spat, speeding up.

He didn't try to stop her as she marched up the castle steps. She should lock him out. Have Accalon blast him back across the boundary line, spare her the commentary on how she wasn't just a disappointment in her own kingdom anymore.

She was about to step inside when something made her glance back. The man remained at the bottom of the steps, his head tilted curiously.

"Who are you?" Analia asked.

"Usually that's the first question a person asks," he commented.

"Usually strangers introduce themselves without prompting."

"Aaron." He sketched a dramatic bow. Straightening, he flashed a grin Analia didn't return. Instead, she turned to head inside.

"Wait." Aaron quickly climbed the steps and lightly tugged on her wrist. "Now you introduce yourself."

"Introduce—you already know who I am!"

"That doesn't mean I don't want a formal introduction." He gently turned her to face him, suddenly serious. "What is your name?"

Analia was about to shake him off, but Brenn's warning flashed through her mind.

"Princess Analia Valarus," she said stiffly. "It's a pleasure."

"Analia," Aaron repeated softly to himself. He looked up, mocking smile in place. "See? That wasn't too difficult, was it, Princess?"

It was official: she hated this man. But Analia quickly realized Aaron was the least of her problems.

# Chapter 4

The Council Chamber was located in the heart of the Ash Castle, hidden behind a thick stone door with carvings of intricate torches. Depending on the route one took, it could be reached within minutes. Accalon, however, decided against this, chatting amiably with the Sun Royals as they toured the Ash Castle.

"What's Uncle doing?" Cadmus asked under his breath, falling into step beside Analia with a cautious glance at their father's back.

"Just watch," she said.

As the tour stretched longer and longer, Othin and Pryanth looked bemused. Deardryn, however, practically twitched with impatience.

"Accalon," she said, "aren't you going to tell us what this is about?"

"Oh, certainly, we'll get to that—now, this painting here was donated to us—"

They turned down another collection of hallways.

"I don't understand why you must be so cryptic," Deardryn pressed.

"Hmm? Oh, there was an oddity on the border that I thought we should discuss—"

"Oddity?" Othin broke in, but Accalon waved the comment aside, finally heading for the staircase that would lead to the Council Chamber.

Their reactions weren't surprising, seeing as the Sun Kingdom was known for its scholars and research. The Sun Castle supposedly contained the largest library in all Elefthia, filled with texts that had been otherwise lost to history. And, if rumors were correct, forbidden arts that weren't so much lost as purposefully erased.

"Is he building their interest?" Cadmus asked, seemingly on the same mental track.

"No," Analia said. She watched as Deardryn and Accalon descended the final staircase, Deardryn forced to remain a half step behind. "He's reminding them where they stand."

Finally reaching the Council Chamber, Aeley politely excused herself to check on Lucilla. Analia made to follow her mother, doubting Brenn would allow her inside, but Accalon put a casual hand on her back. Gesturing for the guards to remain outside, he swung the door open and bowed Deardryn through.

The stone chamber was sparse, consisting of one long table with accompanying chairs. It would have otherwise been plain, except—

"Interesting decor choice," Deardryn murmured.

Paintings of Elefthia's history covered every inch of wall. It was another one of Accalon's early projects, centuries blurring together as one image bled into the next.

Deardryn's gaze lingered on one of the earliest scenes, closest to the door. The Defiants—three men and four women—held the Crystal aloft, a blast of pure white light radiating from the Crystal's translucent, palm-sized surface.

It was a depiction of the Unleashing: the moment magic flooded Elefthia for the first time. Choosing to Bless some humans with varying strengths and styles of magic and not others for reasons unknown. Bringing forth countless varieties of magical organisms.

It was the birth of the once seven, now six kingdoms of Elefthia. But when Analia looked at the Defiants, all she felt was the hollow pit where her magic should be. The only Royal in history without the Defiants' staggering power.

"We mustn't forget our past," Accalon replied. "Otherwise, we become complacent and foolish. And that is when our pasts become our futures."

Othin snorted. "Unless you know how to raise the Defiants and Ancient Ones from the dead, Accalon, I'd say there's a slim chance of that happening."

"I never realized you were so literal, Othin," Accalon said, mildly surprised.

The Sun King scowled. He stalked past Accalon, taking a seat at the table where a tray of drinks already sat—Accalon must have requested those ahead of time.

As Analia and the rest of their company followed suit, she couldn't help the shiver that ran down her spine. The Ancient Ones: all-powerful, all-knowing, everlasting. Tall, clad in black, and pulsating with a dark, malevolent power.

Historians had trouble determining how long they'd ruled over Elefthia—centuries, perhaps even millennia. What was known with certainty was the ruthlessness that they ruled with.

The Ancient Ones preferred to break the humans beneath them rather than bend them to their will: branding their disobedience into their flesh, using loved ones as weapons, and their corpses as messages. The history leading up to the humans finally declaring war was long and bloody, especially since the Ancient Ones were the only beings possessing magic in Elefthia at the time.

Analia's eyes slid to the scene directly after the one Deardryn had picked out: the three Ancient Ones as they dissolved under a tidal wave of magic. Sealed away as the Defiants procured the Crystal and used the Ancient Ones' very own weapon against them, leading to the establishment of the seven kingdoms.

"Now," Deardryn said from her seat across from Accalon, "what is this border oddity?"

"We found a body," Accalon said bluntly.

Analia fought to keep the surprise off her face. Changing tactics so quickly?

Othin exclaimed, "That's a bit more than an oddity, Accalon!"

"Whose body?" Deardryn asked.

"My cousin, Baylen."

Shock rippled across all three Sun faces.

Deardryn pulled a wine glass toward herself with one hand, the other reaching across the table to rest atop Accalon's. "My condolences," she said softly.

"What could have had the strength to kill a Royal?" Othin demanded.

"Interesting you say what," Accalon said, taking a sip from his tea—the only mug provided. "Whatever it was, it left a distinctive signature behind."

Deardryn perked up. "Such as?"

"A circular black mark on the neck."

"Asymmetrical or perfect?"

"Perfect."

Deardryn put a thoughtful finger to her chin.

"How could a mark have killed someone?" Othin asked.

Accalon's brows rose slightly. He hadn't said the mark was the cause of death. Was that just coincidence, or...

Brenn muttered, "That's a fantastic question—"

"Our healers have analyzed the body," Accalon cut in smoothly. "There were no signs of injury. They did, however, find a notable amount of obsidian residue."

Deardryn said, "But if he was discovered near our border, that could have been environmental from the Belt."

"I'm hoping you were smart enough to track the thing," Othin said.

Accalon ignored the jab. "We tried. The creature left no scent behind that our hounds could detect. Even our best Blessed trackers could not identify any trace of footprint, magical trail, not even a hair.

"The killer might as well have been one of the wraiths from the Moon Kingdom, although they still trigger a trackable drop in temperature and a scent our hounds can follow."

Deardryn added, "And I've never come across a variety that only leaves a black mark behind."

"And it wasn't just some sickness that took him suddenly?" Pryanth asked, fidgeting with his sleeve.

Brenn scoffed. "I'd like to know what sickness drops a man out of the blue and leaves a black mark on the neck."

"What are you trying to say, Valarus?" Othin asked.

"I'm not saying anything. Although, it's interesting you reacted so quickly."

"You think we killed him?" Pryanth demanded.

Analia felt Cadmus's leg bounce beneath the table, but he remained quiet. Clearly, he'd come to the same conclusion she had: they were there to observe, not intervene.

But why wasn't Accalon saying anything? He'd spent so much time trying to establish peace between Ash and Sun, and now Brenn was demolishing it like a child kicking down a tower of blocks.

Yet, Accalon remained reclined in his chair, running his finger along the rim of his mug as Othin and Brenn battled on. Curiously, Deardryn remained silent as well.

"Sun had nothing to do with your dead Royal," Othin said, banging his fist on the table.

"You said it yourself," Brenn shot back. "What could kill a Royal? How about another Royal."

"That's enough," Accalon finally said. "Othin, we are not insinuating Sun had anything to do with this."

"That brother of yours just said—"

"My brother and I have lost a cousin," Accalon said. "Grief has a way of raging against any target it can find, regardless of whether it's deserving.

"Surely you understand that. I recall you lost your brother-in-law a few decades back."

"I didn't go around accusing other Royals of killing him."

"No," Deardryn said, placing a hand on her husband's arm, "but you did accuse his wife."

Othin flushed and grumbled something about adultery.

"I apologize for my brother's outburst," Accalon said.

Deardryn nodded, but Othin and Pryanth remained silent. Brenn, on the other hand, looked like he was anything but apologetic. He opened his mouth, but after a sharp glance from Accalon he took a gulp of wine instead.

Analia let out a breath. Did anyone else at the table realize how many strings Accalon was pulling at once? That Brenn's outburst—while completely his own—allowed Accalon to gauge a reaction to a direct accusation, just so he could smooth it over and remain the peacekeeper? But what did those reactions say about Sun?

"Whatever killed your cousin," Deardryn said, "is a threat to not just the Ash Kingdom, but Sun as well. And it doesn't sound like one I wish to face alone."

"We don't need their help," Othin argued.

"Who said you can have it?"

"Brenn," Accalon warned.

Brenn snapped his mouth shut.

Deardryn said, "This creature has proven itself capable of eliminating an Ash Royal. What's preventing it from doing the same to one of our own? Who's to say we would be able to eliminate it on our own?"

Accalon couldn't completely hide his intrigue as he asked, "Are you proposing a temporary alliance?"

"No," Deardryn said. "I'm tired of temporary. I'm tired of these kingdoms being so isolated."

Brenn grumbled into his wine glass, "Oh, it's this speech again."

"Indeed, it is," Deardryn said. "One would think I've delivered it so many times it would have sunk in by now."

"One would think we've ignored you so many times you'd stop talking," Brenn retorted.

Analia tensed. Cadmus lowered his head in despair. Othin started to speak, but Deardryn put a hand over his. He glowered at her, looking like he might rant on regardless.

Deardryn narrowed her eyes in challenge at Othin, only spared Brenn an indifferent glance, and then directed her attention to Accalon, who remained calmly sipping his tea. No wonder she'd earned the nickname the Dragoness.

Deardryn said, "You remember what it was like before the Shattering."

"Yes," Brenn said. "Dictatorships, brutality, and injustice, running rampant like unsupervised toddlers down a corridor. And that was before the seven-year war—"

"I remember before King Hester," Deardryn interrupted. "I remember the centuries of friendship and peace. The willingness to extend a hand to our neighboring kingdoms without fearing we'd lose a finger."

"I remember smoke," Accalon said quietly. Slowly, all eyes moved to him. "Hanging in the air for days after hundreds of soldiers were trapped in the Free Fall Wood that the Star forces set ablaze. I remember the silence of the dead after we burned the Star Castle to the ground, killing not just soldiers, but women, children, and other innocents because we told ourselves that was justice."

One by one, Accalon met the gaze of every person in the room, eventually turning to face the section of wall dedicated to the moments that he spoke of. "Yes, there was unity, there was peace, but there was also a counterbalance that you seem to be overlooking."

"Every political system has the chance to build or destroy," said Deardryn. "It's the figurehead of that system that makes the final decision. And we allowed one bad king to raze centuries of trust in a successful system to the ground."

Deardryn gestured with her wine glass, which was completely untouched. "In the past hundred years, we have clung to our new autonomy like a child to her blanket."

"Unlike children," Brenn said, more subdued than angry, "we actually have monsters in the dark."

"All the more reason to have someone who can shine a light," said Deardryn. "That is all I'm proposing."

"And how do you suggest we do that?" Accalon asked warily.

Deardryn lifted her chin. "A pact between our kingdoms. An alliance, forged between the family trees—"

"A marriage pact?" Analia blurted.

The momentary calm erupted once more.

"You can't be serious!" exclaimed Othin.

"Marriage pact?" Pryanth spluttered.

"So, she *has* gone mad," Brenn said dismally.

Cadmus and Analia swapped disturbed looks. Flicking her gaze to Pryanth, Analia raised her eyebrows at Cadmus. He kicked her under the table.

"I thought there were laws prohibiting the mixing of Royal magics," he said as the others argued.

"No," Analia said. "It just rarely occurs because Royals are so possessive of their Blessings."

There were only a few cases Analia knew of with Royals born to two kingdoms. Just enough to discover that both Blessings didn't get passed down. It seemed to be a gold piece toss to see which Blessing won out, meaning no magical advantage, but a disadvantage in giving another kingdom access to one's own power. What was Deardryn thinking?

The arguing escalated, Brenn and Othin kicking back their chairs and rising to their feet. But Accalon remained silent, scrutinizing Deardryn with narrowed eyes. Deardryn, however, didn't back down.

"By joining our kingdoms," she said over the noise, "we not only obtain mutual benefits, but the reassurance that we can trust one another."

"Why do we need a marriage in order to trust one another?" Othin demanded.

"Why do we need an alliance in the first place?" Brenn asked.

In the oddest turn of events, Othin seemed to agree with Brenn. Turning to his wife, he said, "Deardryn, if you are worried about the killer, we can take care of it ourselves. Even if for some reason we do need assistance, there's no reason to make it so... permanent."

"The reason is the long term," Deardryn insisted. "I see a way to not just help my own kingdom thrive, but through our example, all kingdoms.

"We're suffering, Othin. Royals being killed, trapped behind the walls we built to keep others out. Don't you see? This is the first step the six kingdoms need."

Analia felt her own protests bubble against her lips, but she choked them back.

"You seem to be forgetting," Accalon said, barely raising his voice. "I have no heir."

Quiet.

Analia didn't miss the shadow that passed across Accalon's face. She could practically see his mind flash to the two marble tombstones.

"I didn't forget," Deardryn finally said. "May the gods cherish their souls."

She hesitated. "I couldn't imagine the grief, the heartache, of losing my child or my husband, let alone both. I can't comprehend how I would wake up every morning."

Othin and Brenn slowly sank back into their chairs.

"That's not something I want to contemplate, ever," Deardryn went on. "And even though Brenn's children are not your own, I know they might as well be in your heart. And I know you don't want to think about losing them, too.

"Uniting is our best chance, Accalon, of making it so none of us have to lose another loved one."

A lump rose in Analia's throat as Accalon's loving gaze rested first on her, then Cadmus. She reached for his knee under the table, and he touched her hair.

"Consider it, Accalon," Deardryn said into the silence.

"I am," said Accalon after a moment. "But the decision still lies with my brother, since he is their actual father."

Judging by the smug look on Brenn's face, there was no doubting what his answer would be.

Accalon continued, "Especially since I presume the bride would be departing our kingdom to reside in yours."

"Our only son would certainly not come here," Othin huffed.

A muscle in Pryanth's jaw jumped.

"Well, if that's the case," Accalon said, putting down his now empty mug, "I can definitely see why this marriage pact would be appealing for Sun. You'd get an alliance, access to our resources, a guarantee of safety with one of our princesses in your castle. And this is all after our killer has been taken care of. Although, there seems to be a great deal of confidence it *will* be taken care of."

Accalon leaned back in his chair. "After all, when combining the Royal magic of fire with that of the Royal magic of life, well, that certainly creates a formidable force. Especially if one already knows what the enemy is. Whom it might strike next. Whom it *won't* attack."

Deardryn's eyes narrowed. "I thought you said you weren't accusing us, Accalon."

"I wouldn't dream of such a thing. I'm simply outlining hypotheticals with the information I have. And what I've gleaned from this meeting is we have one ruler utterly opposed to the idea of unification, while the other fights for it like a flame dancing across damp tinder. You see why I hesitate.

"Especially when our attention should be directed toward what killed Baylen, and how we plan to proceed. Whether that be together, or separate."

Deardryn opened her mouth but shut it once more as Accalon finally removed the careful leash he kept on his magic. Unrivaled power rolled off him in waves, sending vibrations through the chamber.

"We've exhausted the topic for today," Accalon said. "You and your guards are more than welcome to stay the night so we may continue this conversation tomorrow. Hopefully, with our minds refreshed, we will be able to stay on topic instead of being diverted."

Deardryn's lips thinned, but there was no arguing with Accalon. He pushed back his chair, power sizzling out. His face was more troubled than anything. Oddly pale as well. Especially in contrast to the bright red of Brenn's angry flush.

Not long later, Analia and Accalon walked back through the empty corridors, having finished a tense dinner before showing the Sun people to their chambers.

"That was certainly an unexpected twist," Analia said.

Accalon nodded distractedly. A cold sweat had broken out across his brow, but he wiped it away.

"If Sun is responsible for Baylen's death," he said, "it certainly wasn't a joint effort."

"You think one of them could've done it without telling the others?"

"It's easy to keep secrets. Especially if you have deep enough pockets and know which throats to slit."

"But why do it in the first place?" Analia asked.

"To whittle down an enemy," Accalon suggested. "A scare tactic of sorts. I wouldn't put it past Pryanth to have done it just to see if he could. The child is unmistakably haughty, which was at odds with his quiet demeanor throughout the night."

They reached Accalon's chambers.

"So, what you're saying is we got nowhere today," Analia summed up.

"Today wasn't about getting anywhere," Accalon said, wearily leaning against the wall. "Today was about establishing a baseline. In that regard, we obtained a great deal of information."

Before Analia could respond, Brenn rounded the corner, heat radiating off him in waves.

"What in the name of the Crystal was that?" he demanded, storming down the hall.

Accalon sighed. "Must we do this now, brother?"

"Why? Would you rather table this for tomorrow as well?"

Analia decided to take that as her cue to leave. She unpinned the phoenix pin from her dress, making to return it to Accalon.

"No," he said, "hold onto that for me." He folded her fingers back around the pin. "I trust you'll keep it safe."

He pulled her into a quick hug, kissing the side of her head. "Love you, little fledgling."

"Love you, too." Analia stepped away, catching a glimpse of the resentment that flashed across Brenn's face. Then, she turned, heading for her chambers and leaving Brenn and Accalon to bicker in the corridor—one blazing, the other an exhausted flicker.

# Chapter 5

Analia woke the following morning to the pounding of rain on stone. There was no point in going to the roof then. Not even Accalon's flames could survive that downpour.

Analia dressed quickly, thankfully moving fast enough to avoid Lynette and Mardie. As she opened her door to leave, she was surprised to find Rois waiting for her.

He was a tall man in his early twenties, with copper hair and a splash of freckles across his nose. This morning, he wore a gray military uniform, the Crystal Guard's phoenix-marked dark gray cloak draped over his shoulders.

The Crystal Guard existed in all kingdoms. Each iteration consisted of the seven deadliest, most skilled soldiers in the kingdom, charged with protecting the Royal family. It was a lifelong vow, which could mean several hundred years since most were Blessed and Demiblessed—those with one Blessed and one human parent. Rois, however, was one of the few humans ever anointed.

"Why are you skulking outside my chambers?" she asked, ignoring the way her heart twisted.

"I wanted to check on you," he said, pushing off the wall where he leaned. "I don't like having an enemy kingdom so close by. Some of their guards are already causing trouble."

"You know the rules, Rois."

Analia stepped around him and marched off down the corridor.

Rois jogged after her, "Brenn doesn't have to know."

"Because that worked out so well for us last time."

"Anna." Rois tried to touch her arm, but Analia jerked away.

She couldn't feel that touch again. Not when it came with the whispers, the memories that had twisted into a lump of rejected steel in the belly of a forge fire.

You should be thanking me, Brenn's voice echoed in her mind. Now you know he was only using you.

Rois let his hand drop. "How many times do I need to apologize?" he asked, regret in his eyes.

Analia had no pity.

"If you want to show you're sorry," she said, "then leave me alone."

She sped up. This time, Rois didn't try to follow.

Analia didn't have a destination in mind as she stormed through the halls. Nor was she surprised when she ended up outside her uncle's chambers. She had just rapped on the door with the iron phoenix knocker Accalon insisted on having, when Aaron, of all people, rounded the corner.

"Are you lost?" she asked, a bit terser than was polite, but this seemed to amuse him.

"Constantly." He sketched a dramatic bow. "Although I seem to have stumbled upon the correct place this time."

Aaron looked like he had just stumbled out of bed. His dark brown hair was tousled in a way that Analia couldn't tell was purposeful or not. Those shadows under his eyes certainly weren't.

"Why are you looking for my uncle?" she asked.

"Othin decided he wanted to get an early start on today's discussion. Which naturally means he sent me in his stead."

"Naturally?"

"Oh yes. I've been told I'm rather delightful to wake up to."

"I imagine it's quite the treat," Analia muttered. "Like a songbird that coos in your ear just to hear its own voice."

Aaron grinned with wicked delight. "Now why are you imagining waking up to me, Princess?"

Analia only spared him a look. Arrogant, lecherous guard. Where was Accalon? Deciding to risk impropriety, Analia shoved open the door, Aaron unabashedly peeking over her shoulder.

Where Analia's chambers were bare, Accalon's chambers were almost cluttered. An entire wall was taken up by a massive bookcase, stuffed to overflowing with books. An ornate writing desk sat beside it, placed beneath a wide window that looked out across the castle courtyard.

Now, however, thick orange, scarlet, and gold curtains were drawn, blocking out the gloomy gray light. In one corner, a small fire was dying in Accalon's hearth. And slumped at the foot of Accalon's bed...

"No," Analia breathed. Before Aaron could speak, she pushed inside, something cold settling in her stomach.

Accalon was still in the clothes he had been wearing the night before. His face was smooth. Too smooth. His body motionless.

"No," she whispered again, crouching beside him. "No. No, no, no, no, no."

Analia was only vaguely aware of Aaron and Rois shouting for help—so Rois had followed her after all. All she knew was Accalon's chest wasn't moving. There was no thud of a pulse beneath the finger she rested first on his neck, then either wrist.

Footsteps—so many footsteps—thundered down the hall. Someone crouched beside her.

"Analia..."

"Where's the wound?" Analia struggled to unlace Accalon's tunic. "We need to find the wound—"

"Analia—"

"If we can just find the wound, then it will be all right. Then we can fix it. He'll be fine." When had she started crying? "Dammit! Where's the wound?"

A hand lightly touched her shoulder.

"Don't touch me! Help me find the wound! Why is no one helping?"

Power thrummed to life behind her. Deardryn swept through the door, glowing with golden light.

"Remove her," she ordered.

Hands immediately latched onto Analia's arms.

"No! Stop! What are you doing?"

Analia writhed in their grip, trying to hold onto Accalon's hand. But she was no match for whoever tugged her through the crowd of people flooding into the chamber.

Voices, exclaiming, yelling, confused, shocked. Ringing in her ears. So loud. So cold. And Accalon...

Analia lunged forward, but the hands around her tightened. Rough, calloused hands. She twisted, expecting to see Rois. But those were silver eyes staring back at her.

Analia tried to shove him away. "Let me go!"

"Analia, stop," Aaron said calmly.

"He's my uncle!"

"I know, but you can't help him. Only Deardryn can, and she's already there."

There came a flare of golden light as Deardryn leaned over Accalon. Analia cringed away from the light, Aaron's words—she didn't care. She couldn't think. She was an animal, cornered, desperate, afraid.

Analia whipped her head back, cracking it against Aaron's cheekbone. He swore, his arms loosening out of surprise more than anything. Analia lunged forward, but within seconds Aaron seized her again. The two grappled, Aaron unable to get a solid hold.

"Dammit, Analia," he swore. "Am I going to have to pin you to the gods-damned floor?"

"Take your hands off Her Highness," Rois said, appearing in Analia's line of sight.

"Back off," Aaron spat. "My queen is trying to heal him."

Finally, he wrestled Analia's arms to her sides. "She'll only get in the way."

In the way. Underfoot. Nuisance. Duckling.

"At least let me do it." Rois tried to shove Aaron aside, but Aaron knocked his hands away. Analia made to break away once more. Aaron crossed his arms in front of her, lifting her up and bringing her down with her legs trapped beneath her.

"You can't," Aaron said tersely.

Something caught between a scream and a sob escaped past Analia's gritted teeth. Why was he doing this to her?

Aaron turned them away from Rois with a brazen finality. "Look away," he said in her ear, almost gently. "Don't watch this."

But she twisted her head, gaze locked on Deardryn's glowing palms pressed to Accalon's chest. Pryanth knelt on Accalon's other side, trying to assist, but his own golden light was nothing compared to Deardryn's blaze. Still, Accalon did not stir.

Analia watched, helpless, as seconds bled into minutes. She listened to the yells, demands to know what was going on, the sobbing, the confused exclamations. Chaos cast in the sunshine light of Deardryn's magic.

"He's gone," Analia whispered. And something fractured inside her that she knew could never be fixed.

Aaron didn't respond. He only held her tighter. Why? It wasn't like she could escape.

Finally, Deardryn looked up, a haggard expression marring her beautiful features. "I'm sorry."

Shock moved through the chamber like an electric current, rooting everyone to the spot. All until a shriek of disbelief broke the spell.

In a flash of gold and flame, Lucilla darted out the door. Aeley was quick to follow, hand clapped over her mouth. Brenn let out a howl of rage that sent the chamber into a new form of chaos: grief.

Analia turned in Aaron's arms. "I hope you're happy," she spat.

Aaron opened his mouth, but no words came out. His hand went to the chain around his neck—why was there pain in his eyes?

Not missing her opportunity, Analia shoved Aaron's arm aside, escaping his grip once more. This time, however, he didn't try to pull her back.

Deardryn remained beside Accalon. Pryanth had risen to his feet, stumbling away with a look of utter confusion.

"I must have done something wrong," Deardryn muttered to herself. "Why didn't it work? What did I do wrong?"

Noticing Analia, her expression softened. "I'm so sorry I failed."

Analia barely registered she was there. She sank to her knees, taking Accalon's limp hand in hers, a sob rising in her throat as she realized it was already cold. She pressed their joined hands to her cheek, ignoring Brenn and Othin's raised voices.

It couldn't be real. Accalon couldn't be gone. Because that would mean she was truly and utterly alone. And that tidal wave of realization threatened to swallow her whole.

Analia felt someone crouch beside her. Expecting Aaron, she whipped her head around, an acid retort on her lips. But it was Cadmus. Pale, shaking, and silent, he stared vacantly at their uncle's corpse. At the faint black mark on the side of his neck.

"My brother is dead!" Brenn roared. "First my cousin, and now my brother. Someone here is killing my family!"

He stood on one side of Accalon's bed, a nonplussed Othin on the other. Analia could feel their power buzz through her skin and into her blood as their tempers flared. Just as she could feel something stir inside her. Something burning.

"My queen just spent up most of her magic reserves trying to save his life!" Othin exclaimed. "Wouldn't that be a little counterintuitive?"

"How do we know she was actually healing him, huh? How do we know it wasn't just some—some facade?"

"Facade!" Othin repeated incredulously. "We're the only foreign kingdom here! How stupid do you think we are?"

Analia's hand clenched around Accalon's. What good was screaming doing? Call the guards. Take Sun for questioning.

"Unless you knew we wouldn't suspect you because we would think you weren't that stupid."

Othin threw up his hands.

"I'm done playing your mind games," Brenn announced. "I want you out of my kingdom immediately."

No! Get the evidence first! What was he thinking?

All around, there came the rasp of leather on steel as weapons were drawn. Grief was igniting into rage, and Brenn was presenting an all-too-easy outlet.

"You're accusing us," Othin said, "with no proof."

"No." Analia's voice was as silent as the smoke before the flames. Not even Cadmus or Deardryn heard. But that initial release of air was the first step—always the hardest step.

Brenn made to respond, but a voice cut through the throng. And to everyone's surprise—especially her own—it was Analia's. "No!"

Everyone froze. Then, eyes roved across the chamber, searching for the source, locking onto her.

"No?" Brenn repeated calmly.

Normally, that would have been enough to have her scuttling back. But the ice had completely melted. Now? Now, she was burning.

"Accalon would never act on conjectures alone," Analia said. "Especially one that threatened to burn every shred of friendship that he'd cultivated to the ground."

"My brother would want his killer to be brought to justice," Brenn said. Too calm.

"It's not justice if you punish the wrong man," Analia said. "Accalon would question, he would push, and he would be suspicious, but he believed in innocence until proven otherwise. And right now, you have no proof."

Deardryn's eyes were wide with amazement. But Analia's gaze was only for Brenn.

"Sun stays until we get answers," she told him. "They will be guarded at all times, but not treated as prisoners until we prove their innocence or guilt."

Silence.

For a moment, Brenn's mask slipped, and Analia saw a level of hatred that she knew deep in her bones would come to kill her. But for now, Brenn had to respond, regain control.

With a great deal of effort, he summoned a look of pride that scared her most of all. Then, he barked a list of orders to his soldiers about Sun regulations. As soon as he finished, his eyes found Analia once more.

"Little duckling," he said. "What a queen you will be. If the crown ever makes it to you."

Analia didn't miss the threat. Her hand tightened around Accalon's, the fire draining out of her like water out a leak. Within moments, she was left empty, broken and grieving once more.

Crystal spare her, what had she done?

After a slight pause, Brenn waved his hand, dismissing the room. It was like a spell had been lifted. Ash guards herded the Sun people into the center of the room, Othin protesting all the way.

Analia glanced to Deardryn, who hadn't moved since her outburst. And to her shock, the look Deardryn gave her was one of approval. Tired, strained, but undeniable.

"Thank you," she said, placing a slim hand over Analia's. "You were magnificent."

Analia only felt hollow.

Someone called Deardryn's name. She gracefully rose to her feet. Delicately dusting the dirt from her skirts, her gaze caught Analia's one last time, and she didn't need to speak the apology aloud.

Analia remained rooted to the ground as everyone filtered out, most still dabbing at damp eyes. She remained motionless as the Ash healers arrived, dressed in their robes of varying shades of green. Ember was among them, her fingers gentle as she uncurled Analia's fingers from around Accalon's so they could take him away.

Slowly, everyone filtered out of the chamber, leaving a heavy silence.

And Brenn.

"You," he seethed, stalking forward.

Analia couldn't move.

"I told you to be invisible. To not embarrass me in front of a foreign power. And yet, you insisted on lingering at every step. And now you have the audacity to challenge me in front of the people who murdered our king?"

At least when he killed her, she would be with Accalon. Not alone with nothing to protect her from Brenn's rage.

"Worthless! You horrible mistake of a girl! I should have killed you all those years ago, spared myself the humiliation. But now?"

Brenn pushed her back with burning hands, her head cracking against the iron post of Accalon's bed frame. "You are going to be questioned. Tomorrow. First thing. And I hope your memory serves you well."

Brenn shoved away from her, striding out of the room and slamming the door behind him.

Silence. Thick and smothering. But Analia welcomed it; allowed it to wrap tighter and tighter around her as the swinging pendulum of time jerked to a halt.

She didn't know how long it took her to raise a heavy hand to feel the lump on the back of her head. How long it took to finally push herself to her feet, one mechanical movement at a time.

She felt herself take that first step as if in a dream. She exited the room, drifting down the corridor, up the stairs, a wraith tracing an ancient, ingrained path.

Chilly rain soaked through Analia's shirt as she stepped out onto the roof. She kicked off her slippers, using her toes to grip the slick stone as she hauled herself up the wall. Reaching the turret's roof, her eyes landed on that gods-damned bench, soaked from the rain, and she finally realized.

She would never see Accalon sitting there again. He would never come looking for her on the turret's roof, ever again. He would never ruffle her hair and call her his little fledgling.

Because Accalon... Accalon was dead.

The pendulum slammed into movement once more. Analia fell to her knees. And as the rain crashed down around her, as the first sobs broke free, Analia knew there was no rising again. Not from this. Not from anything, ever again.

42

# Chapter 6

It had been three days since Ember had slept. But she supposed that was what happened when one was a healer, and the king was assassinated in his own gods-damned chambers.

Ember rubbed her eyes. Everything had started to blur again. Was she remembering to blink? Wasn't she supposed to do that automatically? That would be an inconvenient thing to have malfunction.

She staggered to a nearby set of drawers, rifling through until her fingers found a familiar fuzzy plant. Pulling it out, she crushed a few leaves between her fingers and brought them to her nose, the sharp, sour smell making her eyes water.

Ember doubted Master Lenzi would have approved of her use of devinroot—it was a highly addictive stimulant after all. But bad times called for bad decisions. And all the other times before that? Well, Master Lenzi didn't need to know about that.

Right now, that little beast was the only thing keeping Ember on her feet, and she figured Rosala, patron goddess of healing, would understand.

Ember brushed her light brown hair from her eyes, the back room of the apothecary coming into focus.

The stone building was separated into two sections. The front was much larger, filled with shelves of basic aid equipment that patrons were welcome to browse and purchase. Wide banks of windows—all filled with various plants—stretched across the side walls, letting in light that highlighted the varying shades of blue, silver, and gray in the stone.

The back room, however, was cramped. It was mainly used for storage, with various jars and bundles of dried leaves scattered haphazardly throughout drawers and shelves set into the stone.

The actual healing of patients and the examination of bodies occurred in the Ash Kingdom Healer School, which was also where Ember and her fellow apprentices were supposed to do their studying. Ember, however, had discovered early on that the other apprentices slowed her down—and they were offended when she told them this—so she had taken to bringing her work to this secluded corner. It wasn't like Dane, the apothecary owner, would mind. That required him being around to notice.

Ember gave the crumpled plant in her hand a cursory glance: long trailing stem, vivid orange and yellow leaves. Then, she shoved it back in its drawer—at least, she was relatively sure it was the right drawer. Thankfully, it only needed magic to survive.

Ember had just sat down at her desk to go over her latest ancient and yellowing scroll when the apothecary door softly opened. She was about to swear, just loud enough that the newcomer could overhear and take the hint—the sun wasn't even up yet, for Rosala's sake. But then she saw who it was.

Ember hurried out from her back room. Circling around the main desk, she reached out to hug her friend.

Analia's arms remained stiff at her sides. It took her a moment to offer a hollow greeting, Ember's heart twisting as she pulled away.

"I'm not going to insult you by asking how you're doing," she said, ushering Analia into the back room.

"I look that bad, huh."

"I told you I wasn't going to insult you." Ember pulled out her chair and nudged Analia into it, retreating to lean against one of the shelves. "I haven't seen you since..."

The unsaid words hung in the air like a funeral shroud.

"I just got out of interrogations." Analia idly picked at a thread in her gray shirt, twisting and untwisting it around her fingers.

"How'd that go?" Ember asked.

"It was Ronun. How do you think?"

Ember huffed. That decrepit fossil—thought he knew so much based on observation alone. She didn't care if Ronun was the king's interrogator, no one could completely understand the inside by examining the outside.

Analia went on to explain how Brenn had only ordered Sun's people to be interrogated—plus herself because she was first on the scene. She'd had to convince Ronun to open investigations to servants, staff, guards, any and every person in the castle that could have seen something. But Ember was having a hard time paying attention. She kept searching for something, anything, in Analia's gaze, but there was nothing behind her eyes.

Analia said, "I told Ronun to report to me everything he finds."

"I bet Brenn loved hearing about that," Ember commented.

"Brenn doesn't need to be aware. Just as long as someone's there to smother his flames before he demolishes everything within a fifty-mile radius. And I've had plenty of time to become accustomed to his burns."

What a vile little man. Ember had a few choice herbs she'd like to feed him. But even when they were seven, Analia had shaken her head, asking her not to make it worse.

"I know you said you wouldn't insult me," Analia said, "but you're not looking too well yourself, Em."

"Master Lenzi assigned all the apprentices to the case," Ember explained, rubbing her neck. "Even the ones without their markings."

As healer apprentices moved through their training, they got one white ring inked around their eyes for every area they mastered. After receiving their fourth and final ring, they would travel to the Temple of Rosala where they would swear their healer's oath, and the ink would be turned from white to their kingdom's colors.

Ember only had two rings—one for herbal healing and the other for external healing—and she swore the ink itched. No one listened, though, and blamed it on her being human.

It was widely believed that healers were chosen by Rosala herself. Some argued this choosing enabled the Crystal to Bless healer magic, while others thought Rosala specifically directed the Crystal to bestow such a Blessing. What was known was, in very rare circumstances, a human without a drop of Blessed blood would be chosen and gifted with healer magic—although they didn't receive any other benefits of being Blessed.

"What have you found?" Analia asked.

"Hmm?" Ember stopped scratching her ink markings. "Anna, are you sure you want to hear about—"

"Tell me."

Ember sighed, pushing off the wall. "Well, that's the interesting part. We once again found the black mark on the neck, though much fainter than the one on Baylen's body. But we also found some sort of plant in Accalon's system.

"It's nothing I've ever seen before—which you know is odd, since herbology is my specialty. We've been scouring all the ancient texts we have, but all we've been able to find is its name."

Ember skimmed through a particularly decrepit scroll on her desk. "Yes, here it is, xenol. Nothing else, though. No genus family, no properties, uses. Not even a crude little sketch in the margin. We only found it because of a brief note on its composition, which matched our tests."

Analia peered over Ember's shoulder. "You think it's some sort of ancient poison?"

"I don't know what else it could be," Ember said. "There was no sign of injury, organ failure, brain trauma. And everything else we found in his system was normal."

She reached around Analia to fish out another page, knocking over an entire stack of papers in the process. She'd deal with that later... probably.

Ember skimmed through the list. "Yes, all we found was meat, potatoes, herbal tea, wine—"

"Accalon never drank wine," Analia said immediately. "He said he didn't like his brain being fuzzy."

Ember snorted. "He was dealing with Sun Royals. Can you blame the man for spiking his own drink?"

"No. But I wonder if that was the only spike."

"Well, that's an interesting theory," Ember mused.

"Have you tested his dinnerware for trace amounts of xenol?" Analia asked.

"I tried," Ember said, "but when I went to ask the kitchen staff—"

"Ask?"

"Forcefully insist, whatever, they'd already been washed. But Anna, the xenol was in his stomach. It had to have been consumed, and yet Accalon was the only one poisoned. His plate or cup had to be specifically targeted."

"So, we should be looking at people who had direct access," Analia finished. She sighed, pushing herself to her feet. "I'll do some searching of my own."

Ember frowned, trailing after Analia as she headed for the apothecary door. "Anna, if it's not in our records, I don't know how you'll find it—"

"I will."

"But Anna—"

"I will," she repeated. She stopped at the door, turning to look at Ember fully. Softening her tone, she said, "Thank you," then slipped out.

Analia wrapped her arms around herself as she walked through the kingdom. It was barely cold enough to warrant a jacket, but Analia wanted it colder. Cold enough that she couldn't feel her nose, that her fingers ached when she tried to bend them. Numb. Silent. But she pushed the thoughts aside.

She couldn't think of the grief, the hug from Ember that was supposed to squeeze her back together like a clay pot, but only reminded her of all the cracks she had. The thought alone had her pressing her hand to her mouth, barely managing to contain her sob.

One day. She had told herself she would only have that one day.

Analia climbed the steps to the Ash Castle and reached for her flames. Not the magical kind. These were the flames that had erupted in her chest as Ronun questioned her, mercilessly picking her answers apart as if she hadn't lost everything.

Now, those flames were the only thing that kept her on her feet. One step at a time, feeling the burn of something that would get her killed if she misplayed a single step. She, however, was having a hard time considering that the worst-case scenario.

Not long later, Analia arrived at the Great Hall. Normally, no one would be up at that hour, but a few people sat huddled together at various tables—yes, including him.

Analia looked away. She moved to a side table scattered with fruit and pastries, filling a small bowl. One routine after another. Just another thing she could do without thinking while she let those flames build in anticipation.

"Good morning."

Pryanth—looking slightly rumpled but otherwise pristine—stood behind her, Warack and Kuno to either side of him.

"Hello." Analia bowed her head, then stepped around Pryanth and headed for her family's table.

"Wait," Pryanth said, following. "Is that all?"

Analia took her seat, giving Pryanth a feigned look of surprise. "I didn't realize conversation was desirable given the tension between our kingdoms."

"It's because of you it's tension and nothing more." Pryanth pulled out the chair across from her and tapped its back. "May I join you?"

"Don't you have interrogations?" she asked.

"I've been cleared. Just now, actually, which is the only reason I'm awake at this Crystal-forsaken hour."

Analia warily looked to the guards, both of whom confirmed his story with a nod. "I suppose you may."

Pryanth flashed a smile and settled himself in his chair. Warack and Kuno sat on either side of him.

Yes, certainly haughty with those looks he flashed them. And his conviction that Analia would agree. Well, being a prince with his mother's golden eyes and hair, his father's strong jaw, and his kingdom's sun-kissed skin, she had no problem imagining how Pryanth developed that haughtiness.

Analia let the silence hang between them as she forced herself to eat a grape.

Lately, talking had become the most arduous task she could think of. The past couple meals she'd choked down, she'd purposefully come when no one would be eating. Her only company had been the fire sprites—finger-sized, humanoid creatures made of flame—who liked to perch upon the wicks of candles placed on the Great Hall's tables.

Thankfully, they left her alone. Although the one at her elbow was quite obviously whipping its tiny head back and forth between her and Pryanth, eyes wide with bewilderment.

"My sincerest condolences about your uncle," Pryanth said, finally breaking the silence.

Analia momentarily looked up as she thanked him, then returned her eyes to her bowl. She could feel Pryanth's puzzled gaze on her, but she ignored it.

"If there's anything I can do," Pryanth eventually said, reaching across the table to touch her hand, "please, do not hesitate to ask."

His honey eyes were soft, earnest.

"Do you know who killed my uncle?" Analia asked.

"Well, no, but—"

"Then I don't believe there is anything you can do for me." She softened the words with a gentle pat to the back of Pryanth's hand with her free one, retracting the one under his.

Pryanth gaped. Warack and Kuno struggled to maintain their composure. The fire sprite, however, let out a giggle that sounded like the tiny crackle of a flame.

"Tell me," Pryanth blurted, breaking the silence for a third time. "At the meeting, your uncle and my mother were discussing how he didn't have an heir. I'm not aware of the full story."

"It's not one often discussed."

Pryanth leaned forward. "Are you willing to?"

It was the last thing Analia wanted to do. Especially when talking about Accalon—remembering his past, that he only existed there now—had the sob in her throat threatening to rip free.

"I suppose," she hedged.

She speared another piece of fruit, a bit harder than necessary, taking her time as she chewed. Pryanth practically squirmed with impatience. Finally, Analia swallowed and began.

"There isn't much to tell. A little over two decades ago, Accalon's wife, Arienne, went into premature labor due to the stress of the mob in the square—although I don't need to bore you with that."

Pryanth looked as though he very much would like to be bored by that, but Analia didn't pause.

"Accalon was gone, he had no idea what was happening. He came back to the castle to find his son had been delivered stillborn, and his wife..."

"What happened?" Pryanth asked, enthralled.

"The healers tried, but there was so much blood. And without rapid healing abilities—"

"She was human!" Pryanth exclaimed.

Analia shook herself free of the memories. "It's not unheard of. Royal magic is guaranteed to be passed down, human partner or no." Present company excluded.

"No, I know," Pryanth agreed quickly. "It's just unusual. I suppose human women have the advantage of having more than three cycles a year, but they have completely different social statuses, no magical advantage, different life spans."

"Nothing about Accalon was usual," Analia said quietly.

The fire sprite curled into a ball on the candle wick. Warack and Kuno bowed their heads, no doubt feeling the same crush of grief that threatened to take Analia's breath away. *One day.*

Pryanth bowed his head, but Analia could still see the curiosity in his eyes as he tried to fill in the holes she'd purposefully left.

"I'm afraid the rest of the story will have to wait for another time," she said, rising from the table.

Pryanth quickly looked up. "But—"

"I'm sorry, but I have business to attend to in the library." She grabbed the fire sprite's candle by its ornate metal holder. "Thank you for keeping me company."

Analia nodded to the guards, then retreated from the table. She could feel Pryanth's gaze locked on her, demanding she turn back. Good.

Exiting the Great Hall, Analia looked down at the fire sprite, still curled on the candle wick.

"It will be all right, little one," she promised. "I'll take care of it."

The fire sprite peeked up at her hopefully. And Analia prayed to the Crystal, the gods, anyone or thing that would listen, that that wasn't a lie.

# Chapter 7

Aaron wasn't trying to be difficult. Well, not initially, at least.

The Ash Kingdom's interrogation chambers were in the belly of the castle. Where most of the castle's walls were either decorated with banners or paintings, the interrogation chambers were all gray stone: floor, ceiling, walls, uninterrupted by windows or decoration. Well, unless one counted the dried bloodstains that had been pointedly left uncleaned.

Aaron sat in a stone chair, his wrists shackled to the arms. A desk made from a rough slab of stone with a carved-out center stood before him, Ronun seated on the other side as he jotted down Aaron's account for the thirty-seventh time.

How Deardryn had the Sun's Crystal Guard on rotating shifts. How Aaron had been dragged out of bed—after already having done his shift, mind you—to guard with Dannel because he and Lev had gotten in an argument over a prostitute they'd both fooled around with, and Lev had stormed off. How Othin had then sent Aaron to retrieve Accalon because he wished to continue their discussion immediately.

"And you were the first to find the body?" Ronun asked. Again.

If Aaron had to guess, he would say this man was Blessed, although he couldn't pinpoint what his magic was. The hands he rested on the table between them were heavily scarred. His light brown hair was peppered with gray, which combined with his weathered face had Aaron wondering if he had some non-Blessed blood in him.

The Blessed—Royals in particular—usually exhibited incredibly slowed-down physical aging by their late twenties to early thirties. Talitha was over six hundred when the Defiants all mysteriously disappeared, and it was said that she didn't get a wrinkle until she was in her three hundreds. Demiblessed, however, seemed to bounce around a middle ground between humans and Blessed, with more pronounced signs of aging.

"Yes," Aaron said. Again. "Princess Analia and I were the first to find him. Although that Ash guard showed up soon after. The sad, twitchy one."

"Rois?"

"Sure."

Ronun launched into another round of questions, and Aaron stifled a sigh. He knew he should have stayed in the Sun Kingdom. It was the opportunity he'd been looking for the past three months he'd been there as a guard: a chance to search the castle, no Royals around to question him.

Yet, the moment Deardryn received the letter from Accalon and subtly bullied Othin into agreeing to go, there was Aaron. Volunteering his services as a guard on the journey. Squandering his chance. All because of her.

A sudden shift in conversation jerked Aaron out of his reveries like a sharp tug on a tether.

"Poisoning the king the night before," he mused. "Remind me, when did I say that?"

Ronun tugged his notes closer to himself. "I'm not going to allow you to see what you said in order to corroborate your lies."

"Well, if I must resort to corroborating my lies, I mustn't be much of a liar in the first place—although if you haven't caught me yet I believe that says more about your skills than it does mine."

"You can stop there," Ronun said wearily.

"Why? Because we both know I'm innocent?"

Ronun glared. Completely unfazed, Aaron reclined in his seat, his cuffs chafing.

"Anything else you think we both know?" Ronun asked.

"Well, we both know I make for delightful company, and you must be incredibly reluctant to let me leave as a result. But we also know this is getting tedious. We both know I'm innocent and that I don't know anything I haven't already told you. So, I would say it's about time that you release me."

Ronun eyed him, and for a moment, Aaron thought he was going to do just that. Instead, Ronun dropped his pen and looked down his nose.

"Do you know why I am the Ash Kingdom's interrogator?" he asked.

"Lack of applicants?"

"Because I'm good at reading people."

Aaron didn't doubt that for a second. He'd clocked those sharp, observant eyes the moment he was first escorted into the chamber.

"Everything about your body language, your tone, your words even, says you're perfectly at ease. Yet, your muscles are coiled. You're ready to spring into motion at any moment. That mild amusement on your face hasn't budged an inch from the moment you walked in here, and I want to know what hides beneath it."

"A tender heart, charming wit, and deep-rooted existential dread," Aaron deadpanned.

To his credit, Ronun managed to maintain a remarkable degree of decorum. He tapped his pen on the desk, each tap echoing off the stone.

"You keep building those walls," Ronun said eventually, "and soon, they'll be too tall for you to see what's important anymore."

Aaron bit back a response. Seeing what's important was the precise reason he needed his walls. Nevertheless, Aaron figured it was time he wrapped this up. Time to summon that tender heart of his.

"I understand this is important," he began, leaning forward and meeting Ronun's gaze. "You lost your king, and a special one from what I could tell. And I am sincerely sorry, but I had nothing to do with his murder.

"I've told you everything I know. I wish I could be more helpful—and I know that scoff means you don't believe me—but I do. Because I *know* what it's like to lose a king. I am intimately familiar with the rage, and confusion, and the heartbreak you pray will be assuaged if you can get some answers. But you're not going to get those answers from me. So please, stop wasting your time and continue searching elsewhere."

Aaron didn't flinch under the interrogator's scrutiny. Instead, he allowed Ronun to see the jagged pieces of himself he'd been slowly smoothing out for so long.

And to his surprise, Ronun replied, "I know."

He pushed back his chair and stood. Then, gathering his things, he strode out of the chamber without further comment, leaving Aaron alone. Still shackled.

Aaron rolled his eyes. Letting out a breath, he carefully tucked those pieces away once more. He'd stopped hiding from them long ago, but some were still sharp. He preferred to be delicate with them, give them the respect they deserved.

Twisting his wrist, Aaron managed to wiggle the silver pin he'd stashed in the lining of his sleeve into his hand. A few seconds later, he was free, rubbing his wrists as he followed Ronun out the door.

Clearly, they'd both realized he could've escaped whenever he wanted. So then why had he stayed so long?

It had been four days since Analia had breakfast with Pryanth, and she had spent nearly all that time in the library.

Floor-to-ceiling polished wood bookcases wrapped around the room, the floors covered in a soft, sandy-orange carpet. Accalon—to the horror of the bookkeepers—had decided to organize the books by color and not subject, creating a rainbow effect as one turned about the room.

Gods, when would that stab of grief go away? Analia shoved the thoughts aside, hunching her shoulders over her book.

"Something wrong?" Pryanth asked from a nearby chair.

She was surprised it had taken as long as it had for him to come looking for her. Bored, haughty, and from the Sun Kingdom, Pryanth was looking for something to catch his attention. Something like a story left hanging by a disinterested teller. One that turned Analia into not only a mystery to solve, but a challenge.

As a result, Pryanth had arrived about two hours after that first breakfast, guards in tow.

"I thought you might like some company," he'd said, hovering in the doorway. "And if not company, then tea."

For the past four days, Analia entered the library to find Pryanth waiting for her, a steaming mug of herbal tea already waiting in her usual spot.

"Nothing's wrong," she said, reaching for the teapot.

Pryanth didn't look completely convinced. "Are you ever going to tell me what you've been so diligently looking for?"

"Honestly, I'm not sure." She took a sip from her mug, burning her tongue, before closing the book on her lap. *Herbology: A History.*

"Perhaps a distraction," Pryanth said, his voice softening slightly. "Although, why you're looking for it in plants of all places..."

"And where would you look for a distraction?" Analia asked.

"History," he said immediately. "Think about it, Analia. Story after story, of brave soldiers, crafty Royals, bloody battles, and the psychological warfare of politics. And they all happened!"

"I bet your library is full of those stories."

Analia stood from her chair, crossing to the green section of the bookcases and replacing her book.

"Like you wouldn't believe," Pryanth said. "If you're looking for a distraction, you should come to our library."

"Is it truly as expansive as the whispers claim?" Analia asked, grabbing the next book on the shelf and returning to her seat. So far, she hadn't found even an allusion to xenol.

"Better," Pryanth said proudly. He waved the book on the Ash Kingdom's history that he'd been reading. "You only have books pertaining to your kingdom here. We have books on all kingdoms. Even Star."

"I bet you don't have any books on plants that we don't. They're too boring."

"Every good performance needs its background characters. Without them, the leads don't stand out."

"And if I *were* to come see your magnificent library, which would I be?"

Pryanth met her gaze. "That's up to you."

He flashed her one of those "adore me" grins he'd given her at breakfast.

"I'd like to see it," Analia murmured, carefully keeping her face averted.

"I think you should," said Pryanth softly.

That night, Analia slipped through silent halls, ducking into an antechamber near a back staircase. Fitting herself into a shadowy corner, she didn't have to wait long before there came the sound of approaching footsteps.

"Ronun," she said coolly.

Ronun stalked through the antechamber entrance, clad in his typical gray-and-black robes. He jerked his chin in greeting, not bothering to speak.

A part of her was tempted to point out that he was late. Instead, she cut straight to the point. "What's your report?"

Ronun looked down his nose at her, but for once, this didn't bother her. He did that to everyone.

Unfurling a scroll he had tucked in his sleeve, Ronun read, "All of the Sun people have officially been interviewed and cleared—"

"How?" Analia exclaimed.

"All Ash guards have been interviewed," Ronun droned on, "and all kitchen, serving, and related staff are still in the process of being questioned. Thus far, no one has reported seeing anything that has led to solid, incriminating evidence."

"Have you spoken to the servant who delivered the drinks?" Analia asked.

"Yes, I talked to her," Ronun said, glancing up from his scroll. "I am capable of doing my job without your unsolicited assistance."

Analia had the urge to point out that, if it weren't for her, he wouldn't have talked to them in the first place. Once again, she choked down the words. It wasn't worth the battle.

Ronun went back to his scroll. "Upon asking, she confirmed no odd ingredient had been placed into Accalon's drink—although the term odd is ambiguous. There was no hint of deception, though it's possible she didn't see it happen."

"And what about the guards?"

"Ash guards on patrol confirmed no attempted break-ins to Accalon's chambers at any point throughout the night. One of the Sun guards—the arrogant, smart-mouthed one—"

"Aaron?"

Ronun nodded. Analia sighed.

"He alluded to a dispute between two of his fellow guards that concluded with one storming off—"

"Was he spotted by any of our people?"

"I don't appreciate being interrupted, Your Highness."

Analia's cheeks flushed. She had been pacing the tiny antechamber, mind moving so fast her mouth could barely keep up. "My apologies," she muttered.

Ronun gave her an austere look before continuing. "Yes. Warack reported seeing him stomping throughout the halls. He first made a loop through the Sun corridors, then wandered into the Ash halls—although he did not attempt to enter Accalon's chambers.

"When Warack made to question him, they apparently engaged in a noteworthy squabble. The first of many, it seems. Rois reported separating them before the Sun guard returned to his corridors. Beyond this, this guard has been spotted entering and departing the king and queen's chambers on numerous occasions all throughout their stay."

"He's a guard," Analia said. "Why wouldn't he be doing that?"

"Usually," Ronun said, "guards remain outside unless summoned specifically or carrying news."

Analia paused her pacing. "Who was this guard?"

"Lev."

Of course it was. Analia resumed her pacing.

"And you're positive all of Sun is cleared?" she asked.

"Are you questioning my work, Your Highness?"

"What? No, no of course not."

She was questioning how her uncle was murdered and yet the castle seemed to be full of checked-out alibis.

"Who was the last to see him?" she asked.

"His Highness, Brenn."

"Did you speak with him?"

"Briefly. He wished for me to prioritize Sun interrogations while we still had jurisdiction to keep them here."

For once, Analia agreed with him. "So," she said, leaning her head against the wall, "with all of Sun cleared, what does that mean?"

"It means," Ronun said, "while investigations will be continuing, we do not possess a strong enough reason to hold the Sun people here. They will consequently be returning to their kingdom on the morrow. It also means you have encountered a dead end."

"We'll see about that," Analia said to herself.

Despite Ronun's claims, she knew his methods weren't infallible. His Blessing was a subtle variety. One that enhanced his observational abilities, allowing him to perceive, take note of, and interpret a person's every move, down to their microexpressions.

It created an uncanny ability to spot deception. Yet, if he didn't ask precisely the right question, he could identify deception, but not what it was related to.

"How did the Sun Royals react when being interrogated?" she asked.

Ronun raised his brows, giving her a look of—was that approval? "Queen Deardryn was cool and collected, although noticeably distraught. King Othin blustered his indignation the entire time, particularly about the marriage pact that was discussed. And Prince Pryanth seemed bored, as if he couldn't understand why I was wasting his time."

And Lev had obviously been conferring with the Royals about something. They all had motives, ranging from destroying the possible marriage pact to weakening a kingdom that could declare war.

Yet, it was as Othin said: killing Accalon in his own kingdom, when they would be the obvious first suspects, was incredibly risky. Were any of their motivations strong enough to make that risk worth it?

Analia toyed with Accalon's pin on her chest, her head starting to ache. "Thank you for your report," she said, jerking her chin at Ronun. "You're dismissed."

Ronun gave her an indifferent look. Rolling up his scroll, he dipped his chin and made to leave. Yet, he glanced back.

"Your uncle always turned to me first when questioning a person," he said. "But he was always the one to make the final say. And it was not always the one I suggested. Do not forget, I am only one of many advisors."

Analia nodded, and Ronun finally departed. Yes, he was only one advisor, and Analia was only one princess. But sometimes, one was enough.

# Chapter 8

*R*ise again. It was the Ash Kingdom motto, Accalon in particular fond of it due to its easy applicability. Analia had lost count of how many times he'd said it to her, either with a pat on her shoulder after a failure, or an all-consuming grin at her success. But how was she supposed to rise again from this?

From the top of Mt. Vasolus, Analia peered out across the crowd gathering at various heights across the volcano's face. Many wore the burnt orange and smoky gray of their kingdom's colors. All were wiping tears as Accalon's body, wrapped in an orange-and-gray funeral shroud, was walked through the crowd by the Crystal Guard on their long trek up the volcano.

Analia held her breath, trying to force the lump down her throat. She'd cried enough on her turret. It was a miracle she'd been able to stop, and she had a feeling her luck had ended there. Instead, she let the kingdom cry for her as she watched Accalon's body climb closer and closer.

At the top, the Ash Royals from lower branches of the family tree—about fifteen total—stood in a line, Analia, Cadmus, Lucilla, and Aeley in its center. All wore long, flowing gray robes, hoods pulled up to hide their faces.

The hoods were supposed to be symbolic: the obscuring smoke after a phoenix had died, flung back after the new phoenix, the new ruler, rose from the volcano's flames. Now, she was certain the only things those hoods were obscuring were the Royals as their composure shattered.

Reaching the top, the guards rested Accalon's body a few feet from the mouth of the volcano. They bowed to the assembled Royals, quickly retreating into the crowd as Brenn stepped forward.

"The power of the Ash extends back centuries," he called, his voice echoing. "All the way back to the moment when the Defiants procured the Crystal, abolishing the tyrannical rule of the Ancient Ones and Blessing the lands with magic. It was Azar whom the Crystal chose to Bless with the Royal magic of flame, and every descendant that followed him.

"Stone by stone, he built the foundation of our kingdom. But more importantly, he entrusted those who followed in his footsteps to cherish it, take care of it. And that is exactly what King Accalon Valarus did.

"My brother gave everything he had to this kingdom over his thirty-five-year reign. In the end, he gave his life." Brenn crossed to where Accalon lay at the edge of the crater. "Now, it is time that we as a kingdom thank him for all he has given us."

Analia expected Brenn's words to hurt. Instead, she felt a fierce wave of pride as Brenn raised his hand, summoning a column of golden flames from the volcano's mouth.

She told herself Accalon deserved to be at peace. He would have wanted the rest that the volcano's flames provided as Brenn directed them toward his wrapped body.

It was just the smoke and heat that made her eyes burn as the tongues of flame licked across the shroud. The fire sprites that danced in the flames were celebrating Accalon's life, not mourning his death. The heavy, yawning hole inside her was a reminder of everything she'd had, and not everything she had lost in an explosion of smoke and flame.

The volcano's flames consumed her uncle's body. She could have sworn the lava seemed to hum with power—which wouldn't have surprised her. But why hadn't the lava turned blue after touching Accalon's network like it was supposed to?

The volcano itself wasn't considered active, having not erupted for millennia and no longer releasing its toxic gas. Yet, curiously, whenever it came time for a new Ash ruler to be crowned, lava always had a way of blasting forth, somehow able to reduce even bone to ash.

And ash was all she saw as the smoke cleared, the pile protected from the wind by a group of fire sprites. One by one, each Royal stepped forward, taking a handful of ash and releasing it on the wind.

As the new heir to the throne, Analia was the last to approach. A part of her recoiled at the thought of her skin touching her uncle's ashes. But as the dusty ash slipped through her fingers, as she lifted her hand to the warm spring winds, Analia didn't want to let go.

"Rise again, Uncle," she said, her voice cracking as she watched the last of him spiral away toward the Phoenix Gate.

When she glanced down at her palm, a small pinch of ash remained. She knew she should blow it away. Instead, she idly traced the edge of Accalon's pin with a finger as she hesitated, finding a groove with her nail. Raising a brow, she dug in her nail and the front of the pin popped off, revealing an odd black stone beneath the phoenix.

Feeling her mother's eyes on her back, Analia quickly added the pinch of ash and reattached the front, trying to hide her surprise. It was already a miracle Brenn hadn't tried to reclaim the pin. She would give him no reason to snatch it back now.

As Analia fell back in line, voices rose up from the crowd, combining into a chant. It took her a moment to make out the words, but once she did, she was shocked she didn't crumble to ash herself.

"Rise again! Rise again! Rise again!"

Brenn listened to the cries for a moment, head bowed. "My brother always had a saying," he finally said. "No king can ever last forever, but his kingdom can. And it's the decision of the one that follows whether that kingdom will remain, or be razed."

The volcano rumbled.

"Kings may not last forever, but this king should have lasted much longer. He should still be here with us today, and we should be nowhere near this volcano. But the gods have reclaimed my brother's soul, the Crystal his magic. And every phoenix must rise again."

Brenn raised his hand. Once again, a column of flames erupted from the volcano. The path of the flames curved in unison with the movement of Brenn's hand, coiling down until it engulfed him. The golden lava turned the vivid orange of his magic, swirling around him like a fiery cocoon.

"As your king," Brenn said within the flames, "I swear, I will not just help this kingdom remain. I will build. And we will start by getting justice for my brother."

The cocoon blasted apart, sparks flying as Brenn stepped forward. He threw back his hood—the fabric protected by his magic—revealing the face of the new Ash King for the first time.

"Today, we mourn. We remember our king and all he has done for us. And we will not forget his story. Especially how it ended."

Brenn took a moment to soak in the cheers below. Then, he shadowjumped to the base of Mt. Vasolus, the volcano releasing a blast of dry heat in his wake like a mighty exhale of approval. But Analia only felt cold. Of course, Brenn had to end his speech with a threat so thinly veiled a blink could blow it away.

Analia pushed back her hood and silently took Cadmus's hand. He was the only one that had offered to not just jump her to the top, but also back down.

Yet, the moment they stepped out of the darkness, Cadmus quickly stepped away, leaving her to watch as her family emerged around her. They immediately split off, finding friends and acquaintances in the crowd, scattering farther and farther until she was completely alone.

Analia wasn't fazed, not even surprised. It was nothing new. What was new was the shockwave of pain in her chest as she automatically looked back, searching for someone who wasn't there. Who would never be there again.

It took Analia a moment to notice Pryanth had emerged from the crowd before her—what was he doing there? His mouth was pinched, undoubtedly from Brenn's impromptu speech, but the squeeze he gave her hand was comforting.

"How are you?" he asked, leading her back into the crowd.

Analia cringed under the bewildered looks nearby people gave her. "I'm fine," she said, quickly retracting her hand from his.

Pryanth's face twitched, but he didn't try to reclaim her hand.

"I'm surprised you came," she went on.

"Mother said we should pay our respects before leaving."

"You're all here, then?"

"We stayed close to the back to avoid drawing attention."

"I appreciate that," Analia said, her stomach twisting. Her uncle's murderer came to his funeral? That just felt violating.

Pryanth rested a hand on her arm. "And I wanted to make sure you were all right."

Was he serious? Why would he care? No one cared.

"Analia," he said, stepping closer, "I truly am—"

Pryanth cut off as a commotion broke out behind them. They turned with the crowd as a servant girl stumbled into their midst, sobbing the same four words over and over. "There's been another murder!"

Aaron was starting to get tired of stumbling upon bodies.

"You picked an incredibly bad time to get yourself stabbed, Lev," he growled, pressing down on the wound in Lev's stomach.

Lev groaned but didn't try to explain.

The Sun Royals had decided to leave behind half their guard while attending Accalon's funeral. Deardryn hadn't wanted to make a stir and, more importantly, had wanted to make sure no one tried to enter their chambers when they were gone.

She and Othin had been paranoid of an Ash citizen attempting to take justice into their own hands. They doubted anyone would have the audacity to do something while surrounded by witnesses at a funeral, but if someone could slip something into Accalon's drink or food without notice?

Aaron had just finished his lap of the Sun corridors when he stumbled upon Lev's crumpled body on the ground, the idiot only wearing a tunic and not his leathers. Thankfully, a serving girl with red, puffy eyes had been passing at the opposite end of the hall. The poor girl had nearly jumped out of her skin when Aaron ordered her to get help, but at least she'd complied without hesitating.

Now, footsteps pounded down the hall. Aaron looked over his shoulder, noticing with relief that Deardryn was part of the mob that clogged the corridor.

She assessed the situation with one rapid sweep of her eyes. Then, she dropped to her knees beside Lev, golden light flaring from her palms. Behind her, the crowd parted to let Pryanth through, Analia hurrying in his wake.

They crouched beside Deardryn, Pryanth adding his flickering light to hers. And as Analia looked up at him, Aaron felt like he'd been punched in the gut.

How many times had he seen this image? Analia, soot-stained and shrouded in gray so dark it could have been smoke. Eyes haunted—although the tapestry he was thinking of had failed to note her fury as she looked up at him.

"You," she said, voice shaking slightly, "are followed by death."

She had no idea.

"Technically," he said, "I believe I'm following death."

"Not this time." Deardryn sat back, golden light fading. The color had returned to Lev's face, although he still grimaced as he opened his eyes.

"I've stabilized his life force," Deardryn said to no one in particular, "but he's still going to need help healing the internal damage."

"I can take care of that, Your Majesty."

An elderly woman with gray-streaked brown hair emerged from the crowd. Her eyes were rimmed with vivid orange rings, complementing the hints of red in her copper skin. Behind her came an apprentice with two white rings and light brown hair, her green healer robes matching her master's.

Deardryn bowed her head to the healer and moved aside.

"Ember," the healer said to her apprentice, "watch closely. Everyone else who's not essential, leave."

The crowd did as ordered, the hall rapidly clearing. Aaron, however, always considered himself important, so he remained, as did Deardryn, Analia, and Pryanth.

As the master healer reached for Lev, the guard blinked and slurred a question. The master healer gave Ember an expectant look, but she was already soothing the disoriented guard.

As she turned her attention back to her master, Aaron couldn't help but be impressed. He knew healers were neutral, that they swore an oath to heal all beings, not just the ones in their kingdom, but he'd never seen it in action before. Especially not when the injured party was attached to a kingdom accused of murdering the healer's king.

Ember and her master were just leaning back, healing complete, when Othin and Brenn rounded the corner, guards close behind.

"What is this?" Othin roared.

Aaron helped Ember prop the still-groggy guard against the wall.

Othin rounded on Brenn. "First you threaten us at your brother's funeral, and now you've stooped so low as to attack one of our guards?"

"Who says this was us?" Brenn protested. "You saw that crowd. Every citizen was at the funeral!"

"That's convenient," Pryanth muttered. Analia shot him a look.

"I knew we shouldn't trust them," Othin seethed, rounding on a drained Deardryn.

"Trust us?" Brenn muscled his way back into Othin's face. "Says the man who intruded on my kingdom the day our king was murdered."

"We were invited! Just so you could stab us in the back the moment we let down our guard."

"How convenient you let your guard down after the man who invited you here was dead."

Aaron swore under his breath as guards drew their swords. "Stand down," he snapped, but they didn't listen.

"Shouldn't we ask Lev who attacked him?" asked a voice from the back.

Aaron whipped his head around to see Cadmus shifting awkwardly from foot to foot. He quickly stopped once others noticed him, mumbling, "Before we go about stabbing people."

"Yes," Deardryn said, shaking herself slightly. "Yes, that is true, Prince Cadmus."

Deardryn reached out and touched Lev's knee, his eyes opening. As Deardryn gently asked who stabbed him, Lev's eyes roved over the crowd. First the Sun soldiers—briefly pausing on Dannel, then Aaron—and then...

"Him," Lev whispered, pointing a weak finger at Warack. "He attacked me."

Warack's eyes widened in astonishment. "What in the name of the Crystal are you talking about?"

"Out of nowhere," Lev breathed.

Dannel immediately turned on Warack. "Well, I'm not surprised. Those two have been bickering nonstop the past week."

"There's a big difference between bickering and a stab wound," Warack retorted.

"Definitely an 'out of nowhere' difference," said Dannel.

He took a step toward Warack. Warack raised his sword.

"I'm telling you," the Ash guard said, "I had nothing to do with this."

"Are you calling Lev a liar?"

"He's certainly not telling the truth."

"And how convenient he's unable to defend himself."

The two moved toward each other, but Aaron was on his feet in a flash. He hooked his foot around Warack's ankle as he charged forward. Warack fell, Aaron pivoting to catch

Dannel's sword tip on his dagger hilt. Sliding his blade down to the base of Dannel's, he twisted, the sword falling to the ground with a clatter.

Warack rose and charged empty-handed, but Aaron stepped forward, grabbed him by the wrist, and yanked him over his shoulder.

Warack crashed to the stone with a thud, Aaron landing on top of him a moment later. Ash soldiers made to grab Aaron, but the sad, twitchy one called for them to stop.

Aaron pressed his forearm to Warack's throat, leaning in close. "Knock it off," he said, deadly calm.

Warack glared up at him. All around them, Royals still raged, power roiling throughout the corridor like an impending storm. But Aaron didn't take his eyes off Warack until he finally sagged, still fuming with indignation.

Aaron helped the Ash soldier to his feet, Othin still roaring behind him.

"Sabotage! This was all a setup, wasn't it? You accuse us of murder just to lure us here, pin another murder on our backs, and then stab us in the dark!"

"Oh, get over yourself." Brenn shoved aside the finger Othin had jabbed in his face. "This wasn't us. Warack said it wasn't him."

"So, we just decided to attack our own guard."

"It wouldn't surprise me."

Aaron glanced at Dannel, currently being restrained by two other guards. No, it wouldn't surprise him, either. The most surprising option was that Othin was actually aware of what was going on in his ranks.

Deardryn stepped between the arguing kings, her expression hardening into the mask of the Dragoness. "Regardless of what happened," she said, "it's over. The important thing is Lev is alive. He claims it was Warack who attacked him, but he's not one of our men.

"Brenn, you can punish him the way you see fit, and we will take Lev and the rest of our people home to heal. We're even."

"No, we're not even," Othin shot back. "We didn't kill anyone."

"Oh yes you did," Brenn argued back. "And even if you hadn't, we're still not even. You almost lost a soldier. We lost a Royal and *our king*."

Othin sneered, sarcastically asking, "What, Brenn? Would you like a truce marriage?"

Aaron braced himself to rip apart two Royals, but it turned out, he didn't have to. She had been so quiet, he'd almost forgotten she was there.

"Yes," Analia said, stepping out of the shadows and directly into the thrumming knot of power between Brenn and Othin. "Take me."

# Chapter 9

Analia had no time to second-guess her decision.

After the corridor erupted into chaos, Brenn eventually dragged Analia, Cadmus, and Aeley into the Council Chamber. Just as expected, Brenn fumed and ranted, no longer muzzled by Accalon's imposing presence.

But this was the moment Analia had been waiting for. The one she had been angling toward since that day on the turret when she'd screamed and sobbed, raged until she thought her body would dissolve into flames, then sat frozen, still for so long that she didn't know if she would ever move again.

*One day,* she told herself as morning turned to afternoon. One day to listen to the pounding rain, the sound of her everything blasting apart, crushed into ash that she could taste on her tongue. One day to crumble right along with it.

As afternoon darkened to evening, Analia could only wonder: what was the point? The point of screaming, of silence, of feeling the hot blood that oozed from her broken nails, and icy rain that pelted her skin. What was the point of caring about anything, when her everything had been ripped away with a brutal nonchalance?

It wasn't until evening darkened to midnight that Analia found her single reason. Accalon had deserved better, had deserved more. And he couldn't rise again.

As the rain eased around her, Analia clutched her newfound spark to her chest. She gazed up at the stars, her only company now, and let her one day come to an end. There was no more time for tears. She had to find her uncle's killer. And then she had to kill them.

Analia didn't speak as Brenn blustered on. That was the thing about Brenn: his flames were quick to blaze, but if they went without kindling, they would put themselves out.

"What were you thinking?" Brenn finally demanded.

Analia carefully kept her trembling hands tucked beneath the table where she sat.

"I'm thinking," she said, "that now that Sun has been cleared, we have no ability to hold them here. As soon as they leave, they will be too far for us to investigate. Unless we have someone on the inside."

Brenn glared, but he didn't interrupt.

"Even if somehow, it wasn't someone from Sun that killed Accalon," Analia said, "their library is our best chance at figuring out who did. We've already exhausted our resources here. We have nothing on the plant the healers found.

"But I got Pryanth to confirm that not only do they have herbology books, but books on all seven kingdoms. If there is record of this plant, it's there."

Brenn asked, "You think you have the skill to infiltrate an enemy kingdom, investigate them without their realizing, find the evidence you need to firmly accuse them, and then bring them back to Ash to stand trial?"

His tone made it perfectly clear he did not think she could do this. Across the table, Cadmus stared at her with large, solemn eyes. He didn't speak his uncertainties, but they were plain enough. Only Aeley remained unreadable, leaning against the far wall with arms crossed.

"I..." Analia's eyes darted to Accalon's usual seat, his paintings, then to the table. She was alone. Completely, utterly alone. Analia could barely speak through the pain, "I think I have the best chance."

"How reassuring," said Brenn sarcastically.

"Well, the marriage pact was Deardryn's plan," Cadmus said from across the table. "She'll automatically be in favor of it."

Analia shot Cadmus a grateful glance.

Brenn said, "Othin won't be—"

"Othin isn't the Royal," Analia said.

Brenn's eyes flashed. Analia despised how quickly she scuttled back, "I'm sorry."

Analia looked to Cadmus for help, but he refused to meet her gaze.

"It's true, though," she said. "Deardryn is the Royal, making her the final say. Othin may protest, but he always submits to Deardryn in the end."

Brenn pushed out of his chair, prowling about the room. "I don't want Sun having access to an Ash Royal. Even if there's no chance of you passing down the magic, I don't like them thinking they have leverage."

"Can you think of any other way to get an Ash person in?" Analia asked tentatively.

Brenn paused and glared, and Analia ducked her head. He resumed his pacing. "There has to be someone else we can send."

"The only other person is Lucilla," Analia mumbled. "Sun won't accept anyone from a lower branch."

Brenn's face darkened. She didn't have to add the fact that Brenn would actually mind putting Lucilla in danger.

Cadmus lowered his head even more, playing with his fingers. Analia braced herself to go another round.

"Analia's right," Aeley said.

Brenn stopped beside her and folded his arms. "How so?"

"She's the only person we can send in without them being suspicious," Aeley said. "They already know we don't want them having access to our magic, so Analia is the obvious choice. They'll be expecting her.

"Even if they suspect her, her utter lack of abilities will make them complacent. And if she does fail, when they kill her, we'll have an undisputed reason to go to war."

Cold, hard logic. Analia expected nothing less from her mother.

Aeley held Brenn's gaze, her expression surprisingly hard. "Send her away."

Analia knew Brenn was running out of time to consider. Yet, the speed in which he made his decision nevertheless felt like pressure on a bruise.

"You leave tonight," he said, barely turning his head to look at her. "Don't waste our chance, duckling."

Brenn touched Aeley's cheek, and her shoulders slumped. Then, he flung open the council door, Deardryn and Othin's debate ricocheting off the stone hallway. Aeley made to follow but looked back as Analia called after her.

"Thank you, Mother."

"You never deserved to be heir to the throne," she said, her expression cold. "That title belongs to Cadmus. Go to Sun. Marry that prince, rule as their princess, or die seeking justice, I don't care. Stay away from our crown."

Analia couldn't fight back her flinch as Aeley exited. Across from her, Cadmus went completely still, a look of horror creeping across his face.

Just as Analia suspected, Deardryn won out in the end. Brenn, begrudgingly, agreed to suspend Warack from the Crystal Guard—and by suspend, Analia was positive he meant until the Sun Royals had left, at which point he'd be rewarded. Then, the deal was sealed.

Analia descended the Ash Castle steps. She wasn't bringing anything with her, only Accalon's pin, firmly affixed to her chest. She was just glad she was leaving before the rumors could spread; before the looks could start up again, just like they had when she and Rois—

"Anna, wait!"

Rois hurried down the steps, followed by Ember. No, no more goodbyes.

"Have you lost it?" Rois asked, stopping before her.

Analia's eyebrows shot up. "What are you talking about?"

"Anna, this is dangerous. You're going into enemy territory, alone, without training."

"Yes, Rois," Analia said. "Believe it or not, I've thought this through."

"I don't think you have." Rois didn't flinch away from her glare like he usually did. "You just lost your uncle. The person that meant everything to you. You need time to feel that."

"I had my time."

One day. That was all the time she could handle.

Rois fought back an eye roll. "Anna, please, it's not too late. Stay here. Give yourself a second to breathe, let us help you."

"I told you," Analia said through gritted teeth, "I'm fine."

"But you're not! You're running away! And you can't outrun this! You're just going to kill yourself trying!"

Analia cringed away from his words, her own flying past her lips. "What a shame you lost the right to have any opinion the moment you chose Brenn and your position over me."

Rois took a step back, then glanced to Ember for help. She gave him a look of, *No, you deserved that,* then shifted her blue-gray gaze to Analia.

"Are you sure you want to do this?" she asked.

Analia gave a sharp nod.

"Well, all right, then."

"Ember!"

Ember ignored Rois and gave Analia a hug of farewell. "I collect herbs by the border every full moon," she whispered before letting go. "Find a harp while you're there," she said in a normal volume. "Something that will make you happy."

Analia nodded, although she quietly knew she wouldn't be doing that. She doubted she would be seeing Ember at the border, either. But she only offered her a farewell before turning away, leaving Rois to splutter on the castle steps as she headed off toward the Phoenix Gate.

There were no more farewells after that. Cadmus had given her a quick hug in the Council Chamber, and Lucilla was nowhere to be found.

Analia was left to follow Pryanth into the Sun carriage, the sun dragons obviously anxious to take off. Her hand jerked as it brushed against the frame of the carriage, feeling an odd vibration beneath her fingers. Deardryn flashed her a curious look, but before she could speak, the carriage lifted into the sky.

Normally, it took weeks to travel from the Ash Kingdom to Sun. A good portion of the path had been carved into a collection of mountains and ridges by ancient lava flow, making it impossible to have a straightforward journey. The sun dragons, however, only needed the majority of a day to fly over it all.

Due to their late start, the Royals decided to stop for the night at an inn that they then completely bought out. By the following morning, they were off once more, the golden wall surrounding the central Sun Kingdom coming into view just as the sun began to set.

Whereas the Ash Kingdom was comprised of straight lines and sharp angles, the Sun Kingdom was the exact opposite. Coated in glimmering layers of gold, white, and toasted browns, the Sun Kingdom sparkled in the light. Winding streets zigzagged through marketplaces, wound through lush parks, and curved around a giant golden sundial in the center of the square.

"Beautiful, isn't it?" Pryanth asked, following her gaze. "We have a tradition with the dial. Once every three months, our people gather in the square for a night of music and dancing. Mother started the tradition when she became queen. She said it was important that our citizens felt like they knew us, and that way, they would trust us."

"My uncle thought the same thing," Analia said. She anticipated the spike of grief, numbing the point of contact just in time.

Pryanth, not noticing, went on, "The people have taken to calling it Solemnai. And it's there that we'll introduce you."

The carriage landed before the glittering golden castle. A row of towers rose from the roof in varying heights, making it appear as though it was casting off rays of sunlight.

Pryanth reached over and took her hand. And with nothing left to do, Analia let him lead her out of the carriage and up the white marble stairs, taking her first steps into her new home.

# PART 2: FLAMES

# Chapter 10

There were many things Dimitri hated. But there was nothing he hated more than making beds, meaning life as a servant in the Sun Castle was fucking delightful.

Dimitri yanked on the corner of the sheet he was trying to fit to a mattress, just for the other half to spring free. He swore. Clearly, he had the sheet in the wrong direction, although how he was supposed to know that beforehand was beyond him.

Word had come late that afternoon that Princess Analia was returning home with the Sun Royals, although the reason hadn't been disclosed. At least, not to Dimitri. All he knew was Koz had sniffed him out while he skulked in the shadows, avoiding his scrub work—which frankly should have been reason enough to not give him such responsibilities. Nevertheless, there he was, being outmaneuvered by a gods-damned sheet.

It was the last thing he had to do, having already stocked the attached stone-tile bathing chamber, dusted the white curtains that draped across an expansive window, and dumped an armful of rainbow gowns in the carved armoire. He'd even shoved that gods-damned heavy oak desk all the way down the corridor—his fellow servants watching, not helping, the bastards—and managed to maneuver it into the gap between the wall and the fireplace.

"She doesn't need sheets," Dimitri grumbled, struggling with the third corner. "I should just wait to see if she says anything. Oh, apologies, Your Queenliness, I didn't realize they used sheets in the Ash Kingdom. My mistake, I'll fix it immediately."

He snorted, finally wrestling the last corner in place. Not a moment too soon, either.

Dimitri's ears pricked as voices echoed from the hall. He kept his head bowed as Deardryn swept through the door, followed by Pryanth, what had to be the Ash girl, and the silver-eyed guard that reminded Dimitri of a cat about to pounce.

"These will be your chambers," Deardryn said. Her gaze flickered over Dimitri as if he was a part of the scenery.

"It's beautiful," Analia said, barely glancing around.

This girl was a walking contradiction. Chin high, but shoulders curled. Polite tone, but constantly shifting eyes.

Apparently, she had no magic, either. Although His Royal Brat-Highness actually looked engaged as Analia conversed with him and his mother about the room, so there must be something to her.

"And thank you," she said, turning to face him, "for—"

Her gray eyes widened in astonishment.

Dimitri should've been used to that look by now, but it never failed to set his teeth grinding.

"Did you forget how to blink?" he asked. "Or do all Ash people have a staring problem?"

Analia's cheeks flushed as red as her hair.

"Watch your tongue, servant," Pryanth snapped.

Ah, so the fickle wheel of Pryanth's love life spun again. It always started out so kind. And yet, for some reason, they never stayed. Oh, no, that's right, *he* left *them*. And now, the Old Hag had to step in, judging by that gleam in her eyes. Dimitri suppressed a snort.

"Dimitri," Deardryn said, "that's enough. It's a perfectly understandable response given the circumstances."

Her words were soft, slick as serpent scales, but Dimitri could see the thickly veiled resentment in her honey eyes. Great news, Old Hag, the feeling was mutual.

Dimitri mumbled an apology, the obnoxiously formal words sticking in his throat.

"I'll be speaking with Koz later," Deardryn told him. "You're dismissed."

Dimitri bowed his head. Translation: more scrub work. Crystal spare him.

Seemingly satisfied, they all looked away from him once more. All except those unnerving silver eyes, lingering a moment longer than the rest.

Dimitri shuddered as he slowly gathered his things. Those eyes saw too much. But so did Dimitri's. He hadn't missed the fact that Aaron's puzzled gaze had previously been unwaveringly fixed on Analia, who pointedly ignored him.

A slow smile crept across his lips as he fiddled with the extra sheet he was folding. This was going to be dramatic.

"Before we leave you for the night," Deardryn said, placing a hand on Analia's shoulder, "I thought you should be informed that each Sun Royal is assigned a specific guard. Usually, this only applies when we're out in the kingdom for protection's sake. I, however, thought it would be prudent for your guard to also accompany you when in the castle while you are still finding your way."

"And who is this guard?" Analia asked slowly.

She knew. That was dread in her eyes. Dimitri could barely suppress his glee.

"Aaron."

Analia's head whipped around. Dimitri swore Aaron's brows contracted slightly, but he sketched a dramatic bow. Analia's eyes flashed.

Dimitri let out an inadvertent snort. Leave it to the Old Hag to stir up some chaos. That was when true colors were revealed, after all. Especially the colors of loyalty and betrayal. And it wasn't just the Ash girl being tested.

Pryanth's eyes shot to Dimitri. "Why are you still here?"

"My apologies, Your Highness," Dimitri replied automatically. "I was just leaving."

He was honestly surprised he'd lasted so long. He'd been fully expecting to have to skulk outside the door to get the rest of the story. But as Dimitri slipped back into the corridor, he felt as though he'd seen enough.

Dimitri wandered through the halls, skirting around groups of servants with an ease that came from years of practice. He figured he could get away with a few more minutes of freedom under the guise of still setting up Analia's chambers. What he couldn't puzzle out, though, was why she was there in the first place.

Dimitri slid into a shadowy alcove. Who *came* to the Sun Kingdom? If it were up to him, he'd be gone in a heartbeat. Leave this gods-damned kingdom and never look back. He'd almost done it, too. But then...

Dimitri squeezed his eyes shut. He groped in the shadows for the crack in the wall, the stone polished as slick as dagger blades.

That wasn't important. No, what was important was finally getting out. For good this time.

There came a click under Dimitri's palm. He slid the section of wall aside, then disappeared into the darkness beyond.

Analia followed Pryanth through the Sun Castle halls. Deardryn had suggested letting her rest, but Pryanth insisted he wanted to show her something first. While Analia was certainly intrigued, she couldn't quite shake her feeling of wrongness.

She'd spent twenty-two years surrounded by the dark stone and sconces of the Ash Castle. But here, the walls were a polished warm brown. The floor was gold marble, shot through with veins of amber, honey, and orange. Even the sconces were replaced with softly glowing, fist-sized gold stones, inset in the wall in intricate designs.

"They're sunstones," Pryanth said, following her gaze. "They're able to sense Sun magic, and as they conduct those sensory messages between each other, it sets off the glow."

"Amazing," Analia murmured. She paused to place her palm on one of the nearby stones. To her surprise, it was warm to the touch and seemed to hum like a purring cat.

"Does that mean you have to charge them yourselves?" she asked.

Pryanth shook his head. "Usually, when the Sun magic is released during the Solstice Ceremony, there's enough floating around that it keeps the stones going for that year. You can directly influence them, though."

With a mischievous look, Pryanth stepped up beside her, tapping the stone before her. In response, the light brightened to almost blinding levels.

Analia's hand jerked with surprise as she shielded her eyes. Before she could say anything, Pryanth rested his hand on the blinding stone once more, and the light winked out. One by one, the lights lining the hall followed suit, quickly leaving them in complete darkness.

"Impressive, isn't it?" Pryanth said, his hand finding hers in the dark.

"And you don't even need direct contact?" Analia asked.

"Not if you're strong enough." Pryanth radiated smugness. "If you have the skill, you can cut off not just that one connection point, but all of them."

Pryanth shifted, and a moment later, light flickered back to life in the hall. "Come," he said, not dropping her hand, "this isn't what I wanted to show you."

Analia carefully kept track of their path as Pryanth led her up a collection of grand stairwells. Finally reaching the top, he pushed open a heavy steel door, allowing them to step out onto the roof beyond.

Night was just descending upon the Sun Kingdom. Streetlights flickered in the darkness, dotting the kingdom below with hundreds of tiny golden lights.

"You can see everything up here," Analia said, stepping up to the gold battlements. "This is incredible!"

"It certainly is."

Analia frowned at the slight tension in Pryanth's voice. "What's wrong?" she asked.

"It's the servant boy, Dimitri," he said, bracing his forearms on the parapet. "I'm sure you noticed."

"He looks like your father," Analia said softly.

The similarities weren't immediately apparent. Dimitri was shorter than average and painfully thin, whereas Othin was tall and broad. His hair had the same thick texture, but it was dark blond, not black. Even his features were more pointed, almost weasel-like. But the two had the same amber eyes: color, shape, set. Even the constant narrowed, calculating look.

"My father's bastard." Pryanth's gaze remained fixed on the kingdom below. "Twenty years ago, my father engaged in an affair. He betrayed my mother, Queen of the Sun, and had the audacity to sire a son that looked even more like him than I do.

"He didn't even have the decency to hide his bastard away. He gets to live in this castle, under the guardianship of one of the older servants."

"What about his mother?" Analia asked.

"She was a random woman he'd met in the kingdom."

"Then why isn't Dimitri with her? If she had nothing to do with the castle, why not have the two disappear?"

"Because," Pryanth said, "she was executed for treason."

The back of Analia's neck tingled.

"It was kept hushed," Pryanth continued. "We didn't need knowledge of the events spreading to humiliate us even more. But if that were the case, we should have just killed the babe, too."

Pryanth glanced at her, his face softening at her aghast expression. "I didn't mean that," he said, deflating.

"I know," Analia said, unable to meet his gaze.

Pryanth fiddled with his sleeve. "I know it's not... *his* fault, but Analia, he's everywhere. Everywhere I turn, I see him. The child that was more important to my father than me and my mother. The child he chose. Never mind what that meant for Mother, for me."

He finally looked at her straight on. And Analia recognized that look. She saw it every time she looked in the mirror in Ash.

Hesitantly, she touched her fingertips to his hand atop the parapet. "My father didn't give up on me developing magic until my younger brother, Cadmus, started developing his. After that, it was like he had no reason to hold onto hope. He finally had a child with our magic. A child he could flaunt after distancing himself from me and my disgrace. He went so far as to turn our entire kingdom against me in order to protect his reputation."

Analia took a shaky breath. "I suppose what I'm trying to say is, I know what it feels like to be the forgotten child. The one not chosen. And I know it doesn't mean much hearing that, but..."

"No, it does." Pryanth flipped his hand so he was holding hers. "It's not empty words when you say how sorry you are. You don't have to imagine how awful it is because you understand."

Analia looked down at their hands. "I'm sorry you understand."

Pryanth laughed softly. "Toss a gold piece in a crowd and it's bound to ricochet off at least six Crystal-forsaken fathers."

"Not all parents are horrible," she said.

"Like your uncle?"

Analia could feel stone walls that had somehow slid open grinding shut once more. Yes, Accalon. She was here not to look at pretty views with rejected princes, but to find her uncle's killer. Still, she couldn't help the bud of warmth in her chest as Pryanth's thumb moved across the back of her hand.

"I'm sorry it took your uncle dying to get us here," he said. "But I am glad you're with me, Analia."

"Why's that?"

"Everyone in this kingdom is the same," he said. "They're boring, predictable. There's nothing new or challenging about the way they operate. But you?"

Analia looked away. She knew where this was going.

"You are like tugging on a marionette string, just to find it has snapped. Or maybe attempting to move the arm, just to have the head nod. You never respond the way I expect."

"And that's a good thing?" Analia asked.

"It's a fantastic thing," he said. "Just think, Analia. Someday, I will be seated on the throne, you at my side. We'll be the most powerful pair in all six kingdoms. Fire and life."

"We can't be fire and life if I don't have fire," Analia muttered. They were Brenn's words, bitter on her tongue.

Pryanth waved a dismissive hand. "No matter. That just means my heir is guaranteed to have my magic. But Mother's convinced your magic will come, and she's yet to be wrong. About anything. And she doesn't let you forget it, either."

"But what if this time she *is* wrong?" Analia pressed. "What if I really am unworthy to the Crystal? What if something is wrong with me?"

She'd never said those words aloud before. She trained relentlessly instead, desperate to prove her kingdom wrong. Yet, when hearing something so often, it was inevitable it would take hold.

"The only thing wrong with you is that you were born into the wrong kingdom." Pryanth squeezed her hand. "Just wait. You're going to step onto that sundial next month, and everyone is going to love you."

Yes, there was definitely something warm in her chest. The feeling of being chosen, of being wanted.

It wasn't until much later when Pryanth was escorting her back down the stairs that Analia realized she'd said far more than she had intended. It was something about his willingness to share. There was a safety there, almost a compulsion. It was as if she'd watched him take those few steps across uneven footing and the ground hadn't given out beneath him, so why would it under her?

Pryanth left Analia at her door, bidding her good night. But as he closed the door behind him, Analia didn't climb into bed. Instead, she crossed to her desk, rifling through drawers, pulling out paper and pen. Then, she got to work.

All throughout her brief tour of the castle, Analia had been slowly building a map in her mind. Every twist, every turn, what lay behind each door. Every spot of guard density and absence she could find. If she was going to find her uncle's killer, she had to know the castle inside out.

Finishing her map, she stowed it away in the back of a desk drawer. Hopefully, it was hidden just enough so that no one could accidentally stumble upon it, but she could still explain it away if someone was searching with a purpose.

Finally, she turned away, unable to shake the feeling that she was woefully unprepared for what came next.

# Chapter 11

When Analia's maids woke her the next morning, she was prepared for the whispers and suspicious glances. What she wasn't expecting were the two girls that bounced through her door, already chattering at top speed.

Both maids wore white shirts and gold pants, their black hair coiled in a braided knot at the nape of their necks. And before Analia had time to so much as blink, they converged upon her.

The first girl—who introduced herself as Bie—bundled her into a seat before her dressing table. The second, Nadi, rifled through the clothes someone had put in her armoire—all gowns, matching the strict formality of the Sun Royals.

Analia watched, almost in awe, as the two girls gossiped and giggled faster than a flame consuming a dry piece of tinder.

"Kara may not be the brightest sunstone in the castle," Nadi said, "but she is scrappy. I nearly had to take her eye out with a broom handle to beat her to the front of the crowd today."

"Why?" Analia asked.

She waited for the usual dismissal, but Nadi turned to her in excitement. "To be your maid, Your Highness."

"What?"

"What do you mean, what?" Bie asked. "Don't tell me you didn't know you're the talk of the castle!"

Analia's shoulders tightened slightly. "Why? What are people saying?"

"They're saying a beautiful foreign princess has come to steal the frigid heart of the Sun Prince," Nadi said from beside the armoire.

"Oh yes, very mysterious," Bie agreed, sliding a thin gold-and-pearl pin into Analia's hair. "I think it's the eyes."

"Definitely. So dark and alluring."

"And the hair—"

"You're like the one red rose in a sea of white petals."

Or the one unlit wick in a sea of burning candles.

The two chattered on as they finished helping Analia get ready. As she stepped into her soft gold slippers, she couldn't help but wonder: was Pryanth right?

No, that didn't matter. She was here on a mission, and then she would leave. The sooner the better.

Analia shook herself out of her reveries as there came a quick knock on her door, Aaron appearing in her mirror's reflection a moment later.

"Has anyone told you, Princess," he asked, stepping up behind her, "that you have a breathtaking scowl?"

Analia's frown deepened. Smiling to himself, Aaron turned to greet Bie and Nadi, both of whom blushed and stammered before scurrying out the door.

"You chased away my maids," Analia complained.

Aaron—dressed in his gold-and-white fighting leathers—sat on the edge of her bed. "I did no such thing."

"You smiled at them."

"Is that your way of telling me I have a breathtaking smile?" He grinned, and Analia fantasized about the thud he would make after she shoved him off her bed.

"What do you want, Aaron?" she asked.

"Don't you remember? I'm to be your sparkling travel companion for the next Crystal knows how long. And it has been decided that our first destination is breakfast."

Analia's stomach dropped. She quickly turned to retrieve her phoenix pin from her dressing table, trying to ignore the fact she would be walking into a dragon den as a traitor in a matter of minutes.

"Fine," she said curtly. And without further comment, she strode out her door, resisting the urge to push it shut in Aaron's face.

"Didn't you hear me?" Aaron demanded, hurrying after her.

"Breakfast, I know."

"I'm supposed to stay with you."

"I don't need your help," Analia snapped.

Aaron's eyes flashed. "No," he said, "you don't need anyone's help. Not when you have an army of Royals to tell you what to do. Go to breakfast. Bow your head."

"That sounds an awful lot like what you're doing."

"Is that why I bother you?" Aaron put a hand on Analia's arm to stop her. "Is that the reason you'll only glare at me?"

Aaron's fingers burned against her skin. She could practically feel his arms around her, the thrum of Deardryn's magic, Accalon's corpse—*one day*. She only had that one day to break.

"Back off," she said. And slamming shut that box of memories, she moved faster, ignoring Aaron trailing after her.

The Royals' dining room was much smaller than the Great Hall downstairs, which was reserved for special occasions. The walls were covered in banners bearing the kingdom sigil: a coiled gold sun dragon on a white field. Servants breezed in and out of a corner door, offering trays of various foods to the Royals already seated.

Pryanth waved Analia over, pushing out the chair beside him.

"I like that color on you," he said, nodding to her flowing gold gown.

Analia mumbled her thanks as she took her seat, shoving Aaron's words aside. She couldn't deny, however, it was the quiet truth in his words that kept her head up as a server bustled over, filling her goblet and offering her some kind of pastry.

Analia thanked him, once again caught off guard as he bowed his head and smiled before moving on. This had to be some kind of ploy, didn't it? She warily took a bite of the fluffy pastry, her eyes widening.

Pryanth burst out laughing. "I forgot," he said. "The Ash Kingdom is fond of spice."

"This is not spice," Analia said, taking another bite of what had turned out to be a sweet, sticky cinnamon roll.

"It's certainly not." Pryanth licked some honey from his finger and leaned in close. "Sweet and spicy. Isn't that a delicious combination?"

He tucked a stray piece of hair behind her ear, his fingertips sliding down the strands, her neck, before dropping away. Analia could have sworn she still felt his phantom touch long after.

The Sun Royals chatted among themselves as the meal continued, conversations accented by the clink of forks on plates. Analia expected to sit quietly and listen, but she was quickly absorbed into the conversation.

She was introduced to Cabir, Pryanth's cousin—a man with a sharp nose and prominent chin—who raised his goblet in greeting from down the table. Beside him sat Saura, Deardryn's younger sister, although not Cabir's mother.

A frail woman with hair a few tones darker than Deardryn's, Saura didn't speak much. Yet, she still made it a point to give Analia a warm smile as her trembling hands fumbled with her knife.

"What did I tell you?" Pryanth said in her ear. "They love you."

All except for Othin, who still shot Analia a suspicious look as he leaned over to assist Saura. She fondly patted his arm in thanks as he straightened in his seat once more.

As breakfast came to a close, Deardryn turned to Analia.

"Now that we have been properly fed," she said, "I was hoping you would indulge me, Analia."

It had been framed as a request, but Analia knew there was no question in her words.

"May I ask with what, Your Majesty?"

Deardryn primly folded her napkin. "Now that," she said, "is something I cannot tell you until after."

Around the table, eyes flicked to Deardryn with interest. But it was dread that slowly sank Analia's stomach as she nodded.

Not long later, Deardryn led the way into a large, circular room, Analia, Pryanth, Othin, and of course, Aaron, following close behind. Opposite the door stood a grand bookcase. The remaining sections of walls were taken up by a wraparound bench, which Aaron headed toward to lounge on. The rest of them followed Deardryn over to a table off to the side.

Analia eased into the seat across from Deardryn, expecting some sort of preamble. But Deardryn only sifted through a small box of jewelry she'd placed on the table between them, pulling out a deep gray ring inset with rubies.

"Take this," she said, offering Analia the ring.

Analia sucked in a breath as the ring touched her palm.

"What do you feel?" Deardryn asked.

"Hot," Analia said. She made to drop the ring, but Deardryn leveled her with a look. "It's... it's crackling."

She didn't know how to describe it. The ring had burned the second it touched her skin, the heat not quite pulsating or vibrating, but flickering like a flame.

"Would you say, familiar?" Deardryn asked.

Analia nodded. Pryanth shot her a puzzled look. Othin folded his arms.

Deardryn plucked the ring from Analia's palm with long, slender fingers. "And what about this time?"

Deardryn placed a silver ring in Analia's palm. Analia jerked, biting her tongue as a jolt of electricity shot up her arm.

In a flash, Aaron was at her shoulder. Pryanth, looking startled, reached to take the ring from her hand. "Mother, what—"

"Don't touch it," Deardryn ordered.

"But Mother..."

"Give her a moment," said Aaron, sounding thoughtful.

Pryanth glared at the guard, but Analia ignored them as they bickered. Her fingers had spasmed into a fist around the ring, her bones still crackling with energy. Finger by finger, she managed to unclench her hand, sending the ring rolling across the table.

"Lightning," she breathed. "It was like being struck by lightning."

Deardryn beamed. "Fascinating." She rifled through her jewelry box with more fervor.

"What's in the rings?" Aaron asked, taking the seat on Analia's right.

Both Pryanth and Othin shot him irritated looks.

"Who said you could sit?" Pryanth demanded.

"No one, Your Highness," Aaron said. "But I figured you'd rather have me close so I wouldn't have to yell my questions. That would just be rude."

"Check yourself, Aaron," Deardryn warned.

"My apologies, Your Majesty." Aaron bowed his head, although Analia noted he remained completely unperturbed.

Othin looked as though he was about to retort.

"These two rings," Deardryn cut in smoothly, "hold Royal Ash magic and Royal Wind magic respectively."

Aaron's eyebrows shot up. Pryanth snatched the Wind ring, frowning down at it.

"I don't feel any lightning," he said. "It's just power."

Deardryn dug through her box and offered him a gold ring with a massive diamond. "Try this."

They swapped rings, and Pryanth grunted in surprise. "It feels like my own magic," he said, staring at the ring with wonder.

Deardryn motioned for him to hand it to Analia.

"It's like the magic in the sunstones," she mused, warmth—not as hot as the Ash magic—tingling in drawn-out pulses in her palm.

"I was wondering if you'd notice that," Deardryn said, reaching over to reclaim the ring. "Pryanth mentioned you appeared startled when you touched the sunstones last night, just as I noticed your hand jerk when it came in contact with our carriage. Would you say all three feel similar, or different?"

Analia thought for a moment. "The ring and sunstones are the same," she decided. "But the carriage was different."

Deardryn thoughtfully traced the Sun ring's diamond. "Excellent."

Analia thought her curiosity might overflow as she asked, "What does this mean?"

Deardryn looked as if she had been waiting for someone to ask. Settling back in her chair, she began.

"Centuries ago, while we were still ruled by the Star Kingdom, there was a clever blacksmith from the Sand Kingdom named Gavare. He had only been mildly Blessed by the Crystal, so mildly that many whispered that he was a leaky cup.

"Gavare, however, found a fascinating question within those whispers. Could magic be transported from a Blessed and stored somewhere else? That is, could magic be poured out of a leaky cup, and caught in a sealed one?

"For five years, five months, and five days, Gavare experimented in the forges, testing every material he could think of. Yet, his first attempt was an utter failure."

Deardryn pulled a long iron chain from her box, a chunk of rough black onyx dangling from its end. She handed it to Pryanth, instructing him to put it on.

"Now," she said, "try to summon your magic."

Pryanth shot his mother a dubious look. Yet, after a moment, his face paled.

"My magic," he said, panic creeping into his voice. "Why can't I summon my magic?"

He yanked off the chain and hurled it on the table, the stone flaring with golden light as it landed with a thud. The flash of light expanded, growing to encase Pryanth, bright enough Analia had to blink the spots out of her vision.

Othin leaned forward, his attention suddenly caught. Aaron remained perfectly still.

"Mother," Pryanth said, his glow fading. "What is that?"

"That, my darling, is a damper."

"*That's* a damper?" Pryanth repeated.

Analia sat up straight. Accalon had told her about dampers once, but all he said was they could block magic and were incredibly difficult to make.

Deardryn reclaimed the damper, but she didn't put it away. "Gavare discovered that onyx has interesting magical abilities. After it undergoes various carvings and charms, it is able to attract magic the same way magnets attract one another. Consequently, once the magic is attracted, it becomes stuck."

Pryanth shuddered. "It felt so... empty. Like all the magic had been sucked out of me."

Analia gave him a sympathetic look, but her mind was racing.

"How do they work?" she asked.

"Think of it like a plug," Deardryn said. "When worn by the Blessed, the stone is able to attract all the magic from the internal network—where magic is known to flow—and pull it toward itself. It then stores the magic until the damper is removed, at which point the pent-up magic is released back into the network and can be accessed once more. The longer it is worn, the longer it takes to completely transfer back."

"Was that the flash?" Analia asked.

"Indeed." Deardryn offered her the damper. Taking it in hesitant hands, Analia immediately felt a slight suction between her palm and the onyx. Yet, when she hung the damper around her neck...

"Nothing," she sighed, handing it back to Deardryn.

"That's not surprising," said Deardryn briskly.

"But why would anyone want one of these?" Pryanth asked.

"Warfare," Othin grunted. "The dampers are easy enough to remove, but adaptations are able to deprive enemy forces of their magic."

Something about that didn't sit right with Analia.

"More commonly, however," Deardryn said, "these were used in the Star Kingdom. The Royal children usually wore them while learning to control their magic."

Othin spat, "A bunch of children with the Blessing of death. They should have all been dampered. Permanently."

Aaron and Analia stiffened.

"Well, they're all gone now," Deardryn said, returning the damper to her box. "I suppose that makes it irrelevant."

Aaron asked, "But what about the rings?"

All eyes flashed to him.

"Why is he here?" Pryanth asked loudly.

"Necessity," said Deardryn. Pryanth and Othin opened their mouths, but Deardryn continued without pause. "The rings were Gavare's ultimate success, although it took quite some time to create them.

"Many people saw Gavare's damper as a sign that he truly had no magic and the Crystal had deemed him unworthy. But Gavare was inspired.

"For five years, five months, and six days, Gavare went back to his work in the forges. He believed that the existence of a stone that could block magic meant there was also a metal or stone that could conduct it. Thus, he tested everything he could get his hands on. Gold, silver, copper, amethyst, sapphire, all of which proved themselves to have different interactions with different Blessings. Eventually, he discovered the proper combination of metal and stone for each Royal magic. Actually getting his hands on said magic, however, was a difficult task.

"For years, Gavare traveled from kingdom to kingdom, meeting with the reigning Royals and explaining the discovery he had made. While some Royals were cajoled into donating some of their magic, others remained hesitant. Gavare ultimately had to result to more amoral means of procuring their magic. Many times, he barely managed to escape with his life.

"Finally, he managed to collect all his rings. And upon his death, he donated them to my family to continue his research, even though it is from this very kingdom Gavare received the majority of his ridicule. He never disclosed how he managed to capture the magic, however, which might have been his own form of retribution. Thus, these rings remain the only samples we have."

Pryanth whined, "But why was Analia able to tell the difference when I couldn't?"

"That's what's fascinating." Deardryn leaned forward. "When a Royal uses their magic, it's obvious what type of magic it is. Flames from Ash. Air from Wind. Life and light from the Sun. Darkness from the Moon. Earth manipulation by Sand. Water-work by the Mist.

"Yet, for some reason, when magic is in an energetic state—as it is with the rings—Royals are only able to recognize their own variety of magic. As you said, Pryanth, the other magics feel like indistinct power. Yet, Analia was able to not just recognize her own magic, but two other types. Furthermore, she had no reaction to the damper."

Deardryn drifted into thought. She dug through her box, fishing out another gold ring. Analia braced herself, but when Deardryn handed it to her, her stomach dropped.

"I don't feel anything," she whispered. Just one more unlit candle.

Deardryn's lips curved in a satisfied smile. "That's because there is no magic in the ring." She plucked the dainty ring from Analia's limp hand. "That was a test, my dear, and you passed."

On the contrary, Analia felt like she was going to be sick.

Othin asked, "What's your point, Deardryn?"

"My point? I don't have one. I have a theory."

Deardryn steepled her fingers. "There has never been a single Royal without Royal magic. We do, however, know that magic comes at all different times. Granted, I'm not aware of any twenty-year gaps, but I find a twist in the old rules far more plausible than an entirely new subset.

"Thus, Analia appears to have dormant magic. Enough to allow her to sense the magic around her, but not to draw out her own. And since she has not yet specialized, she has the unique ability to recognize all magic as if it were her own."

Pryanth turned to Analia. "You hear that? You're special."

Analia ducked her head. Now that she thought about it, though, the few magical objects she'd encountered throughout her life had felt different to her. She'd just assumed that was true for everyone else.

"Is that what this is all about?" Othin pushed back his chair, rising to his full height. "You're trying to convince me this girl has value after all?"

Deardryn appeared completely unfazed as he looked down at her. "A unique ability that no other being in Elefthia has? Yes, I would hazard that is rather valuable."

Othin scoffed, turning his attention to Analia. "Listen here, girl. I don't care if you can *sense* a gods-damned thing. My son is a Royal, heir to the throne. I will not have him bound to the equivalent of a human girl playing dress-up. Either you shock that network of yours awake, or I'll dump you back in the Ash Kingdom."

"No, you won't," said Deardryn wearily. "You might be king, but this marriage pact has been sealed by the Royal Queen."

"This kingdom runs on more than just your word," Othin said.

Pryanth squeezed Analia's knee beneath the table. But to her surprise, she was calm. She was finally back on familiar ground.

Aaron sized up the king, his face unreadable. Deardryn, however, gave her husband a smile sweet as adder's venom and said, "I suppose we shall have to wait and see."

Othin snorted. Without further comment, he stalked out of the room, the door clicking shut behind him.

In the newborn silence, Pryanth called his father a name that had Deardryn reaching across the table to swat his cheek.

"Don't mind him," Deardryn said to Analia as she gathered her things. "My husband blusters like the winds, but in the end, it's all just noise. Although he does tend to have the occasional idea."

Deardryn nudged the three Royal rings toward her. "Let us see if we can shock your network awake. Put all three rings on at once."

Analia eyed the Wind ring uneasily, remembering the lightning in her bones. But if this could potentially activate her magic...

Not wanting to touch the rings more than she had to, Analia placed her fingertips through the rings on the table. She flexed her fingers, the rings sliding down her knuckles.

For a single heartbeat, nothing happened. Then, her vision went white as the wave of magic slammed into her.

Analia lost all sense of time, direction, and reality. It was just her, caught in a force that threatened to crush her to powder, silence ringing in her ears, a scream rising in her throat.

And abruptly, it was gone.

Analia gasped. She slumped back in her chair, her entire body tingling as her senses filtered back in. Just for her to realize someone had taken her hand.

"What are you doing?" Pryanth demanded.

"My job," Aaron said mildly. He slid the second ring off Analia's finger.

"Mother didn't say you could—"

"That was too much power. She was *convulsing*." Aaron's hand shifted slightly as he turned in his seat. "My apologies, Your Majesty."

Deardryn murmured something Analia didn't catch. She blinked hard, trying to clear the fog from her vision as she watched Aaron reach for the final ring on her finger. The Ash ring.

Noticing her gaze, he paused. "You can take that one off, Princess," he said.

Analia snatched her hand away. Aaron rolled his eyes. Analia, however, didn't immediately remove the ring. Compared to the other two, the power was much more tolerable. She let herself ease into it, slowly becoming accustomed to the pulsations before reluctantly taking it off.

Deardryn remained unmoved across the table. "Now," she said, "try summoning your magic."

Exhausted, Analia reached inside, tunneling toward that well. But she only tasted ash on her tongue.

Analia shook her head. She expected Deardryn to be disappointed, but this only seemed to intrigue her.

"Oh well," Pryanth said, a bit louder than necessary. "At least we tried."

"What do we do next?" Analia asked, struggling to sit up straight once more.

"Next?" Deardryn asked. "Next will not come for a few days. I need to think through what this information entails."

"But—"

"I think that's for the best," Pryanth piped up. He stood from his seat and stretched. "You can spend the day with me instead. That's far more entertaining than staring at a bunch of rings."

No, Analia wanted to stare at those rings. She wanted to feel that power coursing through her veins once more, wanted to shock her own network alive. But looking between Deardryn's and Pryanth's obstinate expressions, she felt her objections bubble up to the surface, just to slowly sink back down again.

"Yes, Your Majesty," she said, bowing her head.

Aaron frowned, but for once, he didn't have a quip to offer. As Pryanth grabbed her hand and towed her out of the room, Deardryn remained, sifting through her box.

"Aaron," she said, "if you see Dannel, tell him I'm looking for him."

Aaron bowed in acknowledgement.

"Mother's personal guard," Pryanth explained in response to Analia's confused look.

"I see."

But as Pryanth pulled her into the hall, all Analia could see was yet another unlit wick.

# Chapter 12

Pryanth towed Analia down the hall, Aaron following in their wake. She tried to pay attention as Pryanth chattered about her magic, but her heart wasn't in the conversation.

How in the name of the Crystal did she expect to investigate these Royals if she couldn't so much as say no to them?

"And only you could sense it!" Pryanth was saying.

"Yes," Analia said, "I was surprised when you couldn't."

"What does that mean?"

"What?" Analia flinched at the sudden sharpness in his tone. "No! No, Pryanth, I was only thinking about how your magic is so strong, and I have nothing. I would have thought that would make you even more capable of detecting differences."

"Oh." Pryanth laughed, his face smoothing. "Why didn't you say that before?"

"I..." Analia shook her head.

Pryanth smiled at her. It was so easy, so relaxed. Had she just imagined the thunder-cloud that had passed over the sun?

"That's no problem now."

He turned to Aaron. The guard had silently approached, looking unnervingly at ease as he leaned against the wall behind Analia.

"You can leave us, guard," Pryanth said. "She's with me. I can take care of her."

Analia expected Aaron to argue. Instead, he looked to her questioningly.

He was leaving it up to her? Analia nodded, and Aaron shrugged.

Pryanth, however, hadn't waited for a response. He was already halfway down the hall, calling for Analia to hurry up.

She hesitated, turning to Aaron. "What did I do wrong?"

Aaron's head jerked back. "What did *you* do wrong?"

"Never mind," she grumbled, turning away. "I don't know why I asked you."

Analia hurried to catch up with Pryanth, ignoring Aaron calling after her.

Pryanth led the way through winding corridors. Analia tried to ask numerous times where they were going, but he insisted it was a surprise. Even as they stopped at his chambers, Pryanth ducking inside and emerging moments later with an armful of books, he only flashed a grin.

By the time the two reached the top of a collection of marble staircases, Analia was thoroughly intrigued. Yet, when Pryanth finally came to a stop at the end of a narrow hall, all she saw was a single door and a bored-looking guard lounging against the wall.

"What is this?" she asked.

Pryanth jerked his chin at the guard, who barely looked up as he stepped aside. "This," Pryanth said, pushing open the door, "is the Sun Castle library."

The room beyond was a work of spiraling art. The first floor was a maze of tables and cozy velvet chairs, carefully spaced away from the three marble fireplaces. Curving staircases wrapped around the circular room, creating ring after ring of bookcase-lined floors that spiraled out of sight.

"The library takes up the entirety of the tallest tower," Pryanth said, head craned back to look at the soaring stacks.

"It's massive," Analia said.

She could smell paper and wood, mingling with the faint smoke from the fireplaces. If she closed her eyes, she could almost imagine she was back in the Ash Castle, reading by the fire with Accalon—*one day.*

"It's even bigger than you think," Pryanth said, gesturing for her to follow as he headed for a staircase. "Some Blessed, Crystal knows when, used their spatial magic on the tower so it could hold far more than the physical space would allow. Now, we have a thousand libraries-worth of books, all stored in one place."

"Amazing," Analia said.

The two reached the second floor. Pryanth called out a greeting as he stepped off the landing, leading the way into what appeared to be an intimate reception area.

Rows of bookcases branched off of the circular space, the sconces mounted to their sides providing a soft, yellow glow. In the center of the space, Saura sat behind a curved wooden desk, piles of books and papers covering its surface.

"I was wondering if I'd be seeing you today," she said, looking up from the pile she'd been straightening.

Pryanth grinned as he crossed to his aunt. "Don't tell me I'm becoming predictable."

"Of course not," Saura said, her soft voice laced with humor. "I've simply had twenty-three years to learn you tend to end up here sooner or later."

"And this time, I have company."

"I see that." Saura accepted the armful of books Pryanth slid toward her, but her honey gaze had shifted to Analia. "It's a pleasure to have you in my library, Analia."

The queen's sister offered a soft, inviting smile. And Analia felt muscles she hadn't realized were tense start to relax. "It's a pleasure to be here, Your Highness. Although I didn't realize you're in charge of the library."

"Aunt Saura does everything around here," Pryanth explained, leaning against the desk. "Not only does she check books in and out, but she also maintains all of our records. Some Blessed incorporated magic into the system centuries ago, and she's the only one that can make sense of it all."

"All by yourself?" Analia asked, surprised.

Saura flushed as she retrieved a small leather book from one of her piles, but she couldn't completely hide her smile.

"That's a lot of work for one person," Analia commented.

"I enjoy it nonetheless." Saura sifted through Pryanth's pile of books, her hands shaking slightly as she marked down their titles in her leather book. "Even before I had this job, I spent all my time in the library. By the time my sister gave me the position, it was simply for formality's sake. That and I think Deardryn liked the idea of me having something to do that wouldn't aggravate my health."

"You're also the only one she trusts with the records," Pryanth added.

Saura flashed Analia a meaningful look. Turning back to Pryanth, she asked, "Does that mean you'll be letting me return your books for you this time?"

"Now how would I get to feel useful if I did that?"

Sliding his books back into his arms, Pryanth leaned across the desk to kiss her cheek. Saura shooed him back, the corner of her mouth twitching.

"We'll be back later today," Pryanth said, turning and heading for the stairs. "I'll take care of any stray books I see."

Not waiting for a response, he started to climb, his rapid steps muffled by the thin gray carpet. Startled, Analia made to hurry after him, then glanced back at Saura.

"It's all right," she said with an easy laugh. "Not only does he have a habit of ending up here, but also speeding off once more."

"He doesn't slow down, does he?"

"No he does not." Reaching out, Saura gently disentangled a lock of Analia's hair from her pin. "Don't forget, if you ever wish to check out a book, all you need to do is bring it to me or leave me a note."

She patted Analia's hair back into place. And to Analia's surprise, she found herself wanting to lean into that light touch. Instead, she took a small step back as she said, "Thank you, Your Highness."

Saura smiled, then waved her away. Casting her one last look, Analia turned and headed for the stairs. She didn't catch up with Pryanth until the fourth floor.

"You two have a whole routine, don't you?" she asked, falling into step beside him on the stairs.

"You mean with this?" Pryanth readjusted his armful of books. "Most people just leave their books for Aunt Saura to take care of, and she's more than capable of handling it on her own. I just like to save her the extra trouble where I can."

Analia wasn't expecting that. She tilted her head, her voice growing thoughtful. "She must really appreciate that."

"Sometimes. Other times, I just annoy her." Pryanth flashed a grin. "Come," he said, taking her hand with his free one. "I promised I would show you how our library is even more expansive than the rumors claim."

So, he remembered that after all.

Pryanth continued to lead the way up the stairs. And if he noticed how Analia's gaze lingered on him, he didn't let on.

Together, the two made their way through the library's levels. Pryanth listed each section by memory as they passed, quickly returning his books to where they belonged. Yet, even when his arms were empty, he seemed to have a destination in mind.

"And here," he said, coming to an abrupt halt, "we have the first history block."

"First?"

The block of bookcases was massive, soaring so high Analia couldn't have reached the top shelf, even if she had a step stool.

"Obviously," Pryanth said. "You have overall history here. But then there's also history by kingdom, which can be broken down into history by subject, which can even be broken down into history by individual."

"And it's all here?" Analia asked, suddenly incredibly overwhelmed.

"If you know where to look. Speaking of which." Pryanth guided her through a few more stacks. "This," he said, "is your mind-numbingly dull herbology section."

Pryanth offered a teasing grin. And Analia realized she hadn't tensed automatically.

"You remembered," she said, quickly looking away.

"Why the tone of surprise?" Pryanth asked. He gently touched her cheek, turning her face to look at him. "It's your distraction." He stepped closer, close enough she could smell the honey-sweet scent of his skin.

Analia looked up into his face. She should've been thinking about her uncle's case; the fact that Pryanth brought her to the herbology section meant he was either an incredibly arrogant killer, or a name she could check off her list. Instead, all she could focus on was the simple kindness of it all.

He had remembered she wanted to visit the library. He had remembered which section she wanted to visit. And the slight tilt of his head told her neither of those things was a big deal to him. Even though that casual thoughtfulness was something so few had ever extended to her.

Still, it was best not to let her investigation leave a trail.

"Perhaps I should find a more enthralling distraction," she mused.

"Hmm?" Pryanth moved his thumb across her cheekbone, sending a shiver down her spine. "What kind of 'enthralling' were you thinking?"

He smirked, and Analia's eyes widened. Oh gods. She didn't mean it like that.

"History?" she asked weakly.

"You tease me," Pryanth crooned. His hand slid down from her cheek, tracing the contour of her neck.

Analia was acutely aware of his fingers as they laced through her hair. "What were you thinking?"

"I had some ideas in mind," he murmured, easing her back against a bookcase. "Quite a few, actually."

He leaned in, close enough she could feel his breath on her cheek. "Tell me if you had different ones."

But Analia didn't say a word. Not as she stood in the heart of the Sun Kingdom's library, and Pryanth's lips softly touched her own.

The kiss wasn't long, but it still sent her spiraling back in time. Stolen kisses with Rois behind the music hall, not knowing what they were doing as melodies drifted through the cracked door behind them. She knew it was those memories that sent the lick of fear down her spine. What she wasn't expecting was the disappointment as he pulled back, resting his forehead against hers.

"I'm sorry I snapped at you," he murmured.

Analia opened her eyes. Warm, liquid gold stared back at her in the dim library light, not burning russet. "It's fine."

Pryanth chuckled and leaned in once more. Slow, deep. Fear melting away into something else.

Pryanth eventually pulled away, wrapping an arm around her shoulders as he continued the tour. Analia's hands shook as they wound higher and higher through the stacks, but to her surprise, it was out of relief. Relief she could tentatively cross his name off her list.

The two spent the rest of the afternoon in the library. Pryanth slowly accumulated a new armful of books for both himself and Analia as he showed her his favorite sections, one of which being a medical block where he grabbed her a book on herbal healing.

Eventually, he brought her to a hidden nook in the wall on the seventh floor. Flopping down on a collection of cushions, he chose a book at random from his stack and set the rest aside. Yet, as he pulled Analia down beside him, it quickly became clear reading wasn't the only thing on his mind.

By the time the two finally rose to go, Analia had skimmed through her herbal healing book and could still taste Pryanth's kiss on her tongue. She also decided it would be safe to check out two herbology books to continue her research.

"Why the guard?" she asked as they exited the library.

Pryanth shrugged, his stack of books sliding dangerously. "Mother prefers access to be regulated. The guard only allows those with permission in, and the magic I mentioned earlier prevents those without permission from taking books out."

"That's a lot of security," Analia commented.

"There's just as much sensitive material."

Like information on what killed her uncle. Analia murmured her agreement, letting Pryanth redirect the conversation.

She couldn't openly spend all her time in the herbology section. Even though Pryanth hadn't put the pieces together, it would be glaringly obvious to the killer. She had been hoping for late nights with fewer prying eyes, but how in the name of the Crystal would she get past that guard?

Had Rois been right? Was she hopelessly in over her head? As Pryanth kissed her goodbye outside her chambers, she knew the answer was yes.

# Chapter 13

Aaron strolled through the creaky door of Sun Fang.

One of the Sun Crystal Guard's favorite spots, the tavern buzzed with the sound of voices, the thud of drinks on tables, and the rattle of dice. But the most defining feature was the sunstones that jutted from the ceiling like dragon fangs. Stained by decades, probably centuries, of the multicolored smoke billowing from patrons' pipes, the stones cast a hazy, psychedelic light throughout the room.

As Aaron passed, he caught a pair of women casting him seductive smiles with red-painted lips. He smirked in return, his eyes roving. Six o'clock on the third day of the week. He was always here—yes, there he was.

Aaron wove through the crowd, coming up on a back table where three men sat in hush conversation.

"Dannel!" he said, beaming as he took a seat directly across from him.

Dannel's eye twitched. "What are you doing here, Aaron?"

He, too, had stripped off his fighting leathers, but where Aaron's tunic was black, Dannel's was a deep green. It was undoubtedly chosen to highlight his golden-brown hair and eyes—although it also contrasted the drunken flush across his cheeks. That would be helpful.

Aaron plucked a handful of cards from the center of the table. "I'm joining your game."

"Actually, we had just—"

"It's a pity, what happened to Lev, wouldn't you say?" Aaron asked over his fellow Crystal Guard.

"What? Uh, I suppose."

Aaron waved down the barkeeper and ordered a drink. "I've spoken to the healers," he went on. "They say he should make a full recovery."

Aaron nodded to one of Dannel's friends to roll the dice. He jumped, quickly scattering the dice and barely glancing at them before shoving them toward his friend. That, too, would make things easier.

"Yes," Dannel said. "It's a good thing Her Majesty came when she did."

He turned away in his seat, clearly an attempted dismissal. Aaron smiled to himself as he scooped up the dice.

"Yes, Her Majesty showed up, just in time. Those Ash guards as well." He rolled the dice. "Did you know about those two? Lev and Warack, I mean."

"The entire castle knew," Dannel said, reluctantly turning back to accept the dice. "They were bickering every night. It was only a matter of time before one of them snapped. Although I'm surprised it was just a stab wound. You and I know how Lev's mouth tends to get him into trouble."

"Yes," Aaron mused, "in more ways than one. Didn't you tell me he was going after that girl you liked?"

Dannel's friends perked up.

"He was," Dannel admitted stiffly. "We sorted that out, though."

"Did you? That's good. It's better not to have conflict throughout the Crystal Guard, wouldn't you say?"

Dannel nodded, his eyes narrowing.

"Too bad Warack couldn't have found that same forgiveness in his heart," Aaron went on. "But what puzzles me is the fact that Warack was at the funeral when Lev was stabbed."

"He and Lev must have gotten into it on his way out."

Aaron reclaimed the dice and rolled. "Well, if that's the case, I'm surprised you didn't stumble upon him sooner. After all, you were patrolling that hall, weren't you?"

"I had that entire block," Dannel said. "I started where he was found. I was all the way on the opposite side of our designated quarters."

"Then Lev must have gotten stabbed right when you left." Aaron let the words dangle.

The barkeeper came over with his drink. Aaron nodded to him in thanks, taking a sip of the cold, cheap beer before setting it on the sticky table.

"What are you insinuating, Aaron?" Dannel finally asked.

He reached to take the dice, but Aaron's hand shot out and snatched them first.

"I think no matter which way you spin things," Aaron said, idly rattling the dice in his fist, "it's not looking too good for you. Either you just so happened to completely miss Lev getting stabbed—which seems unlikely. Or you found Lev bleeding on the floor and decided to leave him there, which also isn't flattering. Or..."

"Or what?"

"You stabbed him."

Dannel's flush deepened. "I did not!"

"Right through the gut."

"Liar!"

"Off center, too. Were you drunk, or is your aim that bad?"

"That's not—"

"You didn't even clean your sword after—"

"Yes, I did!"

"Oh?" Aaron gave Dannel an innocent look, delighting in the way his flush darkened to crimson.

"That doesn't prove anything," said Dannel, not taking his eyes off Aaron as he rolled the dice.

"Just the ale talking?" asked Aaron sympathetically. "Just as it was the lingering wine you'd snuck the night before, on duty, that had your blood boiling, screaming for you to just take that stab and finally shut Lev up. So elated he decided not to rat you out that you immediately piled on his lie."

"You certainly are adept at telling stories."

"Oh, undoubtedly. But I've always found that the truth has a way of telling itself."

Dannel glanced at his friends, both of whom sat with eyes averted. "What do you want, Aaron?"

"Well, for starters, beer that doesn't taste like someone took a piss in it. Although a new sheath for my dagger might be nice. I hear Chia created a new pastry down in the kitchen that I've been trying to charm my way into—"

"With me, smartass."

"Ah." Aaron suppressed a grin.

He didn't think many people would consider being infuriating a talent, but he certainly did. Anger was a powerful tool, after all. It could be a motivator, but also, a mental inhibitor.

"Here's the thing, Dannel." Aaron propped his boots up on the table, smirking as Dannel snatched his tankard as it was almost kicked over. "You and I, we have a few options." He cocked his head expectantly.

"And what would those be?" Dannel ground out.

"I'm so glad you asked. The first option—my personal favorite—is you do a little something for me. Now that I have leverage over you and all."

"And what's the second?"

Aaron grinned. "The second is Lev and I have a little chat about how the blood loss had made him delirious. He couldn't think straight and was only trying to protect his fellow guard, even though he was literally stabbed through the middle by him. Then, we go and speak with the queen about the cutthroat hiding in her Crystal Guard. And we both know what happens to criminals that threaten the peace of the Sun Kingdom."

Dannel's face went from flaming red to deathly pale. Yes, the Sun Kingdom promoted peace, kindness. A beautiful garden of harmony. But just as with every garden, there were weeds that had to be yanked out by the roots.

"Lev said it was Warack," Dannel said, hands clenching around the table. "Why would he change his mind for you?"

And why had he lied in the first place?

"Tensions are high enough between kingdoms right now as is," Dannel went on. "Do you honestly believe anyone wants to hear it was one of our own?"

"No," Aaron said, "I don't. Which is why it's a great thing I have witnesses."

"They wouldn't turn on me," Dannel said immediately, glancing at his friends. But there was uncertainty in his eyes. The uncertainty of a man who never knew where he stood, making him all the more desperate to cling to what he did have. Lovers, his position in the guard, the respect he'd managed to attain.

"Maybe," Aaron said, sliding his boots from the table. "But Dannel, my friend, look around. We haven't exactly been covert. I'd assume the barkeeper overheard, those two gentlemen at the adjacent table with the immaculate beards—I wouldn't be surprised if that man over there sucking on his lady friend's neck overheard."

"You're willing to dissolve the trust of the Crystal Guard for your own selfish reasons?" Dannel asked. "The trust that you just said was so important?"

The trust that Dannel had agreed was so important. The trust he had broken, a fact that, judging by the looks on his friends' faces, they hadn't missed.

Aaron said, "The termites were already there, Dannel. I'm simply shining a light on them before they eat away the foundation. Unless you'd like to do me one insignificant favor."

"That being?"

"I want you to find where Deardryn keeps her jewelry box."

Dannel sneered, bringing his tankard to his lips. "I never took you for that type of man, Aaron."

"The one with all the magical trinkets," Aaron went on.

"Why do you think she'd tell me where it is?" Dannel asked.

"I don't," Aaron said. "I think you're her assigned guard and therefore have the highest likelihood of being able to find out without her realizing. And if she does realize, it's better you than me."

"But—"

"Hey, barkeeper!" Aaron called across the tavern. "Did you know that Lev was stabbed by—"

"Fine!" Dannel hissed.

"Fine...?"

"Fine, I'll tell you where she keeps it. You do understand this is treason, don't you?"

"Curiosity isn't treason," Aaron said, rising to his feet. "It's what you do with that curiosity that gets you into trouble, and I haven't told you anything about that. For all you know, I'm making sure security is top-notch."

Aaron tossed a few copper flecks on the table to cover his drink. He waved to Dannel's friends, who still had not spoken.

Maybe that was why Dannel liked them. He didn't have to worry about them running away. Although tonight, they were the noose around his precious reputation's neck.

"I expect weekly updates," he called over his shoulder as he exited the tavern. "Otherwise..." Aaron slid a finger across his throat and winked.

As Aaron shut the door behind him, the blare of the tavern was abruptly muted. He took a deep breath of the crisp night air, clearing his smoke-induced headache.

Should he have... Yes, it was the only way. He'd exhausted all other options. If he was right about the scroll, then it would be under massive security. Just like those rings.

Aaron turned away, tugging on his chain. Find the scroll, that was all he had to do. Then he could finally go home.

# Chapter 14

Analia shifted uncertainly as she lingered by her chamber door.

The halls were silent. The patrol had just passed. She knew she had a decent amount of time to slip out and back in. Yet, she couldn't bring herself to open her door.

All she could see was Deardryn's look of approval. Pryanth's smile. The feeling of his lips on hers. They were such an intoxicating change from her kingdom's contempt and her father's disdain.

But buried beneath it all, there was her uncle. Those memories she had collected into a pile and promptly locked behind an iron door.

She was doing this for him. And not giving herself time to think, Analia pushed open her door and slipped into the corridor beyond.

Analia had quickly learned that the Sun Castle guards preferred to constantly patrol rather than be stationed in certain locations. Still, she'd been surprised to discover that included no guards outside her chambers. Truce marriage or not, she was a foreign Royal. Yet, when she'd casually mentioned this to Pryanth, he only said, "Mother trusts you."

She, however, hadn't missed how his eyes narrowed slightly. Clearly, Deardryn wasn't the only one testing to see if she deserved that trust. And Analia wasn't foolish enough to believe there would be no consequences if that trust was broken.

Now, her footsteps echoed quietly as she made her way down the abandoned corridor. The sunstones had been dimmed, casting a faint light that sent shadows slinking across the walls.

She had three floors to scale to get to the library, but she still had no idea how to get past the guard. Could she bluff her way in? Say she got permission?

Analia paused at the corner, listening for footsteps. No, bluffing wouldn't work. She slipped around the corner. It was too easy to verify she was lying. But maybe—

"Well, you're a long way from your chambers."

Analia turned, the words out of her mouth before she had time to think. "I was looking for the kitchen. I was having a hard time sleeping and thought they could brew me some tea."

Dimitri stood at the end of the hall, having somehow silently approached. He tilted his head. Did he actually believe—

"You're a shit liar, you know that?"

Analia folded her arms. "I am not."

"You're far better than most," he conceded, "but that doesn't mean you're good."

Analia could see why Pryanth disliked this servant. Even if he wasn't the king's bastard, there was a bluntness to Dimitri that was as subtle as a slap to the face.

"So, why are you really wandering through the corridors at night?" Dimitri asked, creeping closer.

There was a part of Analia tempted to tell him the truth. As a servant of the castle, he was bound to know far more than she did.

But as a servant of the castle, he was also loyal to the Royals. Especially if his father was the king that had made a big enough fuss to keep him close.

"I'm mapping out the castle," she said carefully. "I don't like being in unfamiliar surroundings."

"You map in the middle of the night?"

Analia was about to reply when both of them froze. Footsteps echoed farther down the hall. Multiple pairs, voices coming closer.

Dimitri swore, fast and colorful.

"We have to go," Analia hissed, eyes darting.

"What do you mean, 'we'?"

"You want to be caught by whoever that is?"

"Who says I'll be caught?"

"Who says I'll keep my mouth shut if I am?"

Dimitri gave her a look of grudging approval. "You can't lie, but you can threaten."

"I can lie."

"Great, we can argue about this again, but this time, we can have our new friends weigh in, too—"

"Fine," Analia snapped, voices coming closer. "Shouldn't we be running now?"

Dimitri hesitated. Then, with the air of a sullen child, he shuffled over to the wall.

"Hurry!" Analia hissed.

"I will leave you."

Dimitri put his hand on the frame of a painting of the Sun Kingdom square. The voices were about to round the corner.

With a shove, Dimitri moved aside the painting, revealing a dark opening in the wall. He clambered through, not glancing back as Analia scrambled in after him.

Analia found herself in a narrow stone passageway. A cold current sighed through the space like a ghostly exhale, a faint bluish glow providing enough light that she could see the snaking pathways to her left and right.

"What in the name of the Crystal..."

Analia turned to slide the painting back into place. Yet, just as the entryway was about to clunk shut, she froze.

"What are you doing?" Dimitri hissed.

"It's the king and queen."

Analia pressed her ear to the crack between the wall and the sliding door, not daring to breathe. Dimitri grumbled something, but he didn't leave.

"I don't know what Brenn is up to," Othin said, "but I don't trust that girl."

"It was Analia's idea," Deardryn pointed out.

"Which makes me trust her even less."

"Perhaps she wanted peace between our kingdoms. Something she didn't believe you and her hotheaded father could accomplish by yourselves."

"Or she could be rooting around for something she can bring back to her king."

Dimitri shot Analia a look. Analia's body went cold.

"Othin, were you paying no attention?" Deardryn's footsteps stopped, right outside the entrance. "Did you not see how every person in that kingdom looked at her? The only person she had was Accalon, and the poor thing stumbled upon his corpse."

One day. One day.

"I don't see her in a hurry to run back to them any time soon," Deardryn went on. "I certainly wouldn't."

"Old Hag," Dimitri muttered. "What are you up to?"

Analia's gaze slid to him questioningly, but his ear was pressed to the crack. He tapped his fingers on the stone, and Analia's heart leaped as the wall became a clear window, revealing the king and queen on the other side.

"It's one way," Dimitri whispered, rolling his eyes as she ducked out of sight. "They can still hear you though, so calm the fuck down."

Analia glared, but she cautiously rose to watch once more.

Othin and Deardryn stood on opposite sides of the hall, the king facing Analia and Dimitri. Arms folded, he was saying, "But with that magic? Deardryn, she's dangerous, whether she's collecting information or not."

"Or advantageous. I'd much rather have that power with me than against me."

Deardryn patted Othin's arm. "She's with us now. It's time you adjust to the idea."

Deardryn turned. Analia swore her eyes briefly locked onto the window. But Deardryn's face remained smooth as she swept down the hallway, leaving Othin slouched against the wall, scowling.

Analia made to ease away from the crack, heart pounding, when Othin turned.

"If she does anything suspicious," he said to someone Analia couldn't see, his voice low, "I want to know about it. I don't care if she so much as drinks an extra glass of wine with dinner. You will report it to me."

"Yes, Your Majesty."

Lev. Just out of view.

Othin pushed off the wall, his final words trailing after him as he departed. "Don't forget, accidents always happen. Especially to little mice that try to ruin a Royal's belongings."

Analia pushed away from the window, bracing herself against the opposite wall. Dimitri remained at the crack a few moments longer. Finally, he eased the entrance shut and turned to her with an appraising look.

"Suddenly," he said, "you're a lot more interesting."

Analia didn't respond.

Othin was already onto her. And if he had caught her tonight—no, she couldn't think about that.

Dimitri led Analia back to her room, taking turn after disorienting turn without hesitation. Rapid-fire questions pelted out of his mouth, but she didn't bother answering them. She could only focus on the cold feeling creeping through her insides as Dimitri unceremoniously shoved her out of an entrance above her desk. It wasn't fear. It was something else. Something that promised devastation all the same.

# Chapter 15

Analia didn't know what to expect as she, Pryanth, and Aaron entered the Ring Room, Deardryn already waiting inside. The Dragoness had seemingly decided that today was the day to get to work testing Analia's newfound abilities, although she had once again refrained from sharing any details.

Aaron slipped away to sit on the wraparound bench, leaving Analia and Pryanth to join Deardryn at the table. The queen didn't appear to have her jewelry box, a pen and paper before her instead.

"There's a ring in this room," she said, skipping greetings entirely.

"Where is it?" Analia asked.

"That is for you to discover."

Pryanth asked, "And how's she supposed to do that?"

"By locating the magic field." Deardryn turned to Analia. "When holding the ring, you received a direct burst of its magic. But that magic also emanates out. You may think of it as the cold surrounding an ice cube, or the heat that radiates from a candle flame."

"And you think I should be able to sense it?" Analia asked doubtfully.

"I see no reason why you shouldn't. Although we have no way of knowing for sure until you attempt to locate it."

Taking the hint, Analia closed her eyes. It took a moment, but there. A quiet thrum that wasn't quite sound, or vibration, or touch, but she was aware of it all the same.

"I've got it," she said.

"Good." Deardryn's pen scratched. "Now, identify which variety of magic it is."

"Variety?" Analia opened her eyes.

Deardryn gave her a look of infinite patience. "Indeed. Just as you were able to distinguish the type of magic when holding the ring, you should be able to identify the type of magic through the magic field. It's the same process as before, just without direct contact."

Pryanth, fidgeting with his sleeve, piped up from Analia's left. "Mother, what's the point of this? We already know she can do it. Can't we try something a little more stimulating?"

Deardryn's lips briefly pursed. She picked up her pen, and without warning, she tossed it to Pryanth. Pryanth reflexively caught it.

"What was that?" he asked.

"Anyone could have caught that pen," Deardryn said. "Assuming they were able to see it coming, that is. The distance is negligible, close enough I could reach out and touch you without moving from my seat. As you increase that distance, however…"

Deardryn plucked the pen from Pryanth's fingers and tossed it across the room to Aaron. Barely looking up, the guard caught the pen between two fingers.

"That takes more skill."

Deardryn gestured, and Aaron tossed the pen back to her. She, too, caught it with ease.

"Now," she said, turning back to Pryanth. "If you were to move across the room, do you suppose you, too, could catch the pen?"

"Yes," he muttered, his face turning pink.

Deardryn fondly stroked his cheek. "The task itself is simple: catching. Yet, just because you can do it from a close range doesn't mean you can do it farther away. But with practice, you can widen that gap. And that is what we are attempting to do with Analia's abilities."

"Trading dexterity for sensitivity," Analia said.

Deardryn gave her an approving look. "Precisely, my dear. Now, let us see just how sensitive your abilities are."

Analia sat back in her chair, obediently closing her eyes once more. She found the magic field a bit faster this time. And yet, it was too distant. It was like music playing too softly to make out the words.

Analia strained her senses, acutely aware of the silent seconds ticking by. She could feel Deardryn's gaze on her, waiting, expecting. Pryanth let out an impatient sigh.

Crystal spare her, they were asking too much. Othin was going to send her home, a failure. There would be nothing standing between herself and Brenn.

Analia's grasp on the field slipped. She scrambled to find it again, but every time she tried to latch on, it was like sand sifting between her fingers. What was she doing wrong?

Analia struggled in vain a few moments longer, desperately shoving back images of unlit candles. Finally, she couldn't take the silence any longer. She opened her eyes, crestfallen as she whispered, "I don't think I can do it."

The hope slowly drained from Deardryn's eyes. Crystal spare her.

"It's not your fault," Pryanth said, only making her feel worse. "It's impressive enough you're able to tell the difference." Pryanth rose, reaching for her hand.

Was that really it? Were they truly so quick to give up on her? Was she giving them any reason not to?

"Well, that was fast," said Aaron. "You barely lasted ten minutes before giving up."

"Be quiet, guard," Pryanth snapped, whirling to face Aaron.

Aaron didn't spare Pryanth a glance. "If that's all you can do, Princess, it's no wonder your magic is dormant. That soft of a poke wouldn't wake a raging mother dragon."

Analia glared. "I'd like to see you attempt to find it before you judge my efforts."

"I don't have your sensory abilities," Aaron said. "It's impossible for me to do it. You're just quitting."

"I am not." Analia pushed out of her chair. "No one knew for sure if I could do it. I'm not quitting because we discovered I can't."

But even as the words left her mouth, Analia knew they weren't completely true. Beside her, Pryanth still fumed—although she suspected it was from Aaron ignoring him, not on her behalf. At her back, Deardryn was utterly silent.

"If you insist." Aaron stretched, that doubtful nonchalance sparking something inside her. "Although, remind me, Princess. What's your kingdom's motto, again?"

"Rise again," she said through gritted teeth.

"Interesting. I wonder if your uncle would think that's what you're doing."

Analia stumbled back a step, her knuckles turning white around the back of her chair. "Leave him out of this," she hissed.

"This? Princess Analia, I thought we already established this was over."

"Well, it's not," she snapped.

"Oh? Is this the part when you try to prove me wrong? That should be entertaining."

Fire coursed through Analia's veins. And it positively flared as Aaron gave her a lazy, disbelieving smile.

Analia turned her back on him and closed her eyes. Arrogant, impertinent man. Thought he knew everything, could say whatever he wanted.

She reached for the thrum once more. She wouldn't let him be right, wouldn't give him any excuse to lounge on his gods-damned bench and mock her. She'd had enough of that in the Ash Kingdom. She would not let that follow her here.

Analia found the magic field once more. She shut out the world around her: Pryanth ranting at Aaron, the feeling of Aaron's gaze on the back of her head, Deardryn's expectations. It was just herself and the magic.

She opened herself to the power, letting it lace through her body. Its crackling rhythm moved through her bones. A familiar beat.

"It's Ash magic," she said, cutting off Pryanth midsentence. She opened her eyes, fire still coursing through her veins as she met Deardryn's stare.

"Are you sure?" Deardryn asked.

Analia folded her arms, not breaking eye contact. Deardryn let the question dangle, but Analia didn't waver.

"Fascinating," Deardryn said, her gaze flicking to Aaron.

"Is she right?" Pryanth asked, turning back to them.

"Indeed, she is."

Deardryn lifted her hand from under the table, revealing the Ash ring in the center of her palm. Savage satisfaction crackled in Analia's lingering flames.

Both Deardryn and Pryanth gave her slightly surprised yet approving looks. Only Aaron remained unfazed, a self-satisfied smirk on his lips.

"Come back tomorrow," Deardryn said, standing from her seat. "I'd like to see how far we can push these sensory abilities."

Analia gave a quick nod. Being dismissed, she turned to stride out of the room, refusing to look at Aaron as she passed.

Pryanth hurried to catch up with her in the hall.

"That was amazing!" he exclaimed, taking her hand and pulling her in for a kiss.

For a few moments, that fire still smoldered in Analia's chest. But as Pryanth rested his hand on the back of her neck, she finally felt those flames sizzle in defeat.

"I'm glad it was stimulating enough for you," she said, pulling away.

Pryanth laughed. "Oh, Analia, we all knew you would find it. It was just a matter of when. You had the entire room practically quivering with anticipation."

Was that true? Had she misunderstood? Had she imagined those looks of doubt?

"You really thought I could do it?" she asked.

"Of course." Pryanth smiled down at her. "You were perfect. The flame to my life."

Something soft, something tentative, began to unfurl in Analia's chest. Something that should have unsettled her.

But Pryanth was right: she'd done something no other Royal in Elefthia had been able to do. She hadn't allowed herself to feel the excitement, the hope that maybe this was the key to finally sparking her magic. Even if it wasn't, maybe this ability would be enough for her people. Maybe she would finally be enough. And Pryanth had made sure she realized it.

As the two headed off down the hall, Analia reached for his hand. He startled slightly, but the look he flashed her was pleased. Clearly, he had noticed that she had never initiated any form of contact with him before.

But Analia had found the ring. She enjoyed the way her heart skipped a beat as his thumb stroked her knuckles. And she was going to get into that library.

# Chapter 16

Analia trailed her fingertips along the rough stone wall as she wandered through the secret passageways.

It had taken her quite a few tries to figure out how to open the entrance—tapping on the wall, trying to pry her fingers between the cracks, nothing. It wasn't until she rested her palm on the entrance, contemplating, that she suddenly felt a click beneath her palm. Then, the stone easily slid aside.

Now, with her slowly expanding map in hand, Analia wound through the castle walls. A part of her was exhilarated. This was precisely the tool she needed to sneak around unnoticed. Yet, the passageways themselves made the hairs on the back of her neck stand up.

They were too narrow, had too many turns. Not to mention she had no idea who she might stumble into.

Analia paused at an intersection. A sharp left turn, or a ladder moving up. Well, she needed to get up three floors to find the library.

"You cannot be fucking serious."

Analia whirled.

Dimitri emerged from the gloomy light farther down the corridor. "What are you doing *now?*" he complained, coming to a glowering stop before her. He was only a few inches taller, but he might as well have been standing on a fifty-foot pedestal with the look he gave her.

Analia tilted her head, remembering how his face had twisted with disgust as they listened to the king and queen through the stone. That didn't seem like the typical reaction of a loyal subject.

"I'm trying to find the library," she said truthfully.

Dimitri's eyebrows shot up. "You're not allowed in without permission."

"I doubt I'm allowed inside these walls either."

"And how *did* you get back in?"

Analia shrugged and explained her tests on the wall. Dimitri swore.

"This is how you repay me for saving your ass?" he complained.

"You were saving yourself," Analia said.

"True. Although you still owe me. Scurry back to your chambers, and we can consider ourselves even."

Analia scoffed. Dimitri didn't look terribly surprised.

"So," he asked, "what were you going to do? Dawdle about until you happened to stumble upon the right passageway?"

"I've been mirroring the path," Analia shot back. "Outside to inside."

"It's not a perfect match."

"I'm aware." There had already been a few turns that hadn't lined up, but she thought she had a good enough idea of where she was to stay on track. "I was planning on periodically opening an entrance to check where I was."

Dimitri's eyes widened in horror. He put his head in his hands, "You were planning on not just exposing yourself, but my passageways, too?"

So, that was what this was about.

"Well," Analia said, casually leaning back against the ladder, "you could always just assist me."

"Why would I do that?"

"Think of it as an exchange," she suggested, toying with her phoenix pin. "You help me, and I'll help you."

"Great," said Dimitri. "You go back to your chambers, and I won't report your midnight meanderings to the queen."

Weaselly little bastard.

"Or," Analia countered, "I could ask the queen to make you my personal servant. I can get you off cleaning duty, give you nothing to do—other than get me in the library."

"You think the queen would go for that?" Dimitri asked.

"You heard her last night. She would rather have me with her than against her."

Dimitri scoffed. "You don't have the guts to stand up to her."

Analia made to argue, but the words died on her tongue. She flashed back to her first day in the Ring Room, unable to say no to either Pryanth or Deardryn. Had Dimitri been lurking in the walls even then?

Dimitri slumped against the wall, feet sliding as he said, "You would ask Deardryn, she would say no, you would stammer some argument, and Deardryn's paranoid intuition would activate. You'd end up spilling everything, get my passageways exposed, and then I would have to kill you."

Analia scowled, but Dimitri wasn't done.

"There's nothing you can give me, but there's a shit ton of things I can do to you."

"Rat me out and I'll tell Deardryn about the passageways," Analia threatened.

"No, you won't. That will just incriminate you more."

The ladder pressed into Analia's back. How had this gotten flipped around on her?

"So," Dimitri said, feet sliding even more, "this is how shit's going to go. You're going to go back to your room, you're going to keep your mouth shut about my passageways, and you're going to keep your snooping ass out of them, too."

There was a part of Analia that wanted to comply, duck her head and avoid the conflict. But the part of her that had sensed that magic earlier in the day, the part that burned from the slap of Aaron's words, had her straightening.

"I don't think that's how this is going to go," she said slowly. "You keep saying 'my passageways.' Worrying about me exposing them and what that might do to you. But I'm getting into that library, whether I have the passageways or not.

"Now, my likelihood of getting in and out without being seen is greatly increased by not just me using these corridors, but you helping me. And if I do get caught, I'll have nothing to lose. And you'll have nothing hanging over my head to prevent me from spilling everything."

Dimitri was silent for a long pause. Finally, he folded his arms. "And what's stopping me from ratting you out first?"

"My offer still stands," Analia said.

"So I would get to sit in a library, doing nothing for Crystal knows how long, before escorting you back to your chambers, just so you can try and fail to make me your servant."

Dimitri rolled his eyes, but something had grabbed Analia's attention.

"Nothing to do but read," she said.

Dimitri's eyes darted away. He opened his mouth, paused, then made a dismissive noise. And Analia didn't give herself time to think.

"I can teach you," she said. "I can teach you to read."

Dimitri went rigid. Bull's-eye.

"Get me into the library," Analia said, confidence building, "and I'll teach you to read."

Dimitri didn't respond, his fingers flexing into the crumbling wall. Analia remained quiet, letting that silent battle rage on. One breath. Two. Three.

"Or maybe not," she said. "I can just keep dawdling about until I hopefully stumble upon the correct passageway and not some guards, or even the queen."

She turned away from the ladder, taking the left turn instead. Her heart pounded in her ears with each step, the silence stretching behind her. Had she been wrong? Would he not—

"Why do you think I can be bribed into defying the Royals?" Dimitri called after her.

Analia glanced back. "Because I'm not the only one skulking in these walls."

Dimitri snorted. Finally, he pushed himself off the wall. "If we get caught, I'll fucking kill you."

Then, shoving past her, he marched off down the hall, not waiting to see if she followed.

Dimitri stomped down the corridor, grumbling under his breath as he took turn after turn with barely a second thought. Since when did the Ash girl have a spine? Why did he have to be the one to discover she was a flashfire waiting to happen? Why did she have to offer him the one thing that triggered a tentative excitement?

She was going to teach him to read. He was finally, *finally* going to learn—although that didn't mean he wouldn't slit her throat if she even came close to exposing his passageways.

"You never explained to me how these passageways work," Analia said.

Crystal spare him, she was the talkative type.

"If you need me to explain how gaps between stones work," Dimitri said, "I'll be demonstrating with our tombstones."

Dimitri veered sharply to the right, coming on a hidden ladder. He started to climb.

"Is it magical or manmade?" Analia persisted, following him up. "Can humans get in, or do you have to have magic?"

"If you needed magic to get in, neither of us would be here right now."

"But Othin has magic."

"And apparently, the Crystal doesn't Bless bastards."

Dimitri stepped off the ladder, struggling to unclench his jaw as he headed down the last corridor. It wasn't like the Crystal being fickle with its Blessings was unheard of.

"Well," Analia said, "the Crystal is supposed to Bless all Royals, but look at me."

Dimitri glanced back despite himself. He expected to see self-pity, or even sadness in her eyes. But no, that was anger, which only sparked his own.

"Your magic will come in," he said dismissively. "You'll go off and have obnoxious little Sun babies with your peacock of a prince, and you'll be queen someday.

"I will forever be the bastard son of the king. Born to some brothel worker that was forced to get Othin's jollies off for some pathetic wager. Cursed with his face, and not even Blessed with his magic."

Dimitri turned sharply away before she could respond. Born to royalty, left with nothing. Nothing except these passageways he'd stumbled upon while listlessly polishing a picture frame.

Dimitri placed his hand on the wall, forcing a sharp sigh out of his nose. He'd better not regret this.

"Here's the library entrance," he said.

He had just felt the click of the entrance unlocking when Analia put a hand on his arm, sending a jolt of panic through his veins.

"Wait," she said. "Do you think anyone's in there?"

"I don't know," said Dimitri. "Let's find out."

Without further warning, he shoved the wall aside. The heavy thud reverberated throughout the passageway and library beyond, and Dimitri quickly pulled the entrance shut once more.

Analia gave him a scandalized look. Yet, as the seconds ticked by, no one came.

"Well, there you go," Dimitri said. He clambered out of the passageway.

"You are a battering ram of subtlety," Analia complained, climbing after him.

Just as Dimitri suspected, the library was silent, only dimly lit by the inset sunstones. He was almost positive the passageways had been lost to history, meaning the only known way into the library was through the front door. Seeing as though that was guarded, there was no reason to have any internal security.

Unless he was missing it. In that case, well, there was no telling for sure until it was too late.

"All tiptoeing will ever get you is stepped on," he said, his lowered voice still unnervingly loud in the silence. "Especially by that prince of yours."

It had only taken him thirteen years of trying to keep his head down, just for Pryanth to trample over him, to figure that one out.

Dimitri waved Analia forward, stepping aside so she could pass without touching him. "All right, little mouse, lead the way. If I'm going to die, it better be for something more than bickering in a library."

Analia scowled as she passed. "I'm not a mouse."

"Sure you are," he said, trailing after her. "Quiet, scurrying through the walls. You might as well be nibbling a piece of cheese."

He mimed the action. Analia looked as though she were contemplating which book to smack him with.

"I don't recall being the only one in the walls," she said. "What does that make you?"

"Gutter rat."

Analia shook her head. She led the way to a block of bookshelves, selecting an armful of books and continuing onto a nearby table.

"What about my lessons?" Dimitri complained, plopping down across from her.

"I didn't forget."

Analia moved to a nearby cart that held various note-taking supplies. Grabbing a thin stack of papers and a pen, she returned to the table and scribbled something on the page.

"Do you know the names of the letters in our alphabet?" she asked.

"I'm not that stupid!"

"Just checking. Here." She slid the sheet toward him. "These are the letters. Copy them out until you can write them by memory."

She handed the pen to Dimitri, and without further comment, she flipped open one of her books.

That was it? That was easy!

Barely thirty seconds had gone by when he shoved his completed paper in her face. Analia jerked back, making a noise of protest. She took the page, her eyebrows rising slightly as she scanned through its contents.

"You have beautiful handwriting," she said, handing the paper back to him. "Have you practiced this before?"

Dimitri's ears burned, but he didn't respond.

She didn't need to know about the hours he'd spent eavesdropping on Pryanth's lessons when they were young, silently seething that Pryanth was only three years older, yet far more educated. He'd snatched an alphabet chart left behind after one of Pryanth's lessons and had been trying to teach himself to read ever since. Yet, he still couldn't do it.

He'd even tried bringing the sheet to Toren, the servant who had reluctantly taken him as his ward. But he'd barely glanced at Dimitri's sheet before mumbling something about how no servant can read.

Analia set Dimitri up with more advanced exercises, seeming genuinely impressed. But Dimitri didn't give a damn what Flashfire thought. What anyone thought. Yet, that didn't stop him from fidgeting in the silence.

"What are you looking for, anyway?" he asked.

Analia didn't look up.

"Come on, tell me."

Analia silently turned a page.

"Fine." Dimitri returned to his work. He tapped his pen against the page, his eyes scanning over the collection of letters. "Oh, just tell me!"

For the next couple hours, the cycle repeated: Dimitri pestering Analia with questions, just for the Ash Princess to ignore him. He managed to catch a glimpse of some sort of leaf on one of the covers—was she reading about plants? Dimitri was starting to get annoyed—more so than usual—when Analia finally closed her book with a sigh.

"It doesn't matter," she said. "I haven't found anything." She gathered up her books. "Let's go, we can try again tomorrow."

Tomorrow? He never said anything about a multiday arrangement. Although...

Dimitri glanced down at his filled-out sheets. He'd made more progress in the past four hours than he had in gods knew how many years.

Dimitri carefully collected his papers. Fine, they would keep going. He could always rat her out when she was no longer of use to him.

Dimitri led Analia back through the passageways, leaving her at her chambers. The two didn't speak as she closed the entrance behind her. Dimitri studied the stone for a few moments, touched the folded papers in his pocket, and turned to go.

# Chapter 17

Ember hurried into her back room. She'd just finished up at the Healer School, their lessons temporarily paused as all apprentices focused on researching xenol. Whoever solved it had been promised their medical mystery marking, the hardest marking to earn.

If Ember could do it, she would only need her internal magic marking and she would be a full-fledged healer. And Analia could come home.

She was confident she could do it, too. Most of her classmates were going about researching in the complete wrong way. Well, at least in her opinion.

They were studying samples from Accalon's stomach and researching scrolls she tried to tell them she'd already looked through. They were trying to understand xenol through history, a non-magical lens. But that plant had been enough to take down a Royal. And as Ember reached for her plant box, she was certain she was about to start figuring out how.

Infused with her magic, the box was able to restore even the driest, crispiest of plants back to full health. Granted, Ember had never tried to restore a partially digested sample before, but that didn't stop her from commandeering the sample and smuggling it back here. Nor did it stop her from trying to restore said minuscule scrap of leaf to its original state.

A week prior, she'd used every scrap of magic she had to slowly restore the fleck. Reforming plant tissue, accelerating growth. She was left chilled to the bone and trembling, but she'd managed to regrow the fragment to a scrap of leaf the size of her thumbnail.

Granted, one of the few herbologist master healers had already done this to a different sample. Ember, however, knew there was no chance she could've smuggled it away without notice. Just as she knew none of her fellow apprentices could have replicated her own regrowing.

"Stupid healer neophytes," she grumbled, unlatching the box. "Going on and on about how herbology is a useless gift from the Crystal. Well, the Crystal can Bless my perfectly round—"

Ember's eyes widened.

The box itself was wooden, plain, similar to a typical window box. She, however, had fluttered her eyelashes at a nice boy who knew his way around a wood shop, and had gotten him to build her a lid, allowing her to close the box and trap her magic inside with the plant.

But when she peeked inside, the xenol sample hadn't grown at all. And there was no trace of magic in the box.

"What in the name of the Crystal," Ember breathed.

Did xenol grow off magic? Did she not infuse enough in the box? No, that couldn't be it. Any time she tried to grow devinroot—which also grew off magic—she could always feel the residual magic in the plant itself.

Ember opened her devinroot's box. Yes, she could still feel the magic faintly pulsing as she trailed her fingers down its fuzzy stem. Yet, when she moved back to the first box, the xenol scrap remained utterly magicless.

Was it the lack of roots? That had never mattered before. Was it simply too damaged? But then where did the magic go?

"What in the name of Rosala's saggy left breast are you?" Ember asked the xenol.

For a few minutes, Ember studied her sample, her mind racing through potential explanations and interfering variables. She was so caught up in her thoughts she almost didn't hear the customer calling her from the front room. Something about burn salves?

Ember glanced through her open door—well, that woman was beautiful. Casting the plant box one last look, she hurried off to help the customer.

# Chapter 18

In the following weeks, Analia fell into a rhythm: morning training with Deardryn, afternoons with Pryanth, and late nights in the library with Dimitri. Part of her wondered if her lack of sleep was impairing her ability to sense the magic, but with how little progress she'd made, she doubted her sleep was the only factor.

Every day, she sat in the Ring Room, desperately trying to latch onto the magic field. Deardryn had hidden one of the rings in the room, and while Analia knew it was the Ash ring once again, locating it was proving to be a completely different task.

The magic field was more of a bubble than a single wave. There was no finding a single thread and following it back to the source. Rather, she found the field, but locating its parameters, let alone where the ring happened to be within that field?

She tried sitting still and concentrating. She tried pacing the room and physically tracing the field with her fingers. She tried asking Deardryn for a hint, which the Dragoness promptly scolded her for. Every time she came close to calling it quits for the day, there was Aaron, ready to mercilessly mock her.

As the days stretched on with little to no progress, Deardryn and Pryanth stopped showing up. Pryanth because he was easily bored, Deardryn because she wasn't in the kingdom anymore. She'd informed Analia she had business to attend to, and she expected Analia to have found the ring when she returned in a week's time. Now, only Aaron and Analia remained, the silence between them crackling with tension.

Why couldn't he be the one to leave? There was no one there to make sure he stayed with her; he wasn't doing anything outside of his occasional mocking. Why did he bother showing up?

"Well," Aaron said when she finally asked, "my official title is guard, but between you and me, I think I'm more of a glorified handler."

"I don't need to be watched like a child," Analia snapped. "I'm not going to cheat to find the ring."

"Perhaps *you* don't need to be watched," Aaron said, "but your magic certainly does. You can't deny you're rather inconsistent."

Analia glared. Aaron looked delighted.

"I didn't realize my failure to use magic was such a threat to the lives of the people in this castle."

She rose from her seat to pace the room, Aaron's eyes following her path.

"You never know," he said. "Perhaps one day, all that magic will come roiling to the surface in a magnificent display of flame and rage."

Analia snorted. "Unlikely."

"If that temper of yours is any indicator, I'd have to disagree. And I, for one, would hate to miss that—although I'd appreciate it if you would pick up the pace because this bench is starting to destroy my spine."

"You're free to go any time."

"And deprive you of my incomparable company?"

"Something tells me I'll survive."

Analia wandered past him toward the bookcase, catching a glimpse of his expression from the corner of her eye. Amused. Excited, even.

"What do you expect to be able to do if my magic *does* explode?" she asked, turning to face him fully.

"I'll be company for when you torch yourself," Aaron said, not missing a beat. "No one should spontaneously self-combust alone."

Analia's lips twitched.

Aaron's eyes widened. He put a dramatic hand to his chest, "Holy Crystal above, did you just smile?"

Heat rushed to Analia's cheeks. "You are truly looking for a fiery demise."

Aaron's eyes danced with mirth. He gave her a one-finger salute, and Analia had to turn away to hide her expression.

Why did he care if she smiled, anyway? Most of the time, he seemed far more entertained when she glowered at him.

Besides, surely she smiled every now and again. So then why did her heart brace itself as she thought about it?

*No one should spontaneously self-combust alone.* Accalon would've liked that.

A splinter pierced through Analia's heart. But just for a moment, Analia allowed herself to feel it before shutting it away once more.

The day before Deardryn was to return to the kingdom, Pryanth intercepted Analia on her way to the Ring Room. Ushering her out to the garden behind the castle, he proudly displayed the blanket and basket of food waiting for them—"Far more fun than ring hunting all day."

Plants in all shapes and sizes lined the garden's winding pebble pathways. A fountain softly burbled nearby, blending with the quiet humming of the nymphs.

Appearing incredibly human-like outside of their pointed ears and slit pupils, the nymphs tended to their plants, their green and brown clothing practically camouflaging them amid the greenery.

Analia and Pryanth talked the entire morning, passing a bottle of sweet summer wine between them. Pryanth perked up as Analia offhandedly mentioned how her harp instructor had once applauded her bloody callouses. Before he could inquire, she redirected the conversation to one of the historical battles he'd been reading about recently.

As Pryanth happily chattered, Ember's words rang in Analia's mind. *Find a harp, something to make you happy.* But it was exhaustion that came to mind, as heavy and forced as the first steps outside in the dead of winter.

"You know," Pryanth said, playing with a blade of grass, "you're the only person that will listen to me talk about this. Everyone else's eyes glaze over because they can't keep up."

"I like listening to you talk about history," Analia said, watching his fingers. "It's the one time your entire face lights up."

Pryanth looked momentarily taken aback. He lifted her chin with a finger, his honey gaze searching hers with an intensity that had Analia's mind stumble to a halt.

She didn't think she was breathing as he slowly shook his head. She didn't think she could have moved if she wanted to as his hand curled, almost possessively, around her face. "The flame to my life."

Then, his mouth was against hers. Analia's body melted into him as he pulled her closer, something warm and delicious spreading across her skin.

He'd never kissed her like this before. Deep enough to scar, hard enough to bruise. His mouth was a steady burn that promised to consume her piece by piece, and Analia didn't hesitate to give it all to him.

The fear, the guilt, the heartache. She let him burn it all away with every stroke of his tongue, the slide of his fingers through her hair.

Pryanth dragged his lips along her jaw. "I have something for you," he murmured.

Analia struggled to catch her breath. Especially as Pryanth flicked his tongue around her earlobe before pulling away. He dug through his cloak pockets, pulling out a gold heart-shaped pendant on a delicate chain.

"It's one of our family heirlooms," he explained. "I thought if you were to become a part of the family, you should have something to show it."

A lump rose in Analia's throat. She'd received countless pieces of jewelry before, all out of meaningless obligation. But this was different. This was her, finally being chosen. And it was terrifying how much she loved that feeling.

"Thank you."

"Come here." Pryanth moved behind her, his fingers brushing the back of her neck as he moved aside her hair to clasp the necklace. "Perfect."

Analia ran her finger along the heart, feeling a faint magical pulse. "How can I repay you for this?"

"This isn't something you repay, Analia," Pryanth laughed, settling back in the grass. "Although, if you insist." He reached out, lightly tugging her wrist and nestling her beside him. "I do believe there is a story about an Ash King and his human wife you've yet to finish."

Analia's mouth tasted sour. But as Pryanth leaned in, as his lips found her neck, she felt her pendant chain shift. And for the briefest moment, she wondered what would happen if she spoke.

What would happen if she allowed the memories to tumble free, all their sharpened edges, ready to remind her of the gaping hole where her uncle had been because he was—no. *One day.*

"Analia," Pryanth complained. "You can't just dangle the details over my head—"

"What's that?"

Pryanth pulled back. He looked to where she was pointing straight up in the sky.

"Those are the sun dragons," he said, leaning in once more. "It's just the Sun guard training. We not only have a ground component of our army, but an aerial as well."

His lips skimmed down to her collarbone, his hand moving up her ribs.

"Can we watch?" Analia asked.

Pryanth paused. Reluctantly, he pulled back once more. "I suppose."

Clearly unenthused, Pryanth collected their things. While his back was turned, Analia let out a shaky exhale, hand on her pin. But as they headed off to the training arena a little ways beyond the garden, she felt the faintest whisper of regret.

# Chapter 19

Aaron would never get used to flying.

The twenty or so sun dragons in his unit soared through the sky in a tight formation, Lev taking center point. Off to Lev's immediate left, Aaron leaned back in his saddle.

He'd spent all his time training underground, confined to the constantly shifting tunnels of dirt and stone, where thievery, backstabbing, and blood were only punished because one had gotten caught. It was a childhood of blood, shadow, and steel. One that had the sun baking the back of his head and fresh air in his lungs feeling simultaneously exhilarating and disconcerting.

Below, the Sun Kingdom stretched in varying shades of gold, brown, and cream. So much ground he had to cover. So many places that gods-damned scroll could be hiding.

Dannel had been no help so far in finding the box—which wasn't surprising. It was just one lead anyhow. But staring out across the kingdom, all he could see were the places he hadn't yet checked.

There was something about the woods that ringed the castle that kept drawing his attention. They were too big, too dense, to not have something hidden in there.

Aaron rubbed his face with a gloved hand. Find one little scroll in a maze of trees, thorns, and underbrush. How delightfully easy.

The sun dragons began to bank. Aaron followed suit, his dragon letting out a huff at the sudden jerk of the reins.

"Sorry," he murmured, patting the dragon's hard, scaly neck.

Ahead, Lev gave the signal. Well, this was as good a time as any.

Aaron dug in his heels, curving his descent so that he was right beside Lev. The guard shot him a surprised look. "What are you doing?"

"I just wanted to check in," Aaron said, raising his voice over the wind. "How are you doing after Dannel stabbed you?"

"I'm fine, thank you—"

Lev's head snapped toward Aaron. Aaron gave Lev an admittedly cheeky salute as he swung one leg over his saddle, rolling off his dragon's back.

All around him, his fellow soldiers fell in a synchronized wave. For a few exhilarating seconds, wind whistled in Aaron's ears. Then, he hit the ground.

Aaron rolled with the impact. Coming up on one knee, he let his daggers fly, watching with wicked delight as they whizzed through the air and thudded into the training dummies across the dirt arena. One in the heart, one in the throat, each quivering upon impact.

Technically, they were only supposed to be practicing their landings. Aaron, however, had always been a show-off. He rose to his feet, dusting the dirt from his leathers as he moved across the training arena to retrieve his knives.

Located in a massive pit, the training arena was segmented into quadrants. On one end stood the training dummies—row after row of unnervingly humanoid targets, directly across from the sand pit used for aerial training. The rest were used for sparring practice.

Reaching his dummy, Aaron noted the thick red blood oozing from the puncture marks. He knew it was only pig's blood, but he was still tempted to keep his riding gloves on as he withdrew his blades. But the feeling of blood wasn't something he should forget. It wasn't something he *deserved* to forget.

Aaron shuddered as he wiped the blood from his fingers, his fellow guards casting him not-so-subtle looks of irritation.

He was actually fond of their open disdain. No one back home would dare—

Out of the corner of his eye, Aaron spotted Lev glaring at him. He made a sharp gesture for Aaron to come over, but feigning misunderstanding, Aaron waved and turned away.

It only took a few minutes of puttering about before Lev stormed toward him. Aaron grinned to himself, pivoting to meet the guard.

"Who told you?" Lev demanded.

"Told me what?" asked Aaron innocently.

"About Dannel."

"Oh. Dannel."

Aaron shrugged and turned away. Measuring the distance between himself and the target, he pinched his dagger blade and sent it flying.

Lev muscled his way back into Aaron's sight. "Why did Dannel tell you?"

"Why'd you lie?"

Not waiting for a response, Aaron sauntered across the training arena to retrieve his knives. Lev's rage was palpable as he stormed after him.

"I lied because I had to," he said, grabbing Aaron by the shoulder and spinning him to face him.

Aaron gave Lev a long, practiced look. One that had Lev's fingers flexing before withdrawing.

Jerking his chin at Aaron, he headed for the sparring ring. Aaron followed, not surprised in the slightest.

It hadn't taken the three months he'd known Lev to figure him out. He'd been able to do that in their first fight, that final fight in the gods-damned tournament he'd had to battle through to become a Crystal Guard.

After the last guard, Nikolai, had experienced an accident involving a spooked horse and a very steep ravine, the Crystal Guard had found themselves down a member. Thus, a two-week-long tournament commenced, filled with endless bloodshed between seasoned warriors and children greener than springtime desperate for a shot at glory.

Aaron had been utterly bored with every match, even during the final rounds when he fought each of the Crystal Guards. He hadn't forgotten the look of humiliation on Lev's face as he held a dagger to his throat, the audience roaring their approval.

Aaron could see the hint of that same flush as Lev tossed him a sword. The man in a position of power that wondered deep down if he deserved it. Constantly feeling like he had to prove himself, especially when an arrogant, lower-ranked guard dared to dismiss him.

"Why'd you have to lie?" Aaron asked, letting his sword casually dip down. Lev took the bait.

"Because Othin knew about my feud with Dannel." Their blades clashed. "For some Crystal-forsaken reason, the rat decided to tell him all about it.

"He practically hauled me into his chambers by the ear when we were in Ash and chewed me out for over an hour. Said we shouldn't be dipping our wicks in the same wax."

"Wonder what the wax would say if she heard that," Aaron muttered.

Lev's sneer turned into a wince as Aaron ducked under his guard, shoving him into a weapons bench. He stepped back, allowing Lev to regain his footing, fueling the flush across his cheeks.

"He told me we better sort this out ourselves," Lev spat, his sword swinging up in a brutal arc. "Otherwise, he would do it for us."

"And so, you confronted Dannel."

"Of course I did."

Aaron's lips twitched. He danced back from Lev's blows, Lev's sword swinging faster, harder, angrier as he played chase.

"The rat was jeopardizing my career because, what, his favorite whore decided she wanted to have a little fun? But he kept stammering something about how he had no choice, he had to. Gods-damned liar. Honestly, he's lucky I decided to go easy on him."

"And by that you mean you let him stab you?" Aaron asked delicately.

Lev slashed toward Aaron's face. Aaron hopped up on the bench behind him just in time. He kicked aside Lev's blade, Lev taking the opportunity to shove him off the bench.

Aaron tumbled through the dirt. He popped back to his feet, sword and dagger ready. Now things were getting interesting.

"He got a lucky shot," Lev said, snatching a second sword and leaping over the bench. "Obviously, I couldn't say it was him."

"Because then Othin would know you did the exact opposite of what he'd told you to do. And Warack was an easy target."

Aaron was distantly aware of the soldiers that had stopped to watch their sparring—although this didn't feel like practice. His arms hummed with the impact of their blades, Lev's attacks quick, precise, and deadly. Good.

"The fool didn't know when to mind his own gods-damned business," Lev ground out. "He kept telling me I was in the Ash quarters when I left that night and I had to leave."

"Why were you in the Ash quarters?" Aaron asked.

"Why shouldn't I have been there? I can go wherever I want."

"I never knew you had such a healthy curiosity."

"It's a good thing I do," Lev panted, having lost his second sword at some point. "If I hadn't, I wouldn't have heard the Ash brothers bickering. Something about monthly late-night meetings?"

Aaron kept the intrigue off his face. Knowing that was all he was going to get from Lev, he figured it was about time he wrapped things up.

Aaron let Lev drive him back a few paces. He adjusted his footing in the sand, Lev taking the opportunity to lunge forward for the kill.

Aaron ducked under his blade. He spun around Lev, kicking the back of his knee and sending him toppling. Planting his boot on Lev's spine, Aaron yanked his sword arm behind his back and rested the tip of his sword against Lev's neck.

For a few moments, the training arena was completely silent. Aaron glanced around. And one by one, each soldier tapped their blades together in front of their chests in a salute.

"Would you look at that," Aaron said to Lev as the soldiers returned to their training. "I win again."

Lev swore. Aaron stepped back, dusted the dirt from his leathers, and sauntered away. And he wasn't surprised in the slightest when he sensed Lev come up behind him.

"So, what are you going to do?" Lev asked, his voice low.

"Well, I was thinking I would do some more knife throws."

"Now that you know about Dannel," Lev ground out.

"Oh, that." Aaron stretched. "I suppose I have two options. I *could* keep it to myself."

"What do you want, Aaron?"

Aaron glanced over Lev's shoulder to the forest beyond. "I'll let you know."

Then, without further comment, Aaron strolled away for a third time. This time, Lev did not follow.

Aaron returned to the centerline of the arena. His body moved on instinct, throwing his daggers as his mind wandered elsewhere.

Yes, Othin knew nothing about what was going on within his troops, but he did know his men. He specifically knew that Dannel and Lev came from warring clans from the south, each having noteworthy combat Blessings that led to constant territory squabbles. He also knew just how easily Lev's temper flared.

Aaron tugged on the chain around his neck as he retrieved his knives. How could Othin have expected Lev to react any differently? Unless that was what he had wanted. Could Othin really be capable of thinking that many steps ahead? Was this just one massive setup, a way to justify animosity between Sun and Ash?

The back of Aaron's neck prickled. He pivoted on his heel, his eyes immediately locking onto a pair of smoky-gray ones.

She stood at the lip of the pit, hands clasped behind her back, dressed in a white gown belted with chains of garnets. How long had she been standing there? And where was the usual contempt in her eyes?

Aaron rocked back on his heels. "See something you like, Princess?"

There it was. He knew he shouldn't purposefully provoke her. But getting a glimpse of the fire that swirled beneath the cautious exterior, even though it very well may burn him later? It was too tempting.

Analia adjusted a thin gown strap. "Yes. It was most entertaining watching you fall off a dragon."

Aaron's smile grew. He moved to the foot of the pit, "You must be so disappointed I stuck the landing."

Analia opened her mouth, then snapped it shut. What was that look that flashed across her face? Aaron climbed the short incline, trying to catch a glimpse of her expression, but she turned away—toward Pryanth? Had he been there the whole time?

Pryanth said something to Analia, but Aaron had become adept at ignoring him. He'd been wondering why he'd been released from guard duty that morning, but the stray piece of grass Pryanth picked from Analia's hair told him everything he needed to know. Aaron's insides shifted uneasily.

"I'll have to take you up sometime," Pryanth was saying. "We can fly even higher than we did in the carriage."

He must have been blabbering about Brax. Every Royal, as well as a few soldiers, had a dragon they bonded with at a young age, the attachment running far deeper than that of having a preferred horse to ride. They were a unit, starting their training together and usually ending it as well. No wonder Aaron's dragon was huffy with him—he was the interloper.

"Another time, though," Pryanth said. "We should be getting back."

Ignoring Aaron completely, Pryanth gestured for Analia to follow him as he headed for the castle. Analia hesitated, then stepped closer to Aaron.

"I wasn't disappointed you stuck the landing," she said. "I'm not that horrible."

Aaron looked down at her. That expression was back on her face. But this time, he recognized it.

"I know," he said, his usual wryness gone. "I was only teasing."

His hand twitched, but he thought better of it.

Analia gave a quick nod and stepped away. He didn't try to stop her as she hurried after Pryanth. He simply watched, puzzled, until she rounded the corner and disappeared.

Analia descended the marble staircase that led to the Sun Castle kitchen. She'd told Pryanth she would return their basket; they didn't need to bother one of the servants. Pryanth had given her quite a look at that, but he didn't protest.

As Analia trailed her hand along the railing, her mind kept returning to her conversation with Aaron. Her heart had unexpectedly slammed into her stomach when he made that comment about her. But he'd said he was just teasing, not taunting. Was that just this one time, or maybe every time?

Analia wasn't sure if that made her like Aaron any more or any less. What she truly couldn't figure out, though, was why he was doing it in the first place.

The kitchen was a bustle of activity as Analia stepped inside. A cluster of cooks fussed over various pots on the massive stove off to the side, another group scrubbing dishes in the sink across from the door. Analia quickly located Chia, the head cook, at a central island, chopping a mountain of carrots on a long wooden board.

"Excuse me," Analia said, stepping out of the doorway.

Chia looked up. An older woman, she had a broad face, with muscular arms and close-cropped silver hair.

"Yes, Your Highness?"

"I just wanted to return your basket," Analia said, offering it to her. "And personally express just how delicious everything was."

Chia's admittedly distracted expression brightened. For a few minutes, they exchanged pleasantries, their voices raised over the general clatter of the cooks behind them. Analia made it a point to mention the seasoning on the chicken, prompting Chia to delightedly discuss the careful balance of pepper and oregano.

"Is there that same balancing act with other herbs?" Analia asked, leaning against one of the counters. "Like paprika or xenol?"

"Xenol?" Chia asked, pausing her chopping. "I've never heard of that before."

"Really? Maybe I'm remembering the name wrong. I'm afraid I haven't been able to spend much time in the kitchen."

"Why ever not?" Chia demanded, returning to her chopping. "You Royals," she went on, not waiting for a response. "You study war, politics, how to rule. And yet, after a long day of work, what is it you come home to? A hot meal."

She gestured with her knife, and Analia leaned back to avoid the slash zone. "Cooking is an art form," she declared. "A careful dance between seasonings, a symphony of flavors. So much work goes into each dish, and yet the beauty of the final product is never admired in the way it should be."

"Yes," Analia mused. "The beauties of what we take for granted always seem to shine brightest when they're gone."

A slow, deep ache rolled through Analia's chest.

"Precisely!" Chia scraped her carrots into a nearby pot with the flat of her knife.

"Perhaps xenol is just an Ash Kingdom herb," Analia said after a moment.

"Can't be, Your Highness." Chia accepted a platter of celery from another cook. "I spent my youth traveling the six kingdoms, mastering the art of each kingdom's unique cuisine, and I've never encountered that ingredient before."

Analia hid her disappointment. Exchanging a few more words with Chia, she slipped out the kitchen door, almost colliding with Lev coming in.

Analia jerked back. Lev looked down his hawkish nose at her. "Xenol?"

Analia froze. Before she could respond, Lev shoved past her, striding into the kitchen.

Analia remained in the doorway, stunned. There was a part of her that wanted to chase after him and explain herself. But she knew that would only make it worse. It was better to seem unfazed. Still, Analia's fingers tightened around her phoenix pin as she climbed the stairs.

She knew it would have been more helpful to talk with a healer or snoop through a Sun apothecary, but Analia didn't have easy access to either. She'd figured that a chef accomplished enough to work in the Sun Castle would have enough knowledge to know what plants were safe for consumption and which were not, though. Especially in regard to local plants and herbs.

In that sense, Analia had gotten more than she'd bargained for. Xenol wasn't just absent from Ash records, but Sun as well. Whoever killed Accalon had extensive resources and was smart enough to obscure their trail. She had to be on the right track.

# Chapter 20

In the library, Dimitri rocked back in his chair, balancing precariously on its back legs. Seated across from him, Analia shot him a look as he jostled the table. He purposefully shook the table even more in response.

It had only been a few weeks since their first night in the library, but Dimitri had already blown past all of Analia's expectations.

"I've never met anyone who learned this so quickly," she'd said, scanning over a sheet of sentences Dimitri had copied down.

Dimitri leaned back in his chair, soaking in the praise. He certainly was picking it up quickly, but that was because he'd spent every moment—free and especially not free—agonizing over his worksheets. Staring at letters until the ink seemed to run down the page and the lines blurred together. Drawing out the alphabet on floors with his cleaning rag as he scrubbed them, mouthing the sounds each made when no one was there to watch.

Tonight, Analia had finally deemed him worthy of a real book, something he'd been pestering her about for days. Although when she had said "real book," this wasn't what he'd had in mind.

"This is boring," Dimitri complained, finally breaking the long stretch of silence. He waved the thin, picture-filled children's book in Analia's face.

"It's not supposed to be stimulating," she said, not looking up from her own book.

"It's for children."

"Children who are learning to read."

"But I'm not a child."

"No, but you do a fantastic impression of one." Analia snatched the book out of Dimitri's hand, forcing him to stop shoving it in her face.

Dimitri let his chair fall back to four legs with a muffled thump. "Why can't I help you find whatever you're looking for?" he asked.

"Because I don't need any help," Analia said.

"Oh, I forgot. Two weeks of finding Crystal shit translates to success in mouse code."

"Fine." Analia picked up the children's book once more, flipping to a random page. "You tell me what this page says, and I'll put you to work."

Dimitri gave her a haughty look and tugged the book toward himself. The majority of the page was taken up by a picture of a sun dragon hatchling, grinning as it batted a fluffy white cloud. Dimitri trailed his finger along the words beneath the picture, silently mouthing them to himself. Then, he looked up at her.

"Fuck you," he said, shoving the book back toward her. He only recognized three of the five words, and he wasn't about to embarrass himself even more by stumbling through them.

Analia snorted. Barely glancing at the page, she read, "Sunny played with the cloud."

"That word is cloud?"

"I think the picture was supposed to be a hint."

"I got it," Dimitri snapped. He slumped in his seat, ears burning.

Analia's expression softened. Oh gods, was that pity?

"It was a difficult one," she said, handing him the book once more. "I haven't gone over that word with you before."

"Oh, so you set me up." Dimitri ignored the book, rising from his seat and crossing to the cart with note-taking supplies.

Analia mumbled something about it not being entirely intentional.

"Well, if you'd like to make it up to me," he said, scooping up an armful of supplies, "you could scribble out the name of whatever you're looking for and I can search for it." He plopped a sheet of paper and a pen down in front of her. Then, moving back to his seat, he stared at her expectantly.

"You just want to help because you want to know what I'm looking for," Analia accused.

"What's wrong with that?" He made to tug one of her many books toward himself, but her hand snapped out and stopped him.

"I said I don't need any help, Dimitri."

That momentary softness had gone, her face hardening to stone.

"Why won't you just tell me?" Dimitri whined.

"Because it's none of your business."

"Fuck yes, it is. I'm not risking my neck for blind charity."

"You're not risking your neck, period." She pushed back from the table, snatching up her book and going to return it to the shelf.

Dimitri trailed behind her like a nagging child. "This is pointless. Just talk to the nymphs outside. Why are you willing to die for a fucking plant?"

"Because it was the plant found in my uncle's body after he was murdered!" Analia shoved the book on the shelf and whirled on him, eyes blazing. "Happy?"

Their voices hadn't gone above a normal volume, but they nevertheless seemed to blare in the oppressive hush of the library. Staring into Analia's eyes, Dimitri could see the rage that smoldered there. But beneath that...

"Take me with you," he said abruptly.

Analia stared at him. Then, she made a noise of disgust and stalked toward the table.

"I'm serious," he said, returning to his own seat. "When you flee this gods-damned viper pit, take me with you."

"Dimitri—"

"We both know I'm not going to drop this," he cut in. "Just say you'll do it and stop wasting our time."

He waited for her to argue anyway. A part of him was actually disappointed when she only sighed and muttered, "Battering ram of subtlety."

Dimitri grinned and tipped back in his chair once more. "Now show me the name of that plant."

"You don't have to help me look, Dimitri."

"I know. But now it's personal."

Analia looked confused. Dimitri feigned an air of nonchalance as he remained tipped back in his chair, mentally running a hand over the frigid, iron-clad box he kept all thoughts of the woman that died for him in. And it only took a few moments before Analia's expression softened.

"Dimitri…"

"If you say you're sorry, I will stab this pen through your hand into the table. Got it, Flashfire?"

Analia raised a brow at the nickname. Dimitri pretended as though he had intended for it to come out. It was just another insult. It meant nothing. It had nothing to do with the fact that beneath that rage in her eyes, he could see the grief, just as raw as his own.

"At least you still have your father," she said. "At least he still chose you."

"Chose me?" Dimitri demanded. "Obligation isn't a choice. And it's certainly not love. If anything, it's guilt, which makes me just as alone as you are."

Something flickered in Analia's eyes. Seemingly deciding it wasn't worth pressing, she picked up the pen Dimitri had threatened her with and wrote something on a spare page.

"It's called xenol," she said, offering it to Dimitri. "Don't bother trying to read the surrounding words. Just tell me if you see it."

Leaving it at that, she went back to her own book. Dimitri thudded back down, glancing at the sheet she'd given him. Taking the pen she had dropped, he practiced writing out the word, committing the letters to memory.

It wasn't like he was trying to help her. No, this was all still completely selfish. Dimitri would bleed her dry if that meant getting out of the castle. No second thoughts.

Finally satisfied, Dimitri grabbed a book at random and got to work.

# Chapter 21

Analia made her way toward the Ring Room. Deardryn was returning from her trip that afternoon, meaning it was her last chance to find the ring.

She'd been tempted to sneak into the room after hours and find it the old-fashioned way. Deardryn, however, had clearly expected that of her, for the room was magically sealed each day after she left, not opening until the next morning when she and Aaron arrived.

Despite this, Analia was surprised to note that she wasn't anxious as she spotted Aaron waiting outside the room for her.

"Good morning," she murmured, opening the door.

She hadn't realized she'd spoken until she registered Aaron's nonplussed expression. Then, his face split in a dazzling smile as he followed her through the door.

"Good morning, Princess."

They took up their usual positions in the room: Aaron on his bench, Analia at the table. But something had shifted. Something that enabled her shoulders to remain relaxed when she caught him watching her. Something that let her mind drift, not tumble in desperation as before.

Analia closed her eyes. Mentally reaching out, she found the field once more. She felt for its edges, easing into the crackling pulses of the magic.

It was her last chance. One final opportunity to get this right. And just as every time before, her hold slipped.

But how? The ring wasn't moving. She wasn't—what was—Crystal spare her. What was she doing wrong?

"Hey."

Analia startled. She opened her eyes, glancing at Aaron.

He smiled, his usual wryness nowhere to be found. "You can do this."

Slowly, Analia's muscles relaxed. With a nod to Aaron, she closed her eyes once more, letting his words echo through her mind. She could do this. She could do this. She would do this.

Analia found the field once more. But still, she couldn't grab hold.

Seconds stretched into minutes, but she kept her eyes squeezed shut. She waited, knowing the field would come back to her eventually. Still crackling, still pulsating, just like a quivering harp string after it's been plucked.

Analia abruptly pushed herself out of her chair. She strode across the room to the bookcase, Aaron rising to his feet and following.

Analia reached up, grabbing a heavy leather book off the bookcase. She looked in the empty space on the shelf, her heart sinking. But as she opened the book in her hands, something tumbled out between the pages. Before she could react, an arm brushed her side as Aaron caught the ring.

"You did it!" he exclaimed, his eyes sparkling. He took her hand, pressing the ring into her palm.

Analia didn't flinch at the sudden warmth. She only stared down at the ruby-encrusted ring, crackling with power. Then, putting the book back on the shelf, she silently exited the room, Aaron close behind.

Analia marched through the halls, fingers curled tightly around the ring. Finding it had actually been simple. Annoyingly so.

Each magical energy field mimicked the actual feel of the magic when Analia held a ring, pulsations and all. It wasn't that Analia had been losing the field. It was that the field was moving. Moving with the rhythm of the magic. Analia just had to move with it. It was easier said than done, but that circle of heat in her palm was proof that she could do it.

Analia found Deardryn in her study, the door left ajar. She sat behind a massive desk cluttered with piles of papers, her hair pinned back and head bowed as she scribbled in—was that a diary?

Analia knocked on the door. Deardryn waved her in, not fully looking up until Analia wordlessly dropped the Ash ring in the center of the page she was writing on.

Finally, Deardryn set down her pen. She turned the Ash ring between her fingers, her expression growing thoughtful as her gaze met Analia's. "Excellent."

With that one word, Analia let her careful numbness melt away. She backed out of the room, holding her tiny flame of success close to her chest. It wasn't until her back was turned to Deardryn and the door was firmly shut between them that she let herself grin.

"I did it," she told Aaron, hardly daring to believe it.

"You did," he agreed. "And it's about time, too."

His tone was teasing, but Analia felt his words like a shock to her spine. She folded her arms, her words burning past her lips, "What's your problem?"

Aaron, looking utterly unsurprised, rocked back on his heels. "And the cycle repeats."

"What 'cycle'?"

"The one where I annoy you, you bite my head off, then we have a begrudging truce, and then you inevitably bite my head off again."

Analia's mouth worked silently. "How about we fill in the rest of that cycle?" she finally said. "Like how you mock me relentlessly, then out of nowhere are kind and encouraging, just to mock me again."

Aaron tipped back his head, staring at the ceiling as if he couldn't believe what he was hearing. "You truly don't get it, do you?"

"Enlighten me."

"I'm trying to help you."

Analia let out a sharp laugh. "By belittling me?"

"By not coddling you like everyone else in this gods-damned kingdom."

"Why is that any of your concern?"

"Because while everyone else might have forgotten, I haven't." Aaron took a step closer, his silver eyes frosted over. "That day back in the Ash Kingdom when you stood up to Brenn. Analia, you were mesmerizing. No one could keep their eyes off you, and you didn't even notice. You refuse to notice."

Analia made to argue, but Aaron ranted over her with a cold anger she hadn't anticipated.

"You think no one expects anything from you? Well, why in the name of the Crystal should they if you don't expect it of yourself? Why should anyone look up to that?"

Aaron's words, while controlled in volume, were nevertheless a slap to the face.

"You mean like how people respect you?" Analia spat, temper spiking at dizzying speeds. "You and your pretty eyes and flirtatious smile? Drawing people in just so you can slice them down to the core without hesitation. Constantly surrounding yourself with ambiguity because Crystal only knows what would happen if anyone saw what heartless creature lurked beneath."

Aaron glared, and Analia glared right back. He didn't get to judge her. He didn't know how Brenn humiliated her, turned everyone against her. He thought it was because she expected nothing from herself? Then why did she spend so much time fighting what was most likely a hopeless battle? And why had his words stung so much if they weren't true?

Before Analia could respond, Pryanth rounded the corner. She took a hasty step away from Aaron, eyes shooting to Deardryn's closed door—oh gods.

Pryanth, however, seemed oblivious to what he was walking in on. He pulled Analia into his arms, spinning her around as he congratulated her on her success.

Analia had no idea how he'd found out so quickly, but she didn't care. Instead, she lost herself in Pryanth's enthusiasm, turning her back on the still-fuming guard as he melted into the shadows behind them.

# Chapter 22

That night, Analia sat in the library alone. She had been too busy celebrating her success with Pryanth to track down Dimitri, so she didn't get a message to him to meet her there. She knew she could have tried harder, but Aaron's words were still a hot poker on the back of her neck.

She didn't need Dimitri's help. She didn't need anyone's help. She would find information on xenol by herself.

Analia had to admit, though, that the library was eerie at night when alone. It was too quiet. Too many shadows flickered in the sunstones' wavering light. But it wasn't enough to distract her from the guilt that gnawed at her insides as soon as her temper cooled.

Aaron had started it. He had escalated it. But she had pushed things even higher. She'd wanted to hurt him in that moment, right after she'd told him she wasn't that cruel.

Analia shoved her armful of books back on the shelf, banishing the thoughts. She'd managed to make a fair amount of progress—although she doubted this block was the only section on herbology.

Selecting an armful of new books, she headed back to her table. She'd worry about finding the next block when she had to. *If* she had to.

Analia flipped through page after page. Even her breathing felt too loud. At least when Dimitri was there, the silence wasn't so pressing. This felt like at any moment, she would feel a blade tip at the back of her neck.

She turned another page, and her eyes widened. She'd found it. And somewhere below, there came the quiet hiss of the library door opening.

Panic tingled through Analia's blood. Without thinking, she ripped the page out of the book and darted into the stacks. Crystal strike her down.

Analia waited for the shouts, the rasp of metal on leather as weapons were drawn. Instead, silence continued to press a heavy hand on the library. Had she just imagined it? No. There it was. Soft, unhurried footsteps. Climbing up the stairs. Directly toward her.

Analia crept around bookcases, trying to stay in the shadows. She knew if she ran, she could make it to the passageways, but there would be no disguising her footfalls.

The footsteps prowled closer. Three more rows until she reached the entrance. But they were circling each other, Analia struggling to remain on the hidden side of the shelves. Crystal spare her.

Aaron scanned the dim library stacks. It wasn't his first time sneaking through the library, but of course, he'd found nothing thus far.

He hadn't managed to check the uppermost levels yet—not that he was expecting to find anything. He was honestly checking more out of thoroughness than a genuine belief the scroll was there. What he hadn't been expecting was the flash of red hair slipping around the corner ahead of him.

Aaron tugged on his chain. He knew he shouldn't have taken it so far that afternoon. But as they'd gone back and forth, all he'd been able to think about was Surce's tapestry.

How many times had he stared at that image? Clung to it when everything else seemed to be falling apart around him? Apparently, he still clung to it even as that very tapestry seemed to unravel.

Gods, how did she already know exactly where to sink the dagger in? He knew he had to wear this mask, for his mission, for his people. But that didn't mean he liked how easily it came to him.

Aaron gave the winding staircase a single regretful look. Then, he stepped off, following the sound of Analia's quiet footsteps. He knew he should keep his mouth shut, figure out what she was up to. And yet, he couldn't help calling out.

"I know you enjoy building anticipation, but I sincerely hope you're not planning on whacking me over the head with a book. Not only would it be extremely ineffectual, but also downright demeaning for the both of us."

He rounded the corner, jerking back as he found Analia waiting for him, arms folded and eyes blazing.

A part of him wanted to blurt his apology right then and there. Instead, his lips twitched.

"Oh," he said, "I can't wait to hear this one."

"What are you doing here?"

"What are *you* doing here?"

"I asked you first."

Aaron shook his head. "Analia, must we play that game?"

He noticed the paper she clutched in one hand. Following his gaze, Analia shifted, pressing the paper to her chest.

"We could play the game of you mind your business and I mind mine," she suggested.

"You're officially not in charge of coming up with our games," Aaron told her.

"Since when do we have any games in the first place?"

"Well, I'm fond of the one where I'm incredibly charming and you find it infuriating."

Aaron waited for Analia's temper to prove his point. Instead, she looked at him coolly as she said, "Really? Because I'm starting to find that game rather tiring."

Fascinating. Was she finally starting to get a handle on that temper of hers? Or was she only trying to spite him?

Aaron rocked back on his heels. "So," he asked, "how'd you get in here?"

He'd only managed to slip inside because he was supposed to be guarding the library door—the only entrance. Yet here she was.

Analia made to respond. Just as the library door suddenly burst open with a reverberating clang.

A

nalia scrambled away from Aaron. That's what she'd been waiting for all these weeks: for the silence to be shattered by the screech of metal, the thud of heavy boots. But Aaron immediately launched into action.

He snatched the paper from her hand in a blur, sliding it into a pocket in his cloak. Then, he thrust a random book into Analia's arms.

Analia stuttered, "What are you—"

"Let me handle it."

"But—"

"Let me handle it."

Aaron roughly pushed her down into a nearby seat. Perching on the edge of the table, he lounged back against the wall. All while the pound of heavy boots marched nearer, thudding in harmony with Analia's hammering pulse.

Crystal spare her. This was not going to end well. Even if Aaron looked the picture of ease, sitting so close his leg was flush against her side, warm despite his fighting leathers—

"Hey," Aaron said suddenly. "I know it's tempting, but eyes up here."

Analia scoffed. She haughtily flipped open her book to a random page, just as the guards rounded the corner.

Aaron's face was a mask of mild surprise. His eyes did a lazy flick from head to toe and back again as he drawled, "Lev. I know you don't make it a habit to surround yourself with books, but most libraries prefer you to be quiet upon entering. Hello, Lena," he added, turning to the second guard.

Lena, a tall woman with short, sleek black hair and olive skin, was the only woman in the Crystal Guard. She gave Aaron an apologetic look. Lev, however, didn't try to control his glower.

"What are you doing in here?" he asked.

Aaron's brows rose slightly. "Have you actually never been in a library before?"

Analia ducked her head lower over her book.

"I have," Lev snapped. "And I've been in this specific one long enough to know you're not allowed in without permission—which you certainly don't have since that would leave the door unguarded. And Analia—"

"I let her in," Aaron said.

Analia made to protest, but Aaron's boot pressed against her calf. She shot him a look, but he didn't glance at her.

"Why'd you do it, Aaron?" Lena asked.

Lev let his head fall back in exasperation, Aaron taking the opportunity to give Lena a wink.

"Princess Analia informed me she was having a hard time sleeping," Aaron lied smoothly. "She requested a book to help settle her mind."

Lev rounded on Aaron once more. "You know you're not allowed to do that."

Lena asked, "Why didn't you just request permission first?"

Aaron shrugged. "I saw no harm in it."

"Depends on what book she's reading," Lev said.

Before Analia could react, he snatched the book from under her hand. She whipped toward him, Aaron's boot digging into her calf keeping her mouth shut.

Lev flipped through the pages in silence. Analia's hands tightened around the edge of the table, but she forced herself to remain quiet. Especially as Lev's smug expression began to shift, first into confusion, quickly landing on irritation. And Analia finally registered what book Aaron had given her.

"It's a book on legends for children, Lev," said Lena wearily.

Analia glanced at Aaron. Had he somehow known, or was he just an incredibly lucky bastard?

Aaron's faint flicker of delighted surprise said enough. Bastard.

"And why was she reading that?" Lev insisted mulishly.

"Because," Analia said quietly, "it was the book my uncle would read to me when I was small."

Lev finally looked at her, as did Lena and Aaron. All three seemed lost for words.

Splinters, so many splinters. They stabbed through her chest, burned behind her eyes.

For a moment, she was back in Accalon's chambers: curled on his lap, feeling the vibration of his voice through his chest as he read.

Aaron's foot brushed against her calf once more, drawing her back to the present. Softer this time.

Analia held her breath, forcing back her tears. *One day.*

Lev still tried to argue, but Lena cut him off, telling him to drop it. Aaron silently held out a hand, Lev hesitating before handing over the book.

"Well, Lev," Aaron said, thumbing through the pages. "You should certainly be proud of yourself. You caught a princess, betrothed to the heir of the throne, reading a children's book." He handed the book back to Analia. "How nefarious."

Analia couldn't bring herself to look at the page, keeping her eyes trained on Aaron instead.

"They still broke the rules," Lev insisted, turning to Lena. "Children's book or not, they're not allowed in here without permission. It's an explicit violation of protocol."

Aaron scoffed. But Lena winced.

"I'm sorry, Your Highness," she said to Analia. "But he's correct."

Lev pointed at Lena triumphantly. "Tomorrow morning we're going straight to the queen—"

"The queen?" Aaron interrupted, sitting up straight. "I thought you were Othin's guard. Why the sudden shift in loyalties, Lev?"

"There's no shift."

Analia didn't miss how Lev's hand drifted to his stomach. Aaron's gaze sharpened.

"You didn't let me finish," Lev went on. "We're taking you to the queen and king tomorrow morning."

This was it. This was all Othin needed to get rid of her, and Lev knew it. Aaron, however, remained perfectly placid.

"Well, rules are rules," he said, stretching. "We have to do as we're told. Don't we, Lev?"

Lev narrowed his eyes. "You have something you want to let me know, Aaron?"

Lena frowned slightly. Analia shot Aaron a questioning glance.

Aaron paused, head tilted to the side. "No," he decided. "Not right now." He slid off the table. "All right, Crystal Captain, take me away."

Aaron raised his hands in front of him as if cuffed. Lev's face burned scarlet. He moved around Aaron, shoving him forward with his sword tip to Aaron's back.

As Lev marched Aaron down the stacks, Aaron reached behind him, shifting the tip of the blade ever so slightly.

"You were off center," he said as they rounded the corner. "Don't worry, I fixed it."

Lev snarled.

Lena sighed and rubbed her face. "That boy doesn't know when to keep his mouth shut."

"Lev or Aaron?" Analia asked.

"Yes."

Lena shook her head. She gestured for Analia to follow as she turned to head after her fellow guards. Analia silently complied, only pausing once they reached Saura's deserted desk to leave a note saying she was taking the legends book.

She knew it was too little too late. Either Othin was going to kill her, or she would die of shame when Deardryn looked at her, all approval gone.

But what scared her the most was the stack of herbology books still sitting at her table, waiting to be discovered. And if Lev was smart enough, he would know exactly what she'd been looking for.

# Chapter 23

The Throne Room was dusted with a thin film of gold. It coated the floors, walls, ceiling, even the support beams that hunched beneath the castle's weight.

True to Lev's word, he'd woken Analia first thing in the morning and marched her to the waiting king and queen. Now, she stood alone in the center of the room, Deardryn and Othin seated on matching golden thrones atop a dais in front of her.

She was completely exposed, unable to hide the apprehension that froze her blood. But at least they hadn't assembled the council.

Despite the six kingdoms being so isolated, they continued to have similar political structures: the reigning Royal at the top with the ultimate say, and a small group of councilmen below, acting as flimsy power checks and mainly there to speak varying opinions.

The fact that they weren't there, however, told Analia this case was being interpreted as—what, a family squabble? That didn't stop Othin from looking like he was about to march down the dais's steps to strangle her, outcome be damned.

Deardryn, however, was completely impassive. She remained silent as Analia knelt, head bowed in submission as she apologized, begging for forgiveness and repeating Aaron's lie. Finally, Othin snapped for her to stand.

"A direct violation of the rules," he fumed. "And there were so few we expected you to abide by. We gave you unrestricted access to our castle. Freedom! Trust! And yet you insisted on barreling through the few parameters we set for you."

How was she supposed to react? With Brenn, she knew to keep quiet, knowing it was impossible to prevent the explosion, but with nothing to fuel the flames, he would inevitably fizzle out. But her silence only seemed to fuel Othin, his voice growing louder and louder until it boomed off the walls.

"An utter mutiny! Complete disrespect. Skulking through our books like some conniving little rat. You're lucky we aren't going to treat you like one and snap your neck—"

"That's enough," Deardryn said quietly.

Analia could barely hear her over the blood roaring in her ears.

Othin pivoted with the speed and subtlety of lightning. "So, what were you trying to find, then? Blackmail? Information to bring back to your father?"

Should she interrupt? Defend herself? Or would her sudden talking be an admission of guilt?

"Othin, she was reading a children's book," Deardryn said.

So, Lev had spoken to her. Then why was Deardryn helping her?

"When they found her," Othin said. "Who knows what she was looking at before that."

Did that mean they hadn't found her books? With that train of thought, though, it would only be a matter of time.

Deardryn's expression remained carefully controlled, her bejeweled hands resting in her lap. Seeing he wouldn't get a response, Othin twisted in his seat to face Analia.

"And how did you get in?" he demanded.

It took a second for Analia to realize he was expecting an answer. Mouth dry, she repeated Aaron's lie once more. The lie she had no clue why he'd spun after everything she'd said and hadn't even had the courage to apologize for.

"Aaron did not have the authority to do that," Deardryn told her. She was so calm, a breeze compared to the tornado beside her. But that somehow made it worse.

"I know," Analia mumbled, face burning. "But I didn't want to wake you. I thought it wouldn't be a problem just this once." She bowed her head. "I truly, deeply apologize, Your Majesty."

"What I want to know," said Othin, "is why no one reported seeing you on any of the three floors between your chambers and the library."

Analia fought the urge to toy with her phoenix pin. "I suppose our paths didn't cross. I didn't see anyone, either."

Othin glared, and Analia ducked her head once more. Did he know about the passageways? Did he suspect?

"How lucky," he muttered. "That, however, doesn't explain why none of our hounds detected your scent outside the library."

Analia's breath caught. Deardryn's eyes briefly flicked to Othin, but her face remained unreadable.

He'd sent the hounds after her? She should have expected that. Why stage an accident when she was giving him all the reason in the world. After all, she couldn't argue her scent into existence. Except...

"Your Majesty," Analia said, "that's impossible."

Othin gave her a look she was accustomed to seeing on Brenn's face. One that had her words dying on her tongue. But she also remembered Dimitri, nibbling his imaginary piece of cheese, and she straightened.

"Even if no one can vouch that they saw me walking to the library, both Lev and Lena escorted me back. My scent had to be in the halls."

That, of course, was assuming they had sent the hounds after she'd been caught—although at that point there would be no reason to.

Othin leaned forward in his seat, face red beneath his beard.

"Let it go, Othin," Deardryn sighed. "The child has seen through your ploy." She patted Othin's hand, and Analia could have sworn she appeared pleased.

But Analia didn't relax. That might have been a trick, but it was one that had implications she didn't like—Dimitri certainly wouldn't be pleased.

"Fine," Othin snapped. "We assume she's telling the truth. That doesn't change the fact she broke our rules. There must be a consequence!"

"What do you suggest?"

Analia could practically feel Othin's temper spike at Deardryn's obvious disinterest.

"Banned from the library," he said. "And no one can retrieve books for her. Confined to her chambers with heightened security, of which Aaron will not be involved."

Analia couldn't breathe.

Deardryn examined a jewel that had come loose on one of her bracelets. "That's certainly extreme."

"She broke the rules!"

"My rule," Deardryn interrupted.

"A rule regardless," Othin shot back.

"And Analia is a princess. Not a servant creeping through our stacks."

Analia stiffened. Was that a coincidental comparison?

"It doesn't matter," Othin insisted, slamming his fist down on the arm of his throne. "If we don't punish her, what kind of message does that send?"

"What kind of message does it send if we bury her after a single offense?"

"Then what would you have her punishment be?"

Deardryn considered. She ran her hand down her white silken skirts, Othin visibly struggling to contain himself.

"Banned from the stacks," she finally said. "Although she can still request books be brought to her. She, however, will not be confined to her chambers, nor will Aaron be removed as her guard."

"Aaron broke protocol! He can't be trusted!"

"Aaron has already been dealt with," Deardryn said. "He made a bad judgment call. One he will not be making again. And if he does, we will deal with it then. But unless you would like to trade Aaron for Lev, he remains."

Othin glowered. Deardryn met his gaze evenly.

"You can bluster all you like," she said. "But I am the Royal Queen. I have listened to your thoughts, I have taken your opinions into consideration, and I compromised with you. That is as far as you are going to get." Her lip curled slightly.

Othin sneered and turned back to Analia. "I'm sealing the library to you," he told her. "Even if you somehow get in, my magic will alert me to your presence. And while my wife believes in second chances, I don't believe in a third. Understand?"

Analia nodded mutely.

So, that was how Deardryn had been sealing the Ring Room. Othin's Blessing was that of shielding: creating barriers that could protect people and locations. He could keep anyone out, but also, trap them within.

Now, Analia had no way to continue her research. She couldn't ask for herbology books. She couldn't return to the library. She doubted Dimitri would continue searching alone.

Othin pushed himself to his feet. Giving Deardryn a venomous look, he stalked past Analia, the door slamming shut behind him.

Deardryn let the silence linger. Heavy, uncomfortable.

"Thank you, Your Majesty," Analia finally said.

"You still hesitate," Deardryn said. "You no longer have the look of blind panic the moment a glance befalls you. Yet, you still brace yourself before speaking. Why?"

Because attention meant ridicule, and careless words led to burns behind her ears. Analia opened her mouth, but no words came out.

Deardryn shook her head. "If you say you had no malicious reason to be in the library, act like it. Don't allow Othin to bully you into submission."

"But he's the king."

"And kings are wrong every day." Deardryn's smooth mask hardened around the edges. "You were given a choice the moment you stepped foot in my castle. You could remain the trembling pup you were back in the Ash Kingdom, taking kick after kick for reasons out of your control, or you could learn to sharpen your fangs."

Deardryn leaned forward in her seat. "You have potential, Analia. Abilities no one else has. It's time you start acting like it."

Analia waited for her usual rush of shame. But while it certainly was still there, it was more of an underlying melody. Instead, she felt grounded.

It was a challenge in Deardryn's eyes, not a rebuke. One that had Analia's chin jutting up.

"Understood," she said.

Finally, Deardryn leaned back, releasing Analia from her piercing stare. "Show me," she said. "Tell me where the ring is in this room."

Analia cocked her head. She took a moment, reaching out for the field. "It's under your hand."

Deardryn flipped over her hand, revealing the Ash ring. "Fascinating," she murmured.

Analia waited quietly at the foot of the dais. Noticing she was toying with her phoenix pin, she forced her hand to her side once more.

"Abilities no one else has," Deardryn repeated. She looked up from the ring, stern. "I expect to see you back at work in the morning. And not in the library."

"Yes, Your Majesty."

Analia bowed her head. Taking her dismissal, she turned for the door. Just as she was about to leave, Deardryn called to her.

"He's in the armory."

Analia glanced back. There was a small crease between Deardryn's brows as she rolled the ring between her fingers.

Analia thanked her quietly, then slipped out.

162

# Chapter 24

T he armory was located in the belly of the Sun Castle.

The moment Analia opened the heavy stone door, she was hit by the smell of mold. Countless shelves and racks full to bursting with metal armor crowded the massive chamber, dust motes floating in what little gloomy light she could see. Clearly, this armory had not been used in a long time.

It didn't take long to find Aaron. He stood in one of the narrow aisles between shelves, the sleeves of his gold-and-white military jacket rolled up as he polished a breastplate. Undoubtedly hearing her footsteps, he turned and sketched a dramatic bow.

"Princess Analia?" he drawled. "Gracing me with her presence? To what do I owe the pleasure?"

Analia struggled to ignore his antics.

"I didn't think Sun had metal armor," she said, carefully maneuvering around a pile of helmets.

"They never use it," he said. "Too stiff and heavy for flying and falling."

"And yet you still have to polish all of it."

Aaron shrugged, then returned to his polishing.

"You really don't care, do you?" Analia asked, taking a few steps toward him.

"No," Aaron snorted, as if the idea were ridiculous. "Polishing and a magical jab to the kidney from Deardryn is far from the worst punishment I've had."

"Her magic hurt you?" Analia demanded. "But how?"

"Life goes two ways, Princess. So does the magic. I suspect you would have found that out the hard way as well if you weren't in the middle of a pending truce pact."

Well, that was new: Brenn's tendency to explode first, ask questions later, protecting her for a change. He would be furious to find out. Almost as furious as Deardryn if she knew Brenn couldn't care less what she did to Analia.

Analia's gaze inexorably traveled down Aaron's back. What else must he have gone through to make his tone so flippant?

Aaron's head turned suddenly, catching her looking. "Analia," he said with mock surprise, "is that sympathy I detect? I must really be growing on you—although I can't say I'm surprised. We have established my delightful presence, breathtaking smile, and undeniable charm, after all."

"And next we can talk about your humility," Analia grumbled.

"Epics can be written about that."

Analia rolled her eyes. Aaron winked and returned to his breastplate.

Taking an oily rag from the pile at Aaron's elbow, she asked, "How often have you had to be punished—"

"Are you actually helping me?" he asked, disbelieving. "My gods. Is this more of that sympathy we were talking about, or are you just making sure we're even?"

"Why *did* you help me?" she asked, reaching for a dusty helmet Aaron had obviously skipped. It would have been so easy for him to pretend like he'd caught her in the library. He had no reason to take the fall—not even *with* her, but *for* her.

"Why is it so hard for you to believe I just wanted to help you?" Aaron asked.

"Why can't you just give me a straight answer?"

"Why do you answer all my questions with questions? It's rather elusive of you."

"But that's what—you're just—that's exactly what you're doing to me!"

Aaron turned away once more, but Analia caught his smile. Heat rushed to her cheeks.

"Maybe we should review our cycle of interactions you brought up," she said. "I feel as though that gives a pretty good answer to your question."

"I think it's our conversation about the cycle that makes me wonder why you're so obstinately refusing to believe me."

"Why should I believe you?" Analia burst out, shoving aside the helmet with a clang. "When have you given me a single reason to trust you? Because of you I didn't even get to hold my uncle's hand when..."

Analia couldn't force the word past the lump in her throat. *One day.*

"So, please," she said, voice shaking, "tell me why I should care about a gods-damned thing you have to say."

She could feel the phantom pressure of Aaron's arms around her, the pulse of Deardryn's magic. The screams. Analia tightened her hand into a fist, the cold oil from her rag oozing between her fingers.

"So *that's* what this is about," Aaron said to himself. Raising his voice, he went on, "My gods you hold a grudge. Are we ever going to get past this, or are you just going to hate me forever?"

Analia snatched a leg brace from the shelf. "You don't get to decide when I do or do not forgive you. You have no idea what it feels like to wake up one morning and realize the person you love most is dead. To be told there's not only nothing you can do, but that you'd just get in the way." She raked her cloth down the brace. "No idea."

"But I do," he said evenly.

Analia froze. "What?"

"My mom," Aaron said, still casually polishing. "And unlike with you, what happened to her was entirely my fault. So, I actually know all too well what it feels like."

Aaron's hand eventually slowed to a stop. He bowed his head, carefully setting down his helmet and finally turning to face her full on.

The mask was gone. There was no careful control, wryness, or teasing. Only a grief that turned his silver eyes to fractured glass.

Silence descended upon the armory, not even interrupted by the whispered echo of their breathing. Analia carefully set down her leg brace, flinching at the slight tinny sound the steel made. Gods, that look was too familiar.

"I didn't know," she finally whispered.

"How could you?" Aaron asked, equally quiet. He hesitated. "But that's why I did what I did."

He moved farther down the row, and Analia shook herself as if from a dream. Aaron picked up a dull golden gauntlet and nudged the matching one toward her, and she numbly started to polish.

"Now, granted," he went on, "the whole 'you'll only get in the way' comment, I'll give you that. That was uncalled for. Although you had just bashed your skull into my face, so perhaps you inadvertently loosened my tongue."

He tried for a grin, but it quickly faded. Lowering his gaze back to the gauntlet, his voice became thoughtful as he said, "But besides all that, I was all too familiar with the fissures skittering out around you. I knew there was nothing anyone could do to stop your world from cracking apart. But I thought... I thought maybe I could give you something to hold onto."

Analia felt strangely hollow. *He's dead,* she'd said. And Aaron's arms had tightened around her. She'd thought it was to stop her from trying to escape once more. But now?

"You were trying to help," she said, realization opening the door for guilt to barrel through. Because Aaron hadn't been holding her back. He'd been trying to hold her together as she broke.

Aaron ran a hand through his hair, trailing oil. "Maybe I handled it wrong. But I promise you, I wasn't trying to hurt you. And I'm sorry I did."

Analia believed him. She also knew he wasn't just talking about that day in Accalon's chambers. Which meant she couldn't have been further from the truth in that hallway.

Not looking back, Aaron took the freshly polished gauntlet from her grasp, placing it with his own shining one. Analia glanced at the gauntlets, down at her empty hands, and then quietly moved to Aaron's side. He tracked her warily, but he didn't move away as she hesitantly rested her hand over his.

"I'm sorry, too," she said. Sorry for her words, sorry for misjudging, sorry he had to feel the pain that she wouldn't wish upon anyone.

Aaron looked down at her hand. Then, he slid his hand away, placing it atop hers.

The quiet that wrapped around them wasn't quite as heavy as before. Aaron's hand was warm, slick with oil, but she didn't mind. As his fingers curled around her hand, she wondered if he, too, was afraid of what pieces might break if he let go.

When she looked up, she found him watching her expectantly. Inviting her to ask.

"How did you handle it?" she asked. "When your world crumbled."

"Horribly," he said. He lifted his hand from hers, reaching for his rag and dunking it in his bucket of oil. "At first, I spent a great deal of time raging at the stars. Then, when that stopped doing anything, I gave crying a try.

"So many days, sobbing until I couldn't breathe. Or perhaps because I felt like I couldn't breathe. Gods, there was a day when I noticed a complete stranger wearing the same silver pin in her hair that my mom used to, and that was enough to send me staggering.

"I just didn't know how to exist in a world that didn't have her in it." He paused. "But then," he said on a heavy exhale, "one morning, I woke up, and I realized I hadn't wept in days."

Aaron's voice drifted off. Analia quietly waited for him to continue, watching the emotions as they shifted across his face. How did he do that? Move so freely through shards of glass, unafraid of drawing blood, unconcerned when he bled?

Once his expression cleared, Analia tentatively asked what happened next.

"I thought I was healed," Aaron said, passing her a chainmail breastplate. "But what I didn't notice was that it wasn't just the grief I didn't feel, but nothing at all. Not happy, not excited, not angry. I was only going through the motions."

"Numb," Analia whispered.

Aaron's voice returned to its usual wryness as he said, "And it turns out, you can't selectively numb, either. You either feel everything, or you feel nothing. And just because you don't feel the wound doesn't mean you're not bleeding out."

Analia scrubbed at a stubborn piece of rust on her chainmail. Was that what she was doing? Not numbing with ice, but cauterizing with fire?

"I think I know the feeling," she murmured.

"Well," Aaron said, "if you're ever in the mood for a cathartic wallow in grief and agony, you know where to find me."

"I'll keep that in mind."

"Would you look at that," said Aaron softly. "That's the second smile I've managed to drag out of you. I must really be growing on you. Like a delightful patch of moss."

"Or a fungus," Analia muttered, still smiling.

Aaron laughed. He turned back to his polishing, and though Analia still had countless questions for him, she somehow knew he had reached his limit for the day. He had quietly tucked those shards away, and she wouldn't be the one to pry them forth once more. But there was one question she could ask.

"Is that why...?"

Aaron didn't need her to elaborate. "I told you, Princess—"

"No more titles," Analia said.

Aaron smiled softly. "I told you, Analia, I haven't forgotten what I saw that day."

"And what exactly did you see?" she asked.

He thought for a moment. "I saw someone whose magic might not be awake yet, but has a different type of fire inside her. One I think a lot of people have tried to stomp out."

"There's only so much stomping a flame can take before it's extinguished," Analia muttered.

"Unless it consumes what tries to smother it." Aaron put down his rag. "You're a force to be reckoned with, Analia. Don't let anyone convince you otherwise. Especially not yourself.

"And if being furious with me is what it takes for you to realize that? If you need to burn to avoid the ice, and I'm the easiest outlet? I can take it. Just..." He averted his gaze momentarily. "Let me know that's what we're doing, all right? Now that we're speaking?"

Analia wished the floor would swallow her whole. Here was a man, not only letting her use him as an emotional training dummy if that meant helping her, but encouraging her to do so. And she had swung without a second thought.

Had she become just as bad as Brenn: unleashing her temper on the easiest target because it was harder to be hurt than angry? Or maybe *because* of Brenn she hadn't noticed that while Aaron was undoubtedly amusing himself when poking at her, it was always more than one type of flame roaring back to life.

One thing was for sure, though.

"I don't hate you," Analia said honestly.

She didn't miss his glimmer of relief as he replied, "I hope I at least annoy you, though."

"Incessantly."

Aaron grinned. Leaning around her, he scraped off the last of the rust she'd been struggling to remove with his thumbnail.

"Now you really annoy me," Analia said, surprising a laugh out of him. "But in all seriousness," she said, catching his eye once more, "thank you. For everything."

The words were completely inadequate. But Aaron's face softened with understanding.

"My pleasure," he said. "And I was serious about the wallowing. Whenever you're ready."

"And the same to you."

"Oh no," said Aaron seriously. "You don't want to extend that offer. I've been informed that I'm incredibly high maintenance."

"Well," Analia said, "I've survived this long."

"And despite my best efforts, too."

Analia whacked Aaron with her rag. He leaned away just in time, smug as a cat as he laughed at her expression.

For the rest of the afternoon, Analia remained in the armory with Aaron. He was surprisingly easy to talk to—even when he insisted on telling her stories about the armor many believed to be possessed by the guards who had died in them. And in those moments, she could have sworn that fire, constantly raging beneath the surface, cooled just a few degrees.

At the end of the day, an incredibly uncomfortable scribe came to fetch Aaron.

"I've been released," he said gleefully as the scribe scurried away.

"What ever will you do with this newfound freedom?" Analia asked.

Aaron snorted. Before he could fire off a quip, realization crossed his face.

"I forgot," he said. "I have something for you."

With a flourish, he produced a single piece of paper from within his jacket. Analia's eyes widened.

She'd been wondering how the library's magic would react to Aaron leaving with just a page, not a full book. Apparently, they had found a loophole.

She eagerly took the page, eyes roving. Aaron was just starting to ask why she wanted a page on xenol when she cut him off with a curse and hurried away.

Dimitri reclined against the pillows on Analia's bed, idly flipping the page of his book. Well, Analia's book, which he just so happened to stumble upon in one of the drawers of her desk.

It wasn't all that interesting, though, just one of those legend books for children. Why were children reading books about war, anyway? And why could they read it so easily, whereas Dimitri had to agonize over every word, mainly using the pictures for context?

He was still struggling through the first story about the Defiants—why a bunch of inadequate humans thought they could defeat three omnipotent gods was beyond him. Now, he quietly read aloud to himself, awkwardly sounding out the words.

"The Defiants fought their way up the..."

Dimitri glanced at the picture: the seven Defiants, their swords drawn as they clashed with a wave of demons with exposed gray bones, summoned straight from the Hell Realm. Battling on a...

"Mountain!" Dimitri declared, positively smug.

He turned the page. "Upon reaching the top, the Defiants found themselves face-to-face with the three Ancient Ones, seated on their dark"—Dimitri glanced at the picture—"thrones. Before the Ancient Ones could attack, Talitha, leader of the Defiants and Queen of the Star, was able to distract them long enough to steal the Crystal, the Ancient Ones' most powerful weapon."

Dimitri snorted. "As if. What are you leaving out, you condescending—"

The door opened. Dimitri peaked over his book, relaxing as he saw it was Analia sweeping inside. As soon as she spotted him, she paused midstep.

"What are you doing?" she asked.

"Hiding." Dimitri flipped another page.

Analia continued to stare at him from the doorway. "From?"

"The queen."

"Because...?"

"She wanted me to repolish her entire jewelry collection because *apparently*, I missed a minuscule spot on her beloved sapphire pendant the first time." He rolled his eyes.

"So, you decided to hide. In my room. On my bed."

"I thought if she found me you could just"—he waved a vague hand—"explain it away."

"You mean take the fall for you."

"That too."

Analia shook her head. She finally advanced farther into the room.

"Come on," Dimitri said, rolling over, "the Old Hag likes you. You could handle it."

"She's not a hag," Analia said, pulling the tiny topaz earrings from her ears—she better not ask him to polish those, too.

"Maybe not around you," he said. "Although I'm surprised you're still singing that tune after you got caught." He grinned. "The one time I wasn't there, too. I don't know if that's a sign that it was my sneaky ass keeping us undetected, or your stupidity having remarkable timing."

"And it's the one time you're not there that I actually find something on xenol," Analia replied casually.

Dimitri sat up. "Crystal fuck me, you did?"

"I wonder if it was just you, slowing me down before, or—"

"All right, fine, whatever, Flashfire. What'd you find?"

"Well…"

Analia came to sit on her bed beside him. She pulled a rolled-up piece of paper from her sleeve and offered it to him.

"And you defiled a book, too," he marveled, unfurling the page. "Gods, I didn't know you had it in you…"

Dimitri stared at the page. Finally, he glanced back at her. "Is this a joke?"

"I wish."

Most of the page was taken up by an ink drawing of a plant. Long, thin leaves trailed like skeletal fingers, curled into talons. Starting out a pale green at the base, the leaves deepened until the ends appeared black as tar.

"Xenol," Dimitri read aloud slowly. "Native to the marshes of the Moon Kingdom." He looked to Analia for help.

"Incredibly rare," she read, barely looking at the page, "it is the only known plant whose magical leaves are capable of destroying… And the rest is blotted out with ink."

Her head thudded back against the wall.

"Fuck," Dimitri said into the silence.

Analia didn't reply.

Dimitri went on, "Moon Kingdom? Have you been on the wrong track this entire time?"

"Not unless a Moon Kingdom assassin snuck into our castle," Analia said. "But someone here clearly wanted this information to be obscured, which is confirmation if anything."

"That's dumb," Dimitri said. "If they wanted to hide it, why not rip out the page?"

Analia shrugged tiredly.

Dimitri leaned back against her pillows. "All right," he said. "If this idiot is dumb enough to not destroy all evidence, we just have to keep looking."

"That's not going to work either."

Analia quickly filled Dimitri in on her punishment.

"Definitely remarkably timed stupidity," he muttered.

Analia whacked him with the children's book. "We just need a new approach."

"And what would that be?"

Analia glared. She rose from the bed and started to pace.

Dimitri smoothed the wrinkles from the torn-out page. Why erase some information, but not all?

"Exports," Analia blurted. "Does the Sun Kingdom have trading terms with the Moon Kingdom?"

"How should I know?" Dimitri asked.

"You're a servant in the Sun Castle."

"And when have you ever known me to do my job?" Dimitri scoffed. "Do you know how many rotations I've been banned from? Chia chased me out of the kitchen with a wooden spoon, cursing my bastard bloodline for seven generations after she caught me smuggling food on the job."

Analia muttered something under her breath and continued to pace.

"Then we'll just have to go to the docks," she decided. "Ask around, see what we can find out."

"The next shipment isn't for over a week," Dimitri said, picking at a loose thread in her pillowcase.

"So *that* you know."

"How else would I know when to hide at dawn instead of sunrise?"

Analia sighed, coming to sit at his feet. "We could go anyway. Ask whoever's there."

"Because that's not suspicious."

"Then I guess we're at a standstill for now."

Dimitri shrugged, indifferent. She might be at a standstill, but he certainly wasn't.

"So, how's your reading?" she asked.

Dimitri's brows rose involuntarily. "Fine."

Her eyes landed on the children's book, flicking across the cover that was obviously not one she had given to him. "Should I ask how you got this?"

"I snooped through your stuff."

He waited for the flash of irritation, even anger. But Analia only sighed. Taking the book, she flipped to the page he had marked. Then, she shifted so she was beside him, placing the book half on her lap and half on his.

Dimitri flinched as her leg brushed his. She just hit a massive block, shouldn't she be annoyed or ranting? Why help him when she didn't have to?

Deciding not to waste an opportunity, Dimitri propped himself up on an elbow and started reading. With every turn of the page, he waited for Analia to call it quits, go back to her pacing, walk away. But she never did.

Later, Dimitri snuck into the library, quietly putting away the books that still lay on their usual table. He didn't know if they'd already been found. And he didn't tell Analia regardless.

# Chapter 25

Analia departed for the Ring Room the following morning, Aaron already waiting for her outside her chamber door. As they moved through the halls, she spotted the faintest wrinkle cross his brow, as if he was trying to decipher where he stood with her.

Analia offered a tiny smile. Aaron immediately brightened.

"And that makes three," he declared.

"Must you keep score?"

"I'd keep count of your scowls, too, but I already have a trove of those." He stepped ahead to open the Ring Room door for her. "I find both incredibly endearing in case you were wondering—ha! Four!"

Aaron grinned, absurdly pleased with himself.

Analia hadn't realized she was smiling. As soon as her attention was drawn to it, the muscles in her face trembled, her smile completely fading as she stepped into the Ring Room.

Deardryn already sat at the table, engrossed in hushed conversation with Dannel on her left. But it was Pryanth that made Analia's heart stumble.

For some reason, he'd not only decided to return to her lessons, but he was also not in his typical seat beside hers. Instead, he sat on the bench, arms folded, lips pursed. His gaze flicked up to Analia as she entered, then darted away.

Analia's insides shifted uneasily. She checked that Deardryn was still deep in discussion, then crossed to Pryanth. "Hi," she said tentatively.

"Hello." Pryanth briefly looked at her.

Analia shifted from foot to foot. "What's wrong?" she whispered.

"Nothing," he whispered back. But the look he gave her was sharp as an ice pick.

Before she could respond, Deardryn dismissed Dannel. The guard bowed before stepping away, and Deardryn beckoned to Analia with an impatient hand.

Shooting Pryanth one last look, Analia made her way to the table. She didn't miss the silent exchange that passed between Aaron and Dannel before the latter left, hand drifting to the pommel of the sword on his belt. Nor did she miss how Aaron sat directly next to Pryanth, smirking to himself.

Analia lowered herself into her seat across from Deardryn, the scrape of her chair grating against her nerves. It was far, far too quiet.

"Your Majesty," she said, bowing her head.

Deardryn waved a dismissive hand. "There are two rings hidden in this room. Without standing from your chair, locate both of them."

Analia had expected something like this. She closed her eyes, trying to settle into the silence that stretched taut as a bowstring. Still, it was a few long moments before she was able to reach out with a mental hand.

As usual, it didn't take long to find the fields themselves. This time, however, Analia's brows furrowed.

"What do you sense?" Deardryn asked.

The two fields were intersecting. Two rhythms. Two melodies that tangled together, non-diatonic harp strings plucked in rapid succession.

Analia did her best to explain the tangled magic. Deardryn's pen scratched furiously as Analia tried to latch onto just one melody. One fast and sweeping. The other slow and languid. She chose the latter, carefully keeping in step as she traced the moving field.

"One ring is in the top left drawer of the desk," Analia said. "Your side."

"And the second?"

Analia paused. "Right next to it. Although..."

"Go on."

Analia didn't miss how Deardryn's voice sharpened.

"There's a third ring," Analia said slowly, opening her eyes. Farther away from the other two in the complete opposite direction. But the field was there, rolling in the relentless tumble of a boulder downhill.

"Where do you suspect it is?" Deardryn asked. Yes, that was a sharp satisfaction in her honey eyes.

Blocking out the first two fields, Analia reached out behind her. "Pryanth," she said, twisting in her seat. "Are you holding it?"

The sullen prince had been pointedly staring somewhere above Analia's left shoulder. At her words, his lips turned down. "No."

Had she gotten it wrong?

Pryanth shifted his hand, tightly clenched in a fist, but Aaron was faster. He grabbed Pryanth by the wrist, ignoring his protests and prying apart his fingers.

"Well, would you look at that." Aaron plucked the ring from Pryanth's palm, raising it so Analia could see. "I never knew 'no' was a synonym for yes. That's going to make things confusing."

"Mock me again, guard," Pryanth warned, "and I'll have your tongue fed to a sun dragon."

Aaron cocked his head, eyes glinting.

"Enough," Deardryn broke in sharply. "Aaron, you just returned from a day in the armory. Don't think your prowess with the blade is enough to compensate for the looseness of your tongue. And Pryanth, I expect you not to interfere with the integrity of this experiment."

She stared at each man in turn. Cold, flat, hard.

Pryanth shifted in his seat and dropped his gaze, face flushed. Aaron bowed his head, although Analia could have sworn he muttered something about how everyone loved his tongue. Deardryn—either not hearing or, more likely, ignoring him—turned back to Analia.

"Without looking at them, can you identify the type of magic?"

"Sun and Wind," Analia said, anticipating the question. She'd been trying not to hesitate, but she couldn't help it when considering the third. "I'm sorry," she said. "I don't think I've ever encountered the third."

"You don't 'think'?" Deardryn asked.

"I know," Analia corrected. She sat up straighter, purposefully sitting on her hands to prevent them from toying with her pin.

Deardryn gave her a look of approval. "And if you were to presume?"

"Sand," Analia decided.

Deardryn didn't respond. That bowstring seemed to pull more taut, Analia fighting the urge to snatch her answer out of the air.

"Indeed," Deardryn said.

With that, the bowstring slackened. Deardryn bent to withdraw the two rings from the drawer, giving Analia a moment to smooth the relief from her face.

Aaron rose from the bench and crossed to Analia's side. He leaned down to place the ring in front of her, taking the opportunity to breathe in her ear, "Force to be reckoned with."

Analia tried to catch his eye, but he'd already retreated back to the bench. At the sound of rings rolling across the table, she turned her attention back to Deardryn. True to what she said, both the golden Sun ring and silver Wind ring joined the bronze Sand ring on the tabletop.

Analia made to speak, but Deardryn was scribbling away once more, golden curls falling across her face. Analia had quickly learned if there was anything guaranteed to provoke the Dragoness, it was interrupting her as she worked. Instead, she looked down at the sparkling rings.

This close, the hum of the fields rose to the foreground, forcing her to consciously work to ignore them. She was already intimately familiar with the gold and silver songs. Although...

Unable to help herself, she reached out and lightly rested her palm over the Sand ring. Out of the corner of her eye, she saw Aaron tense, Pryanth indifferent beside him. But she didn't jolt under the force of this magic.

Yes, it was heavy, but not destructive. It was the roll and shift of boulders, cracking apart, fusing back together again.

"That's all for today," Deardryn said, putting down her pen.

Analia's head jerked up. "You don't want to hide the rings again?"

"You have already proven yourself capable of that skill," Deardryn replied, tapping her papers into alignment. "I would not have you wasting your time polishing a blade that already shines."

Analia fought the urge to look at Aaron. True, Deardryn was the one who had told Analia where to find him, but did she know how long Analia had stayed? Did she sense the shift, one that Analia was uncertain she completely understood herself?

"Yes, Your Majesty," she said, lowering her head.

"Don't look so disappointed," Deardryn said briskly, uncoiling to her full height. "I only wish to review my notes before assigning you your next task."

She swept the rings into her palms. "You'll be back to work tomorrow." She paused, giving Analia's hand a pointed look.

She hadn't realized she was still touching the Sand ring. Somehow, the magic had drifted back into the background music once more. She hastily slid the ring across the table toward Deardryn, who studied her curiously.

"You forgot your hand was touching the ring," she said, a statement, not a question. "Explain."

Analia stammered something about adjusting to the magic field. Deardryn nodded, thoughtful, but didn't move to take another note. Instead, she scooped the bronze ring off the desk, depositing it into the jewelry box she had produced from Crystal knew where. Finally, Deardryn smoothed her scarlet skirts and headed for the door. But something had snagged Analia's attention.

She twisted in her seat, looking after Deardryn. "Why can't I sense them anymore?"

The Dragoness turned back. "Astute indeed." She showed Analia the box. "Do you see what the box is made of?"

Analia leaned forward. The box was a simple rectangle the size of a large book. The only access point was the top that swung open and closed, locking with a heavy iron latch. Made from a shining black stone, various swirling runes were carved into its surface.

"Onyx," Analia said slowly. "The box is a damper?"

"Precisely." Deardryn tucked the box under her arm once more. "With all the magic stored inside, the colliding waves and fields would be far too powerful for an ordinary box to endure. With onyx, not only are the objects contained, but so are the magic fields."

Analia nodded, keeping quiet as Deardryn finally swept out the door. Then, she turned to the two men still seated on the bench.

Aaron had a thoughtful finger resting against his chin. Noticing her stare, he let it drop, flashing a congratulatory grin. Beside him, Pryanth remained sullen, picking at the threads in his dark pants.

Something heavy settled in Analia's stomach. Aaron's eyes darted between the two of them. With a look of wanting nothing to do with what was to come, he rose to his feet and headed for the door. He flicked his eyebrows up in a question as he passed Analia, but she shook her head. Shrugging, he slipped from the room.

Analia should've been used to silence by now. But all that her time in the Ash Kingdom had taught her was the different masks that silence wore. And the one that lay between herself and Pryanth was chiseled from ice.

"Are you sure nothing's wrong?" she finally asked.

Her hands tightened around the chair behind her as Pryanth finally looked at her.

"What were you thinking?" he asked quietly.

Chills skittered down Analia's spine. "What do you—"

"How could you do this to me?" he asked. "Do you have any idea how this looks for me? Betrothed to someone sneaking about the castle?"

"I wasn't sneaking—"

"So, you weren't moving around the castle, alone, at night, going places you weren't allowed to go?"

Analia averted her gaze. "Your mother said—"

"I don't care what she said!" Pryanth yelled. "That doesn't change what you did! That doesn't stop the stories from spreading across this gods-damned castle like a foreign disease."

"What *stories?*" Analia asked.

"Saying you're a spy. You're using me. That you're untrustworthy."

Analia took an involuntary step back, bumping into the desk. "Pryanth," she said, "you can trust me."

"But I can't!" He rose to his feet, a thundercloud obscuring the sun. "How can I trust someone I clearly don't know like I thought I did?"

"Pryanth, I'm sorry," she said desperately. "I never meant to hurt you—"

"But you did!" He advanced forward. "You hurt my reputation! You made me look like a fool! Like I was the marionette being jerked around. Were you trying to cut my strings, too, or was that just a happy accident?"

Analia flinched. Did he really think her that awful? After how she'd treated Aaron, was he that far off?

"Pryanth," she pleaded, "I'm telling you, this had nothing to do with you. I wasn't even *thinking* about you."

"You should have been!" Pryanth halted, only a chair standing between them. "I'm a prince, Analia. Heir to the throne. My people need to respect me. I'm already living with the shame of my father's disgrace. I thought you of all people wouldn't add to that."

Analia could practically feel the dagger he twisted in her gut. "Pryanth," she tried again. "I swear, I wasn't trying to drag you into this. I wasn't trying to create this in the first place."

She reached for Pryanth, her heart twisting as he backed away. Just another person that had looked at her like she was worthy, only for that sentiment to rot away. Brenn wasn't even there for her to blame it on.

"Pryanth," Analia whispered.

"No. No, I can't do this right now."

He backed away from her, an accusatory look on his face as she called after him. Then, he left without a backward glance.

Analia raised shaking hands to her face. She should have been furious, offended by his accusations. But all she could hear was the tiny voice in her head, sounding incredibly similar to Brenn as it chanted *your fault, your fault, your fault.*

How had this gotten turned around on her? She was here to find her uncle's killer, and instead she was hitting dead end after dead end, getting caught by the Royals as she did so. Upsetting a betrothed she knew she was going to leave, knew better than to get attached to. Yet, hurting him somehow dealt the heaviest blow.

Pryanth and his friendly smiles. Always quick to grab her hand, unafraid to show the affection in his eyes whenever he noticed his pendant around her neck. All things she had told herself didn't matter. But that didn't stop the all-too-familiar ripping sensation as Pryanth walked away. Just as Rois had done.

Analia pushed herself off the desk, heading for the door. She couldn't fix getting caught, but she could fix this. She *had* to fix this. Because the only thing more terrifying than losing whatever it was that she had with Pryanth was the accompanying realization that at some point, she'd come to care that there was something to lose.

It didn't take long to find Pryanth. He stood in the middle of the gilded entryway, staring up at the ceiling with his hands clasped behind his back. Servants skirted around him, keeping their distance, casting furtive looks over their shoulders.

Analia called Pryanth's name, and he turned. "You can't let it go, can you?" he asked, more tired than angry.

"I'll let it go," she said, hovering in the shadows. "Just as soon as I'm able to apologize."

She waited for him to interrupt her again, but he remained silent. She caught him tracking a pair of serving girls out of the corner of his eye.

Something hot and heavy lodged in Analia's chest. But she forced it down as she asked, "How many times have you told me your mother has yet to be wrong?"

Pryanth's face pinched. "What does that have to do with anything?"

"Please, just answer." She locked eyes with him, then pointedly glanced at two servants, trying to inconspicuously linger at the foot of one of the many marble staircases.

Pryanth scowled, but mumbled, "She's always right."

"Exactly," Analia said. "And she heard the full story of what happened and forgave me. She realized it was a midnight mistake revolving around me reading a children's book."

"You shouldn't have done it," he repeated.

"I know." Analia took a step toward him. Thankfully, he didn't back away.

"Your actions don't just impact you, Analia," Pryanth said.

"I know."

Dimitri descended one of the marble staircases behind Pryanth, scrub brush in hand. Noticing them, he slowed as he reached the bottom of the stairs, wandering over to a nearby pillar and unabashedly listening in.

"You're a princess, Analia," Pryanth went on. "I thought you would have learned all of this by now."

"I know," Analia said, taking another step. "I know all of this, Pryanth. I know this is my fault. I know I wasn't intending to hurt anyone, let alone you, and I did it anyway.

"I understand I broke your trust. And I know that's something I can't force back together. But I hope I can show you it's worth mending, because I truly am sorry."

Analia hesitantly reached out to take Pryanth's hand. He didn't fight it, but his fingers were limp in hers.

"How do I know you won't do it again?" he asked.

"You don't," Analia said simply. "Not unless you allow me to show you that I won't."

Pryanth was quiet, but his hand remained in hers. That cold, hard knot twisted in her stomach, yanked by the truths that should be lies and the lies that should be truths. He was right, after all. He shouldn't forgive her. He shouldn't trust her.

Analia peeked up at him. "Are... Are we...?"

Pryanth sighed. "Yes." He touched her cheek with icy fingertips. "I'm sorry I yelled."

Analia nodded. But he didn't kiss her goodbye as he usually did before turning away. He walked straight past Dimitri, ascending one of the marble staircases and disappearing at the top.

Analia's shoulders slumped. She'd had two victories that day. So why didn't it feel like it?

Dimitri gaped as Pryanth ascended the marble staircase. At first, he'd been looking forward to the entertainment of a Royal squabble. But as it unfolded before him, he could barely hear the words. There was only the hot sunlight on the back of his neck, slowly building until it burned.

"Enjoy the show?" Analia asked tiredly.

"What was that?" Dimitri spat.

"You too, huh?" Analia asked. She rubbed a hand across her forehead, but Dimitri had no pity.

"You just stood there while he sneered in your face," he said. "Staring down his nose at you like he does to every other person in this gods-damned castle."

"He had every reason to be angry with me; it was my fault."

"I don't care!"

Memories flashed through Dimitri's mind in rapid succession. Pryanth purposefully stepping on his fingers as he scrubbed the floor. Pryanth ordering him to a month of scrubbing toilets the one time he'd tried to tell him no. Pryanth towering over him, spitting in his face as he told him how he was the bastard son of a whore, only living in this castle out of a parental obligation. How he was worthless, an everlasting byproduct of a bad decision that should have been washed down the drain.

"Clearly you do care," Analia said softly.

Dimitri glared but didn't respond. Analia turned to go, and Dimitri didn't bother calling after her.

No, he didn't care about the only person that could have stood up to Pryanth but didn't. The only thing he cared about was the fact that he was losing out on an escape route. But he had worked without her before, and he would do it again.

"I have a new book for you," Analia said, pausing at the foot of the stairs.

Her hand toyed with her phoenix pin. And just like the rat Dimitri was, he chomped down on the proverbial hand she offered him.

"Fuck you," he said.

Shoving to his feet, he marched away. It had only been a matter of time, anyway.

# Chapter 26

Aaron took a sip of his beer, the usual thrum of Sun Fang buzzing in his ears.

The last few days had emotionally wrung him out like a sponge. He hadn't been planning on telling Analia about his mother—well, the pieces he could tell. He hadn't expected her to come talk with him in the first place.

But in she'd come, her temper dying down just long enough for him to sneak a peek at what lay beneath. Then, his words had tumbled forth: how he knew just how deep grief could burrow into someone's bones, how it could slowly eat someone alive.

He'd only been trying to comfort her. But there was no denying his own wave of relief when she came closer, touched his hand, looked into his eyes. She wasn't the only one that had found someone who understood her broken pieces. Aaron just hadn't realized how badly he'd needed that, too.

Across the tavern, the door swung open. Aaron glanced up from his dim, back-corner booth, straightening as he prepared for his next performance.

"Dannel," he said brightly as the guard approached. "I haven't seen you in so long. I missed you."

"Don't start, Aaron," Dannel sighed, sliding into the booth across from him.

Aaron frowned. "Fine then," he said. "You want to skip the pleasantries?" He downed his drink, bringing it down on the table with a thud. "What news do you have for me?"

Dannel folded his arms. "I found where she keeps the box."

That was unexpected. Knowing Dannel was prone to dragging his feet, Aaron had been prepared to prod him along far longer before getting anywhere.

"Took you long enough," he said.

"It would have taken you even longer without me," Dannel shot back.

Aaron shrugged, graciously giving him that one. Dannel glared, but unlike Lev, Aaron couldn't play off his anger. Much more effective was his fear—although Dannel's fear was always most potent when under the gaze of his peers.

"So," Aaron said, unsheathing a dagger and spinning it on the table. "Where is it?"

"She keeps it in her chambers," Dannel said, tracking the spinning blade. "Right now, at least. She had it moved from somewhere else."

Since Dannel didn't offer where that somewhere was, Aaron felt safe to assume he didn't know, which meant he was back to the beginning. He'd already checked her chambers and found nothing.

It was no surprise that's where the box was currently, though. Not only would she want to keep it close, but if Analia was working with the rings each day, she wouldn't want to be running back and forth. Especially if its original home was a significant distance away. Aaron needed to find a way into those woods.

The dagger came to a scraping stop. Aaron pulled it close, thoughtfully rubbing the worn leather hilt. Across from him, a muscle feathered in Dannel's jaw.

"All right," Aaron said, leaning back in his seat.

Dannel stared at him blankly. "That's it?"

"That's it."

"You can't be serious!"

A couple of people at a nearby table glanced their way. Blushing furiously, Dannel lowered his voice and leaned toward Aaron. "What was the point of all this?"

The point was to find one of the Royal hiding spots. The point was to get a glimpse into Royal security, and in that regard, Analia had given him far more than Dannel had.

If Deardryn was able to keep those rings in a damper box, it would be foolish to assume the scroll wasn't similarly locked away. And not even Analia could trace through a damper.

Not yet, at least. Aaron quickly pushed the thought aside.

"The point," he said, "was you did something for me, so I would do something for you."

"You're not doing anything for me."

Aaron raised a brow. "Well, in that case, I'll be letting that treasonous secret of yours be the next thing to burn in all the pipes in this tavern. I wonder what color smoke it will produce. It definitely won't burn as sweet as this stuff, although I don't doubt it would give me the same sort of headache—"

"Do you ever stop talking?" asked Dannel wearily.

"I would, but no one ever gives me a reason to."

"Consider this a gift then," Dannel said, rising from the booth. He shook his head at the barkeeper, declining a drink and heading for the door.

"Why'd you tell Othin?" Aaron called after him. The question had been bothering him ever since his conversation with Lev, more so than he cared to admit.

Dannel paused. "Because Deardryn said I had to," he said, not asking how Aaron knew.

"Why'd you tell Deardryn?"

"Because she asked." Dannel returned to grip the back of the booth. "She summoned me into her chambers when we were in Ash and demanded to know what was going on between me and Lev."

"And you told her?" Aaron exclaimed. "You told your queen about your conquests?"

"Have you tried lying to her? She just stares at you in silence until you break."

Aaron smiled blandly. Yes, he was familiar with that technique.

"So, what'd she do?"

Dannel shrugged. "She looked at me with disgust and told me she wanted no part in this, and I should talk with Othin. Why do you care, anyway?"

"Is it so wrong I want to get to know you?" Aaron asked.

Dannel scoffed. "Get to know me and all the places you can stick that dagger of yours." He slapped a hand down on the dagger Aaron had sent spinning again.

Aaron didn't deny it. Instead, he gave Dannel a grin, sharp as the blade Dannel held captive beneath his palm. Speaking of which.

Aaron gave Dannel's hand a pointed look, and slowly, Dannel pulled back.

"Touch my blade again," Aaron said lightly, "and I'll demonstrate just how many places I've already found."

To Dannel's credit, he didn't drop Aaron's gaze. "Any more questions?" he asked stiffly.

"Not at the moment," Aaron said. "Although I reserve the right to change that status later."

Dannel scoffed. Not waiting for permission, he finally managed to escape.

Aaron remained in his booth for a long time after that. What kind of political game were the Royals up to? Whatever it was, Deardryn was clearly winning in the long term. Othin may have provoked just the fight he wanted, but through that very fight—more specifically its stab wound—Deardryn had won the loyalty of Othin's guard.

But did she want it just to put a stop to Othin's peace-defying antics, or was there something else? Whatever she was up to, it told him one thing for sure: finding the scroll—which was almost certainly hers—was going to take a lot more cunning than Aaron had anticipated.

# Chapter 27

Analia sat on the Sun Castle's parapet, legs dangling over the edge as she idly rolled the Ash and Sun rings in her palms.

It was far from her first visit to the roof since that initial time with Pryanth, now almost a month earlier. She'd been drawn there searching for something familiar in the chaos around her—although the chaos itself was disconcertingly familiar, too. Just like the wall of frosty silence that had slammed down between herself and Dimitri.

At least she and Pryanth were all right. He'd come to her chambers not two hours after their fight in the entryway to apologize once more, this time with a pair of delicate sapphire earrings.

Yet, in the days since, he'd been noticeably absent. And Analia couldn't help but feel like it was her fault.

"I step away for two seconds to receive a message, and you flee to the highest ledge you can find."

Analia glanced back as Aaron crossed the roof toward her, his arms folded in mock disapproval.

"Is there a particular reason you have decided to jeopardize my guarding reputation?" he asked, sitting beside her.

"Latest assignment for Deardryn," Analia said, eyes back on her rings.

"That's it?" he asked, disappointed. "No jab? No, 'go away, Aaron'?"

"Do you think if you fell from this height you could still tuck and roll, or does that big head of yours have a bounce limit?"

Aaron grinned with wicked delight. "It depends on if I was pushed or not."

"I'll keep that in mind."

Aaron laughed. He nudged her shin with his foot, "Where's your prickly prince?"

"He had duties to attend to," Analia said.

"Did he."

"He would have been here if he could," she added quickly, wondering if that were true, wondering why she felt the need to convince Aaron it was. "Cabir offered to join me instead, but I didn't want to subject him to my mood. Or anyone, for that matter."

Aaron's lips briefly pursed. "Well," he said, leaning back on his elbows, "fantastic news for you, Analia. You don't have to worry about inflicting your mood on me because I'm already the paragon of a moody bastard."

"Really," Analia said dryly.

"Horribly moody," Aaron confirmed. "It's getting completely out of hand. If anything, you should be worried that I might accidentally blacken your mood even more with my profound moodiness."

"You seem to be hiding it incredibly well."

"It's a constant burden, although I'm willing to continue shouldering it if you tell me why your assignment has us testing the winds of fate."

Analia shook her head, but she couldn't fight her smile. That man was too charming for his own good—and she was certain he was fully aware.

"Deardryn wants to test how close two magic fields can be before their signals become entangled," she explained. "I was just having a hard time concentrating inside with all the interfering magic."

Analia had only just noticed how the castle seemed to hum. She also suspected she was learning to pick up on the networks of every Blessed and Demiblessed in the castle, although she was still unable to untangle them in her mind. Regardless, now that she'd learned how to tune into the magic, she was struggling to tune it out again.

"So now you're on the roof," Aaron said as if it were perfectly logical.

"So now I'm on the roof," Analia sighed.

"How's that going for you?"

"It's still not working. I have to touch the rings to move them, which just gives me a direct blast of their magic."

An idea dawned on her, although she hesitated before asking, "Can you take these?"

Aaron warily glanced at the rings she offered him. "Me?"

"The magic won't zap you. You don't have a network, right?"

She certainly didn't sense one.

"Right." He sat up, proffering his hands for her to dump the rings into.

"Does that mean you're not Blessed?" Analia asked, mildly curious.

"Can you still sense the magic?"

"Of course, why wouldn't I?"

Aaron shrugged. "So, what do I do?"

"Just slowly move them closer together," Analia said. "I'll tell you when to stop."

She expected at least one follow-up question, but Aaron only went about doing as she instructed.

"You know," he said, "you never did tell me why you were looking for xenol."

Analia stiffened.

"Oh, come on." Aaron nudged her tense shoulder. "You said it yourself, we're friends now."

"I did not say that."

"You thought it."

"Funny you didn't hear any other thoughts I had."

"You mean like the ones that considered how I help you, you help me, you tell me about your schemes—"

"What makes you think I'm scheming?" Analia protested.

"I know you," he said simply.

Knew her for a month, maybe.

She reached for the magic fields, finding them hopelessly entangled. She told Aaron, and he moved his hands apart once more, all the while staring at her expectantly.

"How about a truth for a truth?" she suggested.

Aaron looked like he'd rather pry off his fingernails.

"That's what I thought," Analia said.

The breeze swirled around them, blowing her hair into her face.

"What do you want to know?" Aaron asked warily.

Analia felt for the fields. Still far enough to be separate.

"Why did you become a Crystal Guard?" she asked.

"Next."

"What?"

"I'm not answering that."

"But—"

"Next."

Analia glared, but Aaron stared, impassive, right back.

"Fine," she said. "How did your mother die?"

"No."

"You know how Accalon died!"

Aaron shrugged. He inched his hands closer, and the signals clashed. Analia opened her mouth, but Aaron reset before she could speak.

"How about your father, then?"

"Now I really can't tell you that."

"Why not?" Analia demanded, slapping her hand down on the weather-worn wall.

"Do you want to talk about your father?" Aaron asked. "Explain to me how he's been forged from hellfire itself?"

"I never said that."

"You didn't have to. I saw the way he looked at you, like you were something foul he pried off the bottom of his boot."

Analia wanted to protest. Instead, her anger sizzled out.

"He wasn't all bad," she mumbled, twisting to look out across the kingdom. "Not at first, anyway."

In fact, the longer she was away from Brenn, the more she reminisced over her long-buried memories of what he'd been like before. How he used to tuck her in at night. How he used to listen to her play her harp and applaud. It was just in those moments that she wondered: was he really as bad as she remembered?

Analia's eyes drifted to the sundial in the center of the square. She would be standing there in a matter of days when she was introduced to the kingdom on Solemnai. Then, assuming she survived that—survived the unpredictable storms of Pryanth—barely a month later was the Solstice Ceremony.

The six kingdoms would come together to bless the lands with magic. Including Brenn, who would undoubtedly be awaiting an update.

"At least that means you have some good memories with him," Aaron said, voice softening. "That must make it a little easier."

He'd stopped moving the rings, letting his hands rest palms up on his knees.

"Or ten times harder," Analia sighed. She waved a hand, and Aaron started once more.

"How come?" he asked.

"Now you're just avoiding my questions."

"You know," he said, inching his hands closer, "most people enjoy being asked about themselves. It makes them feel special."

"And you're so anxiously awaiting my questions."

Aaron grinned. "I'm already special enough."

Two distinct fields.

Analia picked at a section of crumbling stone. She was tempted to call it a draw, seeing as though the only thing she had indirectly gotten out of him was he wasn't the killer. Unless he was incredibly skilled at playing dumb.

Although now that she thought about it, he had already given a piece of himself to her, hadn't he? Down in the armory, where he hadn't demanded anything in return.

Even now, as she watched Aaron's hands inch closer to one another, she realized—despite his blatant curiosity—he would let his end drop if she did first.

"I was looking for xenol," she said slowly, "because it was found in my uncle's body. No other potential cause of death. And we have no record of it in the Ash Kingdom."

Analia could feel Aaron's eyes on her, but he didn't ask any questions. She was just starting to think he wouldn't say anything at all when he finally spoke.

"My family lives on the outskirts, far outside the central kingdom. And they sent me here to find a scroll."

"What kind of scroll?" Analia asked.

"I have no idea. I don't know what it says, why it's important, or why we need it. I just know I'm here to find it and bring it home."

He made to continue, clearly reluctant, but Analia put her hands over his.

"Right there," she said.

She'd found it. The spot where the magic fields flowed side by side, almost brushing against one another, but still separate enough for her to sense each rhythm.

Aaron closed his mouth, staring down at her hands over his. "That is annoyingly specific," he said.

Analia smiled, almost a full smile, as she replied, "You have no idea."

# Chapter 28

Ember led Cadmus to the back of the apothecary. He used to spend all his days in the training arena, endlessly perfecting his control over his magic. Today, however, she'd found him loitering in the forges, watching the blacksmiths and fire sprites work with a distracted look on his face.

Seeing he wasn't in the middle of anything, Ember marched right up to him, yelling to be heard over the clang of metal and huff of the bellows that she needed him, and he was coming with her. Cadmus had asked multiple times what they were doing, but Ember just told him to wait and see as she towed him back to the apothecary.

"All right," she said, flipping open her plant box. "This is a sample of the plant we're almost certain killed your uncle."

Cadmus peered over her shoulder. "I'm guessing no one knows you have this?"

"Smart man." Ember pulled the tiny sample from her box and placed it on her stone desk. "Now, summon your magic."

"Why?"

"Because," she said, unceremoniously shoving all flammable objects off the desk and onto the floor, "this plant has some sort of odd relationship with magic. It somehow managed to completely shut down, or dissolve, or break down, all the magic I had stored in that box."

"And you want to see if it's strong enough to do that to Royal magic?"

Ember gave Cadmus an appraising look. He really was intelligent. No, perhaps the word was observant. He had a knack for catching the unspoken, finding connections between dots that most would say were completely unrelated. She just wished he'd break the habit of framing all his answers as questions.

Cadmus shifted uneasily under her gaze. She'd been staring again, hadn't she?

"That's exactly right," she said quickly. "Although, seeing as though it's such a small sample, I doubt it's able to handle all of your magic at once."

Cadmus nodded, taking a seat at the desk. Ember hovered behind him.

"Try summoning a tiny flame," she said. "Teeny tiny. As big as Brenn's respect for other people."

"You can't make a flame that small," Cadmus muttered.

Ember snickered. Cadmus flushed. Ducking his head, he summoned a tiny flame to the tip of his finger.

"Put it on the table," Ember instructed. "Don't touch the plant directly. The magic needs to be disconnected from your entire network, just in case it can somehow latch on."

Obediently, Cadmus directed the flame onto the stone. Before it could fizzle out, Ember scooped up the sample and dropped it into the tiny flame.

At first, nothing happened. Then, they watched, eyes widening as the flame winked out, leaving the xenol completely unscathed. Ember flipped over the sample, just to be sure, but even the spots that had direct contact remained remarkably unburned.

"That is not how that's supposed to work," Cadmus said quietly.

"Summon a bigger flame," Ember said excitedly, furiously scribbling on a random sheet of paper she'd retrieved from the floor.

There was an interaction between the xenol sample and magic, she wrote. Not so much absorbing the flame, as snuffing it out.

Ember watched, pen poised, as Cadmus summoned a ball of flame the length of his pinky finger. He deposited it on the desk, Ember feeling its heat as she dropped the sample in. And this time, it crumbled to ash.

"I'm sorry!" Cadmus gasped, turning to Ember with wide eyes.

Larger flames were able to destroy the xenol, although the process wasn't immediate as with other plants. There was a moment where the xenol remained intact before crumbling to ash.

Ember looked up from her notes and waved a hand. "You think I can't pilfer an-other?" Although the idea of going through the magic-sucking process of regrowing said pilfered sample triggered a sharp pain behind her eyes.

Brushing the thought aside, she swept the xenol's ashy remains into her palm and turned to look for something to store it in.

"I shouldn't have made the fire so big," Cadmus said.

"I told you to make it that big," Ember said. "Besides, if Master Lenzi were here right now, she would be giving us a lecture on how this was hardly a failure; it was a learning opportunity or something like that. She's said it so many times, you'd think I'd remember."

Ember spotted an empty glass jar on the top shelf. She stretched on her toes, trying to reach it.

"Maybe she should tell that to my father," Cadmus muttered. Standing from his seat, he came over and easily grabbed the jar.

Ember accepted it with a distracted smile. One child that could do nothing right, and one that wasn't allowed to do anything wrong.

"Cadmus," she asked, "why have you been hiding in the forges?"

Cadmus bit his lip. For a moment, Ember thought he wouldn't respond. Then, "It's the only place he won't look for me."

Cadmus returned to his seat. "Ever since becoming king, all he's talked about is grooming me to be his successor. How I have to become even stronger, more powerful, relentless. Picking apart every micromovement and telling me how to do it better."

Cadmus looked away. "I know he's trying to be helpful. But lately, the only moments I feel like I can breathe are when he's visiting Mt. Vasolus or I'm in the forges."

Ember fought the urge to give Cadmus a hug. She didn't know him well enough to know if that would be helpful, or just make things worse.

"Well," she said, dusting the ash into the jar and screwing it shut, "if you're ever in the mood to watch someone else's mistakes, this little back room of mine is full to bursting with them." Her easy smile faltered, but she quickly recovered.

Something flickered across Cadmus's face. Before Ember could figure out what, he reached out and tapped the jar in her hand.

"Does this mean xenol can somehow suppress magic?" he asked.

"Something like that," Ember said. "And now we have confirmation that it can suppress at least some Royal magic."

Cadmus watched as Ember labeled the jar and carefully tucked it away. Hopefully, she would remember where she put it.

"But is that enough to kill a Royal?" he asked.

"I have no idea," Ember said brightly. "But perhaps this is just the beginning of what this little beast is able to do."

And perhaps this was the beginning of her finally getting her third marking. Although that didn't explain the black mark on the neck. Cadmus voiced this very thought a few moments later, and Ember could only shrug.

Side effect? Hallmark? Something completely different they had missed?

One half answer, and six new questions.

# Chapter 29

The evening of Solemnai, Analia was a calcified knot of anxiety.

Bie and Nadi whipped around her in a hurricane of lace, jewels, and powder, their usual excited chatter somehow reaching new top speeds. They quickly cut off as there came a knock on the door, Deardryn stepping inside a moment later.

Her golden curls wove under and around a crown of moonstone and topaz. Matching stones wrapped around her neck, wrists, and fingers, her silk gown flowing to the ground in a waterfall of gold, caramel, and butterscotch.

"Your Majesty," Nadi breathed as both she and Bie bowed, "that gown is stunning!"

Deardryn flicked a hand in thanks. She met Analia's eyes in the mirror, and something in her expression twitched. She turned back to the maids, telling them she could finish Analia's hair, it was no trouble. Bie and Nadi didn't protest, patting Analia's arm in farewell and scampering out the door. As it shut behind them, Analia made to speak.

"No need, my dear," Deardryn said. "I understand it's a nerve-wracking day for you."

"Thank you, Your Majesty."

Deardryn smiled kindly. She reached for the comb Bie had haphazardly tossed on the dressing table, humming to herself as she went about getting the last of the tangles out of Analia's hair. Analia tried not to squirm as she desperately searched for something to say.

"You have such nice hair," Deardryn said, finally putting down the comb and starting to braid.

"My mother always said it was like a bird's nest," Analia mumbled.

"That's because Aeley has straight hair. She doesn't understand how to work with waves."

Deardryn clicked her tongue as she caught sight of Analia's reflection. "There's that mulish expression again."

"I'm not mulish." Analia hadn't intended for the words to slip out, but she figured Deardryn would be more offended if she tried to take them back.

Indeed, Deardryn didn't react to the minor disrespect.

"No," she said, thoughtful gaze on her fingers, "perhaps that's not the right word. Most days, you are as determined as the young dragons learning to fly, tumbling to the ground just to pop up again.

"So determined to succeed," she sighed. "And just as determined to clutch the past in a stranglehold."

Analia fought to keep her face smooth as Aaron's voice echoed in her head. My gods you hold a grudge.

Was that why Deardryn had come? Not out of some foreign, motherly comfort, but as a warning?

"There's a lot to hold onto," she said carefully.

"I'm not surprised by that," Deardryn said. "There's so much that the moment you let go, it rolls right over you once more."

"You can't be rolled over if you're invisible," Analia murmured.

She tried to recall the last time she let go. With Rois—

"Do you know why my magic is so powerful?" asked Deardryn.

Analia shoved the memories aside, shaking her head.

"It's because when I was a girl, I was chosen by Rosala."

Analia's eyes widened. "I didn't know Royals could be chosen."

"It's rare," Deardryn said, retrieving a golden pin from the vanity and securing one of Analia's braids. "There are rumors Helia exhibited healing abilities beyond normal Sun magic while she and the other Defiants still ruled.

"There's a certain logic in Sun Royals being chosen, though. Our magic runs parallel to that of the healers: mending the minds, lifeforces, and magic networks that healer magic cannot reach. Now, there are few ailments I cannot treat, or at least stabilize."

"Except death," Analia whispered.

Deardryn's gaze softened. She reached around Analia to pat her cheek. "Except death."

Deardryn decided to let the silence hang, returning to Analia's second braid. Analia tried not to move too much as she took a slow, deep breath.

"If you're a healer," she said, "why do you not have any markings?"

"Astute observation," Deardryn murmured. "After first discovering my Blessing, I attempted to split my time between the Healer School and my royal duties. At the school, I advanced rapidly, far too quickly for my fellow students' liking.

"The kinder rumors said I had an unfair advantage. The whispers that passed through the shadows, however, would have you believe I was not chosen by Rosala. I had simply manipulated my Royal magic. I was infiltrating the Healer School on a covert mission to overturn the healers and replace them with Sun Royals."

"That seems a bit far-fetched," Analia said.

"It does, doesn't it? People are rather predictable when you threaten their lives, but when you threaten their pride, there is no telling how far they will stretch to remain intact."

In the mirror, Deardryn's eyes flicked to the pile of pins.

"Does that mean you left the Healer School?" Analia asked, obediently handing Deardryn another pin.

"I did," she said, "but not because of the rumors. My family had remained quiet as I trained in the Healer School, but I knew my mother in particular was livid. She knew that the responsibilities and oaths of a healer directly clashed with being a Royal.

"Swearing to have no offspring in order to view all people as your children meant no heirs. Promising to not see allegiance when faced with someone in need would make playing politics impossible. It was inevitable that I would have to make a choice."

"And you chose the Royals," Analia said.

"I was next in line," Deardryn explained. "If I stepped aside, the crown would go to my sister, and Saura was too frail, spent too many days in bed. If I didn't pick the crown, I would have people calling me selfish, a traitor.

"Yet, in choosing the crown, I was an oathbreaker. A heretic who turned my back on a Blessing."

"You couldn't win," Analia summed up.

Deardryn let out a small sigh. "Not in that regard. But failure and victory, they're both so fleeting. They're always teetering, just waiting for something to knock them over."

"How'd you knock them over, then?" Analia asked.

"I did what many rulers fail to do. I thought multiple steps ahead, and I was patient.

"I knew all the hurdles ahead of me: my reputation, my past. But I fought for trust. I demonstrated that compassion could coexist with authority. I created nights such as these to dissolve some of the divide between Royals and commoners. I became the Dragoness."

Deardryn patted Analia's hair, now twisted in a set of elaborate braids. "You and I, Analia. In our pasts, we've both been shaped by the people around us. It would be unwise to completely forget the lessons they've taught us, but it would be a fallacy to believe we must remain in those shapes."

Just for a moment, Deardryn let the mask of the Dragoness fall, revealing a vulnerability Analia never would have associated with her. Slowly, she unclenched the fists she hadn't realized she'd been squeezing around her skirts. "Yes, Your Majesty."

Deardryn touched Analia's bare shoulder. "This lesson doesn't just apply to you. It applies to all six kingdoms and the rigid shape they've forced themselves into the past century."

She maneuvered around the chair to face Analia. "Next month, I would like to bring you to the Solstice Ceremony as a full-fledged member of my family. I want you to demonstrate how peace between kingdoms can exist, and whether I can do this depends on you, tonight.

"When you step onto that sundial, you will not just be standing for the lower class. Every noble clan will be in attendance, prepared to scrutinize you and my decision to bring you here. And it is they who shall set the precedent as to how the kingdom will react.

"Ultimately, however, it's your choice, Analia. Tonight is your chance to spread your wings and ride the current, or stay planted on the ground. So, little dragoness, will you fly?"

The hard knot in Analia's stomach started to unravel, but the heaviness didn't leave. Now, it grounded her as she nodded.

Yes, she would fly. But not as a dragon.

Before she could respond, there came a quick knock on the door. Deardryn turned away from her, telling the visitor to enter.

Aaron stepped inside, his usual fighting leathers now accompanied by his Crystal Guard cloak: white with a coiled gold sun dragon. There was a look of genuine surprise on his face as he bowed to Deardryn.

"I was expecting my son," said Deardryn.

"Your son is distracted at the moment, Your Majesty." Aaron's gaze drifted past Deardryn, his eyes widening as they landed on Analia.

Deardryn's lips pursed. "It seems as though my son and I will need to discuss his manners." She headed for the door. "I expect not to have to have that same conversation with you while in his stead."

"I wouldn't dream of such a thing," Aaron said, unusually earnest as he bowed once more.

Deardryn studied him for a moment. Then, not offering a farewell, she swept out the door. Aaron's gaze returned to Analia.

"You're staring at me," she complained.

"Oh, Analia," he said, his eyes following the curve of her collarbones before wandering up to her eyes. "I'm aware."

Analia scoffed. She had to admit, though, her reflection was striking.

Elaborate braids pulled half her hair from her face, highlighting her kohl-rimmed eyes. Gold dangled from her ears and encircled her throat and wrists, including Pryanth's pendant. Her gown faded through shades of orange and pink, the lacy gold top layer varying in transparency, so she looked like the dawn sky.

Aaron chuckled as he came up behind her. "Where's your pin, beautiful?"

Analia looked down to where the pin rested on the edge of her dressing table. "I've been trying to decide whether or not to wear it tonight."

She stroked her fingers around the outer ring. On the one hand, she hadn't gone a day without wearing it since Accalon gave it to her. It was a part of her now. She felt naked, exposed, without it. But what would it say if she wore it tonight of all nights?

Analia glanced at Aaron, but his face gave nothing away.

"No opinions?" she asked.

"I always have opinions," he replied. "It's just your choice."

Analia traced the smooth curves of the phoenix's wings. Nodding to herself, she pinned it to her dress, relaxing under the familiar feel of the warm metal against her skin.

"Tonight isn't just about me joining Sun," she said, heading for the door. "It's about showing how two kingdoms can come together."

"More importantly," Aaron said, falling into step beside her, "that pin is who you are." He tapped the pin for emphasis.

Unbidden memories came bubbling to the surface. Memories with sharpened edges that Analia instinctually tried to shove under once more. Instead, she tentatively let them tumble out.

"This pin was originally my uncle's."

"Oh?"

"Once he forged it, I don't think anyone saw him without it. He was always so careful with it, never letting it out of his sight."

"And now it's yours," Aaron said as they descended a marble staircase.

"He gave it to me the night Sun came to our kingdom. That night, he told me to keep it safe. It… It was the last thing he said to me." Analia's words died off.

Aaron paused, putting a hand on her arm to stop her as well. "He made the right choice," he told her.

Analia's fingers tightened around her pin. She could feel the shard as it bit deep, the blood as it oozed.

Aaron's hand on her arm squeezed. "Anna—"

"I'm fine," she said. She forced her hand to unclench around her pin, forced her shaking legs to carry her forward once more.

It had only been a tiny shard. One that seemed to be just a bit smoother now. But that didn't stop her from being more grateful than she would ever say that Aaron did not let go of her elbow until they reached the entryway where Pryanth waited for her.

The Sun Prince was dressed in varying shades of gold and brown, the buttons on his jacket flashing in the light. He appeared to be engrossed in conversation with Lena, but as soon as Analia and Aaron arrived, he gave a sharp jerk of his head and turned away.

"The flame to my life," he said as Analia reached his side. His eyes roved across her dress, a smile lighting up his face when he spotted his pendant. "Perfect."

He ducked his head, stealing a quick, sweet kiss. The pain in Analia's chest eased a fraction.

She hadn't realized how much she missed this side of him. So much so, she didn't have to force her body to relax into his as he wrapped his arm around her shoulders.

Yet, as Pryanth led her out the castle doors, excitedly talking about the night to come, Analia could feel her nerves resurface. She glanced back at Aaron, who followed a few steps behind with Lena.

He smiled and tapped the corner of his mouth. Analia managed a weak one in return. He gave her a one-finger salute as Pryanth nudged her, and she looked away.

Pryanth led her through the streets. A cool early summer breeze moved through the crowds of people dressed in their finest, everyone excitedly talking as they headed for the square. And when they finally arrived, Analia's breath caught.

The square was normally accented in shades of gold, brown, and white. That evening, though, there was an undeniable sparkle. Garlands weaved around every post and pole. Glittering lights wrapped around vendors' stands that sold strawberries dipped in sugar and cream, fizzing flutes of summer wine, and a variety of fluffy pastries that were sweet and melted on Analia's tongue.

Pryanth led the way from stand to stand, his face split in a boyish grin Analia had never seen on him before. He was a never-ending stream of stories from celebrations past: how when he was small, one of the vendors would always cut his pastries in the shape of sun dragons. How during winter gatherings, the snow sparkled in the sunstone light, and there was a group of children who had taken to lining the walkways with snow sculptures.

"To your first gathering," he said, clinking his wine flute against hers. He pulled her close and whispered in her ear, "And many more."

For a time, Analia was able to forget what was expected of her that night. She lost herself in Pryanth's infectious enthusiasm, all bitterness from their past entryway fight carried away on the honey-sweet breeze. But as the sun continued its descent in the sky, a crowd started to form around the sundial, and the pit in Analia's stomach burrowed deeper.

When only the thinnest sliver of sun peaked over the horizon, Pryanth put down his summer wine. If he noticed Analia's hand beginning to tremble in his own, he didn't say anything. He led her around the edge of the crowd, circling around to the backside of the sundial, Analia feeling the stares crawl over her skin.

Together, they climbed the few steps onto the platform that the sundial sat atop. Deardryn, Othin, Cabir, and Saura were already there, standing in a semicircle between the crowd and the dial. Six Royals from the lower branches stood a little farther back, the Sun Crystal Guard lining the platform on the ground.

Analia expected to stand beside the Royals. But with a wink, Pryanth nudged her behind him, hiding her from view as he stood beside his mother.

Deardryn gave her a brief nod in greeting, Cabir going so far as to twist around to squeeze her shoulder. Othin, however, didn't even look up as he softly spoke with Saura.

The pit in Analia's stomach deepened. She craned her neck, getting her first glimpse of the sundial up close.

The golden dial was the size of a large table. A coiled sun dragon had been carved into the stone in extraordinary detail, its body forming a border around the edge of the dial. Elegant. Intimidating.

Gods, what was she doing up there? She couldn't so much as summon a candle flame. Why would the dial find her worthy? How would her mission not come tumbling down around her the moment she failed yet another test?

Analia tore her gaze from the dial, just for Aaron to catch her eye from the ground. Touching his dagger, he glanced to the crowd, then wiggled his eyebrows suggestively.

Analia didn't immediately notice her smile. There was a surprising comfort in his offer—perhaps because she knew despite the humor in his eyes, he wouldn't hesitate to cut her free.

In that moment, she knew she had one person. One person not on the kingdom's side, but hers. And Analia clung to that feeling as Deardryn stepped forward.

"Citizens of the Sun Kingdom," Deardryn called, her hands spread in welcome. "It is my distinct pleasure to welcome you all to Solemnai."

Cheers and applause erupted from the crowd. Deardryn paused, soaking in the noise. Finally, she raised a slim hand for silence. Then, she launched into her speech.

It was a story woven from history, winding all the way back to Helia, the Defiant of the Sun. Centuries of magic and discovery. Hope and war between ideals, tradition, and change. Stories of the past century filled with fear and uncertainty following the Shattering, and its slow, not-always-straight evolution into harmony.

"We are the kingdom we are today because we stand with our hands linked," Deardryn said. "Yes, we have hierarchies, there's no way to completely dissolve them. But we have hands reaching down as well as up.

"It is an honor to be queen of a people who build instead of destroy. But to continue that, we need trust, and that is why Helia gave us this sundial.

"Tonight, we have a new dragoness hoping to enter our ranks. One whose worthiness will be determined by the magic of the dial the moment she steps on it. A worthiness you will be able to gauge based on the resulting glow. The decision, however, is ultimately yours: will you reach out your hand or keep it close to your chest?"

Deardryn paused, allowing the whispers to surge. Pryanth reached back and squeezed Analia's hand, which had gone cold and clammy.

"The sun has set," Deardryn said. As if on cue, golden sunstones winked to life all around the square. "The dial is ready. Are you?"

Deardryn spread her hands, and the crowd erupted once more. "Then let us introduce to you, the Sun Kingdom, Princess Analia Valarus."

Deardryn stepped back in line with the other Royals. Pryanth stepped away, leaving Analia exposed to the mob of people before her.

There were so many voices. They clamored in her ears, too dense to make out a single sound. Just how the whispers had started back home.

So many people—staring, watching, waiting for her to fail. Especially the clusters of noble clans, front and center.

Deardryn met Analia's gaze. Will you fly?

Analia wanted to sink through the ground. How had Deardryn done it? She'd told Analia about her life of whispers and disdain, so painfully familiar. Yet, today, she stood tall before her kingdom, the heretic, selfish queen, and they applauded her. But not just her.

Analia briefly closed her eyes. This was the Sun Kingdom, not Ash. It was untouched by Brenn, oblivious to her past.

Analia dropped Pryanth's hand. She took a step toward the dial. Then another and another, forcing herself to hear the applause, to see the curiosity, to not hesitate as she stepped up onto the sundial and turned to face the crowd once more. And to not flinch away as the dial erupted.

# Chapter 30

The cheers from the crowd were deafening.

Light arced from each segment of the dial, leaving Analia in the small, unlit center circle. She quickly realized, though, that it wasn't light. It was Sun magic. Warm, glittering, pulsating in slow, rhythmic waves.

Analia's stomach twisted as she thought back to Accalon's chambers, but she shoved the thoughts aside. Still, she couldn't help her prick of relief when she felt someone step up beside her and take her hand.

Analia looked up at Pryanth, taking in his all-consuming grin as he led her off the dial. Gods, she loved that smile. He didn't flash it often, but when he did, it was impossible not to lose herself in it.

Just for those moments, she forgot the constant ache in her chest—one she didn't have to explain to Pryanth because he already understood.

"Perfect," he whispered. "The flame to my life."

And when Pryanth kissed her in front of the entire kingdom, Analia felt the roar of approval in her bones. He pulled back, his eyes wild with delight. As he waved to the crowd, Analia caught a glance of the king and queen over his shoulder.

Deardryn beamed, hands clasped before her. But the moment Othin's amber eyes locked on hers, Analia's tentative excitement caught in her throat.

Pure, undiluted rage. The kind she'd only seen from Brenn after she'd disagreed with him in Accalon's chambers. The type of rage that froze her blood in her veins; the type she knew would come back to kill her.

Before Analia's panic could set in, Pryanth tugged her hand. He led her into the crowd, a twelve-person band taking their place and filling the square with the sound of strings and low, pounding drums.

Song after song, strangers' limbs brushed against her sides, her arms, her back. It was a closeness that once would have made her muscles go rigid. But either shock, or awe, or some cocktail of the two had her spinning to the measured, controlled dances of the Sun Kingdom.

She beamed at the citizens who came to congratulate her—introducing themselves, pulling her into embraces whose warmth and familiarity were completely foreign to her. Even those who remained wary clasped her hands in welcome.

It was everything she had ever wanted from her own kingdom. As far as the Sun people knew, they *were* her kingdom now. It would be so easy, just marry Pryanth and leave the ridicule and shame of the Ash Kingdom behind.

But what about her uncle?

"I still can't believe it," Pryanth said again. "Analia, it was blinding! Mother said it hadn't been that bright even when Father stepped on the dial."

Analia perked up. The band launched into a fast-paced song, Pryanth spinning her before pulling her close once more.

"You know," she said, resting her cheek against his chest, "you've never told me their story."

Pryanth shrugged, and Analia reluctantly let him guide her away. "It was just a typical Sun Kingdom arranged marriage. My father was the eldest, strongest available man from the Gardelle Clan. My grandfather had been looking for a way to forge a connection with them for decades because of their social power. But during his lifetime and his reign, there was never anyone appropriate."

"Does that mean the marriage was recent?" Analia asked.

Pryanth's hand on her back nudged her to the side, helping her narrowly miss a stray elbow.

"About half a century ago. Father was somewhere in his early thirties, my mother closer to one hundred and eighty."

Analia nodded. That type of age gap wasn't uncommon among the Blessed and Demi-blessed.

Pryanth went on, "Mother had already been ruling for some time. She actually arranged the marriage herself." He shrugged. "She probably wasn't in the mood until then."

No, Deardryn was making a point. She was waiting until she could win back the hearts of her people, show them she didn't need any help to rule.

"Does that mean she only married your father because that's what her father would have wanted?" she asked.

"Well, it certainly wasn't for love." Pryanth's lip curled. "Maybe Mother loved him and that's why she asked. But Father wouldn't have accepted out of love just to fuck a whore and protect his bastard child."

That decision had bred so much anger. Not just from Pryanth, but Dimitri, too. Somehow, that didn't stop Pryanth from always looking to Othin first, after every comment, every joke, every accomplishment.

When Pryanth pulled Analia close once more, she stretched up on her toes to kiss his cheek. "We won't end up like your parents," she told him.

Although, did she have any right to promise him that? She was supposed to find her uncle's killer and leave. And her heart wasn't supposed to shrink back from the idea.

"Of course we won't," Pryanth said. "We are life and flame. And I don't plan on fucking a whore in a back alleyway like my father, even if they've already lost their chance of finding a husband—what?"

Analia couldn't stop her face from twitching, his words tingling across the back of her neck. He had to be exaggerating, didn't he? There was no way his kingdom upheld such standards. But Pryanth's look of disgust had the music fading in and out in her ears.

"Do you think that's too harsh? I promise, it's nothing anyone else isn't thinking."

"It's..." Could she lie about this? Gods, how had they even gotten here in the first place?

Pryanth's brows furrowed. "What?" he said jokingly. "Are you saying you've had your share of midnight alleyway escapades?"

His eyes glittered with amusement. But Analia couldn't speak. She could only watch, ice creeping down her back, as Pryanth's expression slowly morphed from confusion, to understanding, to rage.

"You can't be fucking serious."

Pryanth threw down her hands, shoving through the crowd. Analia stood frozen where he left her, dancers flowing around her as the music shifted.

The Princess of Ash would have fled by now. The girl who first arrived in the Sun Kingdom would chase after Pryanth, desperate to apologize. But the woman who lit the sundial up like a beacon took a slow breath, pushed back her shoulders, and headed off in the opposite direction Pryanth had gone.

Dimitri did not understand why he was put on serving duty. Not only had he thoroughly burned that bridge with Chia, but he was too gods-damned short to see over the crowd.

But of course, he could see Analia light up that sundial to the point he had to shield his eyes with his drink platter, which promptly spilled icy summer wine down his arm. He could also see Othin storm past him not long after, barely sparing him a glance until he saw past the servant uniform.

"Don't fucking bother," Dimitri said, trying to shove past.

Othin actually looked hurt. He reached for Dimitri's tray, "You don't have to serve."

"Yes, I do," Dimitri said, jerking away. "Unless you're saying you'd like some clandestine father-son time while your wife isn't looking."

It was always the same cycle: Othin only sparing him a glance when they were alone, not so much as acknowledging him when his wife and heir were anywhere nearby. They were his family, the ones standing on that sundial, while Dimitri was left to hand out drinks.

"Dimitri..."

Dimitri cringed away from how Othin formed his name like it was something precious, from the hand that reached for him with a tenderness that always had a way of disappearing. It was certainly never there when he needed it.

Othin's hand hovered. "Keep your head down," he said in a low voice. "Don't draw any attention to yourself. Not until—"

"I told you," Dimitri ground out. "Not. Interested."

He turned on his heel and headed in the opposite direction, trembling with rage. He didn't fail to notice how Othin didn't so much as take a step after him. He never fucking did.

Dimitri stopped in a relatively unpopulated corner, no one paying him much attention. Not until a familiar figure stepped through the crowd a few minutes later.

"Don't even think about asking me for a drink," Dimitri said, not looking up.

"I wouldn't do that," said Analia, stopping before him. "You'd spit in it."

"That I would."

Analia smiled faintly, but Dimitri stubbornly kept his face flat.

"Drop the tray, Dimitri," she said. "I need to talk with you."

"Why would I do that?" Dimitri asked.

Images from her fight with Pryanth played on an endless loop through his mind, over and over until he felt a scream rising in his throat. But who did he want to scream at?

"Fine," she said. "You want to stay here and serve drinks all night? Be my guest."

Dimitri didn't understand. He thought he'd burned this bridge, had spent a lifetime perfecting that very art. Why was she so gods-damned determined to scramble across?

"Look," Analia said, reading his face. "I'm sorry I didn't stand up to Pryanth. I'm sorry that I can, and you can't, and I can't imagine how many times Pryanth has forced you to bite your tongue. But if it makes you feel better, I believe I just thoroughly flattened his pride—and instead of chasing after him, I'm here with you."

She reached for his tray. "So, are you coming, or not?"

Dimitri shifted. Everything in him told him to run, run before she could first. Yet, this was her, chasing after him. He couldn't remember the last time someone had done that.

Finally, he passed her the drink-laden tray. She promptly set it on a nearby table, then headed back into the crowd.

"You could apologize, too, you know," she said.

"For what?"

"For biting my head off," she suggested. "For sulking. For being a petty baby."

Dimitri snorted. "Flashfire, if you expect me to apologize for that last one, I would never stop."

He made to continue forward, but Analia pinched his sleeve, pulling him out of the way of a couple drunkenly dancing to the music. Dimitri looked at them, then down at the hand gripping his sleeve instead of his arm. "Sorry," he mumbled.

Analia nodded and released his sleeve.

"So where are we going, anyway?" he asked.

Aaron kept close to the shadows as he wove through the square, having left Analia in Lena's care. Most buildings had their doors left open, free for people to wander in and out of as the night progressed. Also free for him to peek inside as he passed.

Surce's tapestry had been too focused on the scroll to show much surrounding detail, but Aaron had enough to compare. Gold room. A polished wood shelf with what looked to be dusty books surrounding the scroll.

Too bad everything in the Sun Kingdom was gold. Too bad he couldn't request a fortune-telling tapestry to be more helpful without the fortune-telling seamstress thumping him on the side of the head.

He was just thinking he'd have better luck heading for the woods when he heard his name carry across the quiet street. Aaron turned.

Analia was heading toward him, followed by Dimitri of all people.

"Why are we finding *him?*" Dimitri complained.

"Because he knows everything."

"You told him?"

"Yes, Dima."

Dimitri's face twitched as if he'd never heard the nickname before. Yet, he remained silent as Analia turned to Aaron and asked, "Will you come with us?"

Aaron glanced back at the shops he hadn't hit yet, but his curiosity won out. He nodded to Analia, who turned and headed back into the crowd.

"I can't believe you told *him* of all people," Dimitri went on, trailing after her.

"Let it go, Dima."

"Why would you do that? And when did you tell him? After how long it took you to tell me, he better have gotten the same treatment."

Aaron began, "Well—"

Dimitri rounded on him, "We're talking *about* you, not *to* you."

Aaron grinned.

"He's too pretty to be a soldier," Dimitri went on, skirting around a fellow servant carrying a tray of drinks. "Are we sure he wasn't picked up from the back alley of a bordello?"

"Why?" Aaron asked. "Are you looking?"

Dimitri scoffed. "You wish."

"Your loss. I've been told my services are top quality."

"Oh, I'm sure your left hand has wonderful things to say about you, Bordello."

"Children," Analia muttered, settling herself beneath a large tree at the edge of the crowd. "I am dealing with children."

Dimitri gave a half shrug, but Aaron's laugh was strained as he sat on a gnarled tree root.

"Why are you dealing with us, anyway?" Dimitri asked. "Shouldn't you be with that pompous prince of yours?"

"That prince of mine," said Analia flatly, "is currently dealing with the revelation that I'm not as *untainted* as he'd like me to be."

It took a moment for the words to click in Aaron's mind. Then, he leaned forward, fist tightening around his tree root. "He walked away from you?"

"You had *sex?*" Dimitri shouted.

Analia gave him a withering look. "Yes, Dima. Thank you for informing the entire kingdom."

"I can't believe you did that!" Dimitri said.

"No one cares in the Ash Kingdom!"

"No, I can't believe you told Pryanth." Dimitri cackled, actually drumming his heels on the ground with glee. "Oh, Flashfire, you just took a needle and popped that prick's pride like a soap bubble." He mimed the action, making a popping noise with his mouth.

Analia blushed. "I wasn't intending to do that."

Dimitri laughed even harder, falling back against the tree trunk. Analia turned to Aaron for help, but he, too, was fighting for composure.

"He is rather fragile," Aaron said apologetically. Analia groaned.

Aaron half-heartedly attempted to stifle his spike of wicked satisfaction. As far as he could tell, that standard had fallen away outside of the Royals—although if something so innocuous was enough to set Pryanth off...

"So," Dimitri said with a grin, "who'd you sleep with?"

"Why do you care?" Analia demanded. "It's not like you'd know him."

"Was it Rois?"

"Aaron!"

"Who's Rois?" Dimitri asked.

"A sullen Ash Crystal Guard."

"Really!"

"He wasn't a guard when I met him," Analia broke in, her cheeks flaming.

"So, there's a story, too?" Dimitri asked. He settled back against the tree, clasping his hands and staring at her attentively.

Analia glared at Aaron. "This is your fault," she informed him.

Aaron raised his hands in surrender, but he couldn't help his curiosity. He, too, leaned back against the tree trunk and waited.

Analia toyed with her phoenix pin for a few moments, clearly reluctant. But finally, she began.

"Rois and I met a few years ago in the back of a music hall. Ember had been performing with her harp, and I'd found that if I sat in the back, no one paid much attention to me. Except this one day, when a human boy sat next to me and caught my eye.

"The recognition was sharp and immediate. I swear my stomach sank through my seat, through the floor, and into the Hell Realm itself. It was just a matter of seconds before he sneered at me, or exposed me, or looked down his nose and turned away. But before I could do anything, he winked conspiratorially and turned forward once more.

"I didn't expect the wave of relief to be so intense. But there was something else beneath that relief. Something I didn't have a name for at the time.

"For the next few months, I couldn't go anywhere in the kingdom without spotting him. But he never stopped to say hello, never said anything. He just gave me that secretive smile. And eventually, I cracked.

"I was actually the one who found him. He was training in a back alleyway, and for a moment, I simply watched. I'd never seen someone move with a sword the way he had, like it was an extension of his arm. I'd later learn that it was his dream to be the first human member of the Ash Crystal Guard, to be good enough to stand toe-to-toe with someone that had an innate, magical advantage over him. But that day, I only got his name."

Aaron watched her carefully, but Analia's hand remained steady as she idly twisted her pin.

"Rois was the first person that ever made me feel seen. The first person that truly looked at me after…"

Analia's face briefly pinched. "That's not important. What's important was at that point, I could count on one hand how many people were willing to speak with me, let alone show any form of affection toward me. So, when Rois kissed me, I trusted him. And when he said he loved me, I believed him. And of course, that's when my father found out."

A cold knot formed in Aaron's stomach. Dimitri was enthralled.

"Rois and I had been careful to leave no tracks, let nothing get back to him. We met in alleyways, back rows of music halls, spent most of our time under the cover of night and shadowy hoods. To this day, I still don't know how he found out. When he did, I expected him to kill Rois. Or me. I knew he didn't care about what we'd been doing, just that I'd outwitted him for so long to do it.

"Instead, my father offered Rois a deal. He told Rois that he would accept Rois into the Crystal Guard, Rois's dream, as long as he cut all ties with me, and never spoke to me again outside of necessity."

Aaron spat, "And the bastard accepted?"

"Crystal fuck me," Dimitri breathed.

"And when it was done," Analia said, voice shaking, "my father told me he'd done me a favor. I should've suspected that Rois was only using me. Now, thanks to him, I knew. And I got to see him every day after that."

Aaron scooted closer. He laid his hand over hers, at a loss for words. But when Analia turned to him, her smoky eyes had hardened to flint. And Aaron couldn't look away.

"Well, fuck, Flashfire," said Dimitri.

"There's nothing we can do about it now," Analia said. "And more importantly, that's not why I brought you two here."

She looked down at Aaron's hand still atop hers. Giving him a nod of thanks, she slid her hand away. And Aaron felt a mounting sense of respect as Analia sat with those shards for a few moments, then tucked them away and outlined her investigation.

"So," Dimitri said once she'd finished, "you've ruled out your fragile prince. What about Lev?"

"Lev's out," Aaron said, filling them in on what Dannel and Lev had told him.

"That's only that night, though," Analia said. "What about during dinner?"

"I was watching him the entire time," Aaron said. "He and Warack had already started their pissing contest, and it was my turn to rein in Lev's temper."

"But what about the rest of the guard?" Analia pressed.

Aaron shrugged, unable to vouch for anyone else.

"So, now," Analia said, "we figure out if it's even possible any of the remaining present Sun people could get access to xenol, and we narrow it down from there."

As the three continued to plan, Aaron's eyes kept wandering back to Analia. After everything she'd been through, she was still fighting. Even when faced with a devastation that he himself had collapsed under.

Her resilience nearly took his breath away. He just hoped she realized she could only fight back the grief for so long.

# Chapter 31

In the weeks that followed Solemnai, Analia spent her days wandering the castle.

Now that she had found how close magic fields could be before they blurred, Deardryn wanted to test the opposite direction. Consequently, she had hidden one ring somewhere in the castle, and Analia had to walk the halls until she was able to sense the field. Aaron typically accompanied her, but some days, Pryanth did as well.

Analia had gone to him the day after Solemnai, braced for a thunderclap. Just for him to act as though nothing had happened—which was infuriating. But the more he told her he was fine, the longer the tension stretched, the more Analia started to wonder if her questioning was why things didn't feel fine.

Eventually, her frustration disintegrated into a quiet nudge of guilt. Now, she couldn't help the jolt of anticipation each time she saw him, wondering which version she would see. Bracing herself for the thunderclap, feeling her pull toward the kingdom grow stronger every time she was touched by the warmth of the sun.

As they strolled hand in hand through the castle halls, Analia decided Pryanth simply had moods, like everyone else. Justifiable ones at that. Gods, if she could survive Brenn for twenty-two years, she could handle a little moodiness no problem.

The day finally arrived when the cargo ships would be docking. Not being able to think of a lie, Analia figured asking directly couldn't hurt. Othin was clearly unenthused, but Deardryn waved away his concerns—"It's the docks, Othin."

Now, Analia walked across the crescent-shaped port connected to the Serpent's Tail. One of the three main rivers that ran throughout Elefthia, the wide expanse of water was a near-perfect crystal blue, kept clean by the various river nymphs and other magical species that darted beneath the surface. Massive cargo ships lined the port, bobbing in the gentle current as their crews went about unloading, their shouts echoing off the water.

Analia and Aaron meandered through the crowd, Analia generating small talk while Aaron offered his assistance with the boats. Yet, it became increasingly obvious that their chances of finding xenol were slim.

Even though the Serpent's Tail tumbled down from the peaks of the Wind Kingdom, flowing southeast to Mist territory and curving around to Moon, most exports were domestic. The majority were from the farmers to the south and the miners to the west, taking advantage of the faster water transport. Analia knew there weren't any embargoes, but she supposed she'd severely underestimated just how tense trade negotiations had become.

Unwilling to ask too many questions, Analia and Aaron turned to go.

"Well," he said, leading the way back to their carriage, "at least we know one thing."

"What's that?" Analia asked.

"That if it hasn't come by boat, it's probably come by land."

Analia paused midstep to look at him. Aaron only winked and opened the carriage door for her.

"It's called the Bend," Dimitri said.

Upon arriving back at the castle, Analia and Aaron had grabbed him, the three now sitting on the Sun Castle roof. It was quickly becoming their unofficial meeting spot, the wind carrying away their words from any listening ears.

Dimitri took a folded piece of paper from his pocket and smoothed it out across the sunbaked roof. Analia peered down from where she perched on the parapet, realizing it was an age-worn map of the central Sun Kingdom.

The square sat in the center of the map, all streets fanning out like radiating sun rays. The map even had streets and businesses labeled, notes on the prominent clans that inhabited each zone scribbled along the edges.

Dimitri drew a jagged line across one of the outermost sections with a finger. "It's a network of drug dens, underground taverns, brothels, the seediest shit you can imagine."

"Did you make this?" Analia asked.

"Of course not," he scoffed. "I stole it—don't give me that look. Some councilman left it after a meeting, and I decided it was mine for the taking."

"What are all these lines?" Aaron asked, swiping the map.

Dimitri tried to snatch it back. "They're nothing."

"No, look," Aaron said, sitting back against the parapet and bringing the map close to his face. "We have the taverns, the music halls, a little pathway, oh that's cute, there are little arrows along the side."

"Give me my map before I push you off the gods-damned roof." Dimitri finally managed to snatch the map from Aaron's hands. Ears turning red, he smoothed it out once more, almost reverently.

Aaron turned to Analia, mildly insulted. "I never expected the most popular way to off me to be pushing me off a roof."

"I told you," she said, "we want to see if you'll bounce."

"Or if you won't," Dimitri muttered.

Aaron's eyes sparkled with amusement. Analia smiled to herself.

It was getting easier to do that lately. She hadn't realized how heavily her lies and secrets had been pressing on her spine. Even if she had, she never would have suspected relief would come in the form of sharing the load.

"So," she said, interrupting Dimitri midcomplaint, "why should we look here?" She slid off the parapet, seating herself beside Aaron.

"Drug dens don't play by the same rules as the rest of the kingdoms," Aaron explained. "They're much more... diverse."

"What does that mean?" Analia asked.

Dimitri said, "It means foreign drugs have higher prices than domestic. A dealer from Ash can spend seven silver chips on an ounce of devinroot and sell it for a shit-ton more here where it doesn't grow."

"People go to one of the dens," said Aaron, "looking for a good time. They're offered something exotic, something they've never had before. They think, 'sure, I'll give it a try.' Next thing you know"—he snapped his fingers—"the dealer has a loyal customer and a constant flow of gold pieces."

"Especially since around here," Dimitri said, "drug lords specialize their stash and stake claims to their turf. 'I'm always here, and I'm the only one with your drug.'"

"Sounds like you two are speaking from experience," Analia said.

Aaron scoffed. "I have the distinct pleasure of dragging half the Sun guard out of these very dens at least twice a week."

Dimitri cackled. Analia turned back to the map.

She could see how these dens operated. The square itself was densely populated with stores, vendors, and the like. Heavy flows of traffic made it easy to slip in and out of buildings as one of the crowd, unseen, unnoticed. Especially toward the outer layers, full of hidden cracks that any sort of business could burrow into.

"But would dealers trade in a more-than-likely rare poison?" she asked.

"Uh, yes," said Dimitri.

"Not all of them, though," Aaron said. "Most dens are designed around having a good time and making a quick piece. Black market poisons wouldn't fly in a lot of those places."

Analia drummed her fingers on the roof. "We can probably cross off all the brothels," she decided. She reached to trace her finger across the main section, but Dimitri stopped her with a glare. "Gods, all right, I won't touch it."

"We can axe the more common drug dens as well," Aaron agreed.

"That still leaves fifteen spots," Dimitri said, eyes darting as he counted them up.

"Sixteen," Aaron corrected. He pointed a finger, "You missed Gritta's, top left—"

"It's not going to be there," said Dimitri sharply.

Aaron looked up from the map. "No, I'm almost certain—"

"Fine, you want to waste our time looking there? Then *you* check that one."

"All right, fifteen," Aaron said, raising placating hands. "I'm sorry for questioning your black-market expertise."

"Don't think that wall is high enough to save your ass, Bordello."

"I could move to one of the gaps if that would make it easier."

Dimitri finally looked at Aaron. The guard flashed a grin, and Dimitri rolled his eyes. He dropped his gaze back to the map, and Aaron and Analia swapped a puzzled look.

"So," Dimitri asked, "how are we supposed to hit all of them?"

"Well," Analia said, "I won't be hitting any of them."

Both men looked at her quickly. Analia stretched, returning to her perch on the parapet as she briefly explained her interactions with Othin.

Dimitri complained, "So, because you don't know how to be inconspicuous and have a target on your back, we have to do all the work?"

"I could come," Analia said, leaning back on her hands. "And then I would inevitably lead Othin directly into the heart of what we're doing, which would not only jeopardize my mission, but also your chance of ever getting out of this castle."

She coolly met Dimitri's gaze. He wrinkled his nose, then turned back to his map.

"I still don't know how you expect us to make it through all of these," he said.

Analia stared out across the kingdom, her mind jumping back to one of the first times Accalon had caught her sitting on the edge of the turret roof.

"Little fledgling," he'd said, sitting beside her. "All fledglings know they must fall before they can fly. But the wise ones know they can soar just as high from the fall of a hop."

She braced herself for the slash, but to her surprise, the memory was only a quick prick.

"We go one by one," she declared.

"No," Dimitri corrected, "Bordello and I go one by one."

Analia and Aaron shared an amused look.

"We can speed things up if we divvy the houses between us," Aaron said to Dimitri. He let his hand hover over the map, and Dimitri gave him a begrudging nod.

Aaron swiftly sectioned off the houses. If they were lucky, they would have the location narrowed down within a little less than two weeks. Giving Analia just enough time before the Solstice to have a nice long chat with whatever dealer they manage to find.

Since when did Dimitri's deal with Analia involve doing work?

Every night for the following two weeks, he dragged his sorry ass through the secret passageways, waiting for whatever guard was on watch at the little-known side door to doze off so he could scuttle past. Just as he'd done the first time he'd escaped the castle.

Meanwhile, Aaron could come and go as he pleased. Gods-damned guard privileges. Not needing a reason, permission, to leave the castle. Although Dimitri had to admit, Aaron was helpful in dealing with the guards at the golden gates, somehow getting them to not ask questions as the two slipped out into the kingdom beyond.

Starting at opposite ends of the Bend, the two worked toward each other. Dimitri's nights became a haze of dark, broken veins; hollow eyes and sunken cheeks; fingers that trailed seductively down his arm. Every aspect of the Sun Kingdom the Old Hag wanted to disappear, shoved to the outskirts like dirt swept into shadowy corners. Yet, there was no sign of the drug lords.

"Are you sure we shouldn't check Gritta's?" Aaron asked one night as they passed the well-maintained building.

Dimitri's stomach flipped, and he quickly shut down the idea. Aaron shot him a frustrated look, but Dimitri turned to inspect the nearby buildings.

He didn't care that he could smell the decay around him. Being out every night beneath the open sky was still a cruel tease at freedom.

His gaze drifted back to Gritta's inn. Easy to get out, but impossible to stay out.

He had no desire to go back there. But of course, with each passing night of failures, Dimitri could feel the inevitability looming closer on the cool night breeze.

"Listen," Aaron said one night, stepping out of the darkness with no warning.

Dimitri jumped, nearly stumbling into a sour pool of vomit. Aaron didn't pause.

"One of the dealers from my last spot said there was a new drug lord at Gritta's. Marcos. Came about three years ago, all commodities from Moon."

Dimitri fought back a curse. Of all plants, Analia just had to investigate that one. And he only had this one spot left. And Aaron was giving him that piercing look again.

"Fine," Dimitri snapped, reaching for the doorknob to the den. "We'll check it—"

The knob came off in his hand. For a moment, both men stared down at the rusted knob in Dimitri's palm.

"Tomorrow," Aaron decided.

Dimitri nodded silently. He tossed the knob away with a heavy clang, almost as heavy as the dread forming in his stomach.

# Chapter 32

Analia pushed through the brothel's creaky wooden door, Aaron's arm draped across her shoulders.

Apparently, it was the Sun military's preferred spot, spending enough time inside to keep the place afloat all on their own. Lev in particular swaggered through often enough to have a suite constantly on hold for him, which Aaron got access to, Crystal knew how. But knowing they were likely to find Marcos that night and needed a private place to talk with him, this was their best option.

Analia kept her face hidden beneath her hood as they moved into the dimly lit main room. Aaron had given her his Crystal Guard cloak, and between the shadow of the hood and her pinned-back hair, he was confident she could go unrecognized.

Waving to the workers scattered across nearby couches, he led the way to a small, central table. The dark-haired woman behind it looked up from the papers before her, and Aaron flashed a flirtatious smile.

The woman, who clearly had been briefed ahead of time, didn't remark how it was unusual for men to bring their own companions. She merely accepted the gold Aaron slid to her, blushing under his gaze as she scribbled something down and beckoned them toward a back staircase.

"Top floor," she said, handing Aaron a small brass key.

Together, Analia and Aaron climbed the winding stairs, passing numerous rooms carved into the stone walls, the occupied rooms mostly muffled through the doors. Reaching the top, Aaron unlocked their door and bowed Analia through.

The room was unsurprisingly occupied by a large bed, the dark stone walls lined with wooden chairs. A wide window looked out across the backside of the kingdom square, lined with thick burgundy curtains that Aaron promptly pulled closed.

Analia sat at the foot of the bed, wrapping her arms around her middle. She watched as Aaron checked the room for, what, magical ears? Actual eavesdroppers? Seemingly satisfied, he flopped down on the bed beside her.

"You know," he said, nudging her side with his boot, "we have some time before I have to meet Dima."

Analia's eyes flew wide open. She twisted, her unease melting away, just to see Aaron's mouth quivering. She pulled off her slipper and swatted him with it, his laugh breaking free.

"You're having too much fun with this," she complained.

"Undoubtedly." Aaron sat up and adjusted her hood, then rose to his feet. He would be slipping out through the window, moving across the neighboring roof below and climbing back down to the street. While they couldn't have snuck in this way without risking someone barging into the supposedly empty room, it was the perfect way to slip Marcos in and out unseen.

"What if this takes a while?" Analia asked.

Aaron smirked. "They'll just think I'm another Sun soldier having an extremely good time with the modest maiden I managed to charm."

Analia hid her face in her hands.

"Oh, I almost forgot." Aaron tossed her something he pulled from his pocket. "For while you're waiting."

Analia reflexively caught it, then stared down at the phoenix pin in her hand. She'd reluctantly left it behind, knowing it would destroy their mission if anyone downstairs happened to spot it.

When had Aaron grabbed it? She looked up to thank him, but he was already gone.

Dimitri couldn't suppress his wave of nausea as he stepped into Gritta's.

Everything was just as he remembered. The front room held sagging couches off to one side, sticky wooden tables in another. The majority of the room was open space, people writhing to the music that thudded from some unseen magical source. Smoke hung in a thick haze across the room, sweet and burning as Dimitri inhaled.

Beside him, Aaron picked at the peeling paint on the wall, looking less than impressed. He'd met up with Dimitri after smuggling Analia to the brothel, his fighting leathers replaced with a deep blue shirt and dark pants. Dimitri didn't see any of his usual daggers, but he knew they were stowed away in his boots and Crystal knew where else.

"Dagger marks," Aaron mused, still poking at the wall. "Through multiple layers of paint, too."

"Turf wars," Dimitri grunted. "Just violent and frequent enough to make a point to competition without getting on the Old Hag's radar."

Aaron glanced at him, the question in his eyes obvious even in the dim light.

"So, Bordello," Dimitri said quickly, gesturing to a pretty blonde girl who was leading a stumbling man into one of the side rooms. "Which room was yours?"

"Third one on the left," said Aaron casually.

"Really? How cozy."

"It was. I only had it on Tuesdays, though. They liked to shift us around to make sure no one got greedy with just one of us."

Dimitri snorted. Aaron grinned and beckoned Dimitri into the shadows.

"This place is packed," he said in a low voice. "We should linger for a bit, establish ourselves before asking around."

"Fuck that," Dimitri said, shoving away from him. "You want to waste your time chatting up the crowd, be my guest." Dimitri, however, would be getting out of there before his skin crawled all the way off his body.

Not waiting for Aaron, he marched over to a group of men slumped on a couch, drinks and pipes in hand. He snapped his fingers under the nose of the most lucid-looking man.

"All right, huff-and-puff," he said, raising his voice over the music. "Where's your dealer?"

The man blinked, pale eyes bloodshot. A sluggish smile stretched across his lips. "Why? Are you buying?"

Dimitri stomped away, muttering under his breath. He made quick work of the room, moving from group to group, demanding to know where Marcos was. Most people looked at him blankly before trying to shove him away. One girl giggled at the name, tracing a circle around her eye and blowing a lungful of violet smoke in his face.

"All right," Dimitri said, slamming his palms on a table hard enough that the lone glass rattled. "Where's your dealer?"

The single occupant looked up, revealing a man with the upper half of his face obscured by a black metallic mask—not uncommon in the space—hammered in intricate designs. Dark, wavy hair partially fell across his covered forehead. His deep blue, almost black eyes were far sharper than the ones Dimitri had been looking into all night.

Beautiful. Gods damn it all.

"Well?" Dimitri demanded.

The man took a long drink. "You annoy me," he said, putting down his glass.

Dimitri's ears burned. "Listen here, you masked marauder," he hissed, leaning across the table. "I don't give two copper shits about your—"

"That's enough of that," a chilly voice purred in Dimitri's ear. Just as the cold edge of a dagger slid against his throat. And Aaron stepped into his peripheral vision.

"What the..." Dimitri began, but Aaron cut him off with a glance that could have frozen a candle flame. All around, patrons' glazed eyes flicked in their direction.

Images flashed across Dimitri's mind. Him, stumbling inside. Pinned against the wall. A group of men, stinking of withdrawal. A flash of light—

"Took you long enough to grab him," the stranger said, taking another imperious drink from his glass.

Aaron shrugged, the blade against Dimitri's throat twitching against his pounding pulse. "Where's the fun in a game cut short?"

Dimitri jerked away from the stares to glare at Aaron. The guard's hand tightened on his shoulder, pressing his dagger just enough for a bead of blood to ooze down his throat.

Crystal strike him down. He never should have trusted Aaron, trusted Analia. It was all a setup, wasn't it? How had the Old Hag found out what happened here?

Dimitri writhed in earnest. Aaron shoved him against the table, grabbing one of his arms and yanking it up and behind his back.

"What did I tell you?" Aaron asked the man. He tugged slightly on Dimitri's arm, and Dimitri gasped.

The man watched, indifferent. "Get him outside," he said. "If you figure out what he's hooked on, I might just hand some over." His dark eyes sharpened. "For a price, of course."

Dimitri's eyes widened. Aaron remained unfazed.

"It'll be less work on my part to let him sweat it out," he said. "I apologize he interrupted your evening."

Aaron turned Dimitri around. Without further comment, he swiftly marched him toward one of the side doors, Dimitri squirming under the scrutiny of the crowd.

Aaron dragged Dimitri out into a cramped alleyway, kicking the door shut behind them. Trash bags overflowed out of a nearby dumpster, the scent of sun-rotten trash forcing Dimitri to breathe through his mouth.

Wrenching out of Aaron's grip, Dimitri whirled on him. "What the fuck was that?"

Aaron rocked back on his heels. "That was us, finding the dealer."

"That was *me* finding the dealer," Dimitri corrected, "and you dragging my ass out of there like a drug-addled child!"

"To be fair, you could've just cooperated and avoided that scene entirely. Although I suppose it made it appear more realistic."

"Realistic? You can't be serious! How did you know it was him in the first place?"

"I let you draw him out," Aaron said simply.

*"Let me?"*

"Marcos is a foreign drug lord," Aaron explained, still rocked back on his heels. "He was going to need incentive to show his face, and if he recognized me and thought I was looking for him, nothing would guarantee him fleeing faster. But an angry, passably high servant hunting him down? That would draw his interest. Enough that he was tracking you the moment you marched over to that second group."

Dimitri's ears burned. This man had purposefully wound him up like a spring and set him loose, just so he could sit back, watch, and wait?

"Besides that, though," Aaron went on, "even if for some inexplicable reason he didn't run, those patrons are notorious gossips, and they definitely recognized me. And we don't need rumors of a Sun guard's interest in a drug lord getting back to the castle."

"No," Dimitri muttered, "but it's fine for a servant to be interested. Insignificant, unimportant little servant."

He sent a vicious kick into a nearby garbage bag, trash scattering across the alleyway.

"Just because it makes you angry doesn't mean it's not true," Aaron said. "Nor that we shouldn't use it to our advantage."

"Use it," Dimitri said, "or use me?"

It was so typical. Used, manipulated, tossed aside. The bastard servant that was stared at so often that one more time shouldn't make a difference. Aaron was no better than the rest of them. He didn't even have the decency to look apologetic. No, he had the audacity to fold his arms and glare right back.

"If I had asked you to go in there, make a scene, and then let me drag you out so I could establish contact, would you have done it?"

"Maybe."

Aaron scoffed. "If 'maybe' means 'Fuck you, do it yourself,' then I concur."

"Don't twist this back on me," Dimitri fumed. "I have every right not to want to be used."

"No," Aaron said. "I suppose you prefer to be the user." He idly flipped the blade previously pressed to Dimitri's throat. "Using Analia to get out of the castle. To learn how to read. As leverage with the Royals if something were to go sour for you."

Dimitri's fist tightened around the dumpster's rim. Who was Aaron to judge how he survived? Who was he to trigger the prickle of guilt across Dimitri's skin?

Aaron waited for Dimitri to respond, but he only seethed in silence.

"I'm going back in to talk with Marcos," he finally said, turning to the door. "You're free to go if you like. Scuttle back to the castle and think of fifty different ways to kill me in my sleep.

"Or," he turned halfway to face Dimitri once more, "you can stay and finally decide to help someone other than yourself."

Dimitri made to retort, but Aaron didn't pause.

"This is bigger than you, Dimitri. You're either in, or you're out."

Not waiting for an answer, Aaron slipped back inside.

It was the lack of remorse for what he had done that bothered Aaron more than the act itself. He supposed he had years upon years of practice suppressing guilt. Perhaps there came a point where it all simply disappeared. That possibility bothered him even more.

Aaron wound his way back through the patrons, doing a quick scan of the room. He wasn't surprised in the slightest to discover Marcos was nowhere to be found.

Taking a seat at the counter, he waved over the barkeeper and ordered a drink. While he poured, Aaron casually asked where that masked man had gone. The barkeeper waved toward a side door, saying something about bad business.

Aaron accepted his glass. Then, he slipped off the stool, melting back into the crowd of smoke and bodies. Making sure the barkeeper wouldn't see him, he started off on Marcos's tail, sliding his untouched drink on a random table as he passed.

The door the barkeeper had gestured to opened out onto another alleyway. Aaron gratefully stepped out of the stifling heat, lifting his face to the cool night air.

The alleyway was similar to the one he'd left Dimitri in—the one where he still sulked, if Aaron had to bet on it. But this was the one thing he would do for Analia without her asking. She didn't need another person betraying her.

That faint tapping of guilt started up again, but Aaron pushed it aside. Noticing a slightly disturbed pile of trash to his right, he shrugged and headed off in that direction.

It didn't take long to catch up with Marcos. The alleyway had opened into an uneven street, flanked by dilapidated buildings that a loan figure slipped past. Aaron trailed behind the drug lord, moving farther and farther away from the den. They spiraled to the edges of the central kingdom, eventually turning off the street and approaching a line of buildings, all made from rotting wood and sagging to the side.

Aaron waited until he was in hearing range, then called, "Nice hideout."

Marcos whirled, the glint of steel appearing in his hand. Interesting.

"Personally, I would've repainted," Aaron went on. "Make it a little less inconspicuously conspicuous, but I can see the appeal. Who needs back door escape routes when you have beaten-in windowpanes, I say."

Marcos's eyes flashed with recognition. He slouched back against the building, voice conversational as he said, "I'm surprised you showed your face tonight."

"Why's that?" Aaron asked.

"I would have thought you would fear being recognized. Nice chain, by the way."

Aaron's heart froze.

"Isn't it?" Aaron ran a hand along the icy chain. "It really brings out my eyes, wouldn't you say?"

"I'm more of a gold man, myself," Marcos said. "Gold goblets, gold rings, gold hands."

Marcos's sharp smile sliced through Aaron's insides, but he kept his face relaxed. So that was Marcos's type: poking, waiting to see when something moved. Either he was an incredible guesser, or...

Aaron came to a stop before Marcos, close enough to smell the sweet scent of drug-laced smoke. "You really are rude," he said. "First to my friend, now insulting my fashion sense. And all we wanted to do is ask you a few questions."

"I don't make a habit of conversing with addicts creating a scene just to find me."

"How about Crystal Guards that have orders to bring you in for questioning?"

"Crystal Guard?" Marcos choked on a laugh. "Is that what you are now?"

Three hits, all in a row. Somehow, Marcos knew.

Ignoring his icy fear, Aaron cocked his head, his mouth twisting in a savage smile. "Would you like to bet on it?"

"Gods no," Marcos said. "I'm not that dumb."

"Then I suppose that means you'll be coming with me."

Marcos shook off Aaron's hand on his arm. "I'm not that dumb, either."

"I never would have guessed you were such a damsel in distress, Marcos," Aaron said.

"Knowing who you are? I suspect anyone alone in your presence is."

Aaron stepped in close, lowering his voice. "Knowing who I am, you should know what will happen if you don't come with me."

Their eyes locked. The building creaked behind them, the sound of their otherwise silent clash of wills.

Marcos's eyes jerked to something over Aaron's shoulder. Aaron turned, and Marcos darted to the side. But Aaron was ready.

Aaron grabbed the drug lord by the collar of his shirt, jerking him back and slamming him against the building. Marcos squirmed, obviously livid.

"Well, that was exciting," said Aaron conversationally. But too easy.

Marcos slashed upward. Pain flashed up Aaron's cheekbone as the dagger sliced his cheek. He jerked his head back, his grip momentarily loosening.

Marcos tried to slip away once more, but Aaron wrapped his foot around the drug lord's ankle. He toppled to the ground, grabbing Aaron's arm to yank him down with him.

The two rolled on the stone, fighting for control of the dagger. Aaron caught a slash on his forearm, grabbing Marcos by the wrist with his other hand and twisting. Marcos hissed and let go. Aaron snatched the fallen dagger and slammed the flat of the blade against Marcos's throat.

Marcos gagged, and Aaron grabbed his arm. He just managed to pin it with his knee when Marcos's free hand latched onto Aaron's wrist, sending a burning pain lancing across his hand. He tried to jerk away, but Marcos's grip tightened. Aaron's bones groaned under the pressure, about to snap—so that's what Marcos was.

Aaron flicked his wrist around, breaking Marcos's hold. Grabbing him by the sleeve, Aaron brought his arm down and pinned it with his knee. Marcos squirmed, but Aaron grabbed his head and slammed it back, the crack echoing off the nearby buildings.

Finally, Marcos went limp. But Aaron didn't loosen his hold.

For a moment, the only sound was the two men's heavy breathing. Aaron wiped the blood from his face with the back of his hand, heart pounding.

"You done?" he asked.

Marcos snarled.

Aaron hummed in disappointment. "We're still playing that game?" he asked, voice slipping into an icy purr. "Even after I was so kind as to try and converse with you instead of removing your fingers, one by one."

He flexed his screaming hand on the hilt of the dagger, still pressed to Marcos's throat. Definitely bone cracks at the very least. And all he'd needed was a few seconds of contact.

"What will it be, Marcos?" he asked. "Will you come quietly, or shall I start collecting your knuckles?"

Aaron just managed to catch the blaze of indignation in Marcos's eyes. Then, they were wiped blank along with the rest of his face as he said, "I'll come."

"Good." Aaron helped the drug lord sit up against the wall. And in one quick move, he sliced off the tip of Marcos's left pinky.

Marcos howled, blood gushing from the wound. But Aaron was cold. He allowed Marcos to clutch his bloody hand to his chest, his eyes accusatory.

"I said I would fucking come!"

"And now you know I'm serious when I say you'll be losing more than just a fingertip when you try to slip away at the first opportunity."

Marcos sneered. "Some things never change, I see."

His gaze bore into Aaron's, waiting for the flinch.

Aaron leaned in close, practically whispering as he said, "You won't say a word about who I am. Not a comment, not an insinuation, not a peep. Because at that point, I'll have no reason not to rip you apart. Slowly, joint by joint, just so you can feel every pop, every scream of pain that tears from your throat."

He traced the curve of Marcos's throat with his dagger tip. "Am I understood?"

Marcos's eyes remained stony, but the blood drained from his face. "Fine."

Aaron paused for a long moment. Then, he leaned back, allowing Marcos to straighten.

"So, I guess it's true then," the drug lord said, allowing Aaron to grip him by the arm and lead him back up the street.

"What?" Aaron asked.

"That every story needs a monster."

Aaron's mouth twisted, just as his heart flinched.

They were halfway back to Gritta's when someone stepped out of the shadows ahead of them. Marcos stiffened, but Aaron walked on, recognizing Dimitri as he drew close.

The servant had the look of a dog prepared to bite the hand that slapped it, but Aaron only nodded at him. Obviously perplexed, Dimitri's gaze darted from Aaron to Marcos and back again, ultimately deciding on silence.

"Tell me," Marcos said, clocking Dimitri, "where are we off to?"

"We're going to talk with a friend of ours," Aaron said. And he left it at that.

# Chapter 33

Analia didn't know how long she waited in the brothel suite, anxiously rubbing her pin between her fingers. She was either about to make the biggest mistake of her life or take a massive step forward in the case. Before she could decide which, there came a tap on the window.

Analia hurriedly stashed her pin in a cloak pocket. Then, she crossed to the window, eyes widening when she saw Aaron on the other side.

"I'm fine," he promised as she opened the window.

The slash of blood across his cheek said otherwise.

Checking that her hood was securely up, he leaned across the gap between the roof and window and hoisted himself inside. Dimitri followed, as did a man dressed all in black. His dark eyes swept across the room as Dimitri moved to stand by the door.

"Well, this is unexpected," he said in a voice like velvet, unashamedly looking Analia up and down. "If you would have told me what our evening would consist of, I would have come much sooner."

"You'd like that, wouldn't you," Aaron muttered, shutting the window.

"What did you two do?" Analia demanded, taking in the smears of red across Aaron's and Marcos's skin.

Marcos smirked, raising his bloodstained hand so she could see. Aaron hid his bloody arm behind his back.

Analia turned back to the bed, muttering under her breath as she reached for a pillow-case. Behind her, Marcos laughed.

"Oh, I understand now."

There came a muffled thump and a snicker from Dimitri. Yet, when Analia turned back, she saw nothing amiss.

"Honestly," she muttered, taking one of the daggers hidden in Aaron's boot without asking. She sliced the pillowcase into strips, hoping they were somewhat clean and noting how everyone would definitely think they had a good time now.

She passed the dagger and a strip to Aaron, then turned to Marcos. "May I?"

Marcos proffered his hand. As Analia wrapped his finger, she was surprised to note the rough calluses against her skin. Clearly, she wasn't the only one examining, either, for Marcos crooned, "Musician's fingers."

Analia's face twitched.

"So attentive," he purred. He leaned in, lowering his voice, "If I let you feel the knocks on the head your friend gave me, do I get to feel something in return?"

His hand moved for her hood.

"Not happening," Aaron said, smacking Marcos's hand aside.

Marcos's lip curled, but he looked back to Analia as she tapped his mask.

"What about this?" she asked. "How much fun can we have when I can only see half your face?"

"How much fun can we have when I can barely see any of your face?" Marcos countered.

Analia tilted her head. "I suppose you have a fair point." Then, before Aaron could stop her, before she could second-guess, she flung back her hood.

Dimitri took a half step toward them, face comically shocked. Aaron jerked as if to pull her hood back up. Marcos's eyes widened. He lifted her chin, leaning close enough she could smell the smoke on his breath.

"Princess Analia Valarus," he breathed. "What kind of trouble are you getting yourself into?"

Analia's pulse thudded in her ears as she tapped his mask. Marcos pulled back. For a moment, she thought it hadn't worked. Then, Marcos pulled off his mask with a bravado Analia knew she hadn't achieved.

"Well, that explains it," Dimitri muttered.

Marcos's face was handsome: a strong jaw balanced with sharp cheekbones and arched brows. A silver piercing winked in his left eyebrow, and around his eyes were four purple rings, the ink separated at the corners of each eye.

"Don't we make for a fascinating pair?" Marcos said, tucking his mask inside his cloak. "A foreign, treasonous princess, and an oath-breaking healer from Moon."

Analia didn't respond. It had been a risky plan, one that popped into her head the moment she caught sight of that mask. One that had her reaching for the very tool she'd watched Accalon wield time and time again: trust.

Now, understanding they both had something to lose, Marcos would hopefully be inclined to talk. But those rings suggested a type of power and intelligence she wasn't completely prepared for.

"So, what will it be?" Marcos asked, taking a chair. "Love potion for that prince of yours? Although I'll warn you, those don't work on impotence."

Aaron's lips twitched despite himself. Dimitri cackled openly from the door. Analia kept her face smooth as she returned to the bed.

"Or perhaps some obsidian," Marcos continued. "Summon a demon. Now that would be exciting."

Analia fought back a shudder. Across Elefthia, there were lines where magic collected at such high concentrations that doorways could be opened. To where, or how many, no one knew for sure. What was known, though, was one just needed the proper materials, the right ritual, and an incredible amount of power to force one open for even a moment.

"I didn't know obsidian opened the Hell Realm," Analia said. She didn't know any of the materials or rituals. They had all been banned during Talitha's reign and subsequently lost to time.

"Most would prefer that it remain that way," said Marcos. "Especially since that particular door has a tendency to permit guests that like to devour the fools that try to summon them.

"Most of the time, it ends with the demon getting sucked back through the gate because whoops, it just consumed its anchor before it could completely pass over. But sometimes, the stronger demons are able to claw their way across regardless. And that's when we get rampages that aren't exactly subtle. Now that requires a tamer's touch, which is even more rare. Regardless, I get my gold, and you could be rid of that impotence problem."

"You certainly have a one-track mind," Aaron said, moving to sit on a chair behind Analia.

"I can hardly help it," Marcos said. His eyes did another slow rove down Analia's body.

She knew he was feeling for chinks he could slide a dagger through, but she couldn't suppress her blush. Marcos latched on with glittering eyes, but Analia kept her chin up.

"I'm not looking for a product, Marcos," she said. "I'm just here for information."

"Information has a cost," Marcos said.

Aaron asked, "Would you say it's greater than or equal to your life? I must admit, I have a hard time believing it's less than—"

"You're not going to kill me, guard. You'd be even worse off than you are now."

"I thought we already established it wouldn't be quick."

The quiet ice in Aaron's words sent a shiver down Analia's spine. Marcos remained perfectly still in his seat, his eyes focused somewhere over her left shoulder.

Analia heard Aaron shift behind her. Marcos's gaze flicked down to his wrapped finger.

"Call off your dog," he said, bored. "I'll talk."

That was too quick. Analia glanced over her shoulder at Aaron. He remained relaxed in his seat, but his eyes were narrowed, hand resting on one of the daggers he had slid through his belt.

Analia was surprisingly comforted by that. She turned back to Marcos, not thinking twice as she said, "Tell me what you know about xenol."

Marcos immediately straightened. "Why in the name of the Crystal are you interested in that?"

Well, that answered one question.

"You were the only one who promised to give information," Analia said.

"I never promised that type of information."

"I don't recall you promising any specific type of information," Analia said. "No limits, no boundaries."

Marcos set his jaw and glared. Analia met his gaze.

"Well, this is boring," Dimitri eventually complained. "You're just glaring at each other. At least punch each other in the face or rip each other's clothes off."

There came a quiet rasp as Aaron presumably unsheathed a dagger. Marcos grinned, swiveling in his chair and stretching his legs out across the one next to him.

"Xenol is something the Royals don't want you to know exists," he began. "As soon as it was discovered, not long after the Unleashing, all healers were instructed to destroy every shred of knowledge on it. You can't find any information on it in any of the six kingdoms. Or, at least, you shouldn't be able to."

His eyes pierced into hers, but she didn't look away.

"What does it do?" she asked.

Marcos's face twitched. "You ever heard of a damper?"

Analia nodded.

"Think of that, but better. Onyx requires a ritual, special carvings, whatever else to be transformed into a damper. But the moment you yank xenol from the ground, it's able to eat away someone's magic network."

"Eat, not plug?" Aaron asked.

"Yes, handsome, eat."

"How the fuck can a plant eat magic?" Dimitri asked.

"How do plants grow off sunlight?" Marcos asked, tipping his head back to look at Dimitri. "How do I heal with my hands, and that scarlet beauty summon flames? Well, theoretically."

Marcos gave Analia a toothy grin. Analia's fist tightened around Aaron's cloak.

Marcos waved a lazy, unwrapped hand that was no longer bleeding—why hadn't she sensed him do that? "Magic has an energy to it," he said. "Something we might not be able to touch or hold or sometimes even see, but that doesn't change the fact that it's there. And if it's there, there's something that can destroy it."

"And since the Royals were the ones to try and eradicate it," Analia said, "I'm assuming that means it can even consume a Royal magic network."

"Clever girl," said Marcos. "A Royal magic network is no different from the weakest, most pathetic Demiblessed that the Crystal took pity on." His gaze flicked to Dimitri, who flipped him a rude hand gesture. "It's not the network that's important," he went on, "it's the amount of magic rolling through it."

"So, Royal magic is simply magic, just at higher concentrations," Analia mused. "Which means, in theory, you would just need higher concentrations of xenol to shut it down."

Marcos gave her an appraising look. "Still don't want to join me over here?" he asked, gesturing to his lap. "Far more comfortable. Or I could always join you—"

Marcos twisted as something whizzed through the air. The tiny object thunked against the wall, Marcos's hand flashing out to catch it.

For a moment, he stared at the object in his palm. Then, he glared up at Aaron. "You flicked a button at me?"

"It felt disrespectful to my daggers to throw one of them," Aaron said.

"Where did you get a button?" Analia demanded, twisting to look at him.

Aaron shrugged, running his fingers along the back of his chair. Dimitri snorted, and Aaron gave Analia a lazy smile.

Analia shook her head and turned to face a still-glowering Marcos. "How long would it take to destroy a Royal's network?" she asked.

Marcos looked as though he still wanted to debate the button flinging. Finally, he shrugged, slipping the button and his bloody cloth into a pocket.

"Impossible to say. Depends on the Royal, the plant dose, how it entered the body. The basic rule is the more magic, the more xenol, which means the longer it takes."

"Well, you're a wealth of information," Dimitri muttered.

"Why do you think I'm not a healer anymore?" Marcos asked.

Analia could see Dimitri about to gleefully charge through that opening and swiftly stepped in. "Does that mean you deal it?"

Marcos gave Analia another look over, which she was disgusted to realize she'd become numb to. "Who would want to use that, let alone buy it?"

"We both know they wouldn't be using it on themselves."

Marcos smirked. "Why, little princess. What do you think it could do in the wrong hands?"

"That depends," Analia said. "Is shutting down the magic network all xenol does?"

"Does it need to do anything else?"

Analia flexed her fingers in Aaron's cloak. Careful. She had to play this extremely carefully.

"Well," she said, "if it's going to go through all the trouble to make a Royal easily disposable, it might as well finish the job, don't you think?"

"Interesting theory."

"Any merit?"

"How should I know? No one's been dumb enough to take that high of a dose. At least, not willingly."

That wasn't a no, though.

"And the people who have taken it," she went on, palms starting to sweat. "Were there any side effects?"

"Side effects?" Marcos sat up straight in his seat, gaze sharp with interest. "Like what, pray tell."

Analia only hesitated a moment. "A circular black mark on the neck."

"That's very specific."

"You already knew this wasn't hypothetical."

"True." Marcos stretched, then rose to his feet. He moved toward the bed, waving an exasperated hand at Aaron as he sat beside her. "As far as I'm aware, no. I've never heard of black marks on the neck. But my knowledge, while world-breaking for you, is rather small in the grand scheme of things. It could be completely possible. I just haven't stumbled upon a case of it."

Analia furrowed her brow. Pieces slid in and out of place in her mind, scrambling to form an image.

"Is that not what you wanted to hear?" Marcos asked innocently, resting a cool fingertip between her brows.

"What do you think?" Analia asked, brushing his finger aside.

Marcos leaned in close. "Are there any answers I can give that you want to hear?"

Too helpful. Too fast.

Over Marcos's shoulder, she saw Dimitri shake his head. She didn't need to glance back to see Aaron's expression. I always have opinions. It's just your choice.

Her choice. Her judgment. Based on that glint in Marcos's eyes, she was confident he already knew exactly what she was talking about.

"Who have you sold it to in this kingdom?" she asked.

"Othin," he said immediately. His lips twisted in a grin as Analia leaned away, unable to hide her fresh wave of anxiety.

"And I believe that is a fantastic place to stop," Aaron said, pushing Marcos back as he sat down between them.

Marcos protested, but Analia ignored him. She met Dimitri's eyes across the room, the servant looking as thunderstruck as she felt.

Othin, opposed to the marriage pact from the start. Destroying it through the death of a king and ensuing strife? It would at least explain why he had been suspicious of Analia from the start.

Analia gave herself three seconds to drown in her fear. Then, she turned to face Marcos once more.

"We'll be in touch," she told him, cutting him off midsentence.

Marcos, not seeming to mind, leaned back against the pillows. "And why do you think I'll be assisting you any more than I already have?"

"Because we're not above escorting you back to the healers."

"And you think I won't take you down with me?" Marcos asked. "The princess from the enemy kingdom that is currently looking for any reason to attack us. Consorting with the underground, the criminals, the rebels."

Marcos grinned. Analia could see the story he could tell. One that Othin would be all too quick to latch onto. The one he'd been weaving throughout their entire conversation.

"It's a good story," she said, "I'll give you that. But you're forgetting: it all comes down to your word over mine. The princess who fought for peace between two kingdoms, or the rogue healer with a god complex."

Marcos remained reclined against the pillows, that easy grin still curving his mouth. Analia waited for his next angle, her mind darting. But Marcos only laughed under his breath.

"Fiery indeed," he said. He brushed a booted foot up her thigh, high enough she jerked away. Aaron grabbed Marcos by the cloak, hauling him to his feet and leading him toward the window.

"And now the princess's handsome guard escorts me away," Marcos narrated, running his fingers across the back of her neck as he passed. "What a fairy tale."

"If this were a fairy tale," Aaron said, "I'd be able to get away with shoving you off the roof."

He slid up the windowpane, glancing back as Analia piped up.

"Be prepared to go on trial for me." She felt oddly detached, hearing her words, but not feeling as though she were the one speaking them.

Marcos glanced back, an innocent look on his face. "But if I were to go on trial for you," he said, "that would mean I would also have to reveal your uncle was my top buyer of xenol."

For the briefest moment, Analia felt nothing. Nothing at all. Then, Marcos's words slammed into her with devastating impact.

Aaron quickly nudged Marcos out the window. "Don't forget you're the only one who knows she was here," he said as he followed, pushing off and landing on the roof with a quiet thud. "If word spreads, I'll know who to come after."

The moment they were gone, Dimitri whipped around to face Analia. He opened his mouth, but she raised a hand to stop him.

Analia braced her elbows on her knees, resting her forehead against her fists. With Marcos gone, her sharp focus slowly fizzled out, leaving her cold and heavy.

What had he meant, Accalon was a buyer? Was he just familiar enough with the case, with her, to know that was the best way to get under her skin? Or was there a darker side to her uncle she never would have suspected?

Analia didn't know how long it took for Aaron to return. Dimitri let him back in through the window, Aaron coming to silently sit beside her. Dimitri, however, positively exploded.

"He's hiding something."

"I know," Aaron said, rubbing his face. "And what he did share was rather on the nose."

"But what about the bullshit about him selling to Accalon?" Dimitri asked.

"One lie doesn't mean they're all lies," Aaron said. "Although Lev did mention overhearing Brenn complaining about Accalon's monthly clandestine meetings."

Analia's head snapped up.

"But that could be anything!" Dimitri said.

"Well," said Analia, "that just means we have to verify." She pushed herself to her feet and paced the length of the room. "We treat everything he said as lies until we're able to find the xenol he sold to Othin. And if that turns out to be true…" Her voice drifted off.

Aaron and Dimitri continued to go back and forth. Analia paid little attention as she paced, turning over Marcos's words.

Even if she couldn't believe anything he'd said, the basic facts remained. Xenol was dangerous. Even if it didn't have the ability to kill, it had the ability to harm. Someone had targeted her uncle, and she wouldn't be surprised if they'd dosed him high enough that it became lethal. Analia shuddered.

Dimitri and Aaron eventually drifted off. Dimitri rose to his feet, heading for the window. He flashed Analia a look she couldn't read, then slipped out, leaving Analia and Aaron alone.

"Let me know when you're ready," Aaron said, stretching out across the bed.

Analia paced a few minutes longer. She slowed with every turn, finally coming to sit beside him. Leaning back against his raised knees, her eyes went to his wrapped arm.

"I should have forced him to heal that," she said.

"Do you think he would actually fix it and not make it worse?" Aaron asked.

Analia frowned.

"Although," Aaron went on, proffering his injured arm, "I'm not opposed to the part where you kiss it better."

Analia knocked his arm aside. "Clean your wound."

"And with this face cut, too? Just imagine what they'll be thinking we were up to."

"They'll probably assume you were bad in bed and I had to seek revenge."

Aaron laughed. Ignoring the pins, he ruffled her hair, then pulled up her hood.

"My uncle used to do that," she said, half to herself as they headed for the door.

"Did he?"

Hand on the knob, Aaron's eyes went to her shoulders. Analia made a noise of exasperation. Grabbing his injured arm, she slid it under her cloak and around her waist, hiding the wrapping from view.

"Well," he said, his fingers grazing her ribs, "since he's not here to tell you, allow me." He pulled her close, whispering in her ear, "You, my friend, were incredible."

As Aaron led her downstairs, Analia's fingers tightened around the pin in her pocket. She might have survived this time. But Analia knew her luck was about to be stretched to its snapping point.

# Chapter 34

On the afternoon of the Solstice Ceremony, the Sun Royals and guards gathered in the castle entryway.

Analia lingered at the back of the crowd, hyperaware of both Pryanth's pendant and her phoenix pin resting against her chest. It was a visible reminder of how two kingdoms were coming together. And in a matter of minutes, that story would be displayed in front of the rest of Elefthia.

Yet, it wasn't the other Royals' reactions that had Analia nervously smoothing her tight, metallic-gold gown. It was the tiny voice that wondered if maybe it would be easier if she let that story be true. Maybe she could find a way to bring justice to her uncle and still remain in a kingdom that actually wanted her.

Analia felt like a traitor for even considering it. Brushing the thoughts aside, she forced herself to focus on Deardryn, who stood in the center of the entryway. Her long, golden sleeves fell back from her hands as she moved them through the air, her magic transforming into a crystalline gateway.

The Soul Gates could only be summoned on the Summer Solstice and the days preceding and following, with each kingdom's gate only responding to the magic of the corresponding reigning Royal. They required a sharp blast of power, but in response, the gates allowed direct access to the Star Kingdom where the Solstice Ceremony took place.

One by one, each member of the crowd stepped through the gate, disappearing with a flash and quiet thrum. Analia was one of the last to approach. She could feel her shoulders tighten with every step, but she passed through the gate without pause, magic tingling across her skin as it deposited her in the remnants of the Star Kingdom.

The square was a wide, flat expanse of stone, dotted with scorch marks. Evidence of its past could be seen in the crumbling marble statues, in the dilapidated buildings that had once been shops and taverns that lined the narrow streets. Scraggly plants poked through the stone, trembling in the wind that sent pebbles skittering.

After the Shattering, the six kingdoms had decided against splitting the territory among themselves, allowing it to remain as the only neutral land they could gather on. Well, that and the Wild Lands to the south. Those, however, were saturated with the dark magic of the Ancient Ones that the Crystal had needed to release. As a result, they were wisely left alone.

Analia scanned the square, shoulders loosening a fraction as she realized Ash had not yet arrived.

"Are you ready?" Pryanth came up beside her and took her hand, almost managing to hide his apprehension as Deardryn swept toward the nearest clump of Royals.

"I don't think we have much choice."

Pryanth frowned. Analia stretched on her toes to kiss his cheek, feeling for the flame that had sparked in her chest after her uncle's death.

There was no going back. This was her test. And as Pryanth led the way after Deardryn, Analia found that spark and let it burn.

The Moon Royals were dressed in their kingdom's typical form-fitting clothes. The deep purple and black created a stark contrast with their pale skin, which was twined with intricate tattoos. They sat clustered around a long, stone table, voices hushed in conversation.

As soon as Deardryn stepped brazenly into their midst, their king rose to his feet.

"Sylas Ruanega," Deardryn greeted him, extending her hand with palm out.

Tall and lean with blue-black curls, Sylas examined Deardryn's hand with slightly narrowed eyes. Across his doublet was his kingdom's sigil: a black moon bisected by dark swords on a deep purple field.

Reluctantly, he pressed his palm to hers, his voice the low rumble of thunder. "Deardryn Oshar."

The two engaged in admittedly stiff small talk, Pryanth slowly squeezing Analia's hand tighter and tighter. Out of warning or comfort, she couldn't tell. Regardless, she didn't need it. She remained tall and straight beside him, watching as Sylas's unimpressed gaze slowly flicked from face to face, meeting his stare as his eyes landed on her.

"Who are you?" he asked, bored despite asking the question.

Well, that was a new reaction.

"Princess Analia Valarus, Your Majesty," Analia said, bowing her head.

Sylas gave her a blank look.

"My love, you've met her before," came a tired voice. A man rose from the seat beside Sylas, revealing the dark brown hair and brilliant green eyes of Patryclas.

Sylas's gaze flicked from his husband to Analia, unconvinced. Eventually, he zeroed in on the phoenix pin on Analia's chest, and she caught his look of faint recognition.

He turned to Deardryn, his thick brows raised. "How did this happen?"

Deardryn beckoned Analia and Pryanth forward, immediately launching into her tale of friction, peace, and harmony between Sun and Ash. Sylas's expression rapidly shifted from skeptical, to unimpressed, to bored, but Analia refused to look away. She'd stood up to Othin, the Sun Kingdom, and a drug lord. She would not flinch now.

As Deardryn finished her story, Sylas's gaze bounced from Pryanth's hand in Analia's to his face. "And you didn't choose Lucilla?"

Analia jerked as if slapped. Pryanth made to retort, but Deardryn gave him a deadly glance that had his mouth shutting with an audible click of his teeth. Behind Deardryn, Othin looked as though he agreed.

Sylas continued, "Accalon is barely dead for two months and Brenn is already setting a torch to everything before him—"

"Sylas," Patryclas hissed, "that's enough." He turned to Analia, his face softening. "My deepest condolences, Anna. The loss of Accalon is truly one that is felt in all six kingdoms."

Analia nodded, not trusting herself to speak.

Patryclas shot a pointed glare at Sylas.

"Yes," said the Moon King gruffly, "our condolences, Ana."

"Anna," corrected Patryclas.

"That's what I said."

Patryclas shook his head, not looking the least bit surprised.

Conversation became clipped after that, Deardryn's original warmth cooling considerably, and Sylas not having been particularly hospitable in the first place. Analia paid them little attention.

She should have been expecting this. She'd been attending these meetings for as long as she could remember. Everyone here knew her story. And one sentence from Sylas had been enough to send her flame guttering. Crystal strike it all.

The two groups finally broke apart. At some point, Pryanth had dropped her hand, and now, he moved past her. Before she could force herself to follow, Patryclas put a hand on her arm.

"I would like to apologize for Sylas," he said gently, the crowd thinning around them. "He can be... well, he can be a miserable wretch sometimes. But I am truly sorry for your pain."

She'd forgotten Patryclas's Blessing allowed him to sense the emotions of the people around him. Apparently, no amount of masking, numbing, or denying was enough to fool him either.

"Thank you," she said tightly. She could not break. Not here.

Patryclas gave her a sad look. "There truly could not have been a worse time to lose Accalon," he said, taking a seat once more and nudging out the one beside him.

"Why's that?" Analia asked, sinking into the chair. Out of the corner of her eye, she spotted Aaron lingering a few feet away, watching them closely.

Patryclas said, "Accalon was the six kingdoms' voice of reason. He couldn't squash every squabble, but he was certainly the only one trying."

"What about Deardryn?"

Patryclas kept his gaze trained on the crowd. "Deardryn may fight for peace, but it's a battle all the same. And she's not afraid of ruffling feathers."

That was certainly true.

"And tonight," he continued, "there's a tension. More so than usual. And I cannot figure out why."

"Is there anything you can do?" Analia asked. "You're rather levelheaded."

Patryclas laughed softly. "I'll try. But Analia, I'm not a Royal. I'm afraid my word doesn't hold the same weight."

Analia looked away. Patryclas patted her hand, obviously sensing her spark of resentment.

"I will do my best," he promised.

Analia nodded, lost in thought. Patryclas rose to his feet. He took a few steps toward Sylas, seated farther down the table. Then, he turned back.

"I didn't know Accalon particularly well," he said quietly, green eyes locking on hers. "But I did know just how fiercely he loved you. He would want you to remember that."

Analia flinched back. Crystal spare her, she hadn't had time to prepare for that wave of grief.

Patryclas's eyes were sad as he watched her—although something odd flickered across his face as Aaron came to take his seat. He didn't say anything, though. He only turned to quietly sit beside Sylas.

Something was off in Aaron's eyes as he dropped into his chair, but surprisingly, he made no comment.

"He's right," he said instead. "Look at them. They're all isolated in clumps. No one is mingling—what's wrong?"

Analia had also been watching the crowd, allowing her to see the moment the Ash Royals arrived. She braced herself, but that didn't stop her from recoiling as Brenn caught her eye.

Aaron's gaze followed her own. He swore, twisting in his seat to look at her.

"You do *not* have to do this," he told her.

"Yes, I do."

"Let me come with you, then."

"Aaron, you can't. He can't know that you know."

Aaron looked as though he wanted to argue but knew he couldn't. He tugged on the chain around his neck, clearly frustrated. Finally, he raised a hand, middle, ring, and pinky fingers extended.

"This is our signal," he told her, taking her hand and bending her fingers into the proper shape. "You make this behind your back, and the moment I see it, I'm getting you out."

For a moment, Analia couldn't speak as another wave of emotions slammed into her. But this time, it was mostly gratitude.

"See if you can figure out what has everyone on edge," she finally said, rising to her feet.

Aaron gave her a mocking salute. But as she headed off, Analia caught his wry smile falter.

Dimitri meandered through the secret passageways, occasionally sliding open an entrance just enough to eavesdrop on the guards and servants beyond. He was more tired than usual, undoubtedly because of Analia's scheme. Even when he wasn't physically running in gods-damned circles for her, his mind was. Especially after talking with Marcos.

Dimitri had genuinely wanted to believe Marcos had been lying about Accalon. But Dimitri knew people, and he especially knew liars. And something deep in his gut told him Marcos had been telling the truth. The only thing more shocking than that realization was the sudden twinge of sympathy he had for Analia.

Dimitri shoved the feeling aside, cracking apart the wall in the entryway. Sure, he had agreed to help Analia, and fine, he'd allowed Aaron to force a commitment out of him, but he refused to get emotionally involved. That was when things always went to shit. Speaking of which...

There seemed to be a commotion in the doorway. He easily recognized Koz's shrill voice, but who was the second voice?

Dimitri dissolved the wall, peering through the one-way window. But of course, the door was out of view.

Not wanting to get caught, Dimitri quickly backtracked. A moment later, he slunk out of the passageways and into a nearby deserted hallway, his intrigue sharpened to a serrated edge.

Every step toward Brenn was one back in time—rewinding past the Sun Kingdom, every wall slamming back down. A part of her was terrified by how easy it was to slip back into that familiar mold. Yet, just as she approached and opened her mouth, Brenn brushed past her.

Analia blinked. Once, twice. Then, she hurried after him. "Father—"

"Not now, duckling."

A jolt traveled down Analia's spine. Somehow, his voice alone had her painfully aware of how two months had stripped away two decades of calluses. Now, every raw, exposed instinct screamed at her to back away, disappear while he gave her the chance. But Analia forced herself to speed up.

"I thought you would want an update," she said.

"Have you identified Accalon's killer?" Brenn asked.

"Well, no, but—"

"Then I don't care."

Brenn spared her a single, disdainful glance. Then, he continued toward the rest of the reigning Royals at the mouth of the path to Mt. Raegyr, leaving her alone in the center of the square as they departed.

That was it? He had just dismissed her, brushed her off as if it wasn't even worth his time to taunt her anymore.

But she had finally done something right. She'd narrowed down the suspect list, she'd tracked down Marcos and learned all about xenol—although the truth in Marcos's words was admittedly murky at best.

Across the square, Analia spotted a Mist guard—dressed in her kingdom's colors of silver and soft blue—accidentally brush against Warack. Warack whirled, snapping something Analia couldn't hear over the buzz of voices. Rois grabbed Warack and yanked him back. The Mist guard glared and continued on her way.

Yes, Patryclas was certainly right. Knowing Brenn's tendency to yank on tension until it snapped in his favor, perhaps it was best she hadn't said anything. She was right not to march after him and demand his attention.

Analia was utterly ashamed of how strong her wave of relief was. She brought a shaky hand to her phoenix pin. And someone grabbed the back of her neck.

Analia wheeled around, coming face-to-face with Othin.

Dimitri leaned back against one of the gilded pillars in the entryway, watching the argument devolve before him.

"I told you," Koz said in his nasally voice, "Her Majesty isn't here."

"I'm aware she's at the Solstice Ceremony. But I must deliver a message to her."

Dimitri peered over Koz's thin shoulder at the woman before him. She was tall and willowy, her dark brown hair pulled back in a severe bun that drew attention to her harsh jaw and wrinkled golden-brown forehead. Four golden rings circled her small, sharp hazel eyes.

Koz demanded, "How do you expect to deliver a message if she isn't here?"

"I'm assuming she'll return eventually."

Dimitri stifled a cackle.

"I can't have you sitting on the steps until she arrives," Koz insisted.

"You could always allow me inside so I may drop off my note."

The woman's gaze locked on Dimitri over Koz's shoulder. Dimitri grinned and twirled a finger around his ear. The woman's gaze shifted from glinting steel to sparkling amusement.

Koz whipped around. Dimitri slid around to the other side of the pillar, skinny enough that Koz didn't notice him. He waited until Koz was speaking to the granny healer once more, then finished his rotation.

"You need permission to enter the castle."

"You mean besides my markings?" The woman swept a stray piece of hair out of her face as though she were afraid it had been obscuring her rings. "They were enough to get me through the gates."

Dimitri could practically see the crimson shade of Koz's cheeks as they bickered back and forth. Finally, he threw up his hands and stalked away, leaving the woman smiling vaguely in the doorway.

"Get back to work," he spat at Dimitri as he passed.

"Nothing I'd rather do more," Dimitri drawled after him.

He waited for Koz's footsteps to fade down a corridor. Then, he sauntered toward the woman, offering a sarcastic applause. "Bravo, granny."

The healer's eyes twinkled with amusement. "What a vile little man," she said conversationally.

"Funny," Dimitri said. "Usually people are saying that about me."

The healer laughed. She took a half step forward, "I don't suppose you, too, will prevent my entering."

Dimitri shrugged. "I don't care if you want to see the Old—Her Majesty. But Koz wasn't lying when he said she's not here. What do you want to talk to her about, anyway?"

The woman's expression slammed shut. "That is between me and Her Majesty."

Dimitri knew his face must have lit up like a sunstone chandelier. There was nothing he loved more than secrets.

"Well, I could sneak you inside," he said, pretending to consider. "Let you drop off whatever message you have for her in her chambers, although she won't be back until tomorrow."

"You 'could'?" the healer repeated.

"Granny, I would love nothing more," Dimitri said. "But I doubt I could keep Koz away from you long enough. Well, I probably could, but I can't be bothered."

"I am perfectly willing to wait on these steps," the healer said.

"That's dumb. Just give it to a servant to deliver."

"I told you, this information is private."

"Have you ever met a servant that can read?" Dimitri asked.

This seemed to take her aback.

"They purposefully keep us illiterate around here to prevent us from snooping through their letters," Dimitri confided.

The woman's face softened slightly.

"All you'll find in here are servants who can't read a lick of what you wrote. Well, *you* won't find them in here because you can't enter."

He didn't have to mention the guards that Koz had undoubtedly dispatched to ensure she had left, nor the fact that, despite having questionable intelligence, they could read a string of words across a page.

The healer wavered. Dimitri shifted from foot to foot. Finally, he extended his hand.

"Come on, granny," he said. "I may be illiterate, but I'm not patient."

"Clearly." The healer finally dug in the pockets of her emerald robes. "I expect to be hearing from Her Majesty."

"I'll put it on her bedside table," Dimitri promised.

The healer reluctantly produced a folded note and handed it to Dimitri. And Dimitri, like the good servant he was, didn't check to make sure she was leaving as he strolled away.

Dimitri scrambled into the passageways moments later, giggling like a child as he unfurled the note. The Royals could kiss his letter-reading ass. Because indeed, as his eyes roved over the page, he understood the words before him.

Well, he could read them, but it took him a second to process. And when he did...

Dimitri's eyes widened. Clutching the note to his chest, he hurried off toward the library.

"**Y**ou just can't help yourself, can you?" Othin demanded.

Analia cringed. How much had he seen?

Othin released his hold on her neck and jerked a thumb behind him, not watching to see if she followed as he stalked off. Enough, then.

"Your Majesty," Analia began, hurrying after him with the unavoidable air of a misbehaving child, "I was only trying to speak with my father."

She couldn't lie, that would only make it worse. But if she was fast enough, somehow managed to cut off the winds before they could build—

"Yes, I'm sure you had a great many things to say to him."

Too late.

"Were you going to tell him how you manipulated our sundial?" Othin asked. "How you used our people's customs to twist them onto your side?"

"I didn't—"

"Or perhaps you were going to tell him of all the herbology books you've been reading—yes, I know about those. Lev discovered them after escorting you back to your chambers. Not many legends or fairy tales in those. Although the way they disappeared certainly could have been taken from one."

Analia stumbled on the uneven stone. How had—Dimitri. Crystal spare her, how could she explain that one?

"Your Majesty," she began.

"Who is it?" Othin demanded, voice trembling with rage. "Who have you poisoned against my family?"

"No one!"

"Is it that guard of yours? You certainly spend a great deal of time with him."

Chills ran down Analia's spine.

"Or perhaps it's someone outside the kingdom entirely. You and Patryclas seemed to be getting on nicely—"

"He was sharing his condolences," Analia blurted.

Othin's face spasmed, but it was too late to stop.

"He was being kind," Analia said, voice shaking slightly. "Just as Aaron was trying to be kind when he let me into the library when we were found, with a legends book, in the legends section."

"Kindness," Othin spat, "is that your excuse? Kindness is only a tool to soften your target so the knife will go in easier."

Analia scrambled for a response as they rounded a building, temporarily obscuring them from view. Othin immediately slammed her against the wall, her head whipping back against the stone with a painful crack.

"Here's the thing about kindness," he said, leaning in close. "I don't need it to dig my knife in. You may have Pryanth and even Deardryn fooled, but I see you testing the line. And the second you step across, I will be there, and I will not hesitate."

His hands tightened on her shoulders. "I will not let you harm my family. Understand?"

Analia stared mutely into his eyes. She knew that look, knew Accalon was the only one that had ever stood between her and that type of hatred.

Othin didn't wait for a response. He shoved away and headed off once more, Analia refusing to touch the lump on the back of her head as she followed.

Othin was getting far, far too close. Although if Lev had found the books, why hadn't he told Othin about their brief encounter in the kitchen? Had he forgotten? Not put the pieces together? Or perhaps he had told Othin, but Othin didn't want her to know.

If that were the case, Marcos's story was starting to become more and more plausible. And Othin's threats more acute.

They stepped back into the group of Sun people. Othin jerked his chin at a nearby bench, the message clear: sit here, and don't move.

Analia silently complied. She watched Othin stalk past Pryanth, who was seated on some nearby steps, instead heading for Cabir. He clapped Cabir on the back, Cabir saying something that had him letting out a booming laugh a moment later.

Pryanth frowned. Clearly, he noticed how once again, Othin had ignored him in favor of someone else.

Analia vaguely wondered if she should say something, but Pryanth didn't look at her. So, she remained quiet, focusing on calming her nerves until Aaron appeared beside her. He sank down on the bench, his face far more sober than usual as he stared out across the square.

Analia rested her knee against his, finally earning a brief glance. "What's wrong?" she asked.

"I've never seen it before," he replied, eyes on the one preserved marble fountain. "I know all the stories, what happened here, but it's different actually seeing it."

Analia didn't know what to say to that.

Countless minutes ticked by, the only sound Othin and Cabir's conversation and the whistle of the wind across stone.

"Did you find anything out?" she finally asked.

"Yes," Aaron said on an exhale. "And you're not going to like—"

"Kira!" Pryanth yelled suddenly, sitting up straight on the steps.

Kira, a younger Wind Princess who had been trying to skirt around the group, paused midstep. She wore her kingdom's colors of lavender and navy, her cloak lined with fur made necessary by the kingdom's cold temperatures. She looked over at Pryanth, her expression unreadable.

"It's been too long," Pryanth said with far more eagerness than usual. His eyes darted first to Analia, then Othin. "We must catch up."

"We will," Kira said with what Analia suddenly realized was rage. "At the post-release meeting. When we discuss who has been killing our Royals."

# Chapter 35

It was tradition to share a glass of wine in the Star Castle's Council Chamber while the Royals recovered from such a massive release of magic. As far as Analia could remember, these gatherings had been civil, some even managing lukewarm. This year, however...

The magic released at the foot of Mt. Raegyr felt more like an explosion. Shock waves blasted outward, slamming into Analia and sending her tumbling back to the bright white light, the same muffled silence that had seized her when she put on the three Royal rings.

She didn't know how long Aaron shook her by the shoulders, calling her name. All she knew was he didn't let go of her as she sagged against him, power still tingling through her mind.

It wasn't long until the sources of all that power came stalking back into the square. Judging by Brenn's outrage, Sylas's vague displeasure, and Deardryn's disturbed expression, news of the Royal deaths had reached them. But they didn't speak a word as they gathered their people, leading the way to the elegant silver castle.

Even though the Star Castle had been restored enough for an annual stay, pieces of its past still lingered. It could be seen in the cracks in the geometric windows, the black marks that marred the silver stone walls and midnight-blue carpets. Marks not just caused by flame or wind, land or water, light or darkness, but the destructive force of all six.

Relics of the late King Hester could be found in the rubble that lay at the center of the Throne Room. Everyone had been sealed inside as the Royals' blast shot through the corridors, so powerful that Hester's bone fragments were the only remains to be found.

"This feels wrong," Aaron mumbled as he looked away. "Like we're walking through someone's grave."

Analia didn't respond. As far as she was concerned, with all the lives King Hester and Queen Elspeth had taken, it was.

It wasn't that King Hester had originally done anything particularly egregious. He'd simply done what many kings with power tried to do: obtain more. It wasn't until the kingdoms fought back that they discovered just how deep King Hester's and Queen Elspeth's cruelty ran.

It had been seven years of wartime atrocities. Prisoners of war taken from the Battle of the Fist, tortured to the point that their screams were said to be heard through the layers of rock that separated their dungeon cells and the Star Castle above. The horrific practice of suspending suspected spies in the square, stomachs slashed open and forced to slowly bleed out. The worst had been when Elspeth had trapped an entire legion in the Free Fall Wood and set it ablaze, killing every person inside with smoke or flames.

That type of fury? Well, perhaps it rivaled that rolling off the six reigning Royals, magic networks flaring as they silently stalked ahead.

Finally, Deardryn pushed open the Council Chamber door. The room was large, with the back wall replaced by a floor-to-ceiling window that displayed the sunset outside. Crystal chandeliers shone with balls of silver light, the Royals not bothering to maintain the electricity in the castle that worked in tandem with magic across the rest of the kingdoms.

Analia could feel the barely suppressed power roll across the chamber like an impending storm. Yet, the Royals remained terrifyingly silent as they sat around the massive table, its surface painted with the Star Kingdom's sigil: a silver constellation of the Crystal on a black field. And only when the last Royal received their goblet of wine did the accusations begin to fly like a volley of arrows.

"Four of us!" Diantha, the Wind Queen, eventually called over the noise, brushing back her shoulder-length, dark brown hair. "A Wind Prince, two Ash Royals, and a Sand Princess. We've never lost so many Royals from so many kingdoms in one year's time."

"Could we have displeased the gods?" asked Roka, Queen of the Mist Kingdom. Her dress wrapped around her slender frame like a sheath, the brilliant blue and silver bringing out the vibrant blue of her eyes and cooler tones of her dark brown skin.

"Well, we certainly haven't done anything," Oberon said. The Sand King was built like a boulder, with a bald head and toasted-brown skin. He folded his arms, the fine burgundy-and-bronze fabric of his jacket stretching across his muscles.

"What's that supposed to mean?" Brenn demanded.

"Well," Sylas mumbled, "Ash is the only one to have lost not one Royal, but two."

Brenn kicked back his chair and jolted to his feet. "Are you suggesting my brother could have done anything to anger the gods?"

Aeley grabbed Brenn by the lapel of his gray jacket and jerked him back into his chair. Analia waited for Brenn to round on her, flames blazing. But Brenn only took a gulp of wine, his face red.

"I don't think anyone here was suggesting that," Patryclas soothed. He put a hand on Sylas's arm, but the Moon King had already returned his gaze to his wine glass, appearing almost painfully bored.

"He makes a fair point, though," Oberon said. "Who said it had to be Accalon that displeased the gods?"

Brenn's eyes flashed to Analia. *Worst decision I ever made.*

Analia took a long sip of wine, provided by Wind. She'd originally found it to be too dry, but now her puckering taste buds felt appropriate.

"Why are we so convinced this is the gods' doing?" Diantha demanded, her almond-shaped eyes darting. "It's not one kingdom being struck, but three. How likely is it that all of us angered them?"

"What are you proposing, then?" Deardryn asked.

"It seems far more likely that it's some sort of creature," Diantha declared.

"That wouldn't surprise me," Oberon muttered.

"Here we go." Brenn threw up his hands. "The annual speech about how we disrespect the land by eating its creatures and using them for work."

"With the way you disrespect your fellow humans," Oberon said, "I'm surprised you don't eat them, too."

"I would if they weren't so stringy." Brenn bared his teeth in a grin. "Don't forget, Oberon, just because you survive off of twigs and berries doesn't change the fact that you lost a Royal, too."

The stone rippled beneath Analia's chair.

"A land creature makes sense," Patryclas said smoothly, his face oddly pale. "It would explain some of the details that seem like oddities to us, like its movement patterns. Perhaps it is a being capable of tracking Royal magic."

A collective shudder rippled across the table. Multiple voices battled over each other, but something bothered Analia.

How did they know this was the same thing killing their Royals? No one had disclosed their causes of death. And if this was actually xenol—

"That would certainly be convenient for you," Othin yelled over the noise. He sat on the edge of the empty seats that bridged the Sun and Moon, Patryclas on the other side. "That would easily explain why you haven't lost anyone yet."

"If I recall," Sylas rumbled, "you haven't lost a Royal either, Othin."

"I lost my brother-in-law!"

"Yes, and what a strong correlation there is between twenty years and twelve months."

Othin leaned across the open chairs. Patryclas's green eyes flashed, reflecting back his rage. He reached for his goblet, the anger draining from his expression as he took a long sip.

"No one is accusing anyone of sabotage," Patryclas said, remarkably calm once more.

This only triggered a new round of yelling. But Analia hadn't missed how Cabir had flinched on her left.

So, that's what had happened to his father. Analia had never gotten the courage to ask what happened to Saura and Deardryn's younger brother. What she really wanted to know, though, was if he'd also had a black mark. If any of them had the mark.

To Analia's surprise, amid the chaos of voices, she made to speak. Brenn's ferocious gaze immediately locked onto hers, and her mouth snapped shut.

Diantha yelled, "Mist, Sun, and Moon have all gone unscathed! It could be any one of them—"

"Do we even know if these deaths are connected?" Roka cut in.

Silence slammed across the table.

"Well?" Patryclas asked, wiping a bead of sweat from his brow. "What were the causes of death?"

No one moved. Deardryn's eyes met Brenn's, and he gave her the visible equivalent of a scoff.

Analia's hands clenched around the edge of her chair as the silence stretched on. The sun had officially set, casting the Royals' guarded expressions in the flickering light and shadows of the chandeliers and candles Cadmus had surreptitiously lit.

"A black mark," a quiet voice finally said.

Brenn's head whipped toward Cadmus beside him. He flushed under Brenn's outrage, but he went on, "Perfectly circular, on the side of the neck."

The hush across the table seemed to deepen, darken.

Analia stared at her brother. Had something shifted in the solemn, perfectionist brother, molded by Brenn's very hands? Something that allowed him to make the smallest crack? Regardless, he'd certainly created a few cracks himself.

A young Sand Princess murmured, "No magical, physical, or scent trail."

"And no other discernible cause of death," breathed a Wind Prince.

A collective shiver seemed to run down the spine of every Royal.

"Something is hunting us," Roka whispered.

Those quiet words resulted in a cacophony of voices rising once more. But what did they mean, "No other discernible cause of death"? Did that mean they couldn't identify xenol in the dead Royals' bodies? Or they had, but they were keeping those details private until they found out what it did.

A part of Analia was tempted to speak, Brenn be damned, but he seemed to know exactly what she was thinking. His eyes locked on hers, and she once again lowered her head. *Duckling.*

"Enough!" Deardryn finally yelled, voice rising above the din. "This is absurd! This is bigger than the petty territory disputes and fickle trading negotiations that divide us. Someone, or something, is hunting Royals. Successfully. We should be working together, not pointing fingers like a cluster of squabbling children."

"Why in the name of the Crystal should we work with you?" Diantha demanded. "We already lost our Royal."

"And Ash lost two," Deardryn countered.

Diantha's lips pressed into a line, but she didn't argue.

"Look around," Deardryn said, gesturing broadly. "There was once a time when every single one of these seats was filled. Now, due to fear or death, we are surrounded by empty chairs."

And just as Deardryn said, Ash had two of those chairs.

"How many of you have those same empty chairs at home? How many of you want to have even more, only left with memories as you move through the deepening quiet as voice after voice is silenced?"

Both had black marks, both had no trace of any other cause of death. But Analia hadn't asked if Baylen also had xenol in his system. She did know there was no trace of a killer, which made xenol more likely over some creature. But how could Baylen have been dosed?

"Death after death, all because you were too stubborn, too prideful, to accept help. To reach out a hand. How many of you want to live with that weight on your shoulders?"

"Why should we listen to you?" Oberon demanded. "You haven't lost anyone."

"No, I haven't," Deardryn replied. "But I know someone who has."

Analia had been waiting for the moment Deardryn revealed her grand victory. All night, she'd felt the glances flitting around her. Now, Deardryn gave them an excuse to land.

"This woman, in her darkest, most painful hour of grief, refused to withdraw into herself and never come back out, even though no one would have blamed her for doing so. Instead, she reached out."

Beside her, Pryanth sat tall, unfazed. Analia, meanwhile, wished her seat would swallow her whole.

"It's because of her that Sun and Ash are united against this threat," Deardryn said. "And if I were you, I would be wondering why I couldn't do it if she could."

Analia slumped as the gazes flicked away, now tinged with indignation.

"So that's your grand scheme?" Sylas asked, bored once more. "To shame us by comparing us to a sad, broken little girl?"

Analia jerked upright. Pryanth dug his nails deep enough into her knee she was surprised he didn't draw blood. Sylas, of course, ignored her.

"Give me one good reason besides calling me a child to help you," he said.

"Because," Deardryn began.

Patryclas dropped his goblet back to the table with a clatter. He slumped out of his seat, hitting the ground with a thud.

And chaos erupted.

Deardryn was the first to move. She launched herself out of her seat and to Patryclas's side. Sylas, letting out a bellow that soared over the sudden shrieks, followed suit.

All around, there came the clatter of seats being thrust away from the table as people rose to their feet. Pryanth and Cabir were among them, quickly shoving through the crowd that seemed to concurrently converge on Patryclas and dart away as fast as possible.

And Analia was left, alone, at the table as the wall of ice slammed into her. Numbing her, ejecting her from her body.

She was forced to watch through eyes that were not her own as flares of golden light illuminated the chamber. Forced to listen to the screams, the confusion, the chaos as if in a dream.

She had to move. She had to get up. Run.

"Analia?" Aaron slid into Pryanth's vacated seat. "Analia, what's wrong?"

"It's all the same," she breathed.

She was back in Accalon's chambers. Surrounded by golden flares of magic that made the entire chamber thrum with power. Everyone around her pushing, shoving, the fear in the air sharp enough to draw blood.

"Oh, Anna."

Analia was distantly aware of the confusion that turned to devastation in Aaron's eyes. He turned her face toward him, his fingers on her cheek so warm compared to the ice clogging her veins.

"This is not your uncle, Anna," he told her, close enough he didn't have to raise his voice to be heard over the panic. "It's not Accalon."

"But it's the same."

The same shrieks of fear, confusion, and anger. The same cold stone beneath her. Even Aaron was the same. His voice, his touch, him.

"It's not the same," he told her, cradling both her hands in his free one. "Deardryn got to Patryclas immediately. She has Pryanth and Cabir helping her. He will be all right."

"But why wasn't Accalon?" Analia whispered.

Analia could see the moment Aaron's heart broke for her.

"I don't know," he rasped.

She'd thought she'd been doing so well. She'd thought she was smoothing out the shards that had broken away, fusing the cracks back together again and forming something stronger. But now, she could feel herself fracturing, splintering apart at the seams.

Crystal spare her, she couldn't do this. She couldn't feel the memories that flashed across her mind, too quick to process but slicing her bloody all the same. She had to hold herself together, hold on to control—she could not break.

But there was nothing she could do to stop herself from tumbling toward a bottom that she was terrified of hitting. Because she knew that as soon as she did, she would finally, irrevocably shatter. And she didn't know if she could put herself back together after that.

One day. One day, one day, one day, one day, one day—

"Analia, breathe," Aaron whispered in her ear.

He squeezed her hands, giving her something to hold onto once again. Analia barely choked back a sob. She let one of her hands drop, squeezing back so hard she felt Aaron's bones shift, but he didn't complain.

"There you are," he sighed, his breath warm against her cheek.

Another flare of golden light flashed over Aaron's shoulder. Analia's eyes mechanically moved to track it, but Aaron's fingers lightly curled around her cheek.

"Eyes on me, Anna," he told her. "I'll let you know when you can look."

Analia felt herself nod. And for the next countless minutes, they sat in the heart of the storm.

Waves of magic rolled over Analia's awareness. She swallowed hard against the bile rising in her throat, but she couldn't stop the tear from rolling down her cheek. Aaron caught it with his thumb, wiping it away without comment. Still, the magic raged.

Analia didn't know how much time passed. She only knew there came a final golden flare. Then, the magic around the chamber winked out.

Something seemed to lift in that moment. Movement slowed; voices drifted off. Aaron eventually glanced over his shoulder.

"Look," he said, sitting back and squeezing her hand.

No, she couldn't. She couldn't see the body, so cold, so still. Dark hair, red hair. Green, gray, vacant, blurring, shifting back and forth in her mind.

"Look, Analia."

Analia looked.

Patryclas woozily sat up, leaning against Sylas's shoulder. Murmurs swirled around them, but Patryclas only stroked a thoroughly rattled Sylas's cheek. Then, he found Analia's gaze through the crowd. And he refused to look away until he saw the relief that sent her entire body trembling. His gaze shifted to the side, a look of understanding crossing his features.

"He's fine," she breathed. "He's fine, he's fine, he's fine."

She pulled out of Aaron's grip, resting her elbows on the table and pressing her palms into her eyes. Three more seconds. Because he was fine. She was fine. But why, why couldn't Accalon have been fine, too?

Analia's hand moved to grip her pin, her uncle's ashes. "He's fine?"

Aaron's voice was low, gentle, as he confirmed. "He's fine."

Analia released a shaky breath. She sat back in her seat, against the hand Aaron tentatively rested on her back.

Across the table, Cadmus wore a haunted expression, undoubtedly identical to her own. He held a sobbing Lucilla close with one arm, reaching across the table with the other. Analia stretched, her fingertips just able to graze his. Cadmus's blue eyes glanced to Aaron with a look of gratitude, then moved to Brenn's back at the end of the table.

Analia slid her hand away. She ignored Cadmus's look of regret, turning to the chaos that had erupted between the Royals instead.

"We're leaving!" Diantha yelled, glaring down at Sylas, still seated beside Patryclas.

"No one is leaving until I find out who poisoned my husband!" he snarled, shadows rippling behind him.

"It's not safe here!" Oberon insisted. "This just proves the killer is one of us."

"But it was only one cup," Roka broke in, pushing through the crowd.

Sylas spat, "Which just means someone must have targeted him!"

"But why Patryclas?" Roka asked. "He's not a Royal, him getting poisoned breaks the trend."

"How convenient for you," said Othin, taking a step toward the Mist Queen.

"Excuse me?"

"Your kingdom is the only one left under suspicion. Blame it on something else and you redirect attention."

"Sun hasn't been hit either!"

"My wife, son, and nephew just spent all their magic trying to heal him—"

"Does Patryclas have the mark on his neck?" Oberon interrupted, shoving between them.

All eyes darted to Patryclas.

Deardryn, looking exhausted where she crouched beside the Moon men, gave Sylas a questioning look. He gave a sharp nod, and Deardryn gently turned Patryclas's face from side to side.

"No mark," she confirmed.

Voices clashed once more.

"All that means," Sylas bellowed over the noise, "is it wasn't that fantastical creature you imbeciles are losing your heads over, but one of you."

Analia jerked to her feet. Snatching one of the small candle jars that had burned all its wax, she moved around the table and sloshed some of Patryclas's wine into the jar.

She had to know. It was too similar. She returned to her seat, Aaron taking the jar with one hand and sliding it in his cloak pocket, the other hand returning to her back.

Diantha shouted, "Someone must have poisoned the wine!"

"You *brought* the wine!" Brenn exclaimed, exasperated.

"But it was only in one cup," Diantha pointed out. "The rest of us are fine."

"Any number of you could have spiked it when passing the goblets around the table," Sylas said, tightening his hold on Patryclas.

"But I don't think any of us would target Patryclas of all people," Roka said.

That earned a pause, followed by a collective shrug. Patryclas might have been right that his word didn't hold as much sway, but that didn't mean he wasn't liked. He was certainly far more favored than Sylas, and Analia doubted any of them would purposefully want to evoke Sylas's black temper.

"Are we sure it was poison in the first place?" Othin asked suddenly.

That got everyone's attention.

"What's his Blessing? Emotional Crystal knows what? How do we know he wasn't just overwhelmed by all our bickering?"

Sylas's nostrils flared. Othin ignored him, turning to Deardryn. The Dragoness furrowed her brows, then fluttered her hands.

"It's possible," she said, sounding slightly helpless.

"How do you not know?" Sylas demanded.

"Because I'm not a full healer," Deardryn said. "I could feel his lifeforce was weak, his magic was drained, and I replenished them. Whether or not that could have been magical exhaustion, or somehow enough to expel a mild enough poison I couldn't detect, I cannot say."

"It's possible," Patryclas rasped, rubbing his face. "You were rather overwhelming."

Sylas looked down at his husband, fury softening a fraction. "You've never reacted that way before."

"And there's a first time for everything."

Patryclas struggled to sit upright on his own, Sylas putting a hand on his back to steady him.

"My love," Patryclas went on, "what do you think is more likely? Me getting magically overwhelmed by a table full of incredibly powerful, highly emotional Royals, or someone managing to poison just one cup without anyone noticing?"

"I want to know the truth," Sylas ground out, "not assumptions. For all I know, this could have been one of the kingdoms lashing out from fear."

Mutters quickly turned to outrage. Aaron nudged Analia closer, but she kept her mouth shut. She knew she couldn't bring up xenol. Not yet, not without knowing for sure.

"We're not going to be able to find that out tonight," Deardryn said.

"No. But we'll continue this tomorrow." Sylas rose to his feet, helping Patryclas do the same. "Before we leave, I'm speaking with everyone." Turning to Deardryn, he bowed his head. "I am in your debt."

Then, with a sharp gesture, Sylas turned on his heel and marched out the door, his arm wrapped tightly around Patryclas's shoulders. A wave of deep purple and black quickly followed.

With that, everything seemed to unravel.

Royals broke apart, going in search of their guards, barking orders, setting up patrols. No one was taking chances.

Analia dug her nails into her palms, letting the noise swirl around her. There were so many new pieces she had to juggle, some slamming into place while others were ejected. But slowly, slowly, she was building a picture.

"Are you all right?" Aaron asked in her ear.

Analia turned her head to look at him. There was some emotion on his face. Something she didn't have a name for, but nevertheless had a sob rising in her throat.

She squeezed her eyes shut. "I don't know."

# Chapter 36

A nalia and Aaron followed the group of Sun members up a narrow staircase. Upon reaching the top, the Royals quickly separated, all going into their rooms and slamming the doors shut behind them. Only Cabir paused, patting her shoulder before disappearing as well.

Analia was left alone in the narrow hallway, only faintly lit by the dangling crystal chandeliers. Always alone.

Aaron lightly touched her arm. Telling her to stay put, he joined the cluster of Crystal Guards farther down the hall, hashing out the details of their watch. He rejoined her in a few minutes, leading her by the elbow into one of the unoccupied rooms and closing the door behind them.

The room itself was sparse: thin gray carpet, two beds, tiny circular window with a chest beneath that Analia knew held a change of clothes. She could practically taste the thick layer of dust and cobwebs that stretched across every surface. Clearly, this room had not been used in far, far longer than a single year.

"I'm on second shift," Aaron said from behind her.

Analia nodded. She sat on one of the beds, a puff of dust rising around her as she pulled her knees to her chest.

Once, she would have rushed to her harp. She would have played until her fingers bled, until the rest of the world was gone, and it was just her and the music. Fast, loud, all-consuming.

But there was no harp here. No harp she wanted to touch again. This stillness would have to do.

"You're safe to wallow," Aaron said, sitting beside her and squeezing her shoulder.

"I know."

"But you're not going to."

"No."

Aaron paused. "Do you want me to leave you alone?"

"No."

For a long time, they were quiet, listening to the muffled voices outside through the thick stone door.

"What is going on in that head of yours?" Aaron asked, half to himself.

Analia's eyes darted around the room. They were alone. The door and window were shut. No one could hear.

"Why," Analia asked, "was always-looking-for-a-fight Othin the one coming up with the strongest reason *not* to fight?"

Aaron froze. Then, he shifted closer, lowering his voice. "Marcos. That's what you're thinking about."

"Othin passed Patryclas his glass," Analia said.

The seating plan unfolded in her mind. Wind, who brought the wine, on Sun's left. They passed it to Cabir, Analia, Pryanth, Deardryn, then Othin, who passed it directly to Patryclas.

"If Marcos was telling the truth," Analia went on, "and he has access to xenol..."

"Are you sure it was xenol?" Aaron asked.

"I won't be sure until we get that sample tested. But Aaron, Deardryn said it herself: his magic was drained."

Aaron clenched his jaw. He carefully withdrew the tiny jar from one of the pockets in his cloak and offered it to her. She brought the jar to her nose. Sharp, bitter, with the faint smell of candle wax. But was there something underneath?

Aaron gave her a questioning look. Analia shrugged and passed him the jar. He scrutinized it for a second, his nose wrinkling at the strong scent.

"Could it have been a result of magic overload?" he asked, twisting to put the jar on the chest.

There came a thud directly outside their door. Analia flinched. Aaron's hand flew to her back, the other whipping out a dagger. The two lapsed into silence.

After a few heartbeats of quiet, Aaron let his hand drop, and he pulled away once more.

Analia peeked up at him, practically able to see the thoughts racing through his head. Not trying to disprove her, just trying to think through every angle.

Once, Analia would have bristled at that. But now, she was grateful for the help that she was once too scared to depend on.

"I guess we won't know that, either, until the wine is tested," she murmured. "But Aaron, did you see his face?"

Aaron shook his head.

"His condition followed the same progression as Accalon." Analia ticked them off on her fingers. "Pale, cold sweat, trembling, all after he drank his wine. And that started with my uncle, not after dinner, but when he was drinking his tea in the Council Chamber."

Aaron sat up straight. He hadn't been in the chamber while they talked, having been stationed outside with the rest of the guards. But Analia saw it every night, every gods-damned image she locked away eating her alive in her dreams until she woke in a cold sweat.

"If that's true," Aaron said, "you've got yourself a timeline."

It was the tea. Not his dinner.

"The guards were with us at all times until we went inside," Analia said, "so they're all off the list."

"Leaving Pryanth, Deardryn, and Othin," Aaron finished.

"Although Crystal only knows who had access before it was delivered," Analia muttered.

"And what about the mark on the neck?" Aaron added.

Analia frowned, pinching the bridge of her nose. "Could it be a delayed reaction?"

"Or maybe it only happens postmortem," Aaron suggested.

There were still so many questions that they couldn't answer yet. But talking aloud, she was able to slide even more pieces into place. She was so close.

"There's still one major question," Aaron breathed in her ear. "Why would Othin poison Patryclas?"

That, to Analia's dismay, was an incredibly easy answer.

"Because he saw me talking with Patryclas today. And he accused him of being one of my accomplices."

Unbridled guilt stampeded through her insides.

"Hey." Aaron turned her face to his with a finger. "This is not your fault."

"Why else would Patryclas of all people be targeted?" she asked.

No one had anything against Patryclas as far as she knew. So, for him to be targeted of all people, most likely with a plant Analia knew—well, suspected—Othin had access to, and Othin had been suspicious of him earlier?

"Even if you're right," Aaron said, "do you think Patryclas would want you blaming yourself?"

"Well, no," Analia mumbled. "But mostly because he would be forced to feel it, too."

Aaron flicked her temple. "Don't take that burden on," he said, his voice softening once more.

"But it's still a motive."

Aaron sighed, running his hand through his hair and down to the back of his neck. "We won't know until we find out if anything was in the wine or not," he said.

Quiet. Eventually, Aaron rose and crossed to the other bed. He unlaced his boots, kicking them off as he leaned back against the pillows.

"What are you doing?" Analia asked.

"Sleeping," Aaron said as if it were obvious.

"Aren't you going to change?"

"No. But I'll courteously look away when you do."

"Aaron, you're in armor," Analia protested. She pushed herself up and headed for the chest.

"Leathers, Analia. They won't wrinkle."

Analia shot a quick, incredulous look at Aaron, who didn't notice as he'd rolled onto his stomach and pressed his face into the pillow.

"You can't sleep in armor."

"Not only have I slept in armor before," he said, voice muffled by the pillow, "but I've done it on the ground."

Analia yanked open the chest. "Aaron—"

"Do you just want me to strip?" he asked, sitting up. "Give yourself a chance to gawk at my flawless naked torso—quit it!"

Analia whacked him with a tunic she'd found in the chest. Aaron grabbed it and whacked her back. Analia yanked it away from him.

"Change," she told him, pulling out a cream-colored nightgown.

"Not when I have to be awake and patrol in a few hours."

"You're ridiculous," she grumbled. She closed the chest and stomped over to her bed, flopping down in a cloud of dust. She turned to change, Aaron snickering behind her.

"What?" Analia demanded, looking at him over her shoulder.

"Good night, Analia."

*"What?"*

"Sweet dreams."

Analia huffed and turned away. She didn't realize immediately that just in those moments, she'd managed to forget the guilt, the fear, every wound that had been ripped open that night. But as she drifted off to sleep, they all came roaring back to the surface, slamming her under once more.

Analia woke the following morning to a hand shaking her shoulder. She jolted upright, cracking her forehead against someone's chin.

"What's going on?" she demanded, blinking in the early dawn light that filtered through the window.

To her surprise, it was Lena standing before her, rubbing her chin with a faintly reproachful expression.

"Something's happened, Your Highness. We need to go."

Analia moved to the chest, noticing that Aaron must have taken the candle jar with him when he left for his shift. She quickly dressed, stepping out into the hall behind Lena in a cream tunic and brown pants. The sound of hurrying feet echoed farther down the hall, Analia spotting both Sand and Wind colors.

Analia headed after them, passing Pryanth as he exited his room. It took him a moment to notice her. When he did, he hurried to her side.

"There you are," he said, sliding an arm around her waist. "Where have you been?"

Analia's jaw dropped. Where was she? Where was *he?*

"I was next door," she said, stepping out of his touch.

"What?" Pryanth's hand found her back once more as they descended the stairs and merged with the crowd. "Why didn't you stay with me?"

"Because you slammed the door."

"That wasn't about you."

Analia blinked.

"I was exhausted and drained from bickering Royals and all the magic I'd used," Pryanth explained, his arm sliding up her back and around her shoulders. "I thought you would have realized that."

Analia kept her eyes on her feet as they crossed the arched entryway, following the crowd to the opposite side of the castle.

"I didn't realize," she mumbled, the words slightly bitter on her tongue.

"I had been waiting and waiting for you to come," he murmured. His fingers idly traced her collarbone. "I really wanted to see you last night."

"You did?"

"Always." Pryanth brushed a kiss to the corner of her jaw. "Just think, Analia. We could have been left alone. Betrotheds. In my bed chambers." His voice dropped to a whisper. "No one would have to know what rules we broke."

Pryanth slipped behind her as they ascended a dark, narrow staircase. "Can you imagine it, Analia?" he asked, his voice shivering across her skin. "What it would feel like to have me finally touch you the way I want to? No silk or lace. Just bare skin. You moaning and writhing beneath me."

Pryanth's wandering fingers slipped beneath her tunic, sliding up her stomach, her ribs.

"No one would have to know," he breathed, his fingers unbearably light as he circled her nipple. "Not that I made you beg. That I made you forget the name of every person that had been inside you. All you'd know was me. That you are *mine*."

Analia gasped as he gave a sharp tug. Pleasure and pain tumbled down her spine, washing away the faint unease his words had triggered.

This was Pryanth. His fingers that teased her until she arched into his touch. His mouth that found the back of her neck. She knew him. She could trust him, believe him enough to fall into the soft desire that rolled down her scalp to her toes.

"But alas," Pryanth said, perfectly composed as they reached the top of the stairs. "Not this time. But we can find another."

Analia could have sunk into the sweet kiss he left on her cheek as he stepped back to her side. But as they continued down the hall, she couldn't help but wonder why he hadn't come to find her, then.

Analia swatted the thought aside. Crystal knew she had enough to worry about. If she could remove Pryanth from that list, she wouldn't hesitate.

The two followed the rapidly building crowd into a sitting room. Bright morning light pooled on the stone floor from a wide skylight. A ring of shadows lined the edges of the room, where couches and side tables sat.

A cluster of people had already gathered in the center of the light, shoulder to shoulder, their voices tangling together. It wasn't quite the clamor of the night before, but there was a coldness in the air, lacing icy fingers through the quiet.

Analia stepped out of Pryanth's grip, trying to wedge her smaller frame through the crowd. She could feel the creeping cold behind her, but she had to know.

Analia broke through a section of the crowd, and she felt it before she saw it. The languid roll of Sun magic, followed by the flash of gold that wormed its way through the cracks between people's shoulders and over their heads.

Analia stepped back, back, back, her shoulders meeting something hard. Arms wrapped around her middle—Aaron?

"What's wrong?" Pryanth asked, more confused than anything.

She would not break. She could not freeze.

"Someone... Someone's hurt," she said, struggling for calm. "Your mother is there—"

"Mother?" Pryanth pulled away, squeezing through the crowd that had congealed around them. "She hasn't had enough time to restore her magic. I need to help her."

Analia watched, a single point of silence in the thrum of voices, as he pushed through the crowd without a backward glance. And a part of her wasn't even surprised.

She just had to move. Had to force her mind to start turning again. She had to know.

But the crowd pushed her back. They stepped on her toes, elbows digging into her ribs, the warm press of bodies coming from every side. Analia latched onto each point of contact, pulling her awareness back, forcing herself to focus.

"You shouldn't have to see this again."

Analia hadn't seen or heard Aaron approach.

"I need to know," she said, turning to look at him.

Somehow, finally being able to speak it aloud had the ice coiling back. She waited for Aaron to disagree, but all he said was, "Are you sure?"

Analia nodded. And Aaron—only mildly looking like he might regret this—put his hand on her back.

He steered her through the crowd, quickly reaching the edge of the ring. Just to find Roka kneeling on the ground, tears in her eyes as she cradled her seventeen-year-old daughter's head in her lap.

This time, Analia didn't fight the cold. She wrapped it around herself, chilling her blood, numbing her heart and mind as she watched Pryanth and Deardryn lift their palms from the princess's chest, golden light flickering out.

Aaron's hand tightened around her spine as a low, mournful wail rose from the cluster of Mist people. They stumbled back, some sinking onto couches while others fled the room.

"What in the name of the Crystal happened here?" Diantha demanded, coming up behind Roka.

"We don't know," Deardryn said, touching a hand to her sapphire necklace, glittering with residual magic. "Roka and I were walking the halls with our guards, trying to figure out what could have happened last night when we found her here."

"She must have wandered off last night," Roka breathed, her lips barely moving. "Lielle always hated being trailed by guards. She... She was rather adept at evading them."

"No one else was in this castle beside us," said Oberon. He looked down at the dead princess and shuddered, moving to sit on a nearby side table.

"Are you sure about that?" Brenn asked, shoving through the thinning crowd.

The Royals all exchanged a haunted look. One that was far, far more terrifying than any yell, any explosion of outrage.

Analia stepped out of Aaron's grip. She threaded her way around a kneeling Pryanth, coming to crouch across from Deardryn.

She could feel the eyes on her, hear the demands to know what she was doing. But she let them skitter across her icy cloak, her hand reaching out to touch the smooth, perfectly circular black mark on the side of Lielle's neck.

"Do you know any Royal that could leave such a mark?" she asked no one in particular, echoing Accalon's words from almost three months before. She let her hand drop limply to her side.

"How is this possible?" Diantha asked. "Wind, Ash, Sand, potentially Moon, Mist." She ticked them off on her fingers.

"And Sun trying to heal multiple," Roka murmured. She pulled her daughter's limp form closer.

"And if all of us have been hit," said Oberon, "that means it's not one of us. Something is hunting us."

Something, or someone. Analia's mind flashed to the wine jar.

"Look at her hands," said Aaron suddenly. He stepped out of the crowd, unflinching under the Royals' hostile stares as he came to crouch beside Analia. He gently lifted one of Lielle's hands, which Analia hadn't noticed was curled in a claw.

"Her nails are all broken," Aaron said. He dragged her thumbnail across the back of his hand, leaving a smear of dried blood behind.

"What does that mean?" Roka asked. Her pale eyes were wide, pleading.

Aaron gently placed Lielle's hand back in her lap, his face grim. "It means your daughter fought back."

Fresh tears streamed down the queen's beautiful face. She turned her head to the side, squeezing her eyes shut as her lips trembled.

Analia wished the Royals would start yelling again. Anything other than the terrified silence. She inched closer to Aaron, who shifted so the side of his body pressed against hers. Analia's shoulders loosened a fraction.

She looked up at him, the same questions written across his face. Where was Othin? Was xenol in her system? Who or what was she clawing at? What were they missing, because clearly, they were missing something.

Analia caught Pryanth glancing at her from the corner of her eye. He sat on Lielle's other side, his exhausted mother leaning against his shoulder. His eyes moved between Analia and Aaron, down to where their arms and thighs touched, his expression slowly darkening.

As the Royals murmured around them, Pryanth helped Deardryn to her feet. He led her to a nearby couch, extending a hand to Analia. She rose to sit beside him, her muscles tightening as Pryanth wrapped an arm around her shoulders. Aaron rose as well, melting back into the crowd of guards lining the shadows of the room.

Five Royals dead. One potential attempted poisoning of a non-Royal. Black circles on the neck and broken nails.

If Lielle had been poisoned, it would make sense she reacted after Patryclas. If everyone else was still fine, though, that meant it just had to be her cup poisoned. But why her? Why Patryclas?

Was xenol not the only piece on the board? In that case, there was something far more sinister at play here.

# PART 3: SMOKE

# Chapter 37

The Sun people were muted with unease as Deardryn opened the Soul Gate late that afternoon. Sylas had gotten his chance to speak with all of them and, unsurprisingly, found nothing.

Immediately upon stepping foot in the castle, Analia hunted down Dimitri, finding him sprawled on her bed with a book in hand.

"We need to talk," she said, just as Dimitri said, "I have news."

Now, they sat on the castle roof, swapping stories. To Analia's surprise, Dimitri sat beside her on the parapet instead of on the roof itself.

"So, what did the note say?" Analia asked.

"See for yourself." Dimitri pulled a heavily creased paper from his pocket and offered it to her.

Analia squinted in the fading light, scanning over the numbered list written in Dimitri's precise handwriting. Her eyes snagged on a few of the words that were oddly familiar...

"Plants?" she asked. "Are these rare plants?"

"Fuck yes they are!" Dimitri grinned. "It took me a second to figure it out—granny had shit handwriting—but I thought I'd seen a few of those when scanning books with you in the library."

"Xenol's not on here, though," Analia said.

"No," Dimitri admitted, taking the scrap of paper back. "But they were all in the book that you found xenol in."

"Does that mean you read it last night? Without help?"

Dimitri puffed out his chest. "I understood most of it, too."

Analia made to clap him on the shoulder, her hand barely avoiding contact. "Well done!"

Dimitri eyed her hovering hand but didn't move away. "It took forever," he admitted, "but I found all of them. And guess what they are?"

Analia shrugged.

"They're all rare, *foreign* plants with odd uses."

Dimitri spread his hands as if waiting for applause. Tingles ran down Analia's spine. She shoved to her feet, her mind racing as she started to pace.

"What does this mean?" she asked.

"Black market plant ring?" Dimitri suggested.

"Not necessarily. This kingdom is built on research. Who's to say all the research is magic based?"

"You think the Old Hag has some secret stash of foreign plants?"

"She's not an old hag."

"And I'm as delightful as a fresh summer breeze."

Analia rolled her eyes. Now that she thought about it, though, why had the healer come for Deardryn? And if the healer had been supplying Deardryn with plants, why did Othin need to get xenol from Marcos?

Xenol wasn't on the list, though, so perhaps Othin's trades were separate? What *did* Deardryn have?

"Do you have any idea where these plants could be stored?" she asked.

"Not a clue," Dimitri said. "They have to be somewhere, though."

Analia ran her hand through her hair. This had to be connected, didn't it?

"I need to go talk with the healer," she decided, coming to sit beside Dimitri once more.

"You can't tell her what you're doing," he said.

"I don't have to. I can get information in other ways."

Dimitri cocked his head but didn't argue.

"We just need to know how to track her down," Analia murmured, drumming her fingers on the wall.

"Well, that's easy enough," Dimitri said. "She works at the apothecary right outside the gates."

Analia gave him an exasperated look. "I thought you said you didn't know her!"

"I don't," he said. "But I overheard some servants talking about her after the fact, and they did."

Analia snorted. Dimitri grinned.

"Pryanth is scheduled to go out to get a new sword in a few days," she mused. "If I can worm my way into that outing and then sneak away..."

"Just as long as I don't have to go," Dimitri said with a stretch.

Analia kicked him in the shins. Dimitri made a noise of protest and scooted away. When he looked back at her, Analia caught herself studying his amber eyes. They certainly looked like Othin's. But she was starting to realize just how different Dimitri was from his father.

"Hey," he said suddenly, "where's Bordello?"

Analia looked down at her chest, feeling the cool absence of her phoenix pin. "He's on his way to do something else."

Ember knelt in a cluster of plants, the full moon providing plenty of light to see by as she collected her herbs. Accalon had always made time to shadowjump her to this little garden on the Sun border, sparing her the travel. Now, it was Cadmus who amiably jumped her, promising to retrieve her a few hours later.

Ember sighed, inspecting the leaves of a particularly invasive weed. She'd been hoping to see Analia the past couple times she'd come to tend to her plants. She had so much to share with her—although her tests with Cadmus hadn't progressed beyond that initial experiment.

Ember had actually been caught after stealing the first sample—which she wasn't expecting—and was now patted down upon leaving the room with the samples—which she found extremely flattering. This, however, made it near impossible to steal another. She didn't think it wise to share everything she'd done, either. Not until she had enough information to escape with a slap on the wrist and a "well done."

But beside all of that, she just wanted to know if Analia was… all right? Surviving? Alive? She'd take anything at this point.

Ember's ears pricked at the quiet tread of footsteps on the Sun side of the border.

"I'm allowed to be here," she called, not looking up.

Stupid little soldiers. Tromping around and crushing her plants. Thinking the best way to solve a problem was to stab a hole through its center.

"Not only are you allowed to be here," a voice replied, "but I was hoping to find you."

Ember's head jerked up. Oh, no fair.

"Well, hello," she said, staring up at the oddly familiar man through her lashes.

Honestly, since when were soldiers allowed to be handsome? The man wore a white-and-gold military uniform, his silver eyes seeming to sparkle in the moonlight. He rocked back on his heels, mouth curved in a smile.

"Ember, I presume?"

"You 'presume'?" Ember repeated. "Surely my reputation has preceded me enough that you don't have to 'presume.'"

"And what would that reputation be?" he asked, approaching on quiet feet and crouching before her.

"Sharp of wit, quick of mind. As beautiful as the moonlight, and just as likely to slip between your fingers."

She stroked a finger up the length of a tall, sleek stem, the man's eyes following her movement.

"I suppose it's because none of those fingers are as deft as your own."

Ember smiled. "That's not for my tongue to say."

"No," he agreed, leaning toward her. "Tongues are meant to tell their own stories."

Their eyes locked. Ember's heart stumbled, suddenly unable to look away. Those eyes…

His mouth twitched. Then, he sat back on his heels, letting out a delighted laugh.

"I like you," he said, extending a hand to her. "Aaron. It's a pleasure."

Ember grinned as she loosely gripped his calloused fingers. "Look at you, actually playing along."

A part of her noted how, despite his white and gold, he hadn't raised his palm to her in the Sun's traditional greeting.

"It's too bad I have to dislike you on principle," she went on, casually turning back to her plants.

"What? Why?"

"Because I'm a healer," Ember said as if it were obvious. "I might enjoy my job, but it's one where we all agree the world would be a better place if it wasn't necessary. And *your lot* are widely responsible for keeping *my lot* in business."

"Maybe you'll decide to like me more once I tell you Analia sent me."

Ember looked up quickly. Aaron dug in the pocket of his cloak, pulling out Accalon's pin of all things and offering it to her.

Ember accepted it silently. She ran her finger around the outer ring, her heart aching. Gods, she missed Accalon. She missed Analia.

"You could have very easily stolen this to earn my trust," she said.

The ghost of a smile flickered across Aaron's lips. "Who taught you not to trust?"

"Pretty boys that think they can get whatever they want if they brood long enough."

Aaron's smile grew. "She also told me to tell you that while you give excellent counsel, you'd be an idiot not to heed mine."

Ember sat back on her heels. "In that case, why didn't you tell me that before?"

"I wanted to see if I brooded long enough that I wouldn't have to."

Ember finally laughed. He couldn't have known about that memory on his own. She handed the pin back to Aaron, who slid it into his pocket once more.

This had to be Analia's, what, new henchman? Ember wished she had a henchman. Why *didn't* she have a henchman?

"I'm assuming that was a reference of sorts," Aaron said, pulling Ember out of her reveries.

"Oh, it was," she said. "A little early school years joke."

"You went to school together?"

"Until I was ten and chosen by Rosala." Ember carefully pulled out another plant, roots dangling. "Accalon had insisted all Royal children not have private tutors, but rather attend school with the commoners. And that little code message was from when I forced Analia to be my friend."

The words were bittersweet on her tongue. The morning after Brenn had publicly humiliated Analia, the stares were relentless as she walked into school.

Without thinking, Ember had pushed forward, taking her hand and glaring at that snot-nosed farmer boy before leading Analia back to her seat.

"Don't let them see you cry," Ember told her. "I don't care what your father says, you're a princess, and princesses don't let anyone see them cry."

She pulled out the seat beside hers, shoving Analia down into it. "You sit with me now."

She expected Analia to go along with her will without protest, as everyone learned to do eventually. Instead, she looked up at Ember, annoyed. "I thought princesses don't let people tell them what to do."

"Princesses take counsel, don't they?" Ember asked, taking her own seat. "I give the best counsel. You'd be an idiot not to heed mine."

And they'd been friends ever since. But as much as it was a part of Ember's story, it was also Analia's. It wasn't her place to tell.

She could see the curiosity glinting in Aaron's eyes and braced herself to tell him just that. But Aaron only scooted closer, his hand hovering over one of her plants.

"I can help you with this," he offered.

Rosala curse her, he was completely earnest.

"Don't you dare," she said, swatting his hand away. "You bloodthirsty warrior types don't have the sophistication, the eye for detail, needed to handle my plants. Although, you have managed to keep that bracelet alive."

Aaron jerked back. Ember thoroughly enjoyed his look of bafflement as he stared at her, his hand seeming to slide up his jacket sleeve of its own accord. Ember barely glanced at the bracelet woven from white petals and stems that faded from pale purple to black.

"Enka flowers," she said, dusting her hands. "The plant of communication. Now why does a barbarian like yourself have that?"

"How did you know?" he asked, almost awed.

"I sensed it. Herbology is my specialty."

She waited for the usual look of scorn, but Aaron brightened.

"So," he said, "that's why Anna sent me here."

"She is all right, isn't she?" Ember asked.

"She's..." Aaron's expression faltered.

"As good as you can expect her to be?" Ember suggested.

Aaron nodded. That was true concern in his eyes. Convincing enough that Ember didn't even smack his hand away when he reached for another plant.

As the night darkened around them, the two continued to collect Ember's plants, Aaron telling her everything that had happened over the past two and a half months.

"So, this is it?" Ember asked, turning the candle jar Aaron had passed her between her fingers.

A part of her was utterly astonished that Analia had not only tracked down an oath-breaking, ex-healer drug lord, but she'd also found out that there was a super-secret plant? Hidden from even the healers? Supposedly in this wine sample that was stored in some of the most deplorable conditions Ember had ever seen.

Honestly, they'd poured it into a contaminated container. What were they thinking? But Ember had learned not to be judgmental. Out loud, anyway.

"That's Patryclas's wine," Aaron said. "Only you can figure out if it has xenol in it."

"It's not going to be easy," Ember mused.

Cadmus had noticed the same pattern Analia had between Patryclas's and Accalon's symptoms. He'd torn into her apothecary the moment he returned from the Solstice, his usual composure shattered as he blurted the story in such scattered pieces Ember thought she deserved an award for how quickly she'd put it together.

She'd frankly been surprised he'd come to her first. Yes, they'd been spending more time together, but she'd presumed it was mostly to avoid the burn of Brenn's rule. But Cadmus had started to linger in her back room, even when they'd been forced to put the case aside. Perhaps Analia wasn't the only lonely Ash Royal.

Ember caught a glimpse of the faint line between Aaron's brows.

"Cadmus had the same idea as Anna about the tea," she said quickly. "We're thinking it would be easy enough to pass off as loose tea leaves that Accalon would have swallowed, which is why we have samples large enough to study.

"But with wine?" Ember pursed her lips, tilting the jar in the moonlight. "There would be no excuse for something to be floating in wine. If there's a plant in here, it had to be ground down to powder."

"Would you be able to identify it at that point?"

Ember tossed her hair. "Of course. Who do you think I am, some mediocre healer the Crystal accidentally *sneezed* on?"

Ember dug out a flask from her satchel. She unceremoniously dumped out the water intended for her plants—that was unfortunate—and carefully transferred the wine and screwed on the lid.

"I'll need some time to do it, though."

"How long?"

Ember shrugged. "Hard to say. But I have faith I'll be able to get a message to you soon—yes, covertly, don't give me that look."

Aaron's expression turned sheepish. He quietly helped Ember pack the bundle of plants they had collected into her bag, Ember assuming the conversation was over. But just as she rose and turned to go, Aaron called after her.

"Is what Marcos said possible?"

Ember turned back. Aaron had retreated into the shadows, enough that she could only make out the pale smudge of his face and those silver eyes.

"Honestly," she said, "I have no idea. If he had four inked rings, he had to have been a skilled healer. And if they were broken, he had to have done something bad enough to cause the ink to reject him."

"Would looking into a forbidden plant be enough?" Aaron asked.

"Seeing as though I didn't even know we had forbidden plants?" Ember shook her head. "I would say it's impossible for a plant to do that, but..."

She thought back to the sample she and Cadmus had tested, how it had seemed to eat away the magic in her box. How it hadn't so much absorbed Cadmus's flame as destroyed it.

She briefly explained to Aaron what she'd found. Despite the shadows, she could see his frown deepen. He didn't speak, though, only watched her quietly as she shrugged once more. Then, sensing the end, Ember turned away.

Just for a moment, there came a flash of an icy chill. Not quite the wind, not quite the night. When she turned, Aaron had disappeared.

Puzzled, Ember headed off once more, bag of plants on her shoulder. Yes, she would test the wine. But there was something else she could do, another thing only she could do. By the time she reached the clearing where Cadmus was already waiting, Ember had drafted out her letters in her mind.

# Chapter 38

Joining Pryanth's outing was far easier than Analia expected. Ever since returning from the Solstice, Pryanth accompanied her as she wandered through the castle in search of her ring, shooing away Aaron—who had returned remarkably fast from the border.

Even though Analia was becoming more frustrated by the day—still unable to pull out the ring's magic—she was elated each time Pryanth met her outside her door in the morning. Especially when he brightened as she asked if she could accompany him on his outing.

Now, Analia met Pryanth down in the castle entryway. Her typical uncertainty as to which Pryanth she would see immediately dispersed as he took her hand and kissed her cheek in greeting. But her relief quickly crumpled as she spotted Aaron and Lena lingering nearby.

It was only supposed to be Aaron. Lena was one more person to notice she was gone.

Analia caught Aaron's eye, and he mouthed, "Queen's orders." Analia stifled a groan. Aaron shrugged unconcernedly.

Pryanth glanced over his shoulder, following Analia's gaze. For a moment, his face twisted in a glower. Then, taking Analia's hand, he led her out the door, telling the guards to stay back.

The armory was close enough that taking a carriage or shadowjumping was unnecessary. They meandered down the crowded streets, citizens quickly moving aside and bowing in respect. Pryanth barely noticed, too busy excitedly chattering about his new sword, the bright sunlight flashing off his honey eyes and turning them to gold. And slowly, that anxious part of herself constantly braced for the thunderclap, relaxed.

Maybe she had been too hasty after Solemnai, the Solstice Ceremony. Maybe, the past fifteen years of cruelty and rejection from her father had taught her to expect nothing less at every turn. And somehow, that expectation had convinced her Pryanth was no better than the rest of her kingdom after the slightest provocation.

Yet, as she listened to him talk, his hand in hers, Analia only felt content. Almost elatedly so. He couldn't be as horrible as her mind was telling her, could he?

"They sharpened the blade with a sunstone," Pryanth was saying. "Not just physically honing the blade, but with magic as well—"

"Come back!"

Analia looked up at the cry that rose above the babble of voices.

Pryanth wrinkled his nose. "Children need to learn how to hold onto their things," he muttered, spotting a large, floppy hat tumbling on the breeze.

He tugged on Analia's hand, but she stayed where she was. Stretching on her toes, she barely missed the hat as it sailed past.

Analia turned to follow its trajectory. She ignored Pryanth's protests, watching Aaron track the hat with a softened gaze. Calculating for a second, he took a few steps back, a few to the side, and reached up to snatch the hat out of the air as it passed him.

The little girl broke through the crowd. As she barreled past, Analia finally noticed what Aaron had apparently picked up on immediately. Matted, light brown curls a few tones darker than her skin, bedraggled clothes, and a perpetual wariness in her caramel eyes.

The orphan—who couldn't have been much older than six—flew to a stop before Aaron. She perched lightly on her toes, craning her neck to look at him.

"Your hat," Aaron said, bowing and presenting the hat with a dramatic flourish. The girl laughed in surprise as he placed the hat on her head.

No wonder it had flown away. The hat was clearly made for a head much larger than her own, sliding down far enough Analia had no doubt it was covering her forehead.

Aaron, clearly noticing this as well, knelt in the middle of the street and asked her name. The girl hesitated, rocking back from her toes to her heels.

"Loliette," she finally replied.

"I'm Aaron. Can I show you a trick to help you keep your hat on?"

Loliette nodded cautiously.

"What is he *doing?*" Pryanth mumbled.

"He's being kind," Analia said, watching as Aaron fished out the strings sewn into the hat.

Pryanth ignored her and stepped toward them. Analia tightened her grip on his hand. "Just watch."

Pryanth gave her a long, suffering look, but he stayed put.

Analia watched as Aaron taught Loliette how to tie the strings beneath her chin. Unraveling his own bow, he let her try for herself. It took a couple tries, but clearly, the girl was a fast learner.

"Perfect!" Aaron told her, examining her bow.

Loliette beamed. She chirped a thank you, immediately taking off down the street and disappearing back into the crowd.

Aaron looked up, still kneeling in the shadow of a nearby building. And Analia could have sworn for just a moment, the silver of his eyes had darkened to smoke.

Memories tumbled through her mind, too quick to grasp. But something warm flickered in her chest as Aaron rejoined them, Pryanth giving him a look of exaggerated impatience.

"Something wrong, Your Highness?" asked Aaron innocently.

Pryanth scoffed, heading off once more. "You aren't doing that street rat any favors."

Aaron started to reply, but Analia beat him to it. "There's nothing wrong with a little help."

Pryanth's eyebrows shot up. "Those urchins have no one who cares about them. They need to learn how to toughen up and only depend on themselves."

He patted Analia's cheek, and she could have sworn the warm sun on the back of her head turned to flame.

"Did I tell you my sword—"

"Some would say those people are the ones who need kindness the most," Analia interrupted.

Pryanth gave her an incredulous look. "Why are you still on this?"

"Why aren't you?" A few people shot her startled looks as they passed, and Analia lowered her voice. "That little girl didn't even have a mother to teach her how to tie a knot."

"Which is exactly why he shouldn't have helped her. That type of kindness will only soften her. If she's going to be on the streets, she needs to learn to survive on her own."

"That kindness gave her a skill that will *help* her survive."

"Well," Pryanth said, "maybe if she needed that one act of kindness to survive, she shouldn't survive in the first place."

Analia clapped a hand to her mouth. She waited for him to take it back, but Pryanth turned his head away and fixed his gaze on the armory up ahead.

One step. Two steps. Three. Then, she was burning.

Heat burst from her stomach, up through her chest, across her face, pounded through her veins. How could anyone say that and not take it back?

Pryanth climbed the steps leading to the armory's entrance. As he walked through the door, his arm stretched out behind him, still holding onto Analia, who had rooted herself to the top step.

"Aren't you coming?" he demanded, twisting to look at her.

"I'll wait outside," she said coolly.

It had been her plan from the start: wait outside, slip away. The one part of the plan she was uncertain she could pull off. But now, she let Pryanth see her anger as it blazed.

"With him?" Pryanth spat, looking over Analia's shoulder.

Analia didn't turn to see Aaron at the foot of the five steep steps. She remained where she was, not breaking his stare. Not leaning against the stone railing behind her. Burning.

Finally, Pryanth dropped her hand. "Fine."

He marched through the armory door, his network pulsing. Lena climbed the stairs to follow, shooting Analia a worried look that she ignored.

As the door closed behind the guard, Analia took a slow, deep inhale. Then, spinning on her heel, she strode back down the steps, passing Aaron, who wore a blatant look of impending doom.

Selbi's apothecary was only two streets over. Dimitri had shown Analia on his map, pointing out an alleyway she could cut through as a shortcut.

Analia wove around people she barely registered. Crossed a street with fists balled so tight hot, sticky blood oozed beneath her nails. The moment she stepped into the alleyway, someone grabbed her by the shoulders.

"Hey." Aaron spun her around to face him. "You need to calm down."

Of course, the blaze intensified.

"I thought you liked it when I was fired up," Analia said. "Or does it not get you off when someone else provokes me?"

A muscle in Aaron's jaw jumped. His voice was calm, though, as he said, "You cannot walk into that apothecary like this. You need to be thinking clearly."

"I am."

"No, you're not."

Analia's heart pounded in her ears. She used to be so good at keeping her head down, staying quiet, maintaining control no matter how hot it burned. But now?

"Explode," Aaron told her.

"No."

"Let it out."

"No."

"Right here, right now—"

"He has no right," Analia burst out. "He is a prince. He has had everything he ever wanted his entire life.

"Yes, his father fractured their family. But at least he's spent every day since trying to make things right. Pryanth has no idea what it's like to not have that, to have nothing.

"Yet, he thinks that anyone that has the heart to try and help is a fool? That those people don't deserve help? Why, because he 'toughened up,' so everyone else should be able to?

"What would he have thought of my uncle, who had dedicated funds each month to help the orphans and 'street rats' as he put it? Would he mock my uncle, too, or did he just spit on his memory out of happenstance? Does he think I don't deserve to have survived because he was my one person?"

Analia hadn't expected those last few words. As soon as she said them, something like a cracking sensation ran across her chest, her anger slowly funneling through.

Aaron's hands tightened on her shoulders, almost painfully so, but she relished it.

"Fuck him," Aaron said, carefully enunciating each word, staring directly into her eyes. "Fuck. Him."

Something about hearing someone else say it had Analia sagging.

"He was all I had for so long," she said. "When the children at school would ask how a Crystal-rejected orphan wriggled into the castle, or when strangers on the streets would crane their necks to get a look at me, I reminded myself I at least had him. Not because he was my king, but because he was my family. The only family that mattered.

"He was my one person. And all of that is just…"

"Gone," Aaron supplied. His hands slid down her arms to grip her elbows. "So thoroughly gone, without a pause in between, as if they'd never been there in the first place."

Analia swallowed hard. "Solving this case was supposed to fix this—this feeling. But I feel like it's killing me even faster."

Aaron took a breath. Paused. Finally, "Have you felt it yet?"

"No."

"Anna…"

"I can't feel that, Aaron. I can't survive that."

Aaron looked as though he didn't know what to say. For a few moments, he was quiet, his thumbs absently moving along her arms. Finally, he promised, "We will solve this."

Analia released a long breath, her head drooping forward. Slowly, her breathing returned to normal. But Aaron didn't let go.

"I'm all right," she said after a few long minutes.

Aaron studied her face. Seemingly satisfied, he released her and stepped back.

Analia brought a hand to her pin. Gods, she missed him.

"You were burning," Aaron said quietly.

"What?"

"Your skin." He rested the back of his hand against her forehead. "Not as hot anymore, but Anna…"

She shook her head. She didn't want to even begin to imagine what that could mean.

A cheerful bell tinkled overhead as Analia and Aaron stepped through the apothecary's glass doors, revealing a hot, humid jungle. Countless plants sat neatly arranged on counters and looming wooden shelves, jars of various poultices interspersed throughout their leafy clusters. Most of the ceiling had been replaced by a massive skylight, allowing the midafternoon sun to cast a soft, inviting light over the decently busy shop.

"You remember what it looks like?" Analia asked under her breath.

Aaron nodded. Then, without a word, the two split up.

Analia wandered through the right side of the apothecary, eyes gliding over the plant-strewn surfaces. Perhaps she had been too quick to react to Pryanth. After all, he had been reacting to Loliette, and she'd clearly been reacting to something else.

She couldn't expect Pryanth to read her mind. He had no way of knowing about Accalon, about her.

Although she had told him up on the roof, hadn't she?

Regardless, she couldn't shake what Pryanth had said about kindness. But those words hadn't been targeted at her. He was angry, just as she was. Maybe he didn't mean it? He couldn't have meant it. The man on the rooftop, the one that kissed her in the library stacks, wouldn't have meant that.

Analia's mind flashed back to when she was eight, and Accalon brought her to a council meeting for the first time. As soon as the councilmen shuffled out, she informed him that they were all liars, Accalon laughing as he agreed.

"But I thought lying was bad," she said.

"Little fledgling," he said, "nothing is always one way, just as everything is never the other. Lies and truths are two tools of many that you must learn when to wield, and when to set aside."

"How do you do that?"

"You do that by thinking with your head"—he tapped her temple—"feeling with your heart"—his hand rested over her heart—"and knowing with your gut"—his hand dropped to her stomach. "They won't always be aligned. But when they are, that is when the path is clearest."

Analia gave him a dubious look. Accalon laughed, kissing the top of her head and leading her out of the chamber. If only he had also told her what to do when head, heart, and gut were utterly opposed.

Analia finished her loop of the shop, finding nothing, feeling more confused than ever. She met up with Aaron back at the door, but he shook his head. Fine.

Analia headed back through the aisles, her eyes darting. Finally, in the center of the apothecary, she found a woman standing atop a rolling ladder attached to one of the massive shelves, tending to an overgrown philodendron.

"Hello," Analia said, surprisingly pleasant.

The woman glanced down, revealing gold-ringed eyes. "Princess Analia!" Selbi said, spreading her hands in welcome. "It's an honor to have you in my shop."

The ladder drifted to the side. Aaron moved around Analia to steady it. Selbi seemed mildly surprised by that, but she returned to pruning her plant without comment.

"I've been wanting to come for some time now," Analia said. "My closest friend back home is a healer, so I've spent a lot of time in her apothecary."

"Would I know her?"

"Unlikely. She hasn't received all of her markings yet, so she wouldn't be at your monthly gatherings at the temple."

Selbi hummed. Analia waited for her to speak, but the healer didn't seem inclined. She snipped another section of leaves, letting the cluster plop on the pile below.

"I was hoping to find some plants that I recognize," Analia went on. "To remind me of home. But I don't think I know any of these."

"You don't," said Selbi matter-of-factly. She stuffed her gardening shears into her dirt-stained apron. "All of the plants in here are strictly from the Sun Kingdom."

She clambered down the ladder, patting Aaron on the head as she stepped off. He flashed a smile, albeit slightly bemused.

Leaving her pile of cuttings on the ground, Selbi marched off through her plants. Analia and Aaron exchanged a glance.

"That must make things difficult," Analia said, hurrying after her.

"How so?" Selbi asked, stopping to poke a prickly purple plant.

"I imagine not having access to all plants across Elefthia means you don't have the best plants for every situation. You must have had to learn to make do with what you *do* have."

Selbi paused. She turned slowly to face Analia, her gaze sharp as cactus spines. "What exactly are you asking me, Your Highness?"

Analia could have sworn that gaze pierced straight through her.

"I only want to know if you have plants from home," she said, leaning her hip against a nearby counter.

"Any plant in particular?" Selbi asked.

"My friend always had this fuzzy orange plant around," Analia offered. "I think it grew off magic..."

"Devinroot?" Selbi asked sharply.

Analia shrugged, pretending not to notice as she sent Ember a silent apology.

"I don't keep that kind of plant," Selbi told her.

Analia knew that. She'd purposefully picked something not on Dimitri's stolen list. Nevertheless, she didn't have to fake her blush under that stare. Gods, Ember, how bad was that plant?

"I'm sorry," Analia stammered. "This isn't important, and you're busy and I'm just getting in your way."

She backed away, flashing an apologetic look before turning around. One, two, three steps. Then, she glanced back as if she couldn't help herself.

"It's just…" She looked away. "Seeing my family at the Solstice Ceremony… it reminded me of home. How long I've been away. And I have nothing to remind me of them."

Her hand drifted toward her pin. "But it's fine," she repeated, quickly dropping her hand. "I'm sorry."

She turned once more, heading for the door. Selbi remained silent behind her. Aaron hurried after her, Selbi still not saying anything.

Analia held her breath as she rounded the corner. Had she misread—

"None of my plants from Ash are in my shop."

Analia turned. Selbi's gaze was still sharp, but her mouth had softened.

"So, you do have some?" Analia asked.

"All of my foreign plants are kept in the Royal Garden," Selbi explained, lowering her voice. "My magic isn't strong enough to provide the life force they need to thrive outside their natural climate. But Sun magic is."

All of her foreign plants. Not just Ash? Analia didn't dare ask for confirmation.

Selbi went on, "Shall I tell Her Majesty you would like access?"

"No," Analia said quickly.

Selbi's eyes sharpened once more. Analia bit back a curse.

"Please," she said, "Her Majesty has been so kind to me these past months. It feels ungrateful of me to complain."

"Her Majesty would want to know how you are feeling, Princess."

Analia didn't have to pretend as she wrung her hands. Especially as Aaron stepped up behind her, his hand brushing her back in warning as he examined a display of slick black stones.

Analia didn't dare glance over her shoulder, but she recognized the voices well enough. Lena and Pryanth. Heading straight for them.

"Please," she repeated, clearly desperate. "I don't want to be one more problem they have to contend with. Not after everything they have done for me."

Selbi still didn't seem completely convinced. Analia opened her mouth, but quickly snapped it shut as an arm snaked across her shoulders.

"There you are," Pryanth said pleasantly.

So, it was this game again. Suddenly, the thought of brushing spats aside, pretending they never happened, felt incredibly tiring.

"You already finished?" Analia asked, looking down at the new golden scabbard, designed to look like a coiled dragon, dangling from his hip.

"It was quick," he told her. "But I came outside, and you were gone."

His gaze flicked to Selbi. Don't speak, don't speak, don't speak.

"What a fine place to wait, wouldn't you say, Your Highness?" Selbi spread her arms.

Pryanth said something Analia didn't catch, too consumed by relief. That relief didn't last, however, as Pryanth ushered her out the door, retracting his arm once they were outside.

"You should have told me you were leaving," he said, power pulsating around him.

Analia studied his face. Angry that she'd left? Hurt she didn't tell him? Sunshine, thundercloud, she couldn't tell what she was actually reading, and what she wanted to read.

"I'm sorry," she said. "I just... I needed to collect myself."

"So, you walked two streets over, and into a random apothecary, with him." Pryanth jerked his chin at Aaron beside her, the guard perfectly serene.

All the confidence Analia had had when talking to Selbi seemed to drain through her feet and into the ground below. Once again, Pryanth had filled her up with his presence, just to leave her shriveled in his wake.

Pryanth waited for a response, but seeing he wouldn't get one, he shook his head sadly. And that sadness hurt more than any angry word he could have hurled at her.

Pryanth took Lena by the arm, fading into the shadows around them and undoubtedly jumping back to the castle. A part of Analia was surprised he didn't walk back to give her a chance to catch up and grovel.

Analia took a slow, deep breath through her nose. Then, she turned to Aaron, still quietly beside her.

"How much do you want to bet the Royal Garden isn't the one right outside the castle?" she asked.

Aaron seemed genuinely taken aback. But, Crystal Bless him, he decided to go with it.

"You little liar," he said, almost gleefully. "I never knew you were such a liar."

"Those lies were harmless," Analia said, starting off toward the castle.

"Such a clever force to be reckoned with," he said, falling into step beside her and ruffling her hair.

Analia briefly closed her eyes. "The Ash Kingdom may not want me as their princess," she said, "but I know how to play the political game."

# Chapter 39

The sun was just beginning to set when Aaron and Analia rounded the side of the castle and stepped into the garden beyond. As they silently walked the pebbled paths, Aaron could feel the anger and confusion radiating off Analia. Or perhaps it was his own, lingering after seeing the rage and anguish in her eyes in that alleyway, literally burning beneath his hands.

But despite his questions, Aaron didn't break the silence. He knew she would let him know when she was ready, even if it was just for a distraction.

Instead, he scanned the surrounding plants. The heady scent of jasmine and geranium filled his nose, sending his hand reaching for his bracelet. The apothecary, too—

"That was sweet," Analia said. "What you did for Loliette, I mean."

Aaron pushed the thoughts aside.

"Analia," he said, bringing a hand to his chest, "did you just pay me a compliment?"

Analia whacked him. Aaron nudged her back, earning a small smile.

There had been something about Loliette that snagged his attention. There was too much intelligence in her eyes. Eyes he had sworn flashed pure gold.

"So," Analia said, "how long were you on the streets, then?"

Aaron pivoted, pebbles scattering beneath his heel. "Me?" he asked. "Never." He moved forward once more, knowing he should leave it there. "But my brother was."

"You have a brother," Analia exclaimed.

"Not blood, but he might as well be."

Aaron's muscles remained relaxed, but he couldn't quite keep the tension out of his voice. Of all the distractions she could have chosen.

Analia tilted her head, obviously intrigued. But she remained quiet, a swinging door he knew he was safe to push or pull shut at any time. Gods, when was the last time he'd had that?

"Branten was on the streets by the time he was four," he said. "He had no one. Had to learn how to survive alone at an age when most aren't capable of doing so.

"It took him years to trust all of us. He'd been conditioned so early on to view every good deed as a trick or a way to put you in someone's debt. Never safe to stay in one place for too long. Thinking multiple steps ahead in every interaction."

Aaron's heart gave a slow, aching squeeze.

Analia asked, "When did you two meet?"

"When we were nine and he beat the shit out of me."

Analia smiled, the biggest one he'd ever seen from her. "Really?"

"Oh yes." Aaron grinned, his jaw aching at the memory. "Don't worry, I got him back."

"I'm sure you did."

Aaron laughed. Gods, those were some of his only good memories from the Underground. He and Branten had gone back and forth for a year, never giving the other a break until they finally came to a truce. They were constantly bruised and bloodied, their knuckles scabbed over, even though they both knew Aaron could have—

Something inside Aaron cringed away. His hand flew to the chain around his neck.

"Hey," Analia said, putting a hand on his wrist and bringing him to a stop. "What's that look for?"

"What look?"

"The 'I'm blaming myself for something that isn't my fault' look."

"Oh, Analia, how you hurt me."

Aaron gently stepped out of her grip and kept moving. Too perceptive.

Analia doggedly trailed him. "I know that look because it's the same one I wear every time you call me out for it."

They stepped into the center of the garden. Here, every pebbled path flowed into one circular cleared-off section, a marble fountain softly burbling in its center.

"Is this about Branten?" she asked. "Aaron, you were a child. There was nothing you could have done."

Oh, how little she knew.

"It's not that," he said. "It's just…"

This was his opening. He could brush it aside with a smirk and one of his jabbing comments that always had Analia's temper flaring and attention redirected. But gods, he was so tired of having to choose every word carefully.

Aaron let out a long breath as he sat on the edge of the fountain. "It's not that I blame myself, per se."

"Then what is it?" Analia asked, sitting beside him.

Cold light. A scream of pain. A blossom of red against pale skin. Icy, relentless fury. But how could he tell her that?

"What if I were to tell you Branten and I never would have met if I hadn't done something horrible. Not on purpose, but it was still completely my fault.

"And what if I regret what I did, but if it meant never meeting Branten, never helping him get off the streets? I would do it again without a second thought. What kind of person would that make me?"

"Certainly no worse than me," Analia murmured.

She shot a pointed look at a nearby bramble bush, a pair of green eyes with slit pupils blinking in alarm before disappearing.

"I can promise you it's worse," Aaron said.

Analia didn't respond immediately. Finally, she said, "That's a lot of hypotheticals."

Aaron stole a glance at her, bracing himself for the blow. But there was only a thoughtful crease between her brows.

All he wanted in that moment was to tell her exactly who he was, why he was there, about the home he desperately wanted to return to. But also, the home he had to protect. The one he couldn't risk, no matter how badly he wanted to believe the tapestries had shown her to him for a reason.

Aaron gave a noncommittal shrug, the weight of his decision settling in his stomach.

"All right then," Analia said. "I'll just work with what I do know."

"What's that?" Aaron asked warily.

Analia turned, her knees resting against his thigh. "I know that you've done some questionable things—"

"Terrible."

"Fine, terrible. But from everything I've seen, every choice you make is for the greater good, even if it's unpleasant for yourself.

"You purposefully provoke sullen princesses and allow them to hate you, just so they won't give up. You take the time to teach little orphan girls how to tie their hats to their heads. And I don't know exactly what you're risking being here, but I know it's enough to scare you, and yet, you're still here."

A battlefield, screams, the clang of sword on sword. Bodies sprawled out around him. The feeling of blood beneath his nails. Gods, he wished he could be the person she saw.

"Why are you so determined to torture yourself with the past?" Analia asked.

"I suspect for the same reason you are so desperate to escape to the future."

She didn't flinch back as he'd feared. She just swung her legs, her toes scattering pebbles as she thought.

"I used to want to escape to the future," she said. "To when my magic would come in and my people would finally see me as more than a smudge on the family name."

Aaron stiffened. Analia patted his hand, her tired resignation sending ice creeping through his veins.

"I thought nothing could be as bad as where I was before. But now my uncle is gone, and I'm starting to wonder if the future is truly an escape, or just another pit I haven't stumbled in yet."

How many times had he thought that throughout the decades? When trapped in the Underground, knowing the reason he was sentenced there wouldn't disappear when he finally reemerged. Every day he hauled himself out of bed after his mother's death, just to see to the end of a war he was nowhere near done fighting.

"You know why I torture myself with the past?" he asked.

Analia shook her head.

"Because when I finally dragged my sorry ass out of that pit, it was the only one I could fall back into."

"Who would have thought the most unbearable thing would be present-day solid ground," Analia muttered.

"You learn to adjust."

Analia raised a pointed brow, and Aaron put up his hands. "Mostly," he amended. "But you're allowed to have off days."

Analia thoughtfully rubbed the strap of her gown between her fingers. "Two sides of the same gold piece."

Aaron snorted. "Perhaps a horribly dented piece that was lost in a sewer grate."

"Well, good news for us," Analia said. "Gold doesn't tarnish. We just have character."

Aaron laughed slightly. "Princess Analia," he said, sliding his legs under hers so they crossed at their knees, "how did you get to be so wise?"

"Through all those dents we were just talking about."

"And how are you doing with that most recent one?"

Analia shrugged her hand. "I thought we already covered that."

"We covered it in the moment," Aaron said. "How are you now?"

For a long moment, Analia considered. "I don't know," she decided.

Aaron frowned. "He should've had to face your flame and rage for that."

"He was angry," she said tiredly. "We've all done things we don't mean when we're mad."

"Maybe. But only Pryanth stomps people down before they can realize he doesn't have a spine."

Analia deflated. Without thinking, Aaron reached over and took her hand. And the breath froze in his lungs.

Crystal spare him, what was he doing? He needed to drop her hand, apologize—she was betrothed. But he couldn't help giving her a sidelong look, feeling like a child waiting to see if he got away with his mischief.

Especially as Analia didn't pull away. Instead, she squeezed his hand. And a low buzz started in Aaron's veins.

Dangerous. So incredibly, spellbindingly dangerous.

"Come on," Analia said, finally rising to her feet and releasing his hand. "We've got work to do."

Together, they searched the rest of the garden, coming up empty once again. Eventually, they returned to the castle. And as Aaron watched her go, he couldn't help but wonder what would have happened if he'd said more.

Analia could sense the impending thunderclap at dinner that night. Pryanth excitedly chattered with his mother and cousin about the new sword that proudly dangled from his hip, his eyes never straying to her. Not even as he walked her to her chambers, holding her hand so tight that her bones ground together. She could feel the anticipation building, pounding, twisting with every echoed footstep, climbing to a crescendo the moment she opened her door.

"How dare you?" Pryanth seethed, slamming the door behind him. "How dare you embarrass me in front of my people? Be so blatantly insubordinate in public?"

Analia expected dread to crawl down her spine. Instead, she was eerily calm.

She'd been waiting for this. Not since their first fight in the entryway, but before that. From the first moment he'd turned on her in the hallway. So quick, gone in a flash.

But Analia was a child of chaos. It was her familiar, her baseline. It was waiting for the boom that had been unnerving.

"I should be allowed to disagree with you, Pryanth," she told him, heading for her dressing table. "You shouldn't want me to be just another obsequious sycophant."

Pryanth stalked after her. "What I want is for you not to make a fool of me in front of my people!"

"No one noticed, Pryanth. No one cared!"

"I cared! I cared that, once again, you took his side."

Analia froze, hand resting on the back of her chair. "This is about Aaron?"

"You are my betrothed," Pryanth hissed, maneuvering around the chair to face her. "You are obligated to side with me."

Analia had the strangest urge to laugh. Or maybe sob. Anything to release the almost electrified disbelief swelling in her chest.

"Is that all I am?" she asked. "Always a step below you? Do I not get a say?"

"I never said that," Pryanth said immediately. "You're not listening to me."

Something sparked, deep in Analia's stomach.

"Honestly, Analia," he went on, "what happened to you? I was there for you after your uncle died. I brought you into my home, loved you when no one else has, and this is how you repay me? By betraying my trust and never stopping to consider how your actions impact me—"

"That's not true—"

"I thought I knew who you are—"

"Pryanth—"

"But every time you're given a choice, you choose yourself over me. You choose *him* over me—"

"Pryanth, let me talk!" Analia yelled.

Pryanth reared back. Surprised herself, it took Analia a moment to speak.

"I'm not choosing Aaron over you," she said carefully.

"Maybe not," Pryanth said. "But he's starting to feel like your version of my father's whore."

Analia took a step back, his words feeling like a physical blow. But Pryanth didn't pause.

"My father always chose her," he said, his voice shaking slightly. "No matter how many times he promised she meant nothing to him. Whenever he was given a choice, he always chose his whore. And I won't let myself get dragged behind empty words."

Analia lowered her eyes to her half-extended hand. She knew she should object, immediately, even. But what did it mean that Aaron merely taking her hand in the garden had comforted her more than Pryanth ever had?

"Aaron is my friend," she said carefully. "Not my betrothed, not anyone I'm interested in, but a friend. One of the only friends I have. And I don't know how to make that any clearer."

"Who's the other friend?"

Analia's mouth snapped shut. Pryanth waited. And as the silence stretched on, Analia unable to meet his gaze, Pryanth's face slowly morphed from anger to rage.

"Him?" he demanded. "Of all people to befriend, you have to choose the fucking bastard? Am I truly not good enough for you, either?"

Analia leaned away. "Pryanth, I chose to marry you—"

"I was your only option! You could have befriended anyone, and you chose the servant that destroyed my family—"

"It's not Dimitri's fault, it's your father's—"

Pryanth's hand flashed out, quick as an adder. Analia's head jerked to the side, her cheek stinging in the shape of his hand, the crack echoing in her ears.

For a long, unbearable moment, neither of them moved. Pryanth's face was frozen in shock, his hand still half-raised in front of him. But Analia felt nothing. Nothing at all. Not even the urge to touch her smarting cheek.

"You shouldn't have made me do that," Pryanth finally whispered, face crumpling. "I didn't want to hurt you."

"How could you?" Analia breathed, tasting metal. She backed up, bumping into her bed, slowly sinking down.

Pryanth followed as if in a daze. "You left me no choice," he said, sitting beside her, stroking her arm. "You knew this would upset me, you knew that I would react. But you kept poking. Why, why would you put me in that position?"

Analia stared at him numbly. She wanted him to wrap his arms around her. She wanted to shove him off her bed, out the door, out the gods-damned window. What was she supposed to do when the person she wanted to comfort her was the person who hurt her?

Pryanth took Analia's limp hand in his. Remorse flooded his expression as he kissed her smarting cheek. "I wish you didn't make me do that."

Then, he rose, exiting her chambers without another word. The door closing behind him sounded more like a crack than a thud in Analia's ears.

# Chapter 40

"Not a word," Analia said as Bie and Nadi bounced into her chambers the following morning.

The maids stumbled to a halt, bringing their hands to their mouths as they caught sight of her face. Their heads bobbed in unison as they backed out of the room, Analia telling them to give some excuse—she didn't care what—to keep people away. Then, she started to pace.

She'd already spent the entire night before turning over every word, every decision that led to her split lip and the red, angry mark across her cheek. Yet, all she'd succeeded in doing was confusing herself even more.

Even now, as the sun slowly rose and fell outside her window, Analia had no answers—not regarding how she should feel, if it could have been avoided, why Pryanth had done it in the first place. But she couldn't bring herself to let it go.

Before she knew it, it was almost dinner time. Bie and Nadi timidly entered her room, clutching a pot of powder and brushes.

"We thought we'd help you cover it," Bie said.

Analia nodded once. The two girls guided her into her chair, their usual chatter replaced by the stroke of brush bristles across skin.

It took a great deal of powder, but Bie and Nadi were able to obscure the mark on Analia's cheek, which had faded to an ugly yellow color. It would probably be gone in its entirety in a day or two thanks to her Blessing, but there wasn't much they could do about her split lip in the meantime.

"Keep your head low," Nadi suggested, arranging Analia's hair around her face.

"Try to keep it angled toward the shadows," Bie added.

Analia's voice was distant as she thanked them. The two maids exchanged a teary look, then flung their arms around her shoulders. Analia stared at their reflections, bewildered. But she allowed herself to partially melt into their embrace. Just for a moment, just as she steeled herself for what was to come.

Analia stuck close to the shadows as she made her way to dinner, acutely aware of her lip. She just had to hope she could hide it—

"What's wrong with your face?"

Analia jumped as the wall beside her slid aside, Dimitri popping his head out of the entrance to the passageways. She quickly angled her face away, "Let it go, Dima."

Dimitri's disembodied head gave her a disbelieving look, then retracted back into the passageways. Crystal spare her, what was he going to do?

Analia shoved the encounter aside as she entered the dining room, already a buzz with voices. Thankfully, no one spared her too long a glance as she took her seat beside Pryanth. She kept her head carefully tilted, but she was still able to watch Pryanth as he pointedly ignored her.

The rest of the table was engrossed in discussing Cabir's plans to lead a tightened border patrol around the central kingdom, the memory of the Solstice still dangling like a spear point over their heads.

As dinner continued without accident, Analia started to wonder if she could get away with it. She only had six bites left when—

"Analia, dear," Deardryn said across from her.

Analia dropped her fork.

"How's your headache?" she asked.

"It's still bothering me, Your Majesty."

"I wonder if it's all the magic fields," Deardryn mused. "The more you hone that skill, I can only assume the more sensitive you become."

"Yes, that must be it." Analia's knuckles turned white around her reclaimed fork.

Deardryn made to continue, but Pryanth lazily cut in, "Leave her be, Mother. She's in pain."

Analia's and Deardryn's eyes shot to Pryanth. One astonished, the other shrewd.

"Analia," Deardryn said suddenly, "look up."

"I'm sorry?"

"You haven't looked up from your plate this entire meal."

No. She couldn't show them. She couldn't watch as the shock melted into concern, then pity, and finally disappointment.

"She's fine," Pryanth said. His hand gripped her knee under the table, hard enough to leave another bruise.

Analia had watched that progression back in Ash. First on Brenn's face when he realized she would never have magic. Then on the guards faces fifteen years ago when Brenn humiliated her to make a point.

"Analia," Deardryn said sharply, the table growing quiet around them. "Look at me."

Over and over again, the cycle had turned in Ash. At some point, she'd started to care whether that cycle continued in Sun. And now, the thought of losing what little respect, approval, she had earned stung more than the mark across her cheek.

"For the gods' sake," Othin said, cutting into his meat, "let her be."

Yes, let her disappear. Don't let the shame swallow her whole.

Deardryn ignored him, her honey eyes demanding. "That's an order from your queen."

Reluctantly, Analia looked up. Her eyes darted to Pryanth as she felt the stares land on her cheek, but he refused to look at her.

"Analia," Cabir said quietly.

"It's fine," Analia mumbled, dropping her head once more.

Deardryn demanded, "How did this happen?"

Analia's eyes darted to Pryanth once more. What was she supposed to say? That Pryanth did it? They wouldn't understand, and Pryanth would just get angry again.

Pryanth fidgeted with his knife. "We got into a disagreement."

"And that is how you conclude it?" Deardryn half rose from her chair, golden light flickering around her palms.

Analia flinched. Not just from the memories of golden light and wine glasses, but there was a part of her that didn't want this mark to just disappear, swept away and forgotten with everything else Pryanth tried to bury.

"This is between me and Analia," said Pryanth mulishly.

"No, this is between you, Analia, and *me*. At what point have I ever taught you that that behavior is acceptable?"

"You don't even know the full story!" Pryanth whined.

"Well," Cabir murmured, "you certainly seem no worse for wear."

Pryanth wheeled on him. "When did you become the final arbiter?"

"When did it become acceptable to slap your betrothed?"

"Enough!" Othin bellowed, banging his fist on the table.

Four pairs of honey eyes turned to him. Analia's gaze returned to her plate, fists clenched around the sides of her chair.

"What's done is done," Othin said. "Pryanth, you shouldn't have left such a visible mark."

The skin behind Analia's ears flashed with phantom burns.

"He shouldn't have struck her at all," Saura said.

The queen's sister looked Othin straight in the eyes, her quiet voice at odds with her sudden, unexpected resolve. And to Analia's shock, Othin softened.

"What's done is done," he said gruffly. He turned to Cabir and changed the subject, swift and sharp as a winter wind.

A part of Analia was grateful for the distraction. Yet, the other part was... disappointed? No, that couldn't be it. Because if she was disappointed that they let it go, that meant she thought there was something to defend, which meant she thought Pryanth had done something wrong. And he had done something wrong. But was that the full story?

Thankfully, no one tried to reengage her, especially not Pryanth. And while the Princess of Ash was desperate to rise from the table and disappear, Analia forced herself to wait until the meal was over. Forced herself to take her time as the Royals finally rose to their feet. Only when their voices had faded down the hall did she flee.

Analia paced across the parapet. She didn't care about the drop, the wind that swirled around her. She just needed the height, the night sky flecked with her familiar stars, just needed to think—

"You know," said a voice behind her, "most people pace away from perilous plunges."

Analia didn't look up. "Most people also use sarcasm as a seasoning, not the whole meal."

"It's not my fault few have as refined a palette as I do."

Aaron stepped into her peripheral vision. So that's what Dimitri had done.

She waited for him to tell her to stop, get down. But Aaron only sat on the wall a little ways down, turning so he could look out across the kingdom. Analia continued to pace, back and forth, back and forth.

"Come sit with me," he said eventually.

"No."

"Just for two minutes. Then you can go back to your pacing for as long as you like."

No, she couldn't stop. She had to keep moving, because the moment she stopped and was forced to sit with what was churning inside her—

"Please?"

Analia paused midstep. She almost hadn't heard him over the wind. But there was something in his tone that made her pivot, keeping her face averted as she came to warily sit beside him.

Analia kept her gaze trained on the kingdom below, feeling Aaron's eyes on her unmarred cheek. Her toes flexed in her slippers. Her fingers curled and uncurled around her skirts.

"I suppose you'd like to see it," she finally said.

"Yes."

"Why should I show you?"

"Because it will be impossible to hide it from me forever, and at least if you decide to show me now, it will be on your terms."

He was so calm, so logical. But the thought of his face once he saw had Analia curling in on herself.

He was right, though. How could she hide this from him? From anyone?

Analia squeezed her eyes shut, Aaron waiting patiently beside her. Finally, taking the little control he gave her, she turned her face to him.

Aaron didn't move immediately, giving her a chance to change her mind. But Analia didn't turn away, didn't open her eyes as he lightly wiped away the powder with his sleeve. He tilted her head toward the light, tracing the mark on her cheek with a feather-light touch.

For a few long, unbearable moments, Aaron didn't speak. Finally, unable to take the anticipation, Analia opened her eyes. But Aaron's face was unreadable.

"What?" she asked.

Aaron's eyes remained trained on her cheek. "I'm trying to think of a name bad enough to call him."

"Aaron, it's nothing," Analia said, leaning back. She half expected his hand to move with her, but he let it drop.

"It's not nothing," he said. "He didn't accidentally bump you into the door frame while walking by. Anna, he *slapped you.*"

"I'm aware."

"Then why are you defending him?"

"Because he didn't mean to! He was angry and it just—it just happened."

Analia cringed away from Aaron's disbelieving stare, her words coming faster. "I know his temper. I saw I was pushing him too far and I should have stopped. He was angry because I embarrassed him in front of his people, again, when I'm supposed to be helping him earn their respect. I made a mistake. I should have been trying to calm him instead of making it worse."

Aaron listened quietly. He waited to make sure she was done. Then, "Is that what he told you?"

Analia bristled. "Don't mock me, Aaron."

"I'm not mocking you!"

Analia looked away. Aaron let out a frustrated breath, Analia watching from the corner of her eye as he raked a hand through his hair.

"How often do I infuriate you?" he asked.

"Frequently."

"Have you ever slapped me?"

"That's different," Analia said immediately. But was it?

"Why?" Aaron asked. "Because I'm your friend and he's your betrothed? Because he convinced you that he loves you?"

"Stop trying to corner me, Aaron."

"Don't let him confuse you." Aaron took her trembling hands in his. "Analia, you know this. You know that if he did love you, he would never—"

"Stop," Analia whispered.

"Could you ever imagine your uncle, who *incontrovertibly* loved you, hurting you—"

"Stop!"

Analia wrenched her hands from his. Aaron jerked back, watching with wide eyes as Analia buried her face in her hands.

It was too much. Too much, too much, too much. Because if Aaron was right, what did that mean about Pryanth? What did that mean about her?

She wanted to believe Pryanth, that it was one time, that she could handle it, that she could trust him. But she couldn't ignore Aaron's words, echoing her own thoughts that had strained to be heard through the chaos.

But who was right? Who could she trust? Because clearly, she couldn't trust herself.

Analia peeked between her fingers. Aaron watched her, clearly wondering what he had done wrong.

"I'm sorry," she whispered.

Analia thought she caught a glimpse of pure, undiluted fury cross Aaron's face. He gently gripped her wrists, pulling her hands from her face.

"Never apologize for this," he told her fiercely. "You hear me? This is not your fault."

Analia wanted to believe him. But she couldn't stop the guilt from twining with her relief. Nor could she stop the tears in her eyes. Aaron reached for her.

Footsteps sounded on the roof behind them.

Analia whipped around. But it was only Dimitri, loosely gripping something in one hand.

"I thought I'd find you two up here," he said, perching on Analia's other side.

Why had she been afraid just then?

"Where've you been?" asked Aaron, sitting back.

"Just checking on my handiwork. Flashfire here may not be able to get her revenge, but that doesn't mean a stupid, unimportant little servant like me can't accidentally slip something into His Brat-Highness's wine that would lead to a very enjoyable night with the toilet."

Aaron smirked. Analia was too tired to respond.

Dimitri's gaze flicked across her cheek, letting loose a string of curses that had Aaron humming in appreciation. But still, no pity.

"Don't cover that up anymore," Dimitri told her, passing her what turned out to be a cloth filled with ice.

"Why?" Aaron asked. "You think he'd care if she forced him to look at what he's done?"

"Of course not," Dimitri scoffed. "That requires empathy."

Did that mean they also noticed Pryanth's willingness to stab where it would hurt most?

"The servants will care, though," Dimitri went on. "They all know what a piece of shit Pryanth is, and they actually like you."

But what about the time Pryanth had spun her around after she finally got a hold of the magic? What about the times he would bring her tea in the library in Ash and they would talk for hours? What had happened to that Pryanth?

"You say that like it's surprising," Analia murmured.

"Well," said Aaron, "you can be a bit taciturn at times."

Analia elbowed him.

"And bony," he complained, rubbing his side.

"That couldn't have hurt," she said.

Dimitri chimed in, "Bordello only enjoys pain in the bedroom."

Aaron's eyes sparkled with wicked delight. "Are you sure we haven't met before?" he asked. "Perhaps a drunken night?"

"Please, you would have remembered me."

A small smile tugged at Analia's lips as the two went back and forth. There was a comfort in their familiar rhythm. It was something to hold onto, even though she remained silent between them.

Analia's free hand drifted to her pin as Aaron eventually filled Dimitri in on their trip to the apothecary. *When head, heart, and gut are aligned, that is when the path is clearest.* But what if she was too afraid to see that path, let alone walk it?

"I've never heard of a secret garden," Dimitri said, kicking her ankle as he thought. "I'll do some digging, though."

"You mean snooping?" Analia asked.

She hadn't spoken in some time, but Dimitri didn't miss a beat. "I thought that was implied."

When the three finally peeled themselves off the parapet, the sky was completely black. Dimitri slipped off almost immediately. Aaron, however, walked Analia back to her room, not trying to pull her from her thoughts.

She'd always known there were two sides to Pryanth. But come to think of it, she'd been seeing that duality less and less. But the flickers of him, the moments when she did see that original Pryanth, they were intoxicating. And if he was still in there somewhere, if she waited long enough, maybe he would return.

But how long would she have to wait? Did she deserve to have to wait?

Aaron lightly gripped Analia's elbow, bringing her to a stop. They'd reached her door, and she hadn't even realized.

Aaron's thumb stroked a single line along her arm. He made to say something, but before he could, Analia slipped inside, softly closing the door behind her.

# Chapter 41

In the week that followed, Dimitri and Aaron found excuses to constantly be around Analia. Aaron continued walking the halls with her, looking for the ring or whatever it was they were doing. Dimitri, on the other hand, took to haunting Analia's chambers, pestering her to help him with his reading.

They all knew what they were doing, but that didn't mean Dimitri had to admit it. That maybe, potentially, Dimitri finally getting to progress beyond children's books wasn't his only reason for being there. That yes, fine, not giving Pryanth a chance to corner Analia was also a contributor. But only because Dimitri was furious Pryanth had gotten away with being a tyrant once again, and not because the sight of the rapidly fading bruise on Analia's cheek had stirred feelings he was terrified of naming.

On the seventh day post slap, Dimitri trailed after Analia and Aaron as the former searched for her ring.

"Gods, Flashfire, what are we doing?" he whined. "We're going in circles! I thought you could sense the magic. Since when does a secret location mean a bad signal?"

"You know," Aaron said, glancing back at him, "you don't have to come with us. I know it must be tiring, what with those little legs of yours."

Those little legs of his sped up, coming up on Analia's other shoulder. "You still bounce when you get thrown off your dragon, Bordello?"

Aaron snorted, and Analia smiled slightly.

"Honestly, Flashfire," Dimitri continued, "I think you just have a loose connection in that head of yours. I'd suggest knocking it a couple times, but if Bordello's any indicator, that might only make it worse."

"You could try huffing cleaning product," Aaron suggested. "But I hear risks include becoming a cynical son of a bitch."

"You two are horrible," Analia told them.

Dimitri and Aaron shared a grin. And they immediately sobered as the Crystal-damned himself rounded the corner ahead of them.

Analia slowed to a stop. Pryanth's eyes slid from side to side as he approached, taking in Aaron and Dimitri a few steps behind her.

"Hi," he said quietly, eyes back on Analia as he reached her. "Can we talk?"

Dimitri folded his arms. Aaron rocked back on his heels. But Analia nodded mutely.

Pryanth's eyes flashed to Dimitri and Aaron once more. "Alone."

Why, so he could slap her again? Before Dimitri could speak, Aaron shot him a sharp glance. Dimitri was tempted to ignore him, especially since the look on Pryanth's face said he knew exactly what Dimitri was thinking. He started to speak but paused as Analia turned to face them.

"Please?" she asked.

Was that guilt in her eyes?

Aaron and Dimitri swapped another glance. Without speaking, the two took exactly ten steps back, then sat on the nearby windowsill.

Oh yes, they weren't going anywhere. Especially as Analia's face—hidden from Pryanth's view—relaxed.

"She told you to leave," Pryanth said loudly.

"Apologies," Aaron drawled. "Guard duties. Queen's orders." He waved a vague hand.

Pryanth's irritation was palpable as he rounded on Dimitri. "You. You have scrub work."

"No, I don't," Dimitri lied.

"You most certainly do."

"I thought you were here to talk with Analia."

Oh, how he loved it when Pryanth's face turned all red and splotchy.

Pryanth walked around Analia, partially obscuring Aaron and Dimitri with his body. "So those are the two you're choosing over me?" he asked.

"Pryanth, please, I'm not choosing them. I told them to go. I can't control if they do or not."

"Why would you want to be around people who don't respect you?"

Dimitri's mouth opened before he knew the words about to spill forth. Aaron elbowed him hard in the ribs. Dimitri whipped his head toward him, but Aaron leveled him with a look that had his protests crawling right back down his throat.

"They're staying because they're concerned," Analia said.

"Do you not trust me?"

Analia opened her mouth, but no words came out.

Pryanth stepped closer, raising his hand. Dimitri's fists clenched as Analia fought back a flinch. But Pryanth only ran his fingertips across her cheek.

"I don't want to fight," he sighed. "I'm sorry you got hurt." His finger moved to trace the outline of the lips he had smashed between his palm and her teeth. "Mother told me how I needed to apologize. That I shouldn't have let you push me that far. That that's not something you do to someone you love."

Pryanth's hand curled around Analia's face as he kept talking, but Dimitri could only hear the blood ringing in his ears. Aaron's eyes were locked on Pryanth's hand, his muscles taut.

They waited for her to push him away, to flag them over, to kick his sorry ass down the hall herself. But Analia was a statue under Pryanth's hands, his mouth as he kissed her.

"I'll leave you alone," he murmured against her mouth. He pulled away, letting his hand drop as he turned and continued down the hall, ignoring the two nauseated men seated on the windowsill. All until Dimitri pressed the toe of his boot down on the trailing end of Pryanth's cloak, sending him stumbling.

Pryanth whirled. "You!"

"Sorry," Dimitri drawled. "Bad timing."

"Scrub work. Now."

Dimitri pushed himself off the windowsill, giving a long stretch. Pryanth turned back down the hall, and Dimitri promptly sat back down.

Analia remained rooted to the spot. Dimitri looked to Aaron questioningly, but the guard only leaned back against the windowpane, waiting.

"Thank you," she finally said, her eyes focusing on them.

Dimitri blurted, "Don't tell me you believe a word of what he said—"

"Dima," Aaron cut in quietly.

Dimitri snapped his mouth shut with some effort. Aaron scooted over, making room for Analia on the windowsill. Dimitri's face twitched out of habit, but he surprisingly didn't mind the feeling of Analia's arm pressed against his as she wedged herself in between them.

"Are you all right?" Aaron asked.

Analia leaned her head back against the window. "I'm so tired of fighting."

"That doesn't mean you should let him get away with it!" Dimitri exclaimed.

"Even though he just tried to put it to rest?" Analia asked.

"Was he trying to put it to rest," Aaron asked, "or trying to bury it?"

Analia frowned. "Pryanth is the sole Prince of the Sun Kingdom," she said. "He's gotten everything he's wanted and never had to suffer the consequences. He's never learned to argue or apologize, but that doesn't make him a bad person."

"Then why do you have to keep making excuses for him?" Aaron asked.

Analia didn't respond, out of despair or anger, Dimitri couldn't tell. But there was no denying his rage as it bubbled over.

"What an overgrown fucking fungus," he spat. "I only touched his cloak, but that ooze is so toxic I'm worried I got some on me. You'll have to throw me in the sewers to make sure I'm clean."

"If that's the case," said Analia dully, "then you need to toss me in, too."

"I think you should just shove him off the roof," Dimitri said. "Now *that* would solve all our problems."

"Over a one-time thing?" Analia asked.

"Doesn't matter," Aaron said. "If he did it once, do you trust him not to do it again—what's wrong?"

Analia's face puckered, her hand going to the skin behind her ear.

Aaron froze. Dimitri fidgeted in the sudden silence, struggling to remain quiet even with the look Aaron flashed him. But as soon as Analia began, he had no problem going perfectly still.

"When I was six, I accidentally broke an heirloom. I had been racing past—I don't remember where to—when my arm barely brushed against the goblet, sending it tumbling.

"I don't even know how to describe my terror as Brenn stormed down the hall to see what happened. And the moment his eyes took in the scene before him, I could actually feel the heat of his magic as his temper erupted. He was so consumed by his anger as he shouted at me that I don't think he realized his fingers were burning. Not until I cried out as his fingerprints were scorched into the skin behind my ear.

"Immediately, his eyes flew wide. He yanked his hand back, although his fingers still burned as he grabbed me by the shoulders and spun me around. At first, I thought he was checking to make sure I was all right. But he was only looking to see if he'd left a mark."

Dimitri was all too familiar with the resentment in her eyes, born from the betrayal of the person who was supposed to love her. That, holy gods, she *still* loved.

Dimitri was surprised by the ache in his chest. Not just for her, but for himself as he realized he didn't have a drop of love for his father.

Aaron asked, "Did you tell Accalon?"

"No. But he always had a way of finding out."

"This happened more than once?"

Dimitri didn't think Analia caught how Aaron's hand clenched around the windowsill. She just shrugged.

"He did his best. Keeping me with him and away from Brenn as much as possible, letting him know he knew what was going on, thinly veiled threats. But there was only so much he could do since I refused to rat Brenn out."

Dimitri demanded, "Why the fuck not?"

Analia finally turned to look at him. And Dimitri thought he was going to be sick as she replied, "Because I couldn't stand the idea of him telling me it was my fault."

Her challenging gaze flashed between them. But Dimitri didn't want to give her pity. He wanted to give her a fucking axe to settle the score.

Aaron caught her stare, his own gaze steely. "That was not your fault."

At his words, the fight seemed to drain out of her, replaced by a look that had Dimitri's nails digging into his palms. He managed to keep his voice flippant, though, as he said, "You just have shit luck."

He ticked them off on his fingers. "Pryanth? Parasite. Brenn? Flaming pile of shit."

"Ah," Aaron said, spreading his hands, "but now you have us."

"And we're fucking fantastic," Dimitri said.

"Incomparable, really," Aaron agreed.

Analia's lips twitched. "With such large heads as well."

Aaron and Dimitri snickered. But as they bantered on, Dimitri couldn't quite shake that look from his mind. It had been the look of utter defeat. One that had him leaning into Analia, just a little more than he was before.

Analia returned to her room later that afternoon. She'd told both Aaron and Dimitri she wanted to be alone, and they'd reluctantly left her at her door.

Now, she sank down on her bed, curling into a tight ball under the covers. She used to be so good at controlling her emotions. But these past few weeks had left her feeling zapped dry, yet oddly lighter. It was like the more she talked, the more weight was lifted off her shoulders, which only reminded her just how exhausted she truly was.

She hadn't been lying when she told Aaron and Dimitri she was tired of fighting. What she hadn't mentioned was she felt like she was fighting herself, just as much as she was Pryanth. Especially as she looked at the pain in his eyes as he apologized to her, over and over in that hallway.

Somehow, despite her anger, that look still managed to twist her heart. Or perhaps, despite her feelings for Pryanth, she still resented him. She resented those moments in her chamber that sent her lifeline out of Ash swinging wildly. The only thing she didn't regret was telling Aaron and Dimitri about Brenn.

That memory had been pressing against her awareness the entire week like a cold knife to the neck. Yet, she'd found letting the words spill out instead of bracing herself for the slash somehow made the cut less painful. It didn't stop the blood from flowing, but it was far more painful, more difficult, to plunge through a tensed muscle than a relaxed one.

Analia's brows scrunched. Something Dimitri had said earlier about signals. Tensed, relaxed. Still flowing...

Analia sat up. It couldn't be that simple. She couldn't have been going about this all wrong.

Analia scooted around, pressing her back against the wall. She'd never done this without Aaron before. There was a part of her terrified of what might happen, but as she brought her hand to her pin, she knew she had to try.

Analia opened her mind to the magic fields. She immediately gasped, her shoulders slamming back against the stone.

At some point, she'd built a mental shield between herself and the magic fields throughout the castle. The feedback had been too overwhelming not to. Consequently, she'd been moving through the castle, slowly sifting through each field.

Now, with that shield down, Analia was bombarded from all sides. Her vision faded to white, her hearing fuzzing out.

But she didn't fight it. Instead, she allowed herself to tumble with the magical currents that rolled through her body. Learning the movements, the patterns.

Slowly, the individual fields began to separate. Hundreds of thin, trailing threads slid across her awareness. Analia tried to reach out and grab one, but she became thoroughly lost within the discordance.

Analia braced herself against the wall and pulled back. No hasty movements. Dance with the melodies, move with the rhythms. There.

Analia latched onto that single thread, forcing the other fields to the background. Slowly, slowly, her senses filtered back in, but when she pushed herself to her feet, she staggered into the wall.

Clearly, learning to manage fields and everyday functioning was going to take some work. But Analia made it to her door. And leaning against the wall for support, she slowly wound her way through the castle. Up the stairs, around the corner, down a corridor, into a sitting room.

Analia moved past couches, a table surrounded by cushy stools, legs finally stabilizing beneath her. She reached through thick white curtains, her fingers wrapping around something hot and crackling with energy.

Analia pulled out the Ash ring. She could feel Othin's shield preventing anyone from taking it but her. And just like the first time she'd found it, she could only stare.

It was so simple. Obnoxiously so. She had been calling out to the ring, when she should have been looking for it calling to her. Just like magnets. And magnets pulled from both sides.

Analia curled her fingers around the ring, and without thinking twice, she headed off to find Deardryn. With each step, something seemed to solidify inside her.

She'd had her time to sulk and wallow. But there wasn't anything she could do about Pryanth, Brenn, the past. Now, though, there *was* something she could do. Now, Analia knew how to find the Royal Garden.

# Chapter 42

Analia padded through night-silenced halls. Nodding to the patrolling guards as she passed, she slipped around the final corner, stopping outside the door she was looking for.

For a brief moment, she touched her pin. Then, she knocked.

The door opened a moment later, revealing a thoroughly surprised Pryanth.

"Hi," Analia said, shifting from foot to foot.

"Hello." Pryanth stepped aside to let her in. He closed the door behind her with one hand, the other drawing her closer as she lifted her face to his.

Pryanth's kiss was tentative, dancing on the threshold of the last time they'd spoken. But Analia relaxed against him. She let her mind drift, losing herself in what had, at some point, become familiar: the way he tilted his head when he kissed her, the hard planes of his chest beneath her palm.

He pulled her closer, the tension easing from his mouth as something clicked back into place. Something that had Analia sighing, Pryanth smiling against her mouth in response.

"How are you?" he asked, trailing his lips along her jaw.

Analia tilted her head. "I wanted to see you."

"Oh?"

Pryanth looked up at her, something she couldn't name in his honey gaze. Her hand trailed up his chest, along his neck, stopping on his cheek. "I missed you."

Pryanth sucked in a breath. He tugged her deeper into his room, one that Analia hadn't seen before. Various weapons hung on the walls, sharp and glinting. A stack of books covered a corner desk, placed beneath a sprawling map of Elefthia.

Pryanth sank down on his bed, settling her on his lap. His lips found hers once more, as smooth and deliberate as a sigh of relief.

"I missed you, too," he whispered.

He made to deepen the kiss, his hand sliding up her back and tangling in her hair. But Analia pulled back.

She rested her cheek against his chest, his heart pounding beneath her ear. Smiling to herself, she ran her fingers through his golden hair, coming to trace the curve of his ear.

"Does this mean you forgive me?" he asked, his voice rough.

"I don't like fighting with you," Analia said.

"I don't like fighting, either." Pryanth sighed, resting his cheek against her hair. "I love you."

Analia's face twitched. He'd never actually said that before—was that sincerity in his eyes?

Pryanth caught her looking. He moved his hand to her neck, lifting her chin and locking his gaze on hers. Unwavering.

Gods, it felt like an insult.

It felt like permission.

It felt like something she wanted to hold onto and never let go of.

*I love you.*

Pryanth smiled slightly. "Analia?" he asked, leaning in.

*I love you.*

Analia struggled to focus as his lips lightly trailed up her neck. "Yes?"

"Is this a reconciliation, then?" His hand slipped beneath her tunic, his fingers softly stroking the skin above her waistband.

"Uh-huh."

"Good." Pryanth kissed her cheek. "Because I still have my list of enthralling ideas to work through."

"I'm sure you do—"

Analia's words cut off with a yelp as Pryanth pulled her down on top of him, his mouth colliding with hers.

Pryanth's kiss felt like a shockwave. It tingled across her skin, leaching into her blood and coming to crackle in her core.

This wasn't a kiss of reconciliation. It was a kiss of intent, his mouth as intoxicating as the sweet summer wine she could taste on his tongue.

And this time, Analia didn't pull away. She didn't try to stop him. Instead, she nipped his lower lip, reveling in the way she could feel his body shudder against hers.

*I love you.*

Gods, he truly had become her familiar. A terrifying, exhilarating familiar that had her tongue curling around his, her senses drinking him in until she was drowning.

Pryanth rolled her over, Analia dragging him down on top of her by his shirt.

It was so easy. There were no tangled emotions, no uncertainties, no thoughts that chased each other round and round in her mind. There was only instinct as she ground against him. Fire as he moaned her name. An intoxicating hum as his hand found her breast.

"Fuck, Analia," Pryanth said, "this is exactly where I've wanted you. Flushed and squirming and..."

Pryanth pressed a deep, deliberate kiss to her neck, just as he flicked her nipple. Analia sucked in a breath.

Pryanth chuckled. But Analia's mind slipped back to when he'd first whispered this image to her. Back in the Star Castle, moments before they found the dead Mist Royal.

Analia caught his hand through her shirt, stilling his hand.

"You got to choose last time," she said, slightly breathless. "I feel like that should make it my turn."

"And what if I don't like taking turns?" Pryanth asked, skimming his nose across her cheek. "What if I just want you, all to myself?"

Analia caught his other hand as it wandered down her stomach. "Who said that's out of the question?"

Pryanth finally pulled back to look at her. His cheeks were flushed, his pupils blown. For the first time, he seemed to take in her tunic and pants from the Star Castle.

"What picture do you have in mind?" he asked.

Analia traced his lower lip with a finger. "One that you painted a few months ago."

Analia led Pryanth through the iron door and onto the roof. She wasn't surprised to find a massive sun dragon waiting for them, the golden scales on its long, serpentine body glittering in the moonlight.

Pryanth let out a delighted laugh. He towed Analia forward, reaching up to scratch his dragon behind its ears. The dragon let out a low, rumbling purr, tilting its head in appreciation.

Pryanth glanced back at Analia. "How…?"

His words died off as he spotted the lean figure dressed in white-and-gold leathers sliding from the saddle. His muscles tensed. But as the guard stepped into the light, Pryanth quickly relaxed. "Dannel."

"Your Highness." The guard bowed.

Pryanth turned back to Analia. "You had him bring Brax to the roof."

"I thought we'd save ourselves the magic of having to shadowjump to the roost," she explained. She'd also thought Aaron so much as breathing on the dragon Pryanth had bonded with as a child would have flames actually erupting from his ears. She figured Dannel was innocuous enough, though.

Pryanth's face split in a grin. "And I promised you, didn't I?"

Dannel tossed Pryanth a pair of riding gloves. Promising to return Brax to the roost when they were done, the guard plopped down on the parapet and gave them a shooing gesture.

"Come," Pryanth said, sliding on his gloves. He lifted Analia into the saddle, then swung up beside her using a chink between scales as a foothold.

Analia leaned forward, resting her hand on Brax's neck. Despite the cool night air, his scales were warm to the touch and hard as steel.

"Amazing," Analia murmured.

Brax flexed his wings in appreciation, stirring waves of rolling heat. Pryanth reached around her to grab the reins. "You ready?" he asked.

"As long as you promise not to let me fall."

Pryanth scoffed. "Please."

Then, not waiting for a response, he dug in his heels. And Brax launched himself into the sky with a mighty leap.

Analia sucked in a breath as she flew back against Pryanth's chest, her hands tightening around the saddle horn. Pryanth whooped, nearly lost in the wind as they soared in a curving arc across the kingdom.

"What do you think?" he asked.

Analia took in the kingdom far below—the way Brax shifted beneath her with every wing beat; the wind that blew back her braid.

"It's incredible!" she yelled, smiling so wide her face ached.

Pryanth's responding laugh was pure joy. He shifted the reins, and Brax responded immediately. They banked, wings spreading to catch the current.

As they looped around the kingdom, Analia couldn't help but notice the synchronicity between rider and mount. The moment Pryanth so much as shifted behind her, she could feel Brax beginning to do the same. They were a team. One body, one mind.

But Analia didn't have time to marvel. She had work to do, as soon as they reached the heart of the kingdom. Now.

Analia reached out for the magic, but she was only met with whispers. Crystal strike her down. Was she too high?

"Look!" Pryanth said. "You can see the sundial!"

Brax tilted to the left, far enough that Analia slammed against the hard muscle of Pryanth's arm. He didn't so much as flinch as he nudged her back. Analia peered down, spotting the glimmer of gold in the moonlight.

"Can we drop a bit?" she asked. "I want to get closer."

"Drop?" Pryanth asked in a voice that had Analia's heart skip a beat. Before she could ask, Pryanth yelled, "All right! If you insist!"

He jerked the reins. Then, they plunged.

The wind roared in Analia's ears. She squeezed her eyes shut, a scream of sheer excitement ripping from her throat. Pryanth laughed as he squeezed his arms around her, stopping her from sliding away.

He yanked the reins, and Brax spiraled out of the plunge, arcing straight back into the air. Analia whipped from side to side, the stars swirling around her like reaching hands, promising to catch her if she fell. But Pryanth's hold on her was tight.

Finally, he straightened Brax out. He stretched his wings, gliding on the currents, the kingdom much closer now than it was before.

"So that was a plunge, huh?" Analia asked breathlessly.

Pryanth laughed against her neck. "You should have been more specific."

As he continued to chatter about different types of maneuvers, Analia leaned back against his chest. She slowly lowered her mental shield, just as she'd been practicing the past few days. But nothing could have prepared her for the magic that thundered through her awareness.

Blessed in their homes, sleeping as she'd hoped instead of moving about and confusing her, but still a constant stream. The sundial, the castle, each individual sunstone streetlight. They all echoed through her awareness, vibrated through her bones until she wanted to scream. She wanted to curl into a ball and claw the magic from her veins.

But Analia gritted her teeth. This was her only chance.

She tumbled through the melodies, searching for the loudest three. One, the sundial. Directly below. Two, the castle. Behind her. Where was the third, the constant, languid thrum—there.

Analia found it for a single second. Then, she slammed every barrier back in place.

Analia slumped back against Pryanth's chest, her eyes scanning. The woods. West of the castle. Contained within the castle's long, wrapping gates. She found it. And Pryanth didn't seem to notice.

The rest of their flight passed in a blur. Pryanth had Brax make a wide loop around the central kingdom, pointing out various landmarks and locations as they passed below. At one point, he fell quiet for several moments, just to brush a soft kiss to her hair.

"What was that for?" Analia asked.

"Nothing," he said innocently, repositioning her against him. He paused. "Did I tell you about the time I almost fell off Brax's back in midair?"

Eventually, Brax came in for a smooth landing on the castle roof. Pryanth helped her dismount, his hands lingering on her waist as he steadied her.

As he tossed Dannel his gloves and dragon and guard launched into the sky, Analia couldn't help but wonder if she'd gotten away with it. All she had to do now was extract herself from Pryanth, and then—

"It's been so long since I've been able to do that."

Analia glanced at Pryanth. His eyes were locked on the retreating figure of his dragon, expression wistful.

"In my kingdom, Royals focus first on training their magic, then on learning to fight and fly. As a child, I watched the guards train every day, begging to learn how to fly like them. But they always told me no, or not yet. So, I taught myself.

"I found an ancient dragon-riding guide in the library, and at night, Brax and I would sneak out to practice on our own. We thought we were so clever, especially since I hadn't yet submitted to the idea that my mother knows everything that goes on in her castle.

"That is, until we landed on the roof one day to find her leaning against the parapet, arms folded as she stared up at us. I swear, Brax and I thought we were going to receive the tongue-lashing of a lifetime. But all she said was, 'Your turns are sloppy. Go on, do it again.'"

Pryanth smiled to himself. "As I've gotten older, I've had less and less time to fly. Until tonight." He reached out, tucking the hair that had come free from Analia's braid behind her ear. "All because of you."

Analia felt a thrum throughout her body. This was him. This was the Pryanth she first met, the one a part of her had given up on ever seeing again.

"I hardly did anything," she said, running her fingers along his jaw.

"And that's hardly the truth."

A low buzz started in Analia's veins as Pryanth eased her back against the castle door. She looked up at him, the cold steel behind her such a contrast to the heat radiating off his body as he leaned in.

"You listened to me talk about Brax. You arranged to have him brought to the roof. You nearly drove me out of my mind in my chambers, just to tempt me now with that look in your eyes."

A shiver ran down Analia's spine. She hadn't even realized she was looking at him a certain way. But that didn't stop her from loving how she could feel him, hard and demanding, as he pressed against her. It didn't stop her from feeling wanted, desired, seen in a way so few had ever seen her before. And gods, she just wanted more.

Analia gripped his shoulders, forcing herself to remember the woods, the plan. She had to remember the plan.

"Say it, Analia," Pryanth said, running his lips along her throat. "Who is this because of?"

He shifted against her, sparks of pleasure dancing across her skin.

"Me," she breathed, her hands tightening around his shoulders.

The plan. She had to remember the plan.

"Louder, Analia," Pryanth whispered. He sucked her earlobe into his mouth, his hips thrusting forward.

And Analia's control shattered. She cried out. "Me! It's because of me."

Analia hauled him closer, circling her hips—gods, the plan—

"Yes, Analia," he moaned, pulling her face to his. "All of it was you. Which means this"—he kissed her cheek—"is because"—he kissed her chin—"of you."

His lips captured hers. And this time, there was no question. No hesitation or pretense or buildup. It was all hot, consuming intent, crackling with the same energy he'd had while riding Brax. And Analia was completely swept away.

She didn't remember wrapping her arms around his neck. But somehow, her fingers had found their way into his silken hair, her other hand fisted in the back of his shirt.

Gods, this was not a part of the plan. But neither was Pryanth: his tongue claiming the curve of her mouth, his hands sliding beneath her tunic. She just needed to feel him, lose herself in him, hold onto this side of him because she didn't know when she might see him again.

Pryanth. The man that kissed her in the library stacks. The prince that gave her his pendant. The one who had her grinding against him as he palmed her breasts.

"Yes, Analia," Pryanth said, dragging his lips down her neck. "The flame to my life. Just say my name."

He pinched her nipple. Analia gasped his name, sensations streaking across her nerves like a warning sign.

*Reckless. Destructive.*

But this was the Pryanth she knew. This was something she wanted. This was panic as his hand found her waistband.

Analia pulled away, her heart pounding in her ears. "What are we doing?"

"Don't you want to?" Pryanth asked, lowering them down to their knees.

*"Here?"*

"Why not? You've done this before, haven't you?"

Pryanth kissed her again, his fingers skimming down her side to her hip.

Analia pulled away, "Pryanth—"

"Don't you love me?"

Analia stiffened.

"Because I love you," he went on. "I want to show you I love you." His voice dropped to a whisper. "Show me you love me."

"Not on a roof."

"Then come back with me," he said, pressing his face to her neck. "To my chambers. You are mine."

"Pryanth, no."

Pryanth pulled back, something like betrayal in his eyes. "Why are you willing to do this with someone else and not me?"

Analia's jaw dropped. She scooted away from him on the roof, "That has nothing to do with—will you ever let that go?"

"I will once we make it right." Pryanth shuffled after her, taking her hands in his, stroking the backs of her hands with his thumbs. "Don't you want to make it right?"

He leaned in once more, achingly sweet. His fingers slipped around to stroke the inside of her wrist, each soft pass sending cracks skittering out across her resolve.

Gods, it was so. Easy. It would be so easy to just submit for so many reasons.

Pryanth reached up to touch her cheek.

Analia shoved him back. "Pryanth, stop."

One moment, she could feel the heat of his body, his magic thrumming around her. In the next, Pryanth recoiled. Then, with a look of something more unstable than hurt, he wordlessly faded into the shadows.

For a few long moments, Analia remained frozen where she knelt, the sudden silence ringing in her ears. Gods, what just happened? What had she done? This wasn't a part of the plan. They were never supposed to take it this far.

But they had. And she had let them.

Analia released a long, shaky breath. She knew there was nothing she could do about that now. But that didn't stop Pryanth's wounded expression from flashing across her mind as she rose to her feet. Nor did it stop the tiny voice that whispered she should have fought for him more, fought so they didn't have to reach this point.

A aron and Dimitri were waiting for her when she returned to her chambers, a book between them on her bed. Dimitri had evidently harassed Aaron into helping him with his reading—although Analia doubted it took much convincing. At the sound of the door opening, they looked up.

Analia had done her best to straighten her clothes and re-braid her hair, but that didn't stop the questions in their eyes.

"I found it," she said flatly.

The two immediately rose. Dimitri moved to open the entrance to the passageways, Aaron offering a hand to help her inside.

Gods, she loved those two. They hadn't tried to stop her when she'd told them her plan, Aaron only asking if she wanted assistance, not pushing it when she said no. Even when she showed them her cracks, they refused to see her as broken. So, maybe, it was about gods-damned time she started acting like it.

Now, the three wound their way through the passageways, Dimitri in the lead. Aaron—who had somehow convinced Lev to put him on side door duty—fell in beside her. His eyes moved to her undoubtedly swollen mouth, and she steeled herself for the comment.

"You need a weapon," he decided. He pulled one of the daggers from his boot and placed it in her hand. "Ideally, you won't have to use it, and if you can, you run first. But if that's not an option."

Aaron wrapped Analia's fingers around the hilt, positioning her thumb over her first two fingers.

"You need to be quick, clever, and precise. No wild stabbing. You wait until in range, then lash out quick as you can.

"A slash across the throat is usually your best chance, although a stab to the heart, eye, or up under the chin can do the trick. All of that requires you getting up close, though. At that point, there is almost no way to prevent a counterattack, which is why if you can, you run."

Analia nodded, sliding the dagger through her belt. "What about Dima?" she asked.

"Don't need anything," he called back, dropping down a ladder.

"But—"

"Don't need anything."

A few minutes later, the three climbed out of an entrance beside the side door Dimitri had used to search the Bend. The servant pulled open the narrow steel door, Analia expecting him to continue on without hesitation. Instead, he paused. Studying the darkness for a moment, he glanced back at Analia and Aaron, then retreated inside once more.

"Did you see something?" Analia asked.

"No. And unless the Crystal Blessed you with perfect night vision instead of flames, neither will you." Ignoring Analia's frown, Dimitri grabbed an old, cracked sunstone near the base of the wall and pried it free. "All right, magic magnet," he said, passing her the dim sunstone. "Lead the way."

Analia rolled her eyes, but she didn't hesitate to push through the door. The three kept close to the castle, staying as far as possible from the guards patrolling in the distance. Somehow, they reached the western woods without incident. And exchanging a quick look, the three stepped into the trees.

# Chapter 43

The near-full moon sent slices of silvery light through the branches above as Analia, Dimitri, and Aaron picked their way through the woods.

In the lead, Analia was careful to keep her mental shield up. She'd learned early on that the moment she let it slip, an overwhelming wave of Sun magic would slam into her—which meant her sunstone's light should have been blinding. Instead, the damaged stone only provided a faint, wavering light as they followed the magic deeper into the trees, Analia only daring to check they were on the right track a handful of times.

"We're close," she eventually said, heading down a steep decline.

Descending behind her, Dimitri asked, "And what do we do once we get there?"

"Depends on what we see when we get there."

From the back, Aaron chuckled. Analia could practically hear Dimitri's eyes roll.

The three quickly reached the base of the hill, coming face-to-face with a thick tangle of foliage. Pushing her way through, Analia only saw forest on the other side. Yet, something had her freeze in her tracks.

Dimitri swore as he bumped into her. "What are you doing?" he asked, struggling to regain his footing. "We need to keep going."

Analia didn't move.

Dimitri poked her shoulder, growing increasingly restless. "Flashfire, come on. There's nothing here, let's go."

But there *was* something there. The quiet urge to turn away, continue down a different path. As subtle as instinct.

"Anna?" Aaron asked, his voice tight.

But she knew better. She could feel the faint trail of tingles through her mind.

"There's some sort of magic here," she said.

Dimitri grumbled something. Aaron maneuvered around him, his voice low as he came to stand at her shoulder. "What do you sense?"

"I don't know." Analia traced her fingers through the air, the magic brushing against her senses like a soft exhale. Reaching behind her, she snapped off a decent-sized bracken frond and tossed it into the forest ahead of her.

The three waited for several seconds. Analia's hand drifted toward her dagger, anticipating the blare of an alarm, a flash of magic. But nothing happened.

"Trap?" Aaron asked.

"Or the Royals have gotten cocky," Dimitri said.

"Well," said Analia, "there's only one way to find out."

Then, not giving herself time to think, she stepped across the magic line. Aaron swore, his hand half extending as if to grab her.

But magic already tingled across Analia's skin. Every instinct in her body cringed away, demanding she go back, it wasn't safe, run. Just the thought of taking another step forward had her muscles stiffening.

Analia focused on the tree in front of her. One step, two steps, three, the magic clinging to her skin like a thin, flexible film.

Analia's body shook as she took another step. And abruptly, it was gone: the magic, the fear. But that wasn't all.

"Are you all right?" Aaron asked.

Analia quickly looked back. She could still see Aaron and Dimitri at the tree line, about five paces away. But judging by their expressions, only she had seen the forest shimmer, then peel back like a layer of paint.

"I am," she said. "And you two are going to want to see this."

The clearing before her dipped and curved like a shallow bowl. Tall stalks of grass lined the gently curving edges, the moonlight providing a faint silver glow. And in the heart of the bowl stood row upon row of plants, standing in winding columns and glittering with a thin sheen of golden magic.

Aaron didn't hesitate to join her. He passed through the magic with little difficulty, letting out a low whistle as he reached her side. "This is definitely the place."

Dimitri danced uncertainly at the border a few moments longer, but his curiosity seemed to win out. Keeping his head low, he shoved through the magic, just to release a string of curses as he reached the other side.

"The Old Hag has access to glamors now?" he asked, exasperated.

"Seems like it." Analia pocketed her sunstone, the moon and magic throughout the garden providing more than enough light.

Aaron said, "That at least explains how none of us have seen it from the air." He reached over and tugged Analia's braid. "Reckless."

Analia ducked away, her cheeks flushed. But something still didn't feel right. There was another melody, hidden beneath the quiet glamor and overwhelming Sun magic.

"We have to be missing something," she said, drawing the toe of her boot through the grass.

"Well," Aaron said, "let's use the time we've got before we find out."

Without further comment, the three stepped into the garden. Keeping quiet, they moved through pathways wide enough for two to walk abreast, their eyes scanning the lines of plants.

"Devinroot," Analia breathed, pointing to a cluster of vivid orange plants.

"I don't get it," Dimitri complained. "There's no way the Old Hag—"

Dimitri's voice cut off in a strangled cry. Analia and Aaron whipped around.

A humanoid creature towered over them. A shadowy cloak attached to a silver collar wrapped its thin frame, exposed gray bone peeking out between patches of dark, scaly skin. It had no eyes, only black gaping sockets situated above slit nostrils and a toothless, black-lipped mouth.

The creature gripped Dimitri by the shoulders, hoisting him off the ground and letting out a quiet hiss.

Analia stumbled back. Dimitri writhed, blood sliding down his arms as the creature raised him higher. He twisted, and—

"Dima, duck!" Aaron yelled.

Dimitri did as ordered. Aaron took a few steps back, sending a straight-flying dagger toward the glowing core of the creature's chest, momentarily revealed when Dimitri tugged on its cloak.

The creature lifted Dimitri as a shield. The hilt of the dagger thudded into Dimitri's shoulder—"Ow!"—just as a second, low-flying dagger slammed into its knee at an angle, popping it out of its socket.

The creature hissed. It staggered back, dropping Dimitri as it grabbed its knee. Analia darted forward, helping Dimitri to his feet.

"Move!" Aaron yelled, shoving the two forward. And together, they took off toward the woods.

The creature bellowed as it popped its knee back into place. Then, it swept after them, silent as death itself.

Analia tore through the glamor without difficulty. She glanced over her shoulder, expecting to see the creature bearing down on her, reaching, grasping, reeking of death and decay. Instead, she slowed to a stop.

The creature wasn't following. It had stopped right at the edge of the glamor where it now prowled back and forth, hissing softly.

Aaron had already paused a few paces back, but he retreated to stand at her shoulder. Dimitri, however, was long gone, the sound of his crashing through undergrowth getting farther and farther away.

"He'll be back," Aaron said.

"You sure about that?" Analia asked.

"No."

They turned their attention back to the creature.

"It can't cross the tree line," Analia observed.

"Maybe there's more than just a glamor there," Aaron said. "A way to ensure it guards the garden but isn't able to harm the civilians."

"Which means," Analia said, "there's something worth guarding here."

Footsteps crunched behind them. Dimitri stumbled back into view, the streaks of blood on his arms appearing black in the moonlight.

"What are you idiots doing?" he hissed.

"Nice of you to join us," Aaron said pleasantly.

"The creature can't leave the garden," Analia repeated. "There's some sort of boundary or shield keeping it in."

"Great," Dimitri said. "It can't get out, and we can't get in. Let's leave."

"Oh no," Analia said, eyes back on the creature, "there's a way to get in."

A few long minutes later, Dimitri stomped out of the shadows, grumbling under his breath as he approached the creature. The creature snarled, to which Dimitri swore right back. For a moment, he studied the creature, tantalizingly close.

"Well," he finally said, "you certainly have a face that's hard to love."

The creature slashed with a taloned hand. Dimitri jumped back. Then, he took off around the edge of the garden, a trail of profanities in his wake as the creature immediately played chase.

Aaron smiled fondly. "What a foul mouth our Dima has."

The two stepped back into the garden, the creature no longer barring their path.

"Be careful," he said.

Analia nodded. And without further comment, the two split up.

Analia wove through the garden, eyes darting. There was no telling if that creature was the only one in the garden, or how much time Dimitri could give her and Aaron—

"It's coming!" Dimitri yelled.

Analia bit back a curse. She forced herself to slow down—her footsteps, her breathing, her heartbeat.

Her eyes roved. Blue, purple, orange leaves. Flat, fuzzy, spiked, thorny. She moved deeper into the garden, xenol nowhere to be seen, the magic throbbing against her skull.

The back of Analia's neck prickled. She dove to the ground, the creature's talons slicing through the hair on the top of her head. Crystal spare her.

Analia tried to rise, but the creature flashed out a foot, her ribs screaming as she fell back to the ground. She rolled beneath a tall, drooping shrub, the creature's hand reaching, reaching, reaching.

Analia grabbed Aaron's dagger and jabbed. She didn't know what she hit, only that the creature hissed and drew back. Scooting through stalks, Analia popped to her feet on the other side of the row and took off.

Escape, she had to escape. The magic roared in her ears, melodies demanding to be heard as terror sent cracks skittering across her shield. She vaulted over a stone wall, tearing through another glamor.

And the magic slammed into her full force.

Analia grabbed her head, a muffled scream escaping between her gritted teeth. It was worse than being on Brax. So, so much worse. Because it wasn't a collection of individual fields, all vying for attention. It was one massive field, ripping through her shield with golden claws.

Analia stumbled into something hard. She staggered along its curve, sliding down, down, down, the world fading in and out. She knew she could adjust, but she didn't have the time. Not as there came the quiet thud of the creature hoisting itself over the wall.

She was trapped. Even if she had somewhere to go, her body was shaking too hard for her to stand. She could only lean against what she vaguely realized was a tall, gold temple, radiating waves of magic—the source of the magic.

Analia braced herself. But the creature didn't come for her. Yes, there was the quiet shift of pebbles under its feet as it moved, but not around to the other side of the temple where she slumped, hidden from view. Instead, it moved back and forth, hissing as if confused.

Analia slowly realized the unfamiliar magic was back, a quiet undercurrent to the roaring in her ears. Its core? Could it be tracking her through her magic? Could it be just as rattled by the temple as she was? Enough that, Crystal almighty, she was temporarily camouflaged? But in that case, it would only be a matter of time before it adjusted.

Analia blinked hard, forcing herself to focus. She scooped up a handful of stones and waited until the creature paced toward the right. Then, she tossed her pebbles as far as she could in that direction, the stones softly rattling like footsteps.

The creature immediately took off in that direction. Quick and quiet, Analia moved around the temple in the opposite direction, climbing back over the wall and into the garden.

Analia forced her shield back into place as she staggered through the garden, desperate to hear the whistle that meant Aaron had found the xenol, but it never came. She was just about to give up hope, knowing her little ruse had only bought her so much time.

But there, four rows over. Thin, curling leaves, fading from pale green to black.

Hope flared in Analia's chest. She leaped over the first row of plants, moving to the second. And cold, slick fingers wrapped around her arms.

Analia didn't think. She stomped down on the creature's foot, and there came a crack. The creature snarled, and Analia ripped free. She leaped over the second hedge.

Something slammed into her shoulder. She hit the dirt, dagger flying out of her grip, hand crashing into a cluster of thorny vines that immediately wrapped around her wrist.

The creature lunged for her. Analia rolled to the right, gasping as the thorns dug in. The creature, however, couldn't twist in time to avoid the bundle of vines that wrapped themselves around it in a hungry embrace. It struggled, unable to break free.

Analia's eyes darted around. Spotting her dagger in the grass, she stretched, ribs and shoulder screaming, vines tightening. But she managed to reach it with her foot and draw it back, slashing through the vines a moment later and rising unsteadily to her feet.

Analia staggered over the last row of plants. She fell to her knees beside the cluster of xenol, the creature snarling behind her. She dug her nails into the dirt, scrabbling for the roots—too slow.

Losing patience, Analia grabbed the xenol at its base and pulled. The entire plant came loose with a faint rip, and Analia jerked to her feet. She just had to find the border.

But the garden was suddenly quiet around her. And skeletal hands gripped her arms as something cold pressed against her neck.

Analia was back in the Ash Castle. She floated, somehow separate from her body as she watched herself and Accalon walking toward his chambers. No.

*Remember this?* A voice hissed in her mind as Brenn came around the corner, ranting about the Sun Royals. Analia tried to look away, but everywhere she turned, she saw Accalon. Curling her fingers around the pin. Kissing the side of her head. Herself, walking away.

*You left him,* the voice whispered as Brenn and Accalon argued. *You abandoned the only person you've ever had.*

Analia wanted to cover her ears. But there was no escaping her uncle paling, leaning against the wall for support, practically stumbling through his chamber door as Brenn departed.

*He's dying,* the voice whispered.

Analia struggled, but there was no resisting the invisible line that dragged her after Accalon—Crystal spare her, she couldn't watch this.

*All alone,* the voice said as Accalon moved unsteadily toward his bed. He reached out to brace himself against the mattress, his hand sliding across the surface as if it were a sheet of ice.

Analia felt the thud of his knees hitting the ground in every bone of her body. She thrashed, a sob rising in her throat as he struggled, unable to rise. But all she could see was his face as it drained of color, his body convulsing as he gasped for air, blood flecking his lips that were now tinged gray, everything turning gray.

*You should have come sooner,* the voice said. *But then again, what could you have done?*

Accalon's body went still.

*Duckling.*

Analia screamed. She didn't realize she was moving until the creature let out an ear-splitting shriek in response.

Analia fell to the dirt, the garden slamming back around her. The creature staggered behind her, clutching at its flashing core—had it gotten bigger? Had she stabbed it? No time to question. No time to grieve.

Analia shoved herself to her feet and took off. But something was horribly wrong.

The garden tilted and spun around her. Her body shook violently, sending her slamming into plants, careening into hedges, barely able to let out the shrill whistle to get Aaron out.

But she was so close. She could see the trees, twenty feet away. But she could also hear the creature rally.

Analia tried to run faster, choking on a sob. She tripped over a protruding root, but quickly scrambled up once more.

Ten feet. Five.

Analia rounded the final bend, just to slam to a halt as the creature stepped out before her. She was done. There was nowhere left to run. And finally, Analia gave in to the terror that had been clawing at her, not just in those moments, but for the past fifteen years.

Analia's knees gave out. She stared up, numb, as the creature reached for her throat. Fingers dug into her skin as it lifted her body into the air. Higher, higher, its cold, rancid breath in her face. And Analia barely felt her arm as she plunged Aaron's dagger straight into its core.

The creature screamed. The glowing crystal shattered before her eyes, the dagger in her hand burning.

The creature stumbled. It dropped Analia to the ground, its body wracked with tremors.

Analia tried to push herself up, but her body wouldn't move. All she could do was watch, horrified, as the core slowly knit itself back together. Her fist tightened around the xenol in her other hand. And somehow, she was on her feet.

Analia staggered across the border and back into the woods. Images flashed across her mind as she ran, blurring with the whirling trees and undergrowth. She didn't know how far she'd gotten when her knees gave out, her mind barely registering the ivy around her. All she knew was the taste of bile as she emptied the contents of her stomach.

Aaron had never known the type of fear that raked down his spine as he saw the creature hoist Analia into the air. A yell ripped from his throat, his hand spinning a dagger through the air faster than he could even form the thought.

He knew he was too far away for it to matter. But he ran anyway, watching in disbelief as Analia managed to stab its core, her dagger blade glinting with a faint blue light.

He'd almost reached her when she dragged herself to her feet. Then, she took off, not seeming to hear him calling her name. By the time Aaron caught up with her in the tiny clearing, she was retching on all fours.

"Holy gods," Aaron breathed, coming to kneel beside her. "Analia—"

He reached out to touch her, but quickly jerked his hand back. Heat sputtered across her skin, even hotter than in the alleyway.

Analia wailed and twisted around. Aaron leaned away, grabbing her forearm to redirect her dagger.

"Anna, stop!" he gasped, but she couldn't hear him. "Anna, it's me!"

Aaron plucked the dagger from her hand and tossed it aside. He didn't try to stop her flailing fists from connecting with his chest, his arms. He only took her face in his hands.

"Analia, look at me." Her skin burned beneath his fingers. "Look at me. It's Aaron."

Analia blinked hard, her lips moving silently.

"That's it," Aaron soothed, leaning his forehead against hers. "Just focus on me."

Slowly, the heat faded from Analia's skin. Aaron moved his thumb along her cheekbone as her fist slid down his chest, her fingers uncurling as her hand dropped to her lap. But all she did was stare, that same haunted look from the Solstice in her eyes.

"You're all right," he murmured.

Analia's face turned green. She shoved away from him to retch once more, but there didn't seem to be anything left in her stomach.

Aaron moved back to her side, pulling back the hair that had come free from her braid. What in the name of the five gods had he not seen?

"What can I do?" he asked.

Analia didn't respond. Aaron touched her shoulder, just as a twig snapped behind him.

Aaron twisted, dagger in hand, but it was only Dimitri. He pushed through the foliage, his eyes doing a quick scan, his nose wrinkling at the sour smell of vomit.

"What the fuck happened?" he demanded.

"I don't know," Aaron said desperately. "I think she's in shock. I only saw the end when the creature grabbed her—Analia, are you bleeding?"

He hadn't noticed before in the dim light. But now, he could feel something sticky on his fingers as he flexed them on his dagger hilt.

"Thorns," Analia coughed.

The tightness in Aaron's chest eased slightly. "Can I see?"

Analia spat. Then, she shakily sat up, wiping her mouth with one arm and offering Aaron the other. Aaron angled it toward the moonlight, examining the oozing puncture marks that wrapped like bracelets up her forearm.

"Fuck," Dimitri said, leaning in to get a closer look. Analia mechanically pulled the sunstone from her pocket, the golden glow only making things look worse.

Aaron's eyes swept the clearing. "Dima, go strip the moss from that trunk for me."

Dimitri shot him an indignant look, but for once he didn't argue. "Should I pick some wildflowers, too?" he asked, sauntering across the tiny clearing.

"We're not weaving flower crowns," Aaron said, checking there were no embedded thorns in Analia's skin. "Moss is the next best thing to gauze."

"No shit."

"I can patch your puncture marks, too."

"I got it."

Aaron lightly brushed away what dirt he could from Analia's arm. She watched him silently, her tremors starting to slow, Aaron's pulse following suit.

Accepting the wad of moss Dimitri offered him, Aaron looked to Analia. She nodded, and he went about molding the moss to her arm.

"I heard the creature," he murmured, eyes on his work. "I tried to find you. I'm sorry I didn't make it in time."

Dimitri wandered away, undoubtedly disturbed by all the sudden emotion.

"I didn't need to be rescued," Analia rasped.

"Oh, I'm aware," Aaron said. "Don't think I didn't see your spectacular dagger work—which, by the way, is yours now."

He fished the discarded dagger from the grass beside them and slid it into her boot. He returned his eyes to his work, voice sobering as he said, "I'm just sorry I didn't help you avoid some of the dents along the way."

Aaron couldn't read the look in Analia's eyes. She opened her mouth—

"Crystal fuck me," Dimitri said. "Flashfire, you found it?"

Aaron tore his gaze from Analia's, glancing over to where Dimitri crouched. He snagged something from the grass, raising it so Aaron could see. Aaron's eyes widened.

"Why the note of surprise?" Analia grumbled.

"Incredible," Aaron breathed, ruffling her hair. He'd heard her whistle, but assumed she'd lost the plant when the creature attacked.

"Damn near crushed it though," Dimitri muttered.

"I'm sorry," Analia said. "Next time I'm fleeing for my life, I'll remember to prioritize the delicate nature of leaves."

Aaron's laugh was shaky to his own ears. But it was from the flood of relief at her words, the color returning to her face, the small smile she gave him. He squeezed the moss around her arm and lightly rested it on her thigh.

There was a part of him that didn't want to ask the inevitable question on the tip of his tongue. But when Analia's eyes met his own, they were tired, but steady.

"Analia," he said, "what happened?"

Analia hung her head but didn't hesitate to explain. Dimitri shoved the xenol in his pocket and moved to sit beside them.

As the story continued, Aaron felt the oddest melting sensation.

"I don't know what happened," Analia finished. "I don't know what I did, I don't know what it did, I don't know how I'm still alive."

Aaron began, "You must have—"

"Aaron," Dimitri cut in sharply. "Have you seen this?"

Aaron followed Dimitri's gaze to Analia's neck. He froze.

"Dima?" Analia asked, but the servant was staring at Aaron.

Yes, it had been a melting sensation. It was his fear and concern dissolving as Analia shook herself off. Giving way to the frozen fury beneath as he traced the perfectly circular black mark on her neck.

"Looks like we found your killer," Dimitri said, his voice distant in Aaron's ears. All he could feel was the flat stone against his chest, so cold it burned.

Dimitri snapped his fingers in front of Aaron's face. "Cool it, Bordello."

Aaron's mind traveled on the wind, circling back to where he could still distantly hear the creature snarling. A creature that had latched onto her, fed off her, nearly killed her—

"You going back there to avenge her or whatever heroic bullshit you're thinking about right now isn't going to do us any good, so knock it off."

A distant part of his mind knew Dimitri was right. He bit down on the inside of his cheek, hard enough he could taste blood.

He could not lose control. Never again.

"Aaron."

Aaron's gaze slid to Analia, who watched him carefully. "You're all right?" he asked hoarsely.

Analia took his hand, bringing it to the pulse on her wrist. Slightly faster than normal, but there, her skin warm. He looked to Dimitri—"You're not feeling my pulse, Bordello."

"I'm sorry," he rasped.

"We got the xenol, and we're all alive," Analia said, not releasing his hand. "That's all that matters."

The three remained kneeling for some time, no one ready to move. Analia was the first to stand, just to immediately stagger. Aaron reached for her, but she waved him off.

As she wordlessly led the way back toward the castle, occasionally leaning on trees for support, Aaron rested a shaky hand on the chain around his neck. He had gotten too close. In more ways than one.

Analia barely remembered the hike back to the castle. Only faintly recalled Dimitri leading them through the passageways to Aaron's chambers, where he briskly cleaned and rewrapped their wounds. She dragged herself back through the passageways to her chambers, too numb to feel the success of finding xenol, her lingering terror, even the confusion of what the mark now hidden behind her hair meant.

She slid open the entrance, ready to collapse into bed. But the Crystal, apparently, had other plans. For her bed was already occupied by a sulking Pryanth.

And a fuming Othin.

# Chapter 44

Analia sat on the edge of her desk, watching as Othin's face changed from white, to red, to purple. He stood, completely rigid, behind her dressing table chair, his hands clenched so tight around the back she thought the wood might snap.

"You," he finally said, "have a lot of explaining to do."

Pryanth shot her a petulant look from her bed. But Analia remained silent.

"Would you like to explain where you've been all night?" Othin asked.

Again, she said nothing. There was no stopping this storm, and she was frankly too exhausted to try.

Indeed, the silence between them gave way to the boom of Othin's voice as he shoved the chair aside.

"No, don't speak. The only thing that has ever come out of your mouth is lies. Lies about your magic, where you've been, what you're doing, what you're planning.

"I told you, Analia. The moment I caught you crossing the line, I wouldn't hesitate to sink my dagger through your spine. And here you are, practically presenting your back to me."

She'd escaped the creature, just to be caught by Othin. She'd finally found the xenol, just to be defeated by a blustering king.

"How did you discover the passageways?" Othin demanded.

Silence.

"Fine. Show me your magic, then."

Analia's brow twitched up.

"There's no point in pretending," he said. "Only people with an active magic network can open these passageways, although I'd love to hear how you found them in the first place."

He paused expectantly. "Someone must have told you. You squeezed it out of them, didn't you? No? Unlikely. I can't wait to find out who so I can stick them as well."

He waited for Analia to protest, but she only dug her nails into the desk.

"Fine. Tell me about your late-night adventure, then. You must have gone somewhere exciting, judging by the grass in your hair and the dirt staining your knees. Oh, and what's this?"

Othin strode the three steps between them, snatching the arm Analia had tried to surreptitiously hide behind her back. "You obviously had help, wherever you went," he said, ripping off Aaron's wrapping.

"It's possible to wrap with one hand—"

"Be quiet," he snarled. He twisted her forearm this way and that. "This certainly looks as though there's a story to tell."

Analia's mind moved too sluggishly to respond. But she had no problem realizing Othin had all the evidence he needed to figure out where exactly she had gone. At least the xenol sample was still with Dimitri.

Othin dropped her arm, continuing his tirade. But Analia's gaze moved around him, landing on Pryanth, still sulking on her bed.

A little boy who hadn't gotten his way. A boy who'd come to try and pester it out of her one more time, just to find her gone. Immediately going to tattle to the father he despised because he knew how the winds were straining to be released.

"Would you like to tell me how close I am?" Othin demanded.

Analia hadn't heard the story he had concocted. She was too consumed by her last struggling spark erupting into an irrational blaze.

Not tearing her gaze from Pryanth, she asked, "How much did you tell him?"

Pryanth flushed. "That's none of his business."

"Really?" Analia asked. "It's not his business to know that the only reason you dragged him here was because I refused to—"

"Analia!"

Othin looked as though he didn't know which way his face should contort. He twisted toward a thoroughly mortified Pryanth, "You told me you caught her slipping out of the castle."

"Not unless he was trailing me through the passageways," Analia said.

She could feel the heat building inside her. He'd not only ratted her out, but he'd lied to do so.

"And here she is," Pryanth jabbed a finger at her, "obviously sneaking back inside. Still don't want to tell us where you were, Analia?"

Analia shoved to her feet. "You want to explain why you felt the need to lie—"

"Enough!" Othin bellowed. He flung out his hands, shoving Analia back onto the desk and a half-risen Pryanth back on the bed. "I don't care if one of you tried to push the other off the gods-damned roof! That doesn't change the fact that you have been sneaking through passageways you were not permitted access to, leaving the castle when you were not allowed to, and refusing to explain your whereabouts!"

Both Analia and Pryanth started to argue, but Othin shot them a vicious glare.

"You," he said, wheeling on Pryanth. "Back to your chambers. Until I come for you, I don't want to see or hear a word from you.

"And you," Othin said, turning his back on a stricken Pryanth. "Your chambers will be guarded. You will not be permitted to leave until your questioning is over."

Analia clamped her mouth shut. Othin advanced on her, his hand raised. For a moment, she thought he was going to slap her, too. But his hand flashed past her head, slamming down on the wall behind her. The outline of his hand glowed a brilliant blue, but Analia couldn't sense his magic.

"Just like the library," Othin said, the magic fading into the stone, "you are blocked. The moment you try to so much as breathe on any of the entrances, I will know. And at that point, there is nothing Deardryn can do to protect you."

So, Deardryn was still on her side. Good. She could use that. As for now, it was better not to give Othin any more information. Not while she was too drained to think responses through.

The king was just turning away when Pryanth suddenly spoke up. "Take her pin."

Both Analia and Othin looked at him quickly.

"You want to make a point," he went on, voice strangled, "take her pin."

Analia knew she should've stayed calm. Othin would've most likely ignored him, finding it ridiculous. But she leaned away, her hand resting protectively over her pin.

She didn't tear her gaze from Pryanth's remorseless face as Othin's fingers wrapped around her wrist. With one hard tug, he pulled her hand away, his free hand snatching her pin from her tunic.

For a moment, he studied the burnt-orange phoenix, the steely-gray outer ring. Then, he pocketed her pin without comment.

Analia's chest felt oddly cold as Othin turned away. But as he gestured for Pryanth to follow, as Pryanth's mouth twisted into a cruel smirk, something snapped inside her.

"Traitor," she whispered as he passed her.

"You gave me no choice," he hissed back.

Liar. But Analia didn't speak as the door slammed behind him. She collapsed on her bed, pressing her face into her pillow and letting out something between a scream and a sob.

Othin didn't come for her the following day. She opened her door, just to come face-to-face with Lev and some other guard she didn't know. They started to tell her to go back inside, but Analia had already turned and shut the door.

She knew Othin was forcing her to stew. He was reminding her that he had control, and she would wait until he was ready.

But Analia wasn't afraid. She was biding her time. And Dimitri only kept her waiting until the following afternoon.

"You have shit luck," he said by way of greeting, sliding open the entrance above her desk.

Analia sat up in bed. Despite the time that had passed, she still felt inexplicably exhausted and empty.

"So," she said, "you *are* able to get in."

"Why wouldn't I?"

"Keep your voice down, I don't want the guards to hear you."

Dimitri rolled his eyes as he clambered into her room.

Analia went on, "Othin said he shielded it against me. He claimed he would know the moment I tried to leave, but I wasn't sure if that meant he sealed it as well."

"He probably meant to but did it wrong. What a dope."

Dimitri sat at Analia's feet. Her eyes traveled to his shoulders, hidden by a threadbare cloak he wore over his white-and-gold servant's uniform. She hadn't failed to notice how his puncture marks from the creature's nails had already scabbed when they'd reached Aaron's room.

It wasn't surprising. His father was Blessed, meaning even if the Crystal had withheld its magic, he still had the guaranteed extended life span and faster healing. But now knowing what she did about the passageways...

Analia said, "That dope also said only people with active magic networks can open the passageways."

She expected Dimitri to roll his eyes, at least look intrigued. Instead, he stiffened.

"Bullshit. I have nothing."

"I thought I had nothing, too," Analia said. "Yet, here I am, tracking Royal magic and nearly self-combusting on two separate occasions. And since I doubt the life span and healing aspects on their own are enough—"

"Haven't you noticed that buffoon is all talk?" Dimitri interrupted, leaning away. "He couldn't even seal your room properly. Why are you listening to him now?"

Because Othin was the only one that could have sealed that garden, and he sealed it strong enough to keep the creature inside. Analia opened her mouth, but Dimitri cut her off with a sharp jerk of his head. He almost looked frightened.

Analia raised her hands, then leaned back against her pillows. After a tense pause, she asked, "Have you managed to hear anything about what they know?"

Dimitri eased back against the wall. "They know that you used the passageways and that you made it outside. They think you were in the castle garden, although Othin is having a fit about what in the garden could have left those marks on your arm."

Analia fought the urge to scratch the itchy wounds along her arm. Hopefully, while Othin forced her to stew, they would have time to heal—although the process was moving far slower than usual. And if they discovered the damage to that thorn bush—no. Analia wouldn't worry about that until she had to.

"Do they suspect you or Aaron?" she asked.

"No."

Analia sighed in relief. "Do you know where he is?"

She hadn't thanked Aaron last night for helping her, although she mainly wanted to check in on him. The moment he'd spotted the mark on her neck—which had barely faded as of that morning—something cold and deadly had frosted over his features. He'd managed to wipe it away by the time they'd exited the woods, but his fingers still shook as he cleaned her wounds.

Dimitri said, "They sent him out to join Cabir's border patrol nonsense."

"But he's my guard."

"And what a shit ton of guarding he would be doing while you're stuck in your chambers indefinitely."

Analia scowled. Dimitri waved a hand.

"Boo-hoo, he'll be back. In the meantime, I found something else."

Without further comment, he produced Analia's legends book from within his cloak—how big were his pockets?

"I've been wondering where that went," Analia murmured.

"You clearly didn't wonder very hard. Anyway, I kept thinking I'd seen that ugly bastard in the garden somewhere before. And look."

Dimitri flipped to a page and shoved the book toward her. Analia barely had to glance at the page to recognize the scene: a swarm of creatures identical to the one in the garden, clashing with the Defiants as they fought their way up Mt. Raegyr.

"I always thought this was just a creative interpretation of what the demons looked like," she said.

"Well, they're real enough to suck your neck and to be in a demonology index."

Dimitri pulled a small stack of pages from his cloak. Analia gave him a disapproving look.

"Now is not the time to develop a moral compass, Flashfire. Not unless you'd like to answer all the questions that would come from me trying to check out the book."

"You could've written out a copy."

"How much time do you think I have? Besides, these pages won't be missed. No one goes in the demonology section; they think it's taboo. But look here."

Dimitri grabbed the top page and read aloud, his rhythm impressively smooth. "The Devourist demon is the highest order of demon, capable of being summoned with obsidian salt and the proper ritual, but it is difficult to contain and control. Comprising the majority of the Ancient Ones' army, the Devourist's life force is connected to the glowing crystal core in the center of its chest, powered by the magic and lifeforce it consumes from the necks of its victims.

"And it goes on to explain how its saliva is what induces the fear-based visions, basically as an incapacitation technique while it sucks you dry."

Dimitri tossed the papers aside and posed as if waiting for applause. Analia flashed back to Pryanth hurling the damper on the table, the onyx glowing with absorbed magic. He had said he felt empty when his magic was trapped. Was that what she was feeling?

It would certainly explain her slowed-down healing. But could that also mean there was something in her network that she hadn't managed to tap yet? Although if she'd had her magic drained, shouldn't it be back by now?

It only took the Royals a night to recover from the Solstice Ceremony. But that was a voluntary release of magic, not a demon sucking it away. Analia didn't want to think about what that might mean for her.

She looked at the page, then back at Dimitri. He had done all of this. For her. Without being asked. Once, she would have thought it was purely because he wanted to escape the castle. But now?

"Thank you," she said quietly.

Dimitri looked as though he'd been slapped.

"What?" she asked.

"I can count on two fingers how many times I've heard that," Dimitri said. "And both times have been from you."

Was work as a servant here so thankless?

"How much thanks do you think someone gets when they're specifically told to keep out of sight?" Dimitri asked, reading her face.

"I'm—"

"If you say sorry, I will deck you with this tome," Dimitri said, waving the legends book for emphasis. "Besides, why should I care? It tells me everything I need to know about a person."

He said it so matter-of-factly, like he didn't care in the slightest that everyone saw the worst in him. But Analia couldn't help but wonder just how thick his skin truly was.

Knowing Dimitri would be more annoyed if she responded, Analia rolled out of bed to pace the chamber. "So," she said, "it wasn't xenol leaving those marks after all."

"It wasn't xenol killing them, either," said Dimitri, collecting his things. "Xenol is redundant at that point."

"Unless Royal magic poses a threat to the Devourist," Analia suggested. "Maybe xenol is a way to weaken Royal magic just enough for the Devourist to strike?"

"Then why bother poisoning Patryclas, not Sylas?"

It took a second for them to register what Dimitri had said. Then, "Crystal fuck me," Dimitri said.

"Sylas was sitting right next to him," Analia breathed, hand resting on the spot her pin used to be. "Is it possible?"

"If it was Othin? Definitely."

"And that would have been Moon hit as well."

Analia crossed back to the bed, extending her hands toward Dimitri. He didn't recoil as she expected, but only touched her with his fingertips.

"We have the xenol," she said. "We have the Devourist. Do we have him?"

Dimitri made to speak, but he paused as there came the sound of pounding footsteps. Analia raised a brow and crossed to her door, moving aside the chair she'd stuck under the handle and peeking out.

"Everyone's running," she said, pulling her head back in.

Dimitri sat up straight, eyes gleaming. Without exchanging a word, Analia slipped out the door, Dimitri heading for the passageways.

# Chapter 45

Aaron pushed his way through the bodies that clogged the entryway like blood clots, Selbi marching in his wake.

The morning before, Lev had dispatched him to join Cabir's patrol, seeing as Aaron's charge was locked away. Unable to find a reason to stay, Aaron saddled up and rode across the central kingdom to find them, knowing there would be no clues to discover.

Indeed, there were no clues left behind the following dawn when Aaron found the body at the edge of their camp. There was only the black mark on the side of his neck, staring like an unblinking eye.

Hope was a cooling ember in the ashes as they raced the body back to the castle, Aaron splitting off to collect Selbi. They all knew it was too late. But that didn't stop the healer from stalking forward, a blast of golden light erupting from the place he assumed the body lay.

Aaron retreated, pressing his back to the far wall that thrummed with the power rolling over the entryway.

He should be used to this by now, shouldn't he? The sound of voices as they teetered on the edge, knowing the plummet was inevitable, but still grasping onto hope? So then why did his body feel so gods-damned heavy?

He turned his head from the crowd, his eyes immediately locking on a pair of smoky-gray ones peering out from a nearby alcove.

Before he could think, his feet were moving, his eyes sliding inexorably down to her neck, her pale blue slip.

Too close. Definitely too close as Analia's fingers wrapped around his wrist and pulled him into her narrow hiding spot.

But Aaron kept his voice light as he said, "I thought you were confined to your chambers."

Analia didn't seem to mind as he gently extracted his wrist.

"Hard to confine someone when the guards ditch their posts," she replied. "As long as I stay out of sight, I don't see why anyone has to know."

She looked to the circle of guards shifting restlessly in the center of the entryway, and Aaron struggled to fight back his smile.

"What's going on?" she asked.

"Our new friend paid Cabir's patrol a visit last night."

"What?" Analia's head whipped toward him. She stepped closer, her eyes flashing across his face, "Are you all right?"

"What? Yes, yes, I'm fine."

Aaron stomped down hard on the emotion stirring in his chest. Especially as Analia didn't immediately look away, as if she needed to see it for herself before she could believe it.

"Who then?" she asked.

Aaron released a heavy breath. "Cabir."

The golden light flared. Analia's face was momentarily illuminated, allowing Aaron to see the blow as it landed, still close enough he could feel her wince. And gods damn it all, he immediately reached for her.

"I have to go," he said, jerking his hand back at the last second. He pushed off the wall and stepped around her.

"Hey." Analia touched his arm, immediately rooting him to the spot. "This was not your fault."

Aaron looked down at her hand. Yes, it was.

"I know," he said.

He stepped out of her grip and back into the entryway. There was another flash of gold, but he didn't—couldn't—pause as he headed for one of the marble staircases. He already knew what would happen next. He didn't need to see it.

As he climbed, Othin's howl of anguish echoed behind him. But Aaron kept moving, one step at a time.

Aaron sat on the parapet, one knee raised. He had stopped at his chambers first, stripping off his leathers and scrubbing the sweat and grime from his skin with water hot enough to burn. Even now, though, dressed in a simple black shirt and pants with the late-afternoon sun drying his hair, he could still feel the death that clung to his skin like icy cobwebs.

He didn't know how much time had passed when there came the inevitable footsteps on the roof behind him.

"Hey, this is my brooding spot. Get your own."

"But I was so hoping to see you," Aaron replied, the words rolling off his tongue before he could stop them.

Analia sat beside him, the gentle breeze fluttering her hair. It was starting to seem as though he couldn't avoid her if he tried—and he was not supposed to be pleased by that.

Aaron brushed the thought aside. He raised a questioning brow, and Analia shook her head.

"I'm sorry," he said, shifting so both feet dangled over the edge. "I know you liked him."

Analia sighed. "He was certainly one of the few good ones here."

Aaron wasn't going to argue that. For once, he had nothing to say.

"So," Analia said, nudging him with her foot. "Why are you brooding?"

Aaron bit his cheek. His mission had been so clear: get in, find the scroll, get out. Leave no trail, nothing that could lead back to where he'd come from, nor where he'd gone. His mission, his people, his home. That was what mattered most.

Yet, there he was. Sitting on the roof with a princess whose safety had been enough to slap every shred of control out of his hands, jeopardizing not just his cover, but his everything. The worst part was days later, levelheaded, a part of him still didn't care.

The part that had his hand inching toward hers on the wall between them. The part that had urged him to spill everything to her that day on the fountain because it had been six gods-damn months, and lies and masks made for horribly hollow company. The part that was muffled under the extensive pile of everything that could go wrong if he chose to listen.

"So," she said, leaning around him to peer into his face, "it's the silent brooding, then."

Aaron made to protest. But Analia merely settled back on her elbows and said, "The very reason rooftop brooding began in the first place."

Gods, she was stunning. Sunlight glanced off her upturned face, highlighting the arch of her cheekbones and turning her hair to flame. His gaze wandered down to her mouth, tracing the tiny smile that said she would be content to sit with him indefinitely.

"I feel like there's a story there," he said.

Analia toyed with a loose pebble on the parapet between them. "I first started climbing the Ash Castle turret when I was seven. It started out as a place for me to hide when my father... was being my father. It was the one place I was free to sulk, or rage, or try and force my magic without anyone finding me.

"Part of me thinks it's because they thought I couldn't scramble up there by myself, but the rest of me knows it was because no one was actually looking. No one except my uncle.

"He had a knack for finding me, especially when I didn't want to be found. But after a while, the roof became our spot. The place where we could sit above all the noise and stress and chaos."

Analia's wistful smile faltered, but the sadness was nowhere near as sharp as Aaron had seen it before. That part of himself hammered against the heavy load of what ifs.

"Do you ever wish he would have left you alone?" Aaron asked. "Just so it wouldn't hurt that much more when he was gone."

"I did try to get him to leave," she said, rolling the pebble along a crack in the wall. "But he only chuckled and said, 'Little fledgling, since when do you have to be alone in order to hide?' Then, he sat on the opposite side of the turret and waited until I inevitably started babbling to him."

Aaron gave her a pointed nudge. She flashed a guilty smile.

"Granted," she said, sitting up, "there are some people like Dima who would snap your head off without hesitating if you didn't leave them alone. But I think, for me, it would have hurt far more if I'd never let him stay."

Aaron's mind wandered through his first three months in the Sun Kingdom. Assimilating into the guard, yet never allowing himself to truly be one of them. Talking, smiling, flirting, deftly switching from mask to mask.

He knew he had a life back home, one he didn't need to risk by starting a new, temporary one here. He'd thought he was surviving just fine.

Yet, these past three months with Analia and Dimitri, feeling like he had somewhere, someone to go to? He hadn't felt that kind of relief since he'd emerged from the Underground for the first time in years.

But as good as that relief felt, he knew it would hurt just as bad if anything went wrong. And there were so many things that could go wrong.

But what if it was worth the risk? What if, despite the odds, it was safe to trust his relief?

Aaron's eyes drifted up.

"Analia," he said suddenly, "where's your pin?"

"In one of Othin's pockets, I suspect," she said, unconcerned. "Unless Pryanth has sent it to be melted down already."

"He took your pin?"

"I'll get it back." She said it so matter-of-factly, the same way she'd say her slip was blue.

He made to reply. And Analia's shoulders slumped. He scooted closer, Analia not hesitating to lean against him.

"Could we have been on the wrong trail this entire time?" she asked, her voice small.

"What do you mean?"

"Dimitri figured out what the creature is. A Devourist demon. They apparently power themselves by feeding off the magic of their victims, and those 'visions' are an incapacitation technique."

Aaron made to pull away to look at her fully, but Analia made a noise of protest that had him moving back once more. "Are you—"

"Tired, but all right."

Well, that explained her burning skin that night: it was the last of her magic sputtering out. But if the magic had been there before, then why hadn't she been able to summon—his dagger.

"We know the Devourist is the killer," Analia went on. "We know xenol is involved, and we know Sun has access to both. But how could Cabir have been dosed? Besides that, Othin wouldn't have killed Cabir. You don't fake that type of grief."

She hesitated. "Could we have accidentally released it?"

Aaron had wondered that at first himself. But he shook his head. "No. If it had escaped, we would have been dead before we left the trees."

Analia seemed to accept that, but she kept her eyes on her fidgeting fingers.

"They have xenol here," she said, "but the scrap from the library says it grows in Moon. They summoned the Devourist, but anyone with obsidian and the right incantation could have done that. Although how many people actually know that ritual in the first place?"

"Marcos," Aaron supplied, practically spitting out the word.

"We'll have to track him down again," Analia sighed. "Long shot or not."

Aaron recalled the hungry glint in Marcos's eyes when he realized Analia was wearing his cloak, only sharpening when he discovered who she was. If they had to find Marcos again, Aaron would be making good on his promise to start collecting his knuckles.

"Have we hit a dead end?" Analia asked.

*We.* Not *I.* Because Aaron wasn't the only one with a covert mission, nor was he the only one that had let others get too close—although would Analia agree with that last part?

"Well," Aaron said, drawing out the word, "if we have, that just means we have to start back at the beginning."

Analia hummed, sounding thoughtful. Aaron's attention wandered down to the kingdom below. A group of guards loaded what appeared to be Cabir's body, wrapped in a golden shroud, into a private carriage, their voices floating up to him. A figure—undoubtedly Selbi—slipped inside as well, probably off to perform tests on the body.

"The scroll is in the temple," he said, so quietly he didn't think Analia heard. They hadn't discussed it since that day on the roof, so she might not even remember.

But she looked up at him, her hair shifting aside to reveal the fading mark on the side of her neck. "You think?"

Aaron nodded. He braced himself to go on, to explain that it wasn't the guardian making him hesitate.

Analia rested her head on his shoulder. "We're going to need a strategy for that one."

A lump rose in Aaron's throat. Finally, he realized it had never been a question of trust. It had been one of hope, one of the most terrifying things to hold on to.

But listening to Analia not so much offer her help as act as though it was already his? That made reaching for that hope one of the easiest things in the world.

As Aaron shifted her into a more comfortable position, he felt that part of himself poke its head out of the pile, whispering that maybe it wouldn't be a disaster if his mission, his people, his home weren't the only things that were important.

# Chapter 46

L ev escorted Analia into the Throne Room, the only sound their echoing footsteps. The king and queen sat in their respective thrones, Pryanth standing between them with his new sword dangling from his hip. It was like walking up to a painting, one of red-rimmed eyes and grief-etched faces from the death that couldn't be shaken after two days.

Deardryn waved Lev out with a bejeweled hand. He bowed and quickly exited the room, leaving Analia alone with the unreadable Royals before her.

But as Deardryn beckoned her closer, Analia wasn't afraid. Not quite hopeful, either, but something in between as she stood in Deardryn's silence.

"Well?" Othin finally demanded. He sat with his hands braced on the arms of his throne, as if he were about to push himself to his feet. "Are you going to explain yourself or not?"

Analia fought the urge to touch the nearly healed mark on her neck, its effects still weighing down her mind. "My apologies, Your Majesty, I didn't realize—"

"Spare me," Othin snapped. "Tell your story and get out."

Analia kept her face composed. Pryanth tried to catch her eye, but she only felt the cold absence of her pin against her chest. Instead, she turned to Deardryn, whose mild curiosity clashed with the brittle tension in the air.

"There isn't much of a story for me to tell," Analia said. "Pryanth and I had a disagreement. I was angry and upset, and I left my room to walk it off in the gardens outside."

"And how does one injure oneself when taking a stroll?" Othin demanded.

Analia kept her gaze on Deardryn. "I tripped. It was already dark by the time I got outside, and there aren't many lights to see by."

"What kind of trip leads to puncture marks?"

Analia finally glanced at Othin in surprise. "They weren't puncture marks. They were scratches from a bramble bush. The one right near the fountain."

The one whose nymph would affirm this story, especially after Analia had sent Aaron to remind her how she'd been caught listening in on a Royal's conversation.

"Bullshit." Othin shoved out of his throne, marching down the dais stairs. He grabbed her arm, Analia fighting to remain still as he jerked it up to see.

"Well?" Deardryn asked.

Othin's fingers dug into Analia's skin. Just as she'd hoped, she'd recovered enough to reduce her rings of wounds to a scattering of random scabs. Apparently, just like everyone else, Othin had completely underestimated her—Blessing and otherwise.

Othin tossed her arm aside. He turned to Deardryn, about to speak.

"Othin, that's enough," Deardryn cut in heavily. Her tired eyes moved from a barely breathing Analia to her husband, then back again. "This is absurd."

Analia didn't relax.

Othin stomped back to his throne. "Deardryn—"

"This castle isn't a dungeon," Deardryn said, ignoring his outburst. "She wasn't being kept under lock and key. She didn't flee into the kingdom without protection. She took a walk outside."

"And used the passageways to do so without permission!"

"I wasn't aware I needed permission," Analia interjected.

Othin's lip curled. "So, you thought you would skulk through our walls? Eavesdropping? Sneaking out?" Realization dawned across his face. "Sneaking into places as well."

Analia's fingers flexed, itching to toy with a pin she no longer had. Between Othin and that gods-damned mark still bogging down her mind, she needed to finish this, fast. If she could just convince Deardryn—

"Why did you feel inclined to use the passageways?" Deardryn asked curiously. "You understand you are free to leave as you please, so why not use the front door?"

Othin threw up his hands. "Exactly!"

Phantom ice flashed across Analia's neck. Faster. Gods damn it all, she had to think faster.

She glanced at Pryanth, her cheeks burning. Just as they'd burned with shame after their fight in the entryway. Just like the burn in the shape of his hand when he slapped her. Each time, she'd fled to the roof because...

"I wanted to be alone." Analia averted her gaze. "I knew if someone saw me leave, they would ask where I was going, if I was all right. And I didn't want to have to explain what happened."

A flash of faintly exasperated sympathy moved across Deardryn's face. Analia tried not to squirm.

So, Deardryn knew what happened on the roof. Of all things to discuss with the parents of her betrothed.

"Would you like to say anything, Pryanth?" Deardryn asked, turning to him.

Analia's nails dug into her palms. But Pryanth's eyes weren't the honey-coated steel she'd come to expect. No, she could barely see them as he bowed his head.

"I'm sorry," he said. Analia's jaw nearly dropped as he went on, "She's telling the truth. At least, the parts I'm aware of."

Analia was nonplussed. She frantically tried to untangle his motive, but she was thoroughly knocked on her back foot. Especially as Othin, looking less than impressed, twisted in his seat to face Deardryn.

"And there you have it," he said. "Using the passageways to evade detection. Using them to break into the library and Crystal knows what else.

"Do you still insist on trusting her? The little mouse, scurrying through our walls, getting into gods know what?"

Analia took a half step forward. She was tired of this king, blustering as loud as he could to compensate for the power he didn't have and clearly craved. Just like her father.

"Precisely," Deardryn said. "You have no idea what she's been doing in the walls, nor where she's been going, both of which are irrelevant now."

"That doesn't mean you should sit on your hands and do nothing!"

"Careful, Othin," Deardryn warned. "I don't punish hypothetical offenses."

"So, you're going to ignore the spark until it's a blaze?" Othin asked.

"You've already sealed me from the passageways," Analia said. "How else would you douse that spark?"

Othin half rose from his seat, face turning red behind his dark beard.

"How did you discover the passageways?" Deardryn asked, completely ignoring Othin.

Finally, Analia was back on predicted ground.

"I sensed the magic," she said.

Once again, not a complete lie. Once that part of her mind had been unlocked, the constant, tingling power of the passageways had become the most ubiquitous magic field she had to block out.

"Fascinating," Deardryn murmured.

Othin exclaimed, "All the more reason!"

"You have already sealed the passageways to her," Deardryn said, her patient mask beginning to crack. "It's a punishment in itself. What else would you have me do, set her up in the square for public humiliation?"

"Don't be dramatic," Othin said.

"Don't inflict your grief on the people around you," Deardryn shot back.

Othin's mouth snapped shut. Deardryn almost looked as though she hadn't intended her words, her hand drifting to her chest, her lips parting.

There was a long, crushing pause.

"We've already lost so much," Deardryn finally murmured. She bowed her head, Pryanth moving to put a hand on her arm.

"Cabir's death shouldn't prevent us from seeking justice," Othin insisted hoarsely.

"But you already got your justice, Othin," Deardryn said, almost desperately.

"So that's it? She defies you for a second time, and you forgive her? Am I the only one who must continually repent?"

Deardryn's eyes narrowed. "Analia took a walk outside," she said, magic faintly thrumming around her. "You sired another woman's child. I fail to see the comparison."

"You also fail to see how I've fought to make it right for you, every day following."

"By obsessing over other people's misdeeds to validate your own."

"Because I don't want to lose anyone else!" He stretched out a hand, past Pryanth, Deardryn just out of reach. "Don't you understand that?"

Pryanth inched away from his father's touch. To Analia's astonishment, her heart squeezed.

Deardryn eyed Othin's extended hand, the mask of the Dragoness sliding back into place. "What if I told you we could gain someone instead of losing them?"

One, two, three heartbeats.

Othin slowly retracted his hand. "You don't mean…"

Deardryn nodded.

Analia blinked, feeling as though she had stumbled upon an intimate moment, wondering if she could back away. But she was frozen to the spot as Deardryn said, "I'm talking about a wedding."

# Chapter 47

Analia felt like she was floating. Away from her body, away from Deardryn explaining that their kingdom had just received a massive blow and needed something to pull them back together.

This was a dream. A nightmare. The Devourist had found her again because Crystal spare her, she could not—

"I think it's a fantastic idea," said Pryanth.

Analia slammed back into her body.

Crystal spare her, she wasn't supposed to be in the Sun Kingdom long enough for this to happen. She was supposed to find her uncle's killer and get out.

"Analia?" Pryanth asked.

She looked up as he descended the steps and offered his hand. "What do you think?"

What did she think? She thought that if she were to be married, she would never get out. Never mind she was lost, no leads, back to the beginning—wait.

"When would this happen?" she asked, not taking Pryanth's hand.

Deardryn considered. "We would need to speed up our current arrangements, but I presume we could be ready in six weeks' time."

Analia fought not to sway on her feet.

"We'll need to inform my father," she said.

Othin recoiled, but Analia had no problem ignoring him. It was paying attention that caused her difficulty as she looked over Pryanth's shoulder at the queen.

"Indeed," Deardryn agreed, "we will notify him immediately—"

"He'll want a celebration as well," Analia said, not caring that she interrupted Deardryn. "It will bruise his pride if he thinks he's been excluded from this aspect of our arrangement."

Pryanth's face puckered, but he kept his hand extended. As Deardryn nodded and continued to plan, Analia forced herself to take it. Always so cold, such a contrast to his breath in her ear as he pulled her close and whispered, "This was my idea, you know."

Once, Analia's heart would have skipped a beat at that. Instead, she could feel her lungs folding in on themselves.

But she forced a smile. Forced her hand to squeeze his. Forced herself to remember she'd managed to get herself back to the beginning, just as Aaron had suggested.

Deardryn and Othin argued a few minutes longer. Finally, they rose from their thrones, sweeping past Analia on either side like sliding cell bars and exiting the chamber. Analia frantically scrambled for an excuse to flee as well, but Pryanth squeezed her hand.

"I have something for you," he said.

He dug in the pocket of his cloak, pulling something free and placing it in her hand. For a long moment, Analia stared down at her phoenix pin, completely at a loss.

"I would have returned it to you sooner," he said, "but with Cabir..."

"But you were the one who took it," Analia whispered, cradling the pin to her chest. "Why would you—"

"You didn't honestly think I meant that?" Pryanth looked aghast. "Analia, I was only trying to bring the fight to an end."

Pryanth tried to pull her closer, but Analia resisted.

"How?" she asked. "How was that ending *anything?*"

"You know my father. He blusters until he thinks he's won. I thought if he got your pin, he would stomp off in victory and I could sneak it back to you when he wasn't paying attention."

His thumb moved across the back of her hand, honey eyes staring imploringly into hers. But Analia only felt something sharper than frustration, hotter than anger.

"The fight was already over, Pryanth," she said, taking a step back. "He was walking away when you said it."

"No, he wasn't."

"Yes, he was!"

"Analia, when have you ever known my father to walk away?" Pryanth stepped closer, resetting the distance between them. "He was preparing for another round."

No, he wasn't. He had just sealed the passageways. It was over.

But was she remembering wrong? Had Pryanth misinterpreted?

Gods, she couldn't even think straight anymore. She just wanted it to end: the anger, confusion, guilt, exhaustion.

"I was only trying to help," Pryanth said. He took her hand clutching her pin with his free one, bringing it to his lips. "I wouldn't try to hurt you like that. I love you. And you are mine."

Pryanth took a step closer. Analia didn't move. She didn't stop him as he leaned in. But that didn't stop his kiss from tasting bitter on her tongue.

Three weeks passed in a flurry of measurements and dress sizings by the castle seamstress, lessons in Sun Kingdom politics, and constant, quietly suppressed panic. With so much to worry about, Analia wasn't sure what the culprit was.

Perhaps it was Pryanth, who had reverted back to his usual self: holding her hand throughout her various meetings. Walking with her as she sought out the three rings Deardryn had hidden, and she couldn't track until her mark was completely healed. Kissing her goodbye each night.

Maybe it was Lev, who seemed to be around every corner, making it impossible to be alone with Aaron and Dimitri. Aaron barely managed to whisper to her that he'd checked Gritta's and all of Marcos's other haunts, but the drug lord was gone without a trace.

Yes, Marcos wriggling free was certainly a stress contender. But perhaps it was simply the idea of going home.

Deardryn had written to Brenn the moment Analia's interrogation had concluded, the Ash King replying with reluctant plans for a celebration in three weeks. Just enough time for Analia to stew.

The morning they were to leave for the Ash Kingdom, Analia, Pryanth, and their guards climbed into the Sun carriage, the twin dragons radiating a dry heat. Deardryn and Othin had decided to stay behind. Both were reluctant to leave and potentially open the kingdom up to another attack, and Brenn had agreed that was best—more like he didn't want to deal with any more Sun people than necessary.

Once more, it took the majority of the day to fly. For the entirety of that time, Pryanth was a constant stream of chatter, thankfully not requiring much from Analia to continue.

By the time the carriage landed before the Phoenix Gate with a gentle bump, the sun had completely set. Pryanth immediately sprang to his feet, wrenching the door open and stepping out. He was followed by a line of guards, no one seeming to notice that Analia couldn't move.

"You ready?" Aaron asked, sliding into the seat beside her.

Lev, about to exit, glanced back at them.

"Do I have a choice?" Analia asked.

"Well, we could always commandeer this carriage and spend the rest of our days as outlaws in the Wild Lands."

Analia snorted. Her hand drifted to the dried, dying plant in her white cloak's pocket—courtesy of Dimitri.

Then, she pushed herself to her feet, smoothing her gray satin skirts. She was tired of running away, hiding, being the gods-damned duckling Brenn said she was.

She exited the carriage, Aaron close behind. And immediately, she came face-to-face with her family.

They stood in a line twenty paces away: Cadmus, Aeley, Brenn, Lucilla. Ash guards fanned out behind them, Rois's gaze locking on her as she stepped up beside Pryanth. He took her hand, his chin lifted at an angle that could almost have been construed as confident.

"Analia!" Lucilla made to dart forward, but Brenn put a hand on her shoulder. The little girl looked up at him, then clapped a hand over her mouth.

"Hello, Lucilla," Analia said.

Brenn flashed her a look, and Analia struggled not to look away.

"So," he said after a pause, "our little duckling returns."

Without waiting for a response, he turned, his crown flickering with firelight as he strode back toward the castle.

Analia didn't think. She moved past Aeley, past Cadmus, coming up on Brenn's shoulder, towing Pryanth behind her.

"You've never been one for reunions, have you, Father?" she asked.

Brenn shot her a sidelong look. "My, duckling, have you actually started to develop some plumage?"

"You would be surprised by what has occurred these past three months. Not nearly so surprised if you had made the time to speak with me at the Solstice."

"I knew I would be seeing you again soon, regardless."

Analia's temper sputtered. Had he been expecting her to return because he had thought she would succeed?

"So," Brenn said, looking to a bemused Pryanth. "You still haven't come to your senses?"

Why had she bothered to hope? Of course, Brenn was expecting Sun to dump her back on his doorstep—more likely dead than alive.

He was always expecting her to be a failure. Forever that scared little girl haunting the castle corridors, burning beneath his fingertips, crumbling to ash beneath his stare.

But now, Analia didn't flinch away as he left them at their quarters with a terse invitation to dinner. She was just about to speak, fear a fading echo in her mind, when Brenn sighed, smoothing a hand down her hair.

For a moment, she was small again, Brenn affectionately flattening her flyaway hairs at breakfast.

"Oh, duckling," he said. "I can't wait to hear all you have to tell me."

Before she could jerk away, he let his hand drop, exiting with the rest of the crowd. Cadmus lingered at the end of the hall a moment longer, looking as though he might speak. But he, too, turned away without comment, leaving Analia and her aching heart behind him.

"So," Pryanth said, half to himself. "You really *do* understand."

Analia's mind immediately flashed back to their conversation on the Sun Castle roof, when they'd bonded over their "Crystal-forsaken fathers." Yet, when she looked to Pryanth, his gaze was fixed on the spot Brenn had been, expression troubled.

"He certainly provides little reason to doubt," she said.

Pryanth's lips pursed. Aaron flashed her a sympathetic look from across the hall.

Gods, why couldn't she just hate him? She'd had the thought so many times before. But as Pryanth dropped her hand, retreating into his chambers without so much as glancing at her, she wondered if "him," only applied to Brenn.

Analia touched her pin. Then, without a word, she turned her back on Pryanth, her guards, and walked away. For once she moved down, not up. Straight past Rois—whom she knew would be waiting for her.

"Anna!" He grabbed her hands, bringing her to a stop. His eyes roved across her face, "Are you—"

"Stop trying to make yourself feel better, Rois," Analia said tiredly, extracting her hands. "You made your choice. Stop trying to make me change mine."

Rois opened his mouth. Closed it. Looked down at his boots. "I just thought I could have both," he mumbled. "I thought I could have my dream, which gave me access to the castle, which would make it easier to sneak around with you."

"Did you think we were just going to sneak around forever?" she asked. "Because that's what saying yes condemned us to."

"I didn't think saying no left us anywhere else."

Fair point. Analia looked away. Rois fiddled with his weapons belt.

"I still care about you," he said quietly. "Saying yes didn't change that."

Analia let out a long, heavy sigh. "I know."

But Rois's words no longer triggered a flutter of longing, not even a twinge of resentment. All Analia felt was hollow as she turned away. And Rois did not try to follow as she continued down the hall.

Analia barely remembered her walk through the castle, too lost in thought to pay attention to where she was going. Still, she wasn't surprised when she found herself at the Phoenix Gate, the sentinel on duty turning away once he realized she wasn't trying to leave.

Analia sighed, feeling a faint magical thrum as she leaned her head against the gate. Everything was just too complicated. Rois wasn't a monster, but he broke her heart anyway. Brenn was her father, but he burned her down to nothing. Pryanth—Crystal spare her, she didn't know where to begin with that one.

Who was she supposed to trust? Who could she trust when everyone around her seemed to have daggers hidden behind their backs? What was she supposed to do?

She still had no answers when Aaron found her and touched her shoulder, saying they'd been summoned to dinner. Analia stroked her pin, which seemed to thrum with the faint magic of the gate. Then, rolling her shoulders, she silently followed Aaron back into the familiar chaos.

# Chapter 48

Ember plucked her harp strings, filling the back room with lilting music. She'd always needed something more engaging than pacing to focus. Yet, for all the focusing she'd done, there was only so much she could show for it.

Across the room, her devinroot drooped.

"I know," Ember said glumly. "I'm not too thrilled right now, myself."

Her eyes darted to the pile of opened letters on her desk, then to the container of mush she had extracted from Analia's candle jar. She scowled, her fingers speeding up. This Rosala-forsaken mystery was starting to—

Ember's head snapped up at the sound of the door opening. Gently setting her harp aside, she stomped out of the back room. And as soon as she saw who it was, she flew through the shelves, all irritation forgotten.

"Anna!"

Analia stumbled back as Ember barreled into her.

"This might be the most enthusiastic greeting I've ever had," she mumbled.

Ember laughed and pulled back to examine her. Analia wore a sleeveless blue tunic and leggings. Those shadows were still under her eyes, but there finally seemed to be a flicker of life in the smoky gray.

"Em," Analia said, "you're staring again."

"Sorry!" Ember waved a vaguely apologetic hand, then propelled Analia through the shop. "Come, I've brought my harp. I haven't heard you play in so long, and I think my plants might murder me if they have to listen to my dulcet woes for much longer—"

"Maybe later," Analia cut in, wincing as her gaze briefly landed on the discarded harp.

Ember put her hands on her hips. "Have you played at all since you left?"

Analia became incredibly interested in the recovered devinroot. "Ember, what does this plant do—"

"Analia Valarus!"

"I'll get to it," Analia said tensely. "Just as soon as we get this mystery solved."

Analia sat on Ember's cluttered desk, ignoring Ember's glare. Spotting the container of mush, she raised a brow. "I'm not supposed to recognize that, am I?"

Ember begrudgingly sat on the other end of the desk, knocking the letters to the ground. "It's the contents from Patryclas's wine."

"Do you know what it is?"

"I'm offended you even have to ask that. Although with the conditions you sent them to me in?"

Ember shuddered. The wine had proven itself to be a bit—fine, a lot—more difficult than she'd expected to test. At first, she'd thought she'd test the wine as is, but there'd been far too many contaminants to sift through: candle wax, the plants and herbs used to fragrance the wax, bacterial and fungal buildup.

There was definitely something in there, though. It had only required an extremely fine strainer with some magical enhancements to figure that out. That, however, only left Ember with a pinch's worth of mush, so fine she could barely sense the magic.

She'd tried repeating her trick of forced regeneration, but that had gone horribly. The moment she'd directed her magic toward the wine-soaked pile, it was like her magic had been sucked out of her. Cadmus had needed to smack her hand away and drag her out of the room, pale and trembling.

"You put me through my paces," Ember said. "You're lucky I love you."

Analia's face spasmed.

"Don't tell me you didn't know that!" Ember threw up her hands. "Anna, I have never been known to be ambiguous!"

"No, I know," Analia mumbled, cheeks turning red. "You just never said it before."

"Really?" Ember cocked her head, then shrugged. "I can't remember. I'll say it more often if it means getting to see that look on your face again."

Analia rolled her eyes. She opened her mouth, paused. "So have you figured out what this mush is?"

Ember hid her disappointment. "No. The magic is too faint. If I could just get a sample of xenol to compare it with, I feel like it would be enough to sense if they're similar or not.

"But I, well, may or may not have been caught stealing samples and am now only allowed to look at them under supervision. The one guard who usually watches me is rather good-looking, though, so I suppose it's not all bad."

Ember expected Analia's face to fall. Instead, a slow smile crept across her lips.

"Well, Em," she said, reaching into a hidden pocket running down her thigh, "today is your lucky day."

Ember's eyes widened as Analia pulled out a dying plant.

"No," Ember breathed. She snatched the plant, the leaves crunching beneath her fingers. "And you kept the roots! I might cry."

"Hopefully, this makes up for the candle jar."

Ember waved a hand. "How did you get this?"

As Analia recounted her tale of the Royal Garden, Ember bustled about—repotting, watering, sending a blast of magic through the plant that left her lightheaded as it tried to latch on. By the time Analia finished, the xenol was only contemplating death. Meanwhile, Ember had emotional whiplash.

"There are about fifty things I need to scold you for," Ember informed her, carrying the xenol over to the pile of mush. "But first, we have the moment of truth."

Analia sat quietly, hands in her lap.

Ember placed one hand on the xenol plant, the other in the horribly unpleasant mush. She let her magic sink into the plants like water through soil, settling herself at the roots.

"They're the same," she said after a moment, retracting her hands.

"Did you just use magic?" Analia asked.

Ember nodded, and Analia looked puzzled. She touched the side of her neck, "Why didn't I sense it?"

"What do you mean, 'sense it'?"

Analia quickly explained her new sensory abilities.

"Holy Rosala, Anna," Ember said. "How dare you keep all of this from me! Especially when I am such an attentive audience!"

"I'll tell you all about it as soon as I'm back from Sun," Analia said. "Which, from the looks of it, is any day now."

She hopped off the desk, pacing the length of the room. "Ember, this has to be it. We have proof that they have access to xenol, it's connected to both Accalon and Patryclas, which makes even more sense if that wine had been intended for Sylas. They have the Devourist demon that leaves the marks. They're cornered."

Ember's stomach sank. "That might not be true," she murmured.

A part of her hoped Analia hadn't heard her, but Analia pivoted on her heel. "What do you mean?"

Ember fought the urge to kick the letters under her desk. "Well..."

"Ember."

"Sorry. Well, when you sent Aaron to find me—well done, getting a henchman, I mean, I turned your brother into my own—"

"Ember!"

"Sorry! I thought I'd write to the other healer apprentices. You know, healer neutrality and pompous neophytes looking for any chance to shout their knowledge—"

"Em—"

"I know, paper-thin pedestal. I just thought they had the highest chance of actually telling me what they found in their Royals with the black marks."

"And?"

Ember's fingers twisted into the soft fabric of her healer robes. "Xenol wasn't in any of their systems."

Shock flashed across Analia's face. Quickly composing herself, she said, "Well, we already know that it wasn't xenol killing them, but the Devourist. We theorized that xenol was used to decrease their powers to assist the Devourist."

"Maybe," Ember said. "But Anna."

Ember averted her gaze, spotting the letters once more. Sliding off the desk, she snatched them up and slowly sifted through, Analia's impatience palpable.

"None of the Royals were found with xenol in their system," Ember repeated. "But all of them were found with trace amounts of obsidian."

She waited for Analia to get it, her heart sinking.

"That makes sense," she said. "It's a demon, summoned by obsidian salt. It probably passed into the bodies through the black mark."

"Anna," Ember said gently, "Accalon didn't have any obsidian in his system."

Analia froze. "What?"

"I told you," Ember said, reaching for Analia's hand. "He had xenol, wine, and his dinner. No obsidian."

"But... But he had the black mark," Analia said.

"It was so faint, Anna. It could have been anything."

"But we still don't know if xenol can even kill someone."

"I know."

"Then how—"

"I don't know." Ember squeezed Analia's hand, a lump rising in her throat as she watched the denial warring in her eyes.

"We have to be missing something," Analia said.

"Anna—"

"No!"

Analia snatched her hand back, striding out into the main area. Ember hopped off the desk and followed.

"There are too many pieces that fit for this to be a mistake," Analia said, spinning around in one of the aisles to face Ember once more.

"I agree," Ember said quickly. "I just don't know where to go from here."

Analia dragged her hand down her face. Ember touched her arm, neither of them speaking until the door opened once more.

"Analia, are you sure you can't shadowjump, because you disappear remarkably fast the moment my back is turned."

Ember glanced up. "You again?"

Aaron stepped into view. He touched Analia's shoulder in greeting, his assessing gaze momentarily darting between her and Ember.

"You know," he said to Ember, rocking back on his heels, "most women are delighted to see me."

"Really?" Ember asked half-heartedly. "And how many of those women's beds have you been in?"

"Well, that depends."

"Nice try. Even if I wasn't a healer sworn to celibacy, it would take a lot more than pretty eyes and some flowery words for me to open my legs."

"Which is one of the many reasons why I like you."

Ember smiled slightly. She turned her attention back to Analia, who was studiously examining an aloe plant and ignoring them.

"Besides," Aaron went on, "you don't need to do anything with your legs. They're fantastic on their own."

Ember's head whipped toward him.

"Here we go," Analia muttered.

Ember put her hands on her hips and glared. "You compliment my legs," she said, "but not my spectacular ass?"

"I didn't want to come off as stale," Aaron said. "I figured you've gotten enough of those comments."

Despite her despair, her unease, her heartache for her friend, Ember laughed.

"You're trouble," she said, simultaneously ruffling his hair and smacking aside his hand reaching for a plant.

"You two are horrible," Analia muttered.

"Come on, Analia," Aaron said. "I would never say such things to anyone other than Ember. We already established that's our game, just as you and I have ours."

"I still don't think we have a game," Analia muttered.

"Then what would you call the thing where I'm incredibly charming and you find it exceedingly irritating?"

Analia swatted aside his finger poking her in the ribs. But that was a small smile tugging up her mouth. Rosala curse her, how had he done that?

As Ember stared unabashedly at the guard, Analia quickly filled him in on their findings. Once she'd finished, he ran a hand through his hair.

"Is there any point in checking his chambers one more time?" he asked.

Analia replied, "It can't hurt."

"I'll keep running tests on the xenol," Ember said. "Now that I have a full specimen, I'm not nearly as limited as I used to be."

The group quickly dispersed after that, Analia and Aaron heading for the door. Ember didn't expect to say anything else. But as she watched Aaron lean around Analia to open the door for her, she called out.

Analia glanced back.

"Play your gods-damned harp."

The corner of Analia's mouth lifted. She looked as if she were about to turn without comment. But then she mouthed, "Love you, too," and fled, not catching the fond look Ember and Aaron shared.

Analia and Aaron wove through the crowded kingdom streets. She toyed with the hem of her tunic, her eyes sweeping across storefronts, inns, vendors filling the air with the smell of meat and peppers. Exactly as she'd left it.

"Everything here reminds me of my uncle," she said, half to herself.

Aaron ran his fingers along a phoenix statue as they passed. "I can only imagine."

"He had this tradition where once a month, he would wander out into the kingdom and just talk with people. Everyone from store owners, to noblemen, to prostitutes, to orphans, whoever he stumbled upon. He would ask them questions for hours, his voice scratchy by the time we headed home."

"He took you with him?" Aaron asked.

"From the time I was three. Although during those days he was carrying me by noon because I was tired—I swear to the gods, Aaron, if that smirk is followed by you offering to carry me..."

Aaron's laugh was pure wicked delight.

Analia managed a smile of her own. "He always said a kingdom should know the ruler they're obeying, and a ruler should know the people who obey. It was something he picked up from working in the forges before becoming king. And all those people are still here, going about their lives, following their routines as if nothing has changed. And somehow, their familiarity is only making me feel even more lost than I was before."

Aaron let out a long, heavy sigh.

"When I found out my mother had been killed," he said, "the first thought that pushed through the denial was, how is anyone standing right now? How had they already adjusted when it would take me decades to stop being surprised when I'd walk past her room and not see her reading by her window?"

*Decades?* Analia double-checked, but she still couldn't sense a magic network. But he had to be at least Demiblessed if it had been decades.

Could he just have an extended life span and faster healing, and Analia's sensory abilities only included magic and networks? Then again, she couldn't sense Ember's magic, either.

"How old are you?" Analia asked, absently rubbing the side of her neck.

"One hundred and three," Aaron said, smiling slightly at Analia's shocked expression.

"Why can't I sense you, then?" she asked.

"I'm not entirely sure," Aaron said. "What I *do* know is there's a part of you that will never stop wondering how everyone else kept moving. And you won't quite figure out how you did it, either. But eventually, you'll realize somehow, you've kept moving, too."

They reached the Phoenix Gate. The sentinels swung the gate open for them with a metallic clang, one Analia knew Accalon had always loved for its inexplicable grandeur. A piece of him for when he was gone.

"Does it ever get easier?" she asked as they walked along the winding path to the castle.

"Mostly," Aaron said.

"That's comforting."

"Do you want comforting, or honest?"

Analia gestured for him to continue. He lightly tugged her hair, but his face quickly sobered.

"Sometimes," he said, "there are days where I don't even think about her. Other days, I can look back at the times she would tap me on the nose when I was being a smartass and laugh. And other times... the grief is an arrow through the back."

Analia touched his arm. "What's today?"

"Today," he said, rubbing the back of his neck, "the last arrow wound has scabbed over, but isn't ready to flake away yet."

He patted her hand, and Analia let it rest against the smooth leather for one moment longer before dropping away.

The two didn't speak as they climbed the castle steps. Analia led the way toward Accalon's chambers, their path lit by Everflame sconces. Gold, not blue.

"Ember and I used to play our harps together every day," she said. "It was the one thing I was truly, truly good at. Better than everyone, magic or not."

"Musician's fingers," Aaron said, echoing Marcos's words.

"Musician's fingers that haven't touched the strings in months. Not when feeling that type of joy feels like the hardest thing in the world. It feels wrong, when these sconces used to be lit by Accalon's blue flames and are now perpetually lit by the Everflame."

"Arrow?" Aaron asked.

No, it was just another shard tinged with red. But Analia nodded. "From the front, though, not the back."

"That's to be expected," Aaron said. "But Accalon wouldn't want you to jam it in any deeper."

Analia didn't respond.

They reached Accalon's chambers. Analia registered another slice at the missing phoenix knocker outside the door, but she let it drip in the background as she pushed open the door. Just to find Accalon's chambers had been stripped bare, even the smell of smoke and ink cleared away.

Analia drifted inside, strangely hollow as her mind filled in every missing piece of furniture and pop of color against the stone. So many cuts, insubstantial on their own, nevertheless accumulating until she wondered if there was anything left to chip away.

"No obsidian," she finally said.

"No sign of a struggle, either," Aaron said, moving around the room. "Although that would have been easily scrubbed away."

Aaron continued his search, peering into every crack in the stone. Finding nothing, he came to kneel at the spot where the foot of Accalon's bed used to be.

"Well, that's to be expected," Analia sighed, poking at the ashes in the fireplace with her foot. "It's been three months, after all. Maybe I can get my hands on any written records that were made before the chamber was stripped."

Aaron hesitated. "I'm sorry."

Analia looked back at him. Guilt twisted his mouth, but the look in his eyes told her he wasn't just talking about the last time they were in this room.

"There's nothing to forgive," she said truthfully.

Aaron bit his cheek and looked away.

"How can we have all the pieces, yet still no conclusion?" she asked, coming to sit beside him.

"I've been wondering the same," Aaron said, fingering the chain around his neck. "Could they be two separate things?"

"Maybe," Analia said, "but then why was Patryclas—"

"Poisoned with the same thing," Aaron finished with a sigh.

Could her original theory still be possible? Othin poisoned Accalon because of the wedding pact, then targeted Patryclas because of his potential alliance with her? It would make sense if it were someone else summoning the Devourist that killed Cabir and the rest. But they still had no idea if xenol could kill someone. Besides that...

"Marcos said Accalon was his top buyer," Analia murmured.

She'd been trying to ignore that fact, writing it off as Marcos still searching for chinks he could slide his dagger through. But it was getting harder to do so as everything else he'd said fell into alignment.

Aaron, too, looked as though he would like to argue, but knew he couldn't. He reached over, giving her knee a quick squeeze. Analia sighed, carefully tucking her jagged pieces away.

"The celebration is starting soon," she said, rising to her feet. "I have to get ready."

She offered Aaron a hand up. Together, they exited the room, Analia casting one last look over her shoulder before closing the door behind them.

"What do we do now?" Aaron asked as they headed back toward Analia's chambers.

Analia expected her stomach to roll. Instead, her voice was steady as she said, "Now? Now, I tell Brenn."

# Chapter 49

Standing before her mirror, Analia grabbed her pin from the dressing table and attached it to her gown. Normally, Lynette and Mardie would have been there to help her, but Analia had sharply dismissed them the moment they stepped through her door. The two had given her an odd look, but silently complied.

Analia shrugged it off as she finished getting ready. She'd opted out of the Ash Kingdom's spiraling braids, instead letting her hair fall in loose waves pushed back by a beaded headband. Her dress swirled with shades of gray, the low neckline embroidered with red, orange, and gold. Simple, but elegant. Although the slit on the side and low back bordered on bold.

Well, they were celebrating her impending wedding to a foreign Royal. A potentially scandalous gown matched the theme. Honestly, so would her eventually fleeing her betrothed to return home victorious. In that regard, Analia didn't know if she had any good options left.

Turning, her eyes landed on the gilded harp in the corner of her room. Ember's words echoed in her mind, and hesitantly, she reached for it.

Her fingers slid into position, something settling in her chest. But as Analia made to pluck a string, her hand refused to move. She was frozen, stiff, her mind horribly empty.

Analia quickly turned away. She strode toward the door, needing to get as far as possible from the terror that maybe, it wasn't she was afraid to be happy again—she simply couldn't.

Analia yanked open her door. Pryanth stood on the other side, his hand raised as if about to knock. Seeing her, he let his hand fall and offered a greeting.

He wore a fine, buttoned-up white jacket. The collar, cuffs, and hem were embroidered with gold threads, a coiled sun dragon over his heart.

He gave Analia a quick once over, looking for flaws. Evidently finding none, his face brightened.

"The flame to my life," he said, bending to kiss her. Pulling back, he cocked a brow as if waiting for something.

"You look very handsome," Analia choked out.

Pryanth grinned. "Only the best for your father."

Pryanth flung his arm around her waist and headed off down the hall, not seeming to notice the tension in her shoulders.

The ballroom was already filled with people as Analia and Pryanth entered. Noblemen milled between tables of food, the chamber abuzz with voices and the orchestra on a raised stage in the center of the room. It was nowhere near as extravagant as Analia had seen before, undoubtedly because Brenn could blame the lack of time he had to prepare.

Upon entering, a server offered them crystal glasses of blood-red wine. That wasn't right, either. Servants at all of Accalon's events had always been cheerful, encouraged to mingle as they worked. Now, they scurried around the outskirts, heads lowered in submission.

How had Accalon been so thoroughly erased in so little time?

Pryanth downed his wine. Placing the glass on a random table, he towed Analia deeper into a room that glittered with gold and rainbow-obsidian accents in the Everflame light.

Thus commenced a night of sweeping music, an endless flow of wine, and constant small talk with nobles that openly stared at Analia, who stared back until they looked away. There was only one person she wanted to speak with that night. And of course, she spotted him lurking in one of the many shadowy alcoves that lined the ballroom's first and second levels.

Murmuring an excuse in Pryanth's ear, Analia slipped into the crowd before he could stop her. Weaving between guests, she ducked into the alcove, trusting the swell of voices and strings to camouflage her voice.

"Ronun," she said coolly.

The interrogator, dressed in his black-and-gray robes, gave her a nod, gaze still fixed on the crowd.

Analia leaned against the wall. "It's been some time since we last saw each other."

"Three and a half months," he confirmed, bored.

"Certainly enough time for discoveries to be made."

"Discoveries that can be shared another time, when I am not busy with an assignment from my king."

"To keep watch for suspicious activity, correct?"

A nod. Analia pushed off the wall, directly into Ronun's line of sight.

"Don't forget," she said, "you had an assignment long before that. To report to me whatever you find on my uncle's case. And seeing as though my timeline is far stricter than yours, I would hazard a guess that you do, in fact, have the time."

Ronun didn't respond immediately, his gaze focused up and over her head. Analia waited. When his eyes finally dragged down to hers, she could have sworn she saw a flicker of approval.

"Well?" he asked.

"I assume you finished your interrogations," Analia said. "Kitchen staff, servers, any other staff working that day?"

"Of course."

"And?"

"No one in the kitchen reported seeing anything odd. I inquired about dinner, drinks, individual plates, and nothing was amiss in the kitchen itself."

"We know it was his tea from the Council Chamber that was poisoned," Analia said. "Is there anything to suggest something could have been added before we arrived?"

"If so, it wasn't seen."

Analia nodded to herself. There was no one for Sun to shift the blame to.

"Is that all?" Ronun asked, folding his arms.

"Who cleared out my uncle's chambers?"

That seemed to catch him off guard. "His Majesty."

"My father?" Analia spluttered. "Why?"

"He claimed it was an open wound. He couldn't bear to walk past his brother's room every day, knowing he was gone and having no idea why. He told the servants as soon as evidence was collected, he wanted it stripped."

Erased. Ignored. Shoved aside and forgotten. Analia wrapped her arms around herself, not caring about Ronun's sharp gaze.

"Was there any evidence of note?" she asked.

Ronun studied her carefully. "Is there something in particular you would like to hear?"

"Obsidian," she said, only hesitating a moment.

Ronun shook his head, and Analia didn't know if she should feel triumphant or defeated.

It was official: separate deaths. But what about the mark on Accalon's neck?

Ronun's eyes sharpened. Analia stiffened as a hand touched her shoulder.

"Brenn's heading for Pryanth," Aaron said in her ear.

Just like the rest of the guards, Aaron had been hovering along the perimeter, leathers on and weapons only half-concealed. She'd been wondering if he would slink his way over.

Analia nodded at Aaron, who, spotting Ronun, wiggled his fingers in a wave. Ronun's jaw tightened.

"Not a word of this," Analia told him. Then, not waiting for a response, she headed back into the main area.

Analia stuck to the edges of the room, trying to avoid the worst of the crowd. Aaron caught up with her after a few steps, his face flashing with pride. But also, something else.

"That prince of yours better have told you just how beautiful you look tonight," he said in her ear.

"Of course he didn't."

"Then allow me."

Gripping her elbow, Aaron ducked into the deserted alcove they'd been about to pass. He turned her to face him, his eyes finding hers through the shadows.

"You," he said, "are positively mesmerizing, Analia."

Analia looked up at him. Then, not caring if anyone could see, what they might think, she grabbed his hand. "Thank you."

Aaron's lips parted. He brushed the knuckles of his free hand across her cheek, and Analia felt her eyelids flutter.

"Don't let them forget it," he whispered. He squeezed her hand. Then, he released her and stepped back, quickly disappearing into the crowd.

Analia touched her cheek, the ghost of his gesture lingering across her skin. She didn't have a name for the dull ache in her chest. She just brushed it aside as she moved back into the crowd, coming to stand beside Pryanth—who snatched her hand in a bone-grinding grip.

"There you are, duckling," Brenn said, barely glancing at her. "I was just talking with your prince about your time in the Sun Kingdom."

Undoubtedly trying to figure out if she'd destroyed her cover.

Analia accepted a wine glass from a passing servant. "I'm sure Pryanth did a fantastic job of retelling."

Pryanth puffed out his chest. "Of course."

"Yes, well." Brenn took a long sip of wine. "Now that you're here, I can deliver my congratulations, and express how thrilled I am to be joining our kingdoms."

None of them believed a single word. But they all plastered on smiles and clinked their glasses, no one trying to stop Brenn as he departed. Nor did Analia miss the silent order in his eyes: *follow me.*

Analia took a sip of her wine. It was only her first glass, whereas Pryanth's cheeks were flushed. But instead of scuttling up the stairs to where her father waited in a raised alcove, Analia danced.

Song after song, Pryanth spun her around, the music soaring across the room in a storm of strings. On one of her turns, she caught Aaron's eye across the room.

He truly was handsome. The type of handsome that had her wondering how the proud planes of his face, the perfect tousle of his hair, hadn't been sketched by a pen. But her attention always returned to those silver eyes.

She could feel them watching her as she spun away, following her every movement as if she was a masterful performer he couldn't believe he had the privilege of seeing. *Mesmerizing.*

Something warm blossomed in Analia's chest. It was the same feeling she'd had when Ember had said she loved her. It was so natural for them, just like it had been with Accalon. No convoluted strings that jerked her emotions around like a lantern in a storm.

As Analia finally excused herself and headed for the stairs, she caught Aaron's eye once more. He casually touched his face, his pinky, ring, and middle fingers extended in the same "get me out" gesture he had shown her at the Solstice.

But Analia shook her head. A faint line appeared between Aaron's brows, but he only mouthed, "Good luck."

Ascending the steps, Analia discovered Brenn wasn't alone. Cadmus huddled in the shadowy corner, engrossed in a hushed conversation with their father.

"Hi." Cadmus's blue eyes flicked to her, then down to his boots.

Analia nodded to him, her attention already fixed on Brenn.

"You certainly took your time," Brenn said. He sat on a slick, obsidian-glass throne, matching crown atop his head as he stared out across his subjects below. It was such a contrast to Accalon that it sent a stab through Analia's body. But that wasn't all.

"Things have certainly changed around here," Analia commented.

"Your uncle cast quite a shadow when he was alive," Brenn said. "Some would say it's about time that what has been concealed should come to the forefront."

Cadmus made to slip past Analia and head back down the stairs, but Brenn gestured for him to stay. He stiffened but returned to his position against the wall.

"Does that include his death?" she asked. "Have you stopped caring about that as well?"

"I haven't been informed of any breakthroughs."

"You haven't made yourself available to receive them."

Brenn scoffed. "Come now, duckling. I talked to your betrothed. With all the trouble you've managed to get yourself into, the fact that you haven't been tossed out by now is a testament to the Sun Royals' stupidity, not your own skill."

Analia clamped down on her temper.

"If you believed that," she said slowly, "you wouldn't have summoned me up here."

Analia could have sworn Brenn's throne reflected the flicker of flames across his fingertips. Cadmus shot Analia a quick look. She could see the demand in Brenn's eyes for her to bow her head, fill his silence with an apology. But Analia bit her tongue and waited.

"Fine then," Brenn said, folding his arms. "Regale me with all the information you've found."

Analia paused. Then, choosing her words carefully, she outlined her investigations, only leaving out Marcos's identity, although she wasn't sure why.

As she talked, she could see something slowly evolving in Cadmus's expression from the corner of her eye. Just as Brenn's indulgent, mocking smirk twisted into a sneer. Especially as she reluctantly mentioned Marcos's claim of selling to Accalon.

When Analia finished, the alcove was silent. She let it sit as Deardryn would, keeping her hands relaxed at her sides instead of fidgeting with her pin. Brenn would have to acknowledge her, no weaknesses to pounce on.

"And?" Brenn asked.

Analia blinked. "And what?"

"What is your conclusion?"

Analia opened her mouth, but no words came out.

A cruel smile slowly stretched across Brenn's mouth. "Leads, then?"

Again, Analia did not speak.

"At least tell me you have a suspect."

"I've told you what I know," said Analia carefully. "Including the people I suspect have the most likely motives."

Brenn sighed, shaking his head in disappointment. "Oh, duckling. You certainly know how to make a mess of things."

Analia took a step back. Even Cadmus appeared dumbstruck.

"So blind to the reality staring you in the face," Brenn went on, rising from his throne and advancing toward her.

Analia took another step back, approaching the edge of the stairs. "What do you mean?"

"The lack of connection to the other murders? Analia, that's the only thing you got right, and you have the least amount of confidence in it. It's not connected. Gods, it wasn't even a murder!"

Analia's hand tightened around the railing as Brenn stopped, close enough she could feel the heat of his magic. Her mind scrambled for answers, rapidly shoving pieces together, pulling them apart. Finally, there came a click that sucked the air from her lungs.

"No," she whispered.

Brenn's expression was devoid of pity.

"Your uncle started consuming xenol thirty years ago."

"Stop."

"He told me it felt like he had too much magic. It was hissing in his ears, threatening to consume his mind. And xenol was his solution."

"He wouldn't—"

"He always took it in small doses. Just enough to take the edge off. Until the day we were visited by Sun, and he took just a bit too much."

Analia's legs shook. Behind Brenn, Cadmus's face turned green.

"Then why?" Analia asked desperately. "Why did you let me go to the Sun Kingdom? Why did you let me keep going in circles when you knew all along?"

"Because it was a way to get rid of you!" Brenn exclaimed. "You and your smudge on the family name. A smudge that would be next in line for the throne? Over Cadmus?"

Brenn shook his head violently, fire crackling across his palms. "I still didn't know how Baylen was killed, but I knew you wouldn't be able to find anything. You would fail, run out of time and get married to that insipid little prince, and while I might not be able to get justice for my cousin, at least you would finally be out of the way."

Analia said, "But I did find—"

"A creature that has been killing other Royals, including one from Sun. What do you think would happen if I tried to declare war on Sun with the same evidence Deardryn has used to turn all the surrounding kingdoms into her allies?

"Face it, Analia, it's over. You don't have anything."

Analia's hand on the railing was the only thing keeping her upright. No, Accalon wouldn't have been so reckless. She'd once thought he never drank wine, either, just for him to spike his drink that night without her knowing. Gods, if she had no idea he was using xenol, what else could she have not known?

But what about Patryclas's wine? Why had xenol shown up twice?

"You're still trying to disprove it!" Brenn exclaimed, staring into her face. "Analia, Accalon is dead. Burned to ash, released on the winds, never to return. There's no point in obsessing over his death. He's *gone*."

Each word was a slap to the face. Her eyes moved from Brenn, to a distraught Cadmus, to the empty throne.

"Some things never change, do they, Father?" she asked.

Brenn's eyes flashed. Analia counted to ten in her head. Then, she turned, marching back down the steps and into the crowd, for once the first to leave.

"Slow and steady," Aaron said in her ear. She didn't know when he'd approached. "Don't let him see he rattled you."

Analia didn't care. Cadmus pushed through the crowd, coming up on her other side.

"Anna," he gasped, "I'm sorry. I promise, I had no idea—"

"Don't apologize to me, Cadmus," she spat. *"Defend me."*

Cadmus flinched as if struck. Analia pushed past him, the brother whose good heart was overpowered by cowardice, always at her expense. She shoved through the crowd, away from Aaron, past Pryanth and the knot of noblemen he'd inserted himself into, only aware of the dull roaring in her ears.

She couldn't scream or sob or vomit or fall to her knees. Not until she walked out the door. She wouldn't let anyone see.

But finally, Analia was out. Then, she was running.

# Chapter 50

Analia hadn't been on her turret since the day of Accalon's death. The metal bench still stood in its center, but she couldn't bring herself to sit there. Instead, she sank down on the edge, that same gods-damned candle still miraculously beside her.

Analia hurled it into the night, not listening for the thud as it landed. She only pulled her knees to her chest, numb to the world, the edge she teetered on—in more ways than one.

It wasn't long before there came the quiet scuff of footsteps behind her. For a moment, just a moment, her heart leaped. Then, it positively plummeted.

"You know, the only thing predictable about you is your altitude."

Analia didn't respond as Aaron sat beside her, his silver eyes reflecting the starlight.

"So," he said, "this is the famous spot?"

Analia nodded.

Aaron hesitated. "Is this the part where I go to the other side of the turret?"

Analia flinched, jerking her head to the side. Aaron swore under his breath. He squeezed her shoulder, "I'm sorry."

Analia didn't respond. Aaron waited a few moments. Eventually, he retracted his hand and started to rise.

"Brenn said Accalon accidentally killed himself," she blurted.

Aaron immediately sat back down, closer than he had been before. "What?"

"He said that Accalon had been consuming small amounts of xenol because his magic was too much for him. That the stress of the Sun Royals coming led to him accidentally dosing too high. Which means Marcos was telling the truth."

"Holy gods," Aaron breathed. He offered his hand, but Analia didn't take it.

"He had xenol, and Brenn knew, but he couldn't waste an opportunity to finally get rid of me and my claim to the throne."

"But what about Patryclas?" Aaron asked.

"I don't know."

"Do you think this is at all possible?"

"I..."

She saw the logic in Brenn's story, how all the pieces clicked neatly in a row. It was inevitable that theory would slice her heart down the middle, true or not. But it was her gut that squirmed. Was it because she knew it wasn't true, or because she didn't want it to be true?

"I keep holding on too tight," she said. "Too tight to xenol being involved, even though we still don't know if it can actually kill. Too tight to Othin being the killer, even as his motive and credibility started to crumble. I was so desperate to have a lead and make progress, and all it's gotten me is nothing.

"I have nothing, Aaron. My uncle is dead, I have no leads, I have no idea if Brenn is telling the truth, and I'm sitting on this gods-damned turret knowing all of this, and yet, a part of me is still expecting to hear my uncle coming up here to find me at any moment."

Analia's voice cracked. Aaron offered his hand again. Still, Analia didn't take it, her arms firmly wrapped around her knees.

"Can I tell you a story?" he asked.

"Do you have to?"

"Well, I was trying to be polite, but—"

"Fine," Analia sighed, but Aaron didn't look offended. He tipped his head back, quiet permission for her to look away.

"Where I come from," he began, "we have a legend that the stars are the tears of the sun and moon. Once, the sun and moon inhabited the sky together. They were always side by side, shining their light on the world below in a halo of silver and gold. There was still a night and day that could be tracked, but they were both brighter. Warmer. And this would not do for the Ancient Ones.

"They were creatures of darkness and shadow; pitch-black nights that seemed to stifle not just sight, but all senses—the complete opposite of the perpetual glow of the sun and moon. Finally deciding they'd had enough, the three sliced through the bond that held the sun and moon together with a whip of black magic.

"With their connection severed, the sun was banished to the daytime, forced out of the skies whenever night would descend and the moon would arrive. The two struggled, begged, pleaded, even threatened, but they were never able to find their way back to each other.

"In their despair, the sun and moon flooded the skies with their tears, which transformed into the stars. And the shooting stars we see arcing across the sky are the ones still searching, hoping, for a way back. But all of the stars are reminders from one to the other that they are still out there, and someday, they will be together again."

Aaron's hand drifted toward the chain around his neck, only to find it had been tucked into his leathers. Seemingly deciding to leave it, he let his hand fall back to his side as he finally looked down at her.

Analia could barely choke out her words. "That's such a sad story for something so beautiful."

"I always saw it as the opposite," Aaron said. "Yes, there was grief, and pain, but it was only because their love endured."

He reached out, lightly tracing the outer circle of her pin with a fingertip. "So much love, just with no place to go. But out of that, we got the stars."

Analia thought she could hear the cracking as it radiated throughout her body.

"You're safe to wallow, Analia," Aaron said softly.

Analia opened her mouth, intending to tell him it was fine, she was all right.

"I feel like I failed him."

Aaron shook his head, something like sorrow in his eyes. "Never, Analia. This shouldn't have been placed on your shoulders in the first place."

"But he was my everything," she whispered. And as the first tear traced a burning trail down her cheek, Aaron opened his arms. And finally, finally, Analia didn't hesitate.

Wind buffeted them from every side. But Aaron was warm, solid, smelling of metal and something spicy. His heartbeat steady beneath her ear, his arms holding her tight as her body threatened to shudder apart.

"I know," he whispered into her hair.

She would never hear him call her his little fledgling ever again. She would never feel him ruffle her hair and kiss the top of her head, ever again.

"This is the worst part," Aaron said, his hand stroking long, soothing lines along her spine. "When you finally allow yourself to feel it for the first time. You just have to ride it out."

But Analia didn't know how. Not as a wave that seemed much bigger than it should have been bore down on her, slamming her down, down, down.

She should have known something was wrong when she left him that night. She should have stayed. Would he still be dead if she had? Would he still have died alone? Crystal spare her, he was all alone.

"You will survive this," Aaron promised, his lips finding her ear.

Something ancient inside Analia's chest shuddered. She might survive, but Accalon wouldn't. He couldn't. Because Accalon. Was. Dead.

The last of Analia's strength gave out. She collapsed against Aaron's chest, struggling to breathe as sob after sob wracked her body, those three words hammering against her until she shattered.

Accalon. Was. Dead. Gone, never to return. And Analia was all alone. Still breathing. But how was she supposed to survive when she could feel his absence searing through her soul, burning away her very being until not even the ashes remained?

There was nothing to rise again. Nothing but empty chambers and lonely rooftops and memories that slashed deeper than the fact that she could never make more of them.

Because Accalon. Was. Dead. He was dead, he was dead, he was dead, he was dead.

Aaron shifted, almost as if uncomfortable, but he didn't let go. He leaned his cheek against her hair, no longer speaking, just letting her cry. But there was no amount of tears that could quell the burning in her chest, spreading through her blood, her bones, across her skin until she was completely consumed.

"Anna," Aaron breathed, reaching up to where her arms wrapped around his neck. "Anna, look."

Aaron gently disengaged her arms and leaned back, just far enough to hold their cupped hands between them. Analia tried to catch her breath, see through the blur of tears. But her mind refused to comprehend the tiny flames that flickered across her fingertips. Black, maybe blue?

Analia's eyes shot to Aaron in horror, his silver chain now freed from his leathers. "Did I burn you?"

"What? Why does that matter? Analia, look." He brought their hands closer to her face as if she hadn't seen. "It's your star."

But it wasn't excitement, joy, even satisfaction as Analia felt the heat against her cheek. It was a hot, bubbling resentment. One that had her finally able to catch her breath as she slammed those feelings back down, her flames flickering out like shadows chased away by the sun.

That's what it took? Crystal spare her. It wasn't worth it. Not worth it at all.

"Don't worry," Aaron told her, misinterpreting her frown. "It always takes time to master it. But Analia, you did it!"

Aaron brushed the tears from her cheeks, nudging the corner of her mouth up with his thumb.

"I guess," Analia mumbled.

"No, not you guess. You did it."

Analia tried to force a smile, but Aaron shook his head.

"Analia, that is pathetic," he said, finally earning the faintest of real smiles.

He pulled her back against his chest, starting to say something, Analia still too drained to be enthusiastic. But both of them froze as her fingers brushed the frozen chain around Aaron's neck. And cold, deadly power crackled across her mental shield.

# Chapter 51

Time seemed to freeze around Aaron as he felt Analia's finger brush against his chain. Her body went rigid, his excitement draining into a blood-chilling dread.

Slowly, mechanically, he reached to untangle her arms from his neck for a second time. He leaned away, still acutely aware of the incredible heat radiating off her, the burn of her fingertips across the back of his neck.

He knew he should speak, every instinct screaming to explain it away. But Aaron was transfixed by the frozen look of confusion on her face.

"What are you?" she whispered.

Aaron opened his mouth, but no words came out.

Analia's voice grew stronger, "Who are you?"

Aaron stared, helpless. But Analia didn't need a response.

"Star Royal," she breathed. And her confusion crumbled as Aaron didn't deny it.

"Analia—"

Analia leaned away from him. Aaron felt his hope shatter like glass beneath a boot heel.

"How?" Analia demanded. "How do you exist? How did I not sense you before? Unless..."

Her eyes drifted to the chain of his damper. "A plug," she said faintly. "Containing the flow, and not allowing it to radiate out."

Aaron nodded. Truthfully, he hadn't known that last part. He'd been anticipating the moment she sensed his network for months now. But when she never did, he'd thought the damper completely masked him. He would have never suspected coming in direct contact with the chain would be enough for her.

"I suppose to prevent any magical slip ups as well," Analia went on, face unreadable.

Aaron brought a hand to the chain around his neck, feeling the kick to his gut as Analia warily tracked the movement. But there was something else that shifted beneath his pain.

"Was it you?" she asked. "Has it been you killing all the—"

"No!" Aaron's voice came out louder than he'd intended.

"Why should I believe you?" Analia demanded. "After everything your people have done? After the months of you lying to me?"

Each word was a physical blow, slamming into him over and over until that icy wall shattered apart.

"After everything my people have done?" he spat. "You mean all the stories told about them after they were slaughtered? Everything they had built reduced to rubble, burying every single good deed they'd ever done?"

"How many people did Hester and Elspeth kill first?"

"That wasn't me—"

"How long did Elspeth listen to the screams of the people trapped in the Free Fall Wood?"

"And what do you think drove her to do that?"

Agony ripped a claw through Aaron's insides as he thought of the Star Kingdom square and the one preserved fountain in its center—holy gods that fountain.

Doubt flickered across Analia's face. Aaron wanted to seize on it, wanted to tell her the full truth about himself and his people. But before he could speak, Analia's expression hardened.

This was his warning. His people, his mission, his home—there was no room for what he wanted to be important, too.

"Why are you here?" Analia asked, dragging her hand down her face.

Aaron let instinct take over. Let the icy purr of his voice freeze his heart as he said, "I already told you, Analia. I needed to find the scroll. A more-than-likely magical scroll—"

"That only I could find," Analia finished.

"Why else do you think I would tell you?"

"You were only using me," Analia breathed. "You admit to using me, right after you tried to convince me that your people aren't monsters."

Because she didn't believe him, wouldn't believe that she only knew one side of the story. Wouldn't believe he despised the monster history forced him to be, but that didn't mean he wouldn't sharpen his claws to survive.

"I'm honestly surprised it took you so long to figure it out," he said. "But I suppose that goes back to the whole you holding onto things too tightly thing. The murder, your uncle, your desire to have at least one friend you could trust. Although based on your taste in men, your judgment in that area isn't exactly pristine."

Analia recoiled, sending a wave of self-loathing through Aaron's body.

"I suppose that means you killed the last guard as well," she said.

"Well done," Aaron crooned. "That, however, was only indirectly my fault. True, I waited until he was alone and precariously close to the edge of the ravine before spooking his horse, but that horse was the one who ultimately bucked him off.

"Such a pity, how humans die so easily. A simple fall is enough to do it."

Analia shifted away from the edge.

"Do you have any remorse?" she demanded.

"No," he said truthfully. Not enough, at least. "He was a necessary sacrifice. I needed a reason to get in the castle long term without suspicion."

"And you just had the good fortune of stumbling upon me," Analia finished.

Aaron let his smile answer for him. He waited for her to push to her feet and flee, fast and far and never look back.

But Analia only rested a hand on her pin as she asked, "Was any of it real?"

All of it.

"What do you think?"

Aaron forced himself to watch the fragile hope in Analia's eyes shatter. Because he couldn't afford to hope himself. Hope that she panicked, that she wanted to believe him. That she would have trusted him and everything they'd been through in the three months that were so short in the long term, yet had nevertheless become indelible.

"How could you?" she asked, voice cracking.

But there was nothing he could rebuild here. Nothing that wouldn't do more damage as it inevitably toppled down once more.

"I thought we already covered that."

Aaron rose to his feet. Analia watched him silently, the devastation in her eyes giving way to rage. Good.

"Is that it?" she demanded, standing as well. "Your charade is up, so you make your dramatic exit? No more emotions you'd like to manipulate?"

"No, I think I've had my fill." He turned, not glancing back as he strode across the roof. "I'm leaving as soon as I get the scroll. I hope you're smart enough not to get in my way."

"And what will stop me from exposing you?"

Aaron turned back. Analia's chin was raised, all fear gone.

He forced himself to watch her, Marcos's words echoing in his mind as he ran a suggestive finger along his damper chain. "I think you know what will happen if you try."

Every story needs a monster.

With the image of Analia's anguish burned into his mind, he turned. Descended from the roof. Headed back through the castle.

He didn't know where he was going. All he knew was the moment he stopped, he would fall to his knees. And he didn't know when he might rise again after that.

# PART 4: ASH

# Chapter 52

Seventy-two hours. Not even seventy-two gods-damned hours. Yet, when the Sun carriage landed in front of the castle, Dimitri was greeted by a sight that had him wondering if he had inhaled too much cleaning product after all.

The frost between Analia and Aaron was palpable as they exited the carriage. The two immediately headed off in opposite directions, Analia taking Pryanth's hand and barely sparing Dimitri a glance as she passed him.

He told himself it was indignation that had him storming through the passageways not long after, nothing more. Even though Analia had been the one person he thought would never look at him like that. But when he made it to her chambers, he found something had been shoved against the entrance. Something that looked a lot like the back of an armoire.

Dimitri pounded his fist on the thick wood, demanding to know what was going on. But there was only silence on the other side.

Fine.

It took forever to catch Aaron by himself. He was constantly surrounded by fellow guards, or nowhere to be found, forcing Dimitri to pace through the passageways until Aaron was assigned to late-night patrol duty. Yet, as soon as Dimitri popped out of the entrance, demanding to know what was going on, Aaron froze him with a look and asked if Dimitri had something to scrub.

All sympathy Dimitri had puffed out like a dying star.

As he stormed down ladders and rounded corners, he told himself he didn't care. He had known the return to his isolation was inevitable. The past three months had been a temporary reprieve; he knew better than to get comfortable.

If he was smart, he would go straight to the Royals, tell the Old Hag everything Analia was up to and get his freedom that way. That would serve her fucking right for blackmailing him, forcing him to care. Yet, Dimitri hesitated as he peered into what Analia dubbed the Ring Room.

Analia and Deardryn faced each other in the center of the room. The queen wore a gown of scarlet silk, Analia in pale blue with Deardryn's sapphire necklace around her neck.

"It's not working," Analia said. "I can feel the Mist magic, but I can't direct it."

"You must think of yourself as a cup," Deardryn said, walking over to the nearby table. She seized a goblet of wine, not noticing Analia's scowl as she followed.

"This magic is not your own," Deardryn said, placing a second, empty crystal glass beside the goblet. "You're not pulling the magic out of yourself, you're drawing it in."

"I'm trying," Analia insisted.

"Shoving against the magic where it already lies won't do anything." Deardryn nudged the goblet with the crystal glass, the wine sloshing slightly. "You need to pull the magic into yourself. Let it fill your network, and then you can bend it to your will."

She poured the wine from the goblet into the glass. Swirling the glass, the wine moved in response.

"But how do I pour it in?" Analia asked.

"You must open yourself to the magic."

Deardryn removed the pendant from around Analia's neck. Settling it around her own, she closed her eyes. A thin stream of water trailed from her fingertips, coiling into a tiny sun dragon that swooped into the empty goblet before dispersing.

Deardryn removed the pendant and placed it back around Analia's neck. "Be a cup."

Analia turned away, facing Dimitri once more. He wasn't surprised to note the frustration on her face. But there was something else as her eyes darted to the side—toward the bench?

Dimitri remained rooted in place as the lesson continued, Analia still unable to summon the magic in the pendant. Finally, Deardryn called the session to a close, looking mildly disappointed.

Analia wordlessly handed the pendant back to her. Taking it in one hand, Deardryn smoothed the other down Analia's hair, the closest Dimitri had ever seen her to motherly.

Analia's shoulders shook. She quickly backed away, exiting the room and leaving Deardryn alone.

Dimitri knew this was his chance. But he didn't reach for the entrance as Deardryn settled the pendant inside her box, closing the lid and tucking it under an arm. She swept from the chamber, leaving it silent, empty, and hollow. The same hollow feeling in Dimitri's chest as he finally unpeeled himself from the wall and turned away.

It took Dimitri three days to work up the courage to walk through Analia's door. He sat on her bed, book in hand and thoughts in an anxious tangle as he waited for her to come back from training.

Why wouldn't she just tell him what happened? She didn't get to treat him like shit just because everyone else did. But there was also a smaller voice, one that wondered what he had done wrong.

The door opened. Dimitri jolted upright as Analia entered, looking positively harassed.

Spotting Dimitri on her bed, her face flashed through so many emotions he couldn't keep track. Finally settling on irritation, she slammed her door shut.

"Don't mind me," she said, "make yourself comfortable."

Dimitri only missed a beat as Analia stomped across her room. "I would, but your mattress is fucking awful."

"Have you tried rolling a few inches to the left?"

Dimitri threw down his book. "And here I was thinking *I* was the miserable bastard."

"Is that what we're calling it now?"

"Yes. I'm miserable, Aaron's moody, and you're—"

"Mouse-ish?" Analia supplied, yanking the golden pins from her hair.

Dimitri's temper sputtered. "No," he said truthfully. "You haven't been that for a while now."

"Then what am I, Dima?" she asked, turning to face him.

"Mourning," he said.

It was one word. A hand that he had always snatched away, but tentatively extended now. He held his breath as Analia remained stiff, arms folded across her chest.

He was a fool, wasn't he? A Crystal-forsaken fool that should have learned by now.

"I don't know what to do," Analia whispered.

Dimitri tried not to squirm as she crossed the room and sat beside him, tears in her eyes. What was he supposed to do? He didn't know how to comfort someone. No one had ever shown him how.

"What," he coughed, "what happened?"

"Well," Analia said, slumping against the wall, "we were right. It was xenol in Patryclas's cup. But Ember wrote to the healers from the kingdoms who have lost Royals and had the mark, and none of them had xenol in their system. But they did have obsidian. And Accalon did not."

Dimitri shrugged. "So, they're different murders, then."

If anything, that made things easier: fewer details had to line up across cases.

"No," Analia said. "It wasn't even a murder."

With that, the story from that night came tumbling free. Every word seemed to take something from her, leaving something horribly empty behind by the time she finished. But where Analia was draining out, Dimitri was filling up.

"You can't tell me you believe him!" he exploded the moment she finished.

Analia winced.

"What about Patryclas?" he demanded. "What about the fact that it was your gods-damned father of all people telling you this? You're going to listen to him?"

"The story lines up, Dima. Marcos said he was his top buyer. There was no obsidian. And I know my uncle's power. It was overwhelming."

"And you also knew him. Do you honestly think he would get so frazzled by Royals he invited coming to his territory that he'd choke down an entire poisonous plant without realizing?"

The story was complete bullshit. Dimitri only knew the prior Ash King through what Analia told him, and even he could see how absurd the idea was. He knew Analia thought so as well; he could see the doubt in her eyes. So then why was she rolling over?

"What happened between you and Bordello?" he asked."

Analia's expression shut like a stone door. "Nothing."

Dimitri thought his head was going to explode.

"Is that why you haven't spoken a word to him in over a week?" he asked. "Why you're back to being Pryanth's lapdog, just waiting for him to kick you again? Or should I say slap?"

Analia's head reared back. "Drop it, Dimitri," she hissed.

"You mean just like you've dropped your uncle's case?"

"There is no case!" Analia yelled, slamming her hands down on the bed between them. "There's nothing to solve, nothing to prove. There is nothing left for me to do besides accept the fate my father nudged me into, just like he always has."

"You're giving up," Dimitri said. "On your uncle, this case, on Aaron, on—" Dimitri quickly cut himself off, but Analia's eyes still flashed.

"So, that's what this is about?" she asked. "Our deal?"

No, Dimitri wasn't even thinking about that.

"I taught you to read, Dimitri. You talk about me giving up? Not taking action? Maybe it's about gods-damned time you take your own advice."

"I did!" Dimitri pushed himself to his feet, glaring down at her. "How do you think I found that side door? How do you think I knew about Gritta's? Why do you think I know the passageways as well as I do?"

"Then why are you still here?"

"Because I didn't have any gold!" Dimitri stalked over to Analia's fireplace, the story blasting past his lips. "Servants don't get paid. We get free lodging in the castle, free meals that we prepare ourselves. Apparently, that's supposed to be more than enough. But it's not e-fucking-nough out in the kingdom, and how was I supposed to know that at thirteen, having never stepped foot past the golden gates?"

Dimitri kicked his boot through the ashes. "Slipping out was pathetically easy. I only had to wait for the guard at the side door to fall asleep. Then, it was just a matter of telling the guards at the gate that the queen had sent me, that they were welcome to confirm with her and I was sure they would love the walk back to the castle to speak with a queen who would be just as thrilled to have her authority questioned. I had barely finished the thought when the gates opened, and I was out. I had nothing but the clothes on my back and the map I'd stolen, and it was fucking overwhelming.

"All the people, the noise, not knowing where to go. I only stumbled into Gritta's because it was the closest building and the sun had set.

"I had no idea what I was getting myself into. I just went straight to the woman behind the bar and asked for a place to stay. And the old bat laughed in my face. Said I didn't know what this establishment was, did I?

"This drew the attention of some nearby addicts, who were already a few pints deep if the smell said anything. They were especially interested when I said I had no gold. Gritta didn't so much as lift a finger as they backed me into a corner, mumbling about how only an idiot wouldn't swipe some gold while in the castle."

Dimitri toyed with the poker, his grip painfully tight. He could still feel the residue of his terror from that night. Terror that had built and built and built until it burst forth. But he wouldn't tell Analia that part.

"That's the life of someone without gold," he said instead. "Fighting for everything you have, even when it's nothing. Constantly walking around with a target on your back when you finally get just a crumb."

"And so, you came back," Analia said. "You made it out, you escaped the addicts, and you came back."

Yes. But Analia and that accusatory tone of hers didn't get to know why.

"I had to work my ass off for nothing either way," he said, turning partially to face her. "At least with one option, I didn't have to worry about someone killing me in my sleep."

The lie was so flimsy. But Analia was too angry to notice.

"You're trying to lecture me about giving up?" she demanded, also rising.

"You still have a chance! And you're just going to set all the progress you've made ablaze because what, you're stumped? Because you and Aaron are fighting? Because your father was mean to you again? What would Accalon say?"

Dimitri knew just how deep that last comment would dig, but he didn't care as memories from that night at Gritta's played in his mind. The screams, the confusion, Dimitri shoving the men aside as they clawed at their eyes. Racing for the door, stumbling outside, vomiting on the corner.

He'd known in that moment he would never escape the castle. But Analia had a chance, and she was squandering it. And the look she gave him? It went past fury, deeper than betrayal.

"Maybe if you stop expecting everyone to do what you want," she said, "while letting them know just how little you care about them, you would've been able to stay out. Too bad you don't seem capable of that."

As soon as the words were out, Dimitri could see the regret on her face. But that didn't stop him from flinching.

He'd thought of all people, she'd seen through him. She'd quietly let him know with every smile, every eye roll, every time she casually complimented his reading or his handwriting and looked away while he processed.

But he should have known better. Othin, every servant in this gods-damned castle. Everyone left eventually.

"I'm sorry." Analia extended a hand to him.

But the only reason people stopped leaving was because he stopped giving them a chance to.

"Dima..."

Dimitri stalked to her door, slamming it shut behind him without a backward glance.

It was far easier to leave than be left, after all. But since when did leaving hurt just as bad?

# Chapter 53

Analia felt like she was dying. There was no other way to explain the pain she had barely kept at bay the last three months finally slamming into her. It was relentless, all-consuming, ravaging her entire body until all that remained was grief. Grief and shards and heartbreak.

For so long, the only thing that got her out of bed was the need to solve her uncle's murder. Now, her maids had to half drag her to her dressing table each morning, her eyes red and puffy from tears.

There was no case. Her uncle was dead. There was too much inside herself to control, and she'd already lost the battle with Dimitri.

Gods, she'd tried to stay away from him and keep that last piece she had intact. But it was inevitable she would burn it to ash. And she was terrified of what she might say if she chased after him to apologize.

But it was better Dimitri didn't care about her. Just like Aaron.

Even though she'd moved to one-on-one training with Deardryn, Aaron was still a constant presence trailing her through the halls. Every morning, she wondered if it would be the day he finally disappeared. Yet, every time, she opened her door to find him waiting for her.

One morning, they passed a servant standing atop a ladder, adjusting a chandelier. Analia barely registered the snap when Aaron's arm folded around her waist, hauling her against him and out of the way as the chandelier shattered at her feet.

The servant squeaked in alarm, scrambling down the ladder and apologizing profusely as she clutched the rusted support chain. But Analia barely heard her.

Aaron's body was warm and solid around her. She knew she should step out of his grip. Instead, she had to fight back the question pressing against her lips. Why?

Why hadn't he left yet? Judging from the bruises that blossomed across his temple, he had been up to something, and with his damper on, she doubted there would be any sped-up healing.

Gods, everything went back to that damper: keeping him undetected. Blocking magic she'd been taught to despise. Somehow not preventing her from wanting to know if he was all right.

But Analia was unable to let the words spill forth. Just as she was unable to reveal his secret to Dimitri—to Deardryn, for that matter. Because even though Aaron had used her, lied to her, tossed her aside as if she was as worthless as everyone else claimed, he'd also given her something to hold onto.

Wordlessly, Aaron released her and stepped back. And Analia reassured the servant girl.

*I think you know what will happen if you try.* The words repeated in her mind with every passing day. But it was the same feeling of wrong, wrong, wrong, in her gut that Accalon's cause of death produced. The same feeling she got when Pryanth draped his arm across the back of her chair, whispering in her ear, "I love you."

Until he hated her. Analia bit her tongue before the words could escape.

There was no home waiting for her anywhere else. All she had was the sunstone lights, the gold and marble. The faces of the twenty or so noble families that milled around her, glasses of wine in hand as they enjoyed the gathering Deardryn had thrown together the night before the wedding.

Pryanth, dressed in his princely raiment, chatting with the people that passed. Analia, silent on his arm in a tight-fitting gold gown that threatened to strangle her. Nodding in the proper places, sipping from her sickly sweet wine whenever there was a pause in conversation.

"What are you trying to do?" Pryanth snarled in her ear as they danced. "You do realize you have to speak in order to make an impression."

"I'm sorry," Analia murmured. She'd said it so many times the past few weeks that she didn't have to think before the words were out, the next already set to be launched when Pryanth's mood flared once again.

He didn't even try to control it anymore. Not when she gave him no reason to. Not when she deserved every insult he hurled her way.

Failure. Quitter. Worthless. Duckling.

Analia's feet ached by the time Pryanth walked her to her chambers. All she wanted was to kick off her slippers, cut off her dress, and sleep. Waking up was optional.

Pryanth's arm tightened around her as she reached for her door. "Don't turn this into the worst decision I ever made," he joked. But the warning in his eyes was lethal as he kissed her cheek and released her.

Analia gave a wobbly smile and slipped into her chambers. She only made it a few steps before she fell to her knees, feeling the blade of his words rake down her spine.

"I'm losing my mind," she said faintly. "I am losing my mind."

Ember rested her chin in her hands, Cadmus pacing the length of the back room behind her.

The night of Analia's wedding celebration, Ember had locked up the apothecary, wondering if she had the gall to crash the event she had not been invited to. She had just slipped her keys in her pocket, deciding, yes, of course she did, when Cadmus found her.

The disoriented prince quickly filled Ember in on Brenn's reveal, his expression a mix of grief and guilt as he described Analia's escape to the roof. They'd agreed the story made little sense, especially since they knew Accalon would have been even more careful with Sun's arrival. They'd decided to return to the apothecary first thing the following morning after the xenol had time to recover, determined to solve the mystery once and for all.

"It just doesn't make sense," Ember said for what felt like the thousandth time.

Analia's retrieved xenol plant sat on the desk before her, several leaves already removed and turned to ash by Cadmus's magic. Scattered around it was Ember's collection of scribbled notes and calculations from their various trials.

"Based on plant-to-magic ratios," she went on, "Accalon didn't have anywhere near enough xenol in his system to break down the entire network. Either his magic should've overwhelmed the xenol and destroyed it, or the xenol would've been digested before it could take down his entire network."

"Could we have done the calculations wrong?" Cadmus asked, repeating himself as well.

"Even if we had, Cadmus, this is based off your network. And not to knock you, you're plenty powerful, but Accalon's magic?"

"Incredible," Cadmus agreed, coming to stand behind her and peering at the plant.

"And beyond that," she said, "if he truly had been consuming it for thirty years, you would think he would have built up a tolerance."

It just didn't make sense. Could they have missed the obsidian in his system, and it was the Devourist after all?

No, every shred of evidence from Accalon's body had been recorded. She had assisted in the process and knew that for a fact.

"What are you saying?" Cadmus asked.

Ember tugged on her hair. "I'm saying we're still missing something, and I have no idea what."

Cadmus didn't seem to appreciate just how hard the smack to her pride was. The confidence she had spent so much time padding against the dismissive backs her fellow apprentices turned on her. Herbology specialist without a drop of Blessed blood. What good could she do?

"Well," Cadmus said, rifling through her drawers, "if we're missing something, we just need to figure out what."

Who had she been trying to fool? She was no official healer. Yet she thought she could do something none of them could? Why, because she specialized in plants when everyone else only had a firm familiarity?

Cadmus pulled out a document and moved to sit on Ember's desk. "Everything we need is in here," he said, showing her the original list of evidence found in Accalon's system.

"We've already gone over that," Ember said tiredly.

Maybe it was better to just quit now. She would be choosing to stop, not failing.

Cadmus gave her a sharp look and buried his nose in the pages. "Meat, honey from the tea, wine—Uncle never drank wine."

"That's what Anna said."

"Patryclas," Cadmus said, shoving off the desk, aiming for another drawer. When had he learned her organizational system—or lack thereof? "He was also poisoned with wine."

He quickly scanned over the list of components Ember had found in his jar. "It's the one thing he and Accalon had in common."

"And Accalon ends up dead the one time he drinks it," Ember mused.

"I'll be back," Cadmus said. He tossed the papers on Ember's desk and strode out of the back room.

Ember's mind darted back to when she had first tested the mush from Patryclas's wine. The power had been sucked straight from her veins. She had thought it was because there was a larger sample in front of her compared to that tiny scrap she had first tested, but if that wasn't all...

Ember placed her hand on the xenol plant, willing it to grow. It wasn't long before Cadmus returned, thumping a wine bottle down on her desk.

Ember rose from her seat and grabbed a sample jar, Cadmus uncorking the wine with a pop behind her. Filling the jar to the brim with the fizzing white wine, she ripped off a handful of leaves and dunked them in. The moment she set them on the desk, Cadmus sent a roaring blaze to incinerate them.

Ember leaned away from the heat that rolled off the leaping flames, far bigger than necessary to burn the sample size she'd chosen. The leaves glowed in the core of the flames, Cadmus stiffening at her side as they shone brighter and brighter. Then, the flames sputtered, dying down as if they'd run out of things to consume. Eventually, they shrunk to a spark, and finally, they winked out entirely.

And the leaves remained.

"Holy Rosala," Ember breathed.

Before she could stop him, Cadmus reached out with glowing fingers. First, he touched the plant itself, his body jerking but still able to retract his hand. But when he touched the wine-soaked pile—

"Cadmus, stop!" Ember smacked his hand away.

Cadmus stumbled, nearly doubling over, but his eyes were bright.

"Are you completely stupid?" Ember demanded, heart pounding.

"No comparison," Cadmus wheezed. "The wine pile latched on immediately."

"Idiot," Ember grumbled, rising from her chair and shoving Cadmus into it. "Absolute idiot."

She rested her hand against his clammy forehead, sending a gentle wave of healing magic through his body. Cadmus relaxed under her touch.

"You're good at that," he said.

Ember removed her hand. "Well, I would certainly hope—"

"No, not the magic," he said. "Although you already know that's fantastic, in your words. I... I mean you're good at taking care of people. There are plenty of healers I've met that are there to heal just because they have the magic and they like to use it. But you do it because you like to help people. And I don't think that gets enough credit."

Herbologist. Human healer. Cared about people. All overlooked. But something warm emerged in Ember's chest.

"Thanks." She leaned forward and ruffled his hair. Cadmus made a noise of protest and batted her hand away.

The two turned their attention back to the mess on Ember's desk, the soaked leaves still glowing faintly.

"It must be a catalyst of some sort," Ember mused, prodding the leaves. "Enabling the magical degradation process to move faster than digestion?"

"Or maybe it enhances xenol's magic tolerance," Cadmus suggested.

"Regardless," Ember said. "If Accalon has been consuming xenol, you would think he'd know what to avoid. And that very thing showed up in his mug the night Sun arrived."

"So now," Cadmus said, taking a swig from the bottle, "the question is, who added the wine?"

# Chapter 54

Analia didn't know if she slept that night. She only knew that the light slowly built outside her window, that the frantic knocking at her door announcing Bie and Nadi's arrival meant it was time to get up. Face the day. Face her husband to be.

"Aren't you thrilled?" Bie asked. "Marrying a prince. I would be thrilled if I was marrying a prince."

"That's because you're a servant, Bie."

"So?"

"So, Analia's already a princess."

Princess of a kingdom who didn't want her. Princess of her dead uncle's kingdom. An uncle whose death she couldn't even solve.

But that's why she was here, wasn't it? Because she had failed. Because she deserved Pryanth and the man he so resembled, and she was starting to think she could never escape.

There came a knock at the door. Analia's heart stuttered. But it was only the willowy seamstress, hustling through the door with gown in tow.

Analia barely looked at the mass of gold fabric as Bie and Nadi clapped and bundled her into it. Her new kingdom's colors. Her husband's colors. The man who said he loved her.

So why was her heart pounding? Why couldn't she breathe as Pryanth's pendant wrapped around her throat? Why were the walls closing in, the sunstones' magic throbbing through her skull? *Wrong, wrong, wrong.*

Bie and Nadi pushed open the door, hurrying her before them. Around the corner, down the hall, music slinking up the stairs.

Off to marry the prince whose hand had been branded across her cheek. Whose vicious words snarled in her ear. Who was too consumed by his own past and pain to acknowledge hers unless it was to stab straight through it.

Analia's foot touched the edge of the top step. All she wanted to do was flee. Flee from Pryanth, the Sun Kingdom, her uncle's death, the grief that had swallowed her heart and still searched for more. And the worst part was she knew where she wanted to run to—*whom* she wanted to run to.

Bie and Nadi nudged her forward. Gods, the last person who had escorted her down this staircase was Aaron. She'd told him on these very steps about her uncle's pin because even then, she knew she could trust him with that piece of her.

How could that person have only been a façade? How could she have clung to the history she had been told when the present her own eyes saw told a completely different story? Even on her turret, how much could she believe when she'd seen the flash of terror in his eyes?

A part of her wondered if she was just looking for an escape. But how telling was it that even with all this in mind, her first thought still went to him?

"Analia?" Nadi asked, lightly prodding her back.

"I'll be right back," she said.

They started to protest, saying the ceremony was about to begin, where was she going? But Analia took off down the hall.

She might not be able to avoid this wedding, but Crystal strike her down if she couldn't make things right. She couldn't lose anyone else, not without trying to salvage first.

Aaron sat on the edge of his bed. He stared down at his boots, knowing he would have to bend over to put them on, causing his bruised ribs to shriek in protest.

He'd spent the past three weeks trying to find a way through the garden, hoping his damper would camouflage him to the Devourist. But apparently, it possessed other hunting abilities that made knocking Aaron around all too easy.

He'd been tempted to try without his damper, but he knew he couldn't risk it. Not when the Devourist could suck him dry. Besides that, he'd discovered when shadowjumping to meet with Ember that removing his damper after so long resulted in a glorious silver blast for all to see, as well as the feeling of being dropkicked as his magic returned to his network.

He couldn't risk asking Selbi to heal his injuries, either. Not when she would have questions he couldn't answer. Consequently, Aaron was on his own.

He had just laced up his first boot when there came a knock on the door. He called for them to enter, not looking up as the door opened and shut.

"Hi."

Crystal spare him, he couldn't do this again.

Aaron looked up, an icy retort on his lips. But the words melted away when he saw her.

Analia had been transformed into a sunstone. Her floor-length gown sparkled with magic, shifting the layers of silk and lace in patterns of gold, amber, honey, and brown. It was held up by delicate pearl straps, matching the combs in her hair.

She was the precise image of Surce's tapestry. The first one he'd ever seen. Which meant tonight—

"You're staring," Analia told him.

"I know." Aaron slowly brought his booted foot back to the ground, ignoring the whine in his back.

Analia's mouth twitched. Aaron dragged his eyes away, staring over her shoulder.

"What are you doing here, Analia?"

"I need to talk to you."

Aaron didn't respond.

"I feel like I'm about to make a huge mistake," she said, sinking down on a chair across from him.

Marrying Pryanth? Giving up on Accalon? He didn't allow himself to consider any options that involved himself.

"What do you want me to do about it?" he asked.

"Tell me if I am?"

"Why me?"

"Because you said you always have an opinion."

Gods, it was hard to fight back a smile.

"This is your choice," he told her.

"But—"

"What I *can* tell you," he went on, knowing he should've left it at that, "is to think about what answer you're hoping to hear, and ask yourself why."

Aaron bent to resume tying his boots. For a few long moments, the chamber was silent.

"Pryanth told me not to be the worst decision he's ever made," Analia said quietly.

Slowly, Aaron sat up, his damper a circle of ice against his chest.

"My father has been saying that to me for the past fifteen years, all because I made the mistake of flinching the first time that he said it." Analia's hand half rose, then fell back to her side, her phoenix pin nowhere in sight. "I'm just so gods-damned tired of always being afraid."

Aaron didn't have a name for the emotion clogging his throat. He stood from his bed, still unable to look at her as he headed for the door.

"I think you have your answer," he said. Nowhere near what he wanted to say.

He made to move past her, but Analia caught his hand.

"Aaron," she said, rising to her feet, "I'm sorry. I'm sorry for how I reacted on the turret. All you were trying to do, all you've ever tried to do is help me, and I lashed out at the first opportunity. Again."

No, he couldn't hear this. He couldn't allow the hope pounding against his rib cage to take hold.

He began, "That doesn't change anything—"

"You are not your family, Aaron."

Aaron sucked in a breath.

"Those things were done," Analia said, "but not by you."

"What about the guard?" he pressed.

"You did it to protect your home, and don't try to tell me you still would have done it if you didn't have to."

Aaron took a step back, but Analia moved with him.

"I saw your face," he said. "I know you can't mean this."

"I was unexpectedly faced with death magic, Aaron. It takes more than three seconds to process that. Especially when you're simultaneously doing everything in your power to shove me away—which you're still doing."

Aaron barely choked back his apology in time.

"Why can't you just let this go?" he asked, almost desperately.

"Because you're my friend," she said, matching his tone. "You're the person that takes pleasure in harassing me but can always make me smile, even when I'm falling apart and terrified to do so because you always give me something to hold onto, and I miss you."

Tears pricked behind Aaron's eyes. He could feel the four selfish little words on his tongue: *I miss you, too.* Too selfish.

"Analia, stop," he begged. "You're scared and desperate—"

"Of course I am!" she exclaimed. "The entire time Bie and Nadi were helping me get ready this morning, all I could think about was how I lost Brenn just to find a new version of him. How I'm about to be trapped in another kingdom where I have no one. Who wouldn't be terrified? But what I can't stand is the idea that you think what I said on that fountain no longer stands."

"Anna, *please.*"

Analia's free hand reached up, resting against his damper chain. Her eyes met his, a challenge glinting there as she didn't so much as flinch.

*I see you,* that gaze said. *I know you. I'm sorry.*

"You are not a monster, Aaron," she said. "I trust you."

It was everything he'd dared to hope for, things he wondered if he even deserved to hear. And it cracked his heart right down the center. Because he was leaving that night.

"But I can't keep chasing after people begging for forgiveness," Analia said. "Not when what happened wasn't just my fault. And since I've already said all I can, it's your decision what happens next."

He was leaving. Never coming back. And she had already lost Accalon.

Aaron dropped her hand, stepping away from her hand on his neck.

"There's nothing left to say," he told her.

He quickly turned, hiding his face, not thinking he could bear to see hers. Then, he exited his chambers and headed off down the hall.

He knew she didn't need him tonight. The tapestries proved she would handle it herself. Then, she would return home, and she would hate him. Not miss him, not grieve their loss on top of her uncle's.

And eventually, she would forget. Even though Aaron never would.

# Chapter 55

Analia watched Aaron's retreating back from his doorway, the chill of his magic still zinging through her bones. She knew he didn't mean it. She'd seen the remorse on his face before he turned. She'd also noticed how his collection of daggers she had seen on her first visit to his chambers—one even peeking out from under his pillow—was nowhere to be seen. Which meant tonight must be the night.

Analia leaned her forehead against the doorframe, letting the blow hit home. He was leaving. And she was about to be trapped. A fledgling shoved in a cage.

*I think you have your answer.* Yes, she did.

Analia turned in the opposite direction of Aaron, knowing he'd made it perfectly clear he didn't want her coming after him. But she still had time. She couldn't get into the passageways anymore, but she knew Dimitri's usual haunts. After that, even if she—

"Analia?"

Analia skidded to a stop, nearly slamming into Deardryn as she rounded a corner. The queen wore a white gown, shimmering with gold detailing.

"There you are," she said. "What are you doing? Your ceremony is about to commence."

Analia clasped her hands, summoning a bashful look. "I wanted a moment to collect myself," she said. "When I marry your son, I only want everyone to see my wings."

Wings she would use to fly far, far away—although how, she still didn't know. Not when the home she had thought she found had a price for staying and leaving. One it was determined to collect.

Deardryn's face softened. She lifted Analia's chin with a long, cool finger. "Fly indeed, little dragoness."

A shiver worked its way down Analia's spine. Did Deardryn know? Could she see the magic roiling just beneath Analia's skin? Had she figured out that Analia had been refusing to touch it these past three weeks?

Deardryn's hand dropped. Turning, she gestured for Analia to follow her. And Analia could feel the flames—real flames—crackle beneath her skin as she fell a half step behind Deardryn. But even as her eyes darted, looking for Dimitri, a way out, anything, she was met with nothing.

The corridor opened up ahead of them. Deardryn's hand on Analia's shoulder flexed, claw-like nails pricking her skin, just shallow enough to not draw blood.

She just needed time.

They stepped into the ballroom. The pillars were strangled by glinting chains of beads. Vases choked with blood-red roses clogged the various tables scattered across the room, dappled with wine flutes. Noblemen and women dressed in their finest stood in clumps of white and gold, hushed voices clashing with the quiet orchestra off to the side.

One simple plan. Nothing extravagant.

But Deardryn was speaking to the crowd. The music was picking up. Analia was handed a bouquet of white lilies whose scent crawled down her nose until she was trying not to gag.

Her eyes darted over the crowd. No allies to be found.

Could she fake an illness? That would only delay, perhaps only a few minutes with how desperate Deardryn seemed to keep this going, her hand on Analia's back propelling her down the petal-strewn aisle.

Magic? No, her flames would only make it worse. Injury? No, she would just be carried down the aisle. Straight toward Pryanth, who waited at the other end with glittering eyes.

The music swelled as Analia neared him.

The obvious answer was to say no, but then they would ask why. Because she wanted to go home? No one would believe that. Because she didn't want to marry Pryanth? That would get her beheaded.

Analia reached Pryanth. His icy fingers snaked around hers, gripping so tight she lost all feeling in her hand. She only heard the quiet, *wrong, wrong, wrong,* in her mind as the ceremony commenced, led by the Minister of Bindings in his white robes. Out of time.

The Sun Kingdom's wedding ritual consisted of wrapping ribbons cleansed in each of the five gods' temples. Starting with Pryanth's left wrist, crossing to Analia's, up to Pryanth's right, down to Analia's right, and the figure eight continued.

Analia's lips moved, saying the words, not hearing them. All she could focus on was the shifting color of the ribbon, each dedicated to a different god. Green, pink, purple, white, gold.

It was just another performance. The careful steps of every dance, the formal attire, the relentless sparkle of gold that tried to hide the rot beneath. The sunshine magic that only warmed the surface of the icy death in its wake.

The ribbon tightened around her wrist. Binding her. Trapping her. The unwilling captive of the man across from her, dressed all in gold except for the white family cloak around his shoulders. So similar to Aaron's cloak—Aaron.

Analia barely noticed as Pryanth kissed her. But as the audience applauded and he unraveled their ribbons with a quick jerk of his wrists, Analia raised her fist behind her back with her last three fingers splayed.

She didn't care who saw and dared to wonder. She only knew this was her last hope.

But as wine was passed around the room, as people danced and Analia's careful calm cracked along its foundation, there was no sign of messy dark hair or starlight eyes. There was no voice that rose above the crowd as Pryanth finally led her away.

Up the stairs, down the corridors, Pryanth's grip still vice-like. His footsteps sure as he dragged her to his chambers, slamming the door shut behind them. Sealing Analia's fate for good. The moment the door closed, Pryanth was on her—mouth crushing, hand shoving the delicate straps of her gown down her shoulders. *Wrong, wrong, wrong.*

"Pryanth, wait," Analia said, squirming back.

"Why?" he demanded, pulling her deeper into his room. "All we've done is wait."

His face was flushed with wine. Analia's gaze darted: the window, the entrance to the passageways above his desk, the sharp array of weapons hanging from his walls. Pryanth tried to kiss her once more, but Analia jerked her head to the side.

"Pryanth, stop!"

"Why?"

"Because I don't want to."

Pryanth jerked to a stop in the center of the room. And his look of disbelief was more terrifying than any flash of his temper.

"'Want'?" he asked, bringing his face close to hers. "You're complaining to me about 'want'? You think I wanted this?"

He stabbed a finger into her sternum. "This was your idea. Yours and my mother's."

Analia felt an odd tinge of betrayal. "But you said on the roof—"

"You think that was real?" Pryanth yelled, power thrumming around him. "You think I wanted to be married to the dud Royal from an enemy kingdom when my name has already been dragged through the mud by my father?"

Pryanth shoved her to her knees, pressing her back against his bed frame. She should be relieved, shouldn't she? He didn't want this either. She could use this.

Instead, Analia said, "But you said I was the flame to your life."

Pryanth's laugh went beyond a thunderclap. It was a cloud of hail, pelting her.

"How desperate were you to believe that?" he asked.

What was that flicker in his eyes?

"Then why?" Analia asked.

"Why do you think, Analia?"

Analia didn't even need a moment to consider. "Deardryn."

Pryanth sneered. And something sharp dragged through Analia's chest.

"This was Mother's doing, not mine," he said. "She said that if I ever wanted to inherit her throne, I would have to marry you and solidify her alliance. She was willing to change the laws, turn our kingdom upside down, just to get you here. Why? The only thing that makes you special is how completely *worthless* you are."

Analia tried to push Pryanth back, but he pressed her harder against the bed.

"If you don't want this," she gasped, "just let me go. Let me disappear and you'll never have to deal with me again."

"No," Pryanth spat, "I'll just have to deal with the reputation that my Crystal-forsaken wife abandoned me. A Royal deemed unworthy by the Crystal, saying no to me?"

But that wasn't rage in his eyes. It was heartbreak. Humiliation.

She was one more person not choosing him. The insecure, rejected prince, desperate for love and control after his father's betrayal.

"You love me," she realized, hardly able to believe it. "You tried not to, you're trying to deny it now, but you love me—"

Analia gagged as Pryanth pressed his forearm across her throat.

"Know a lie when you hear it, Analia," he hissed.

Analia did. He continued to talk, but his voice fuzzed out in her ears. All she could do was stare at the man that had trapped her with I love yous—words that only slashed deeper and deeper as time went on. Because this wasn't the man that she had started to fall in love with. He was just the one forcing her to stay.

"You're only prolonging the inevitable," Pryanth said. "One way or another, I will have my birthright." He leaned in close, running his lips along her cheekbone in a horrifically gentle line. "I will kill you if I have to."

A phantom burn flashed behind Analia's ears. She didn't try to stop the terror, grief, heartache, as it thundered through her. Instead, she reached for the tiny, ancient spark that wavered in its wake.

She did not deserve this.

And Analia erupted in a column of midnight flame.

# Chapter 56

Dimitri raced through the passageways, Aaron close behind.

He had told himself he wasn't going to go to Analia's wedding. For once, he wasn't the one that had burned the bridge. Yet, that same feeling that had him sitting inside the passageways, watching Analia's training with Deardryn day after day, had him lurking in the back of the ballroom.

He watched as Analia was shoved down the aisle, her shoulders back, head high, her eyes just a little too wide. But there was nothing he could do as he watched his friend—Crystal strike him down, she was his friend—get married off to a monster. But what was that weird gesture she made behind her back? Dimitri took a step forward, just as Aaron appeared beside him, gripping his arm tight enough to leave a bruise.

"That's the signal," he said. "Get me out."

Dimitri cocked his head. "You couldn't have thought of something more obvious, could you, Bordello?"

"It wasn't meant for this situation." Aaron raked a hand through his hair. "Dimitri, we have to get her out."

"Say no more."

Dimitri made to march forward, not sure what he was going to say but knowing full well words would spew forth anyway. But Aaron's grip tightened.

"Not yet," he said. "Do it now and we make a scene. We need as few witnesses as possible."

Dimitri gave Aaron a look. "And when's that?"

Apparently, that time was now. Both men carried a small bundle as they tried not to bounce off the walls at every racing turn.

"So, what's your plan, Bordello?" Dimitri called over his shoulder. "Just barge in on them?"

"Something like that."

"And what if they're in the middle of..." Dimitri let his words trail off.

"She wouldn't have made the signal if she wanted that, Dima."

"And what if she didn't have a choice?"

They reached Pryanth's chambers. Aaron came up on Dimitri's left, expression nauseated. "All the more reason."

He passed Dimitri his bundle and tried to open the entrance, but it didn't budge. Aaron swore under his breath, tugging the chain around his neck.

Dimitri obligingly stepped forward, unlocking the entrance with his palm, but he made no move to open it.

"This is all you," he said. "I'll come in as soon as I know everyone is clothed."

Aaron gave him a withering look. Then, he slid the wall aside. And the two of them came face-to-face with a wall of roaring black flames, flickering with a bluish tinge.

Dimitri stumbled back, heat blasting across his face. Aaron, not looking surprised in the slightest, clambered through the entrance, calling Analia's name.

Dimitri waited for the cry of pain as Aaron was burned alive. His hands tightened around his bundle of clothes as the seconds ticked by, unable to look away from the flickering flames.

So, Flashfire really was a flashfire after all.

A minute passed. Then two. Fire licked up the stone across the room, seeking purchase, something to burn.

"Come on," Dimitri muttered. "Gods, please..."

The fire gave one last crackling hiss. There was a flash of bright silver light, so bright Dimitri had to look away as something cold raked down his insides. Then, the fire died down. Just as the fire flickered out, there came another flash, this time of black energy, nowhere near the intensity of the silver one before.

When Dimitri finally dared to poke his head out of the entrance, he saw Aaron tucking his silver chain under his leathers once more. He knelt in the center of the room, skin flushed and face twisted in a grimace, but not appearing to have been burned. Analia was curled in a ball in front of him, face hidden as Aaron gripped her shoulders. And at the foot of the bed…

"Fuck," Dimitri said into the silence.

He tumbled onto Pryanth's desk, getting a closer look at the pile of ash and bits of charred bone. There was no coming back for Pryanth. And Dimitri didn't try to stop his wicked lash of satisfaction.

"That's one way to handle it," Aaron said, staring at the ash with something like awe.

Dimitri expected tears, even horror, as Analia lifted her head. Instead, she was eerily calm as she said, "He was going to kill me."

Aaron tensed. He ran his hand down her arm, to comfort her or himself, Dimitri didn't know. But his voice was firm as he said, "You did what you had to do."

"No," Analia said. "I lost control."

She uncurled, twisting in Aaron's grip to face him. Aaron tried to smooth his expression before she could see, but she was too quick.

"Aaron, did I—"

"No," he said quickly. "No, it's not that—just give me a moment."

Aaron leaned back against the bed frame, tugging the chain around his neck.

"Oh," Analia said softly.

Dimitri turned away, having just enough decency to give them some privacy, but nowhere near enough to stop himself from kicking his boot through Pryanth's ashes.

"I didn't think you would come," Analia whispered.

"I told you, the moment I saw that signal, I was breaking you out. No matter what."

"Does that mean…"

Dimitri could barely hear Aaron as he said, "I couldn't be one more person that hurt you."

There came the sound of flesh hitting leather. "You idiot, you think hating you is any better?"

"I know, I know, I promise, I'm sorry." Aaron sighed. "And I'm sorry for the turret, too."

*Finally.*

Dimitri didn't look back until he heard them rise. Aaron sat on the bed, and Analia extended her hand. Dimitri's last kernel of resentment flickered.

"We're good," he grunted. He paused. "Right?"

Analia nodded quickly. Dimitri braced himself, then took her hand and gave a quick squeeze.

As their hands dropped, Analia's eyes drifted to Pryanth's ashes. Dimitri braced himself, for what, he didn't know. But Analia only blinked free a single tear, her lips forming the words, "I'm sorry." Then, she straightened.

"We don't have much time," she said, eyes clocking the night-darkened sky out the window. "They're not going to expect my presence until morning, but at that point, there's nothing we can do."

Dimitri said, "Good thing for you, we think ahead."

He tossed her a bundle of clothes he and Aaron had stolen from Lena's chambers. Analia nodded her thanks, turning her back to them and stripping off her gown. Both men averted their eyes.

"I counted the guards when we left the wedding," she said. "Two at every junction on this floor, and patrols on the ones below. I wouldn't be surprised if above, as well."

"Queen's orders," Aaron confirmed, still looking a little woozy—what was that about? "We were ordered to do everything we can to protect the consummation."

Analia said, "Not so much keeping others out, but keeping me in."

She pulled a dark tunic over her head, slipping something in her pocket. Then, she picked up her gown. Her forehead creased with concentration, and black flames licked across her palms and down the dress, its remains joining Pryanth's on the ground.

Dimitri couldn't help but be impressed.

"Well done," Aaron murmured as she sat beside him once more. He handed her the dagger he'd given her in the garden, retrieved from her chambers. Analia slid it into her belt without comment.

Dimitri asked, "So what, are you going to just blast your way through them?"

"Gods no," Analia said, taking the boots he offered her. "We wouldn't make it down a floor before we were caught."

Aaron asked, "So what are you..." His voice trailed off, his eyes glinting. Analia nodded at him, lacing up her boots.

"The passageways?" Dimitri demanded. "Look, Flashfire, I know we agreed Othin can barely dress himself in the morning, but he definitely shielded you from the passageways."

"No," Analia said, "he put an alarm on. Think about it. He wouldn't want to keep me out. Then there's nothing he can pin me with.

"He wants me to go through the passageways because now he'll know when I do. And then he can nail me."

"Can't you just shadowjump out of here?" Dimitri asked.

"That would require me knowing how to do so," Analia said. She shot a quick look at Aaron, who glanced at Dimitri, then shook his head a fraction.

Well, that was interesting. Knowing he wouldn't get any answers, Dimitri said, "But you can't enter the passageways here. It will lead him straight to the crime scene!"

Aaron said, "He would come here anyway. Even if we were able to sneak out of here and find a different entrance, that would just mean Othin would send two patrols and not one."

"It's not worth the risk," Analia agreed.

"But we'll still have to move fast," said Aaron. "The moment Othin arrives, he'll find the remains and go straight into the passageways."

"Which is why," Dimitri sighed, sitting on Analia's other side, "you idiots need a distraction."

Analia started to protest, her hand coming to hover over his, careful not to touch him. And that little gesture solidified Dimitri's plans.

"You and Bordello go through the passageways," he said. "I'll distract my beloved father."

"Dima," Aaron began, but Analia nodded.

"You won't be able to hide Pryanth's death for long," she told him.

Dimitri cocked a brow. With the sweep of his foot, he shoved the pile of ash under the bed, giving Analia a look of a master performer at the end of his routine. Analia winced. Her eyes darted around the room, lingering on every scorch mark in the rock, the half-melted weapons on the wall.

"We'll come back for you," she promised, rising to her feet.

"Don't lie," Dimitri said, flopping back on the bed.

He'd known the moment he volunteered there was no escaping, no fulfilling that bargain of freedom.

"So, where are you two going?" he asked, turning to Aaron.

"I'm getting her out of the kingdom—"

"No," Analia interrupted, heading for the desk. "We're going to the garden."

"Anna, I can get the scroll later."

"No," she said, just as Dimitri asked, "What scroll?"

"We're going to the garden," Analia repeated. "Not just to get your scroll, but because I finally know who killed my uncle."

Dimitri's eyebrows were in danger of disappearing into his hairline. But he kept his mouth shut as Aaron waged a quick, silent battle with himself. Then, he rose, steady on his feet as he crossed to Analia and pulled her phoenix pin from his cloak pocket.

"Rise again," he whispered, fastening the pin to her tunic.

Analia's face flooded with emotion. She touched Aaron's cheek, looking at a loss for words. Then, the two looked back at Dimitri, who gave a lazy wave.

"We will get you out," Analia vowed. Aaron nodded in agreement.

It took Dimitri a moment to name the emotion that swelled in his chest. Sorrow. It was sorrow as he watched Analia open the entrance, the outline briefly glowing blue as she and Aaron clambered into the passageways beyond. It was sorrow as he realized this could very well be the last time he ever saw them.

The only friends he'd ever had. And Dimitri wouldn't let them down.

# Chapter 57

The Ash Castle corridors were deserted as Ember hurried after Cadmus.

"What are you going to do, Cadmus?" she asked, struggling to match his pace.

The Ash Prince marched down a sweeping staircase, not glancing back at her. "I'm going to figure out who put the wine in Accalon's mug."

He reached the bottom of the stairs, turning down the hall that led to the kitchen without pause. Ember cursed as she scrambled after him.

She'd always known the Ash Royals' flames came with a temper to match, but had Cadmus ever erupted like this before? Golden flames snaked around his hands, combed burning fingers through the deep red of his hair.

"Think this through, Cadmus," she pleaded. "If you go in there ready to torch your way to the truth, you're only going to tip off the culprit and scare your witnesses into silence."

"That's a bit hypocritical coming from you."

Well, he had a point there.

"Then you should trust me and my extensive experience when we say you need to calm down."

Giving the flames around his wrist a warning glare, Ember grabbed Cadmus's sleeve. Thankfully, her fingers remained intact as she jerked him to a stop outside the kitchen door.

"You want to find your uncle's killer?" she asked.

Cadmus nodded.

"Then breathe."

Cadmus glared. But slowly, the golden light and shadows that flickered across his face winked out. Ember didn't let go until every flame was snuffed, her own pulse matching that of the one pounding beneath her fingers.

"Good," she soothed. "I can help with this," she added, tapping her finger on his pulsating vein. "I can slow your heart rate just enough that you—"

"No."

Cadmus firmly pulled his arm back, but the look he gave her was one of gratitude. Then, he pushed through the kitchen door, spine straight, shoulders back, head high. Rise again, indeed.

The kitchen was a hustle of activity despite the late hour. They all looked up as Cadmus marched into their midst, voices fading.

"Who was on duty the night the Sun Kingdom came to our castle?" he asked, eyes sweeping the crowd.

There came the awkward shuffling of feet. Finally, a balding man with a square head and sharp brown eyes stepped forward. "I was in charge, Your Highness."

Cadmus turned on his heel. "Come with us."

"**A**re you all right?"

Aaron glanced at Analia in the darkness, her face faintly illuminated by the damaged sunstone he'd retrieved from her chambers. It was the first time she'd spoken since slipping out the side door, Aaron having slit the guard on duty's throat before dragging him into the passageways.

"I feel like I should be asking you that," he replied.

That was the only thought that had swirled through his mind ever since he left his chambers: was she all right? What if Surce's tapestry was wrong? Gods, what if it was wrong?

"I'm keeping my mental shield down," Analia said. "I'm trying to adjust to the temple's magic now instead of getting overwhelmed by it later."

Did that mean she could still sense the Sun magic, even though her own had awakened? Aaron decided that was a question for another time.

"What about everything else?" he asked.

"It's like you said," Analia said flatly. "I did what I had to do."

Regardless, a first kill always had a way of haunting a person. He knew Analia would discover that on her own, though. Perhaps it was better to let the shock shield her as long as possible.

The two crested the final hill.

"You never answered my question," Analia said.

"About?"

"Are you all right? I saw the look on your face back in Pryanth's chambers. Like you were in pain."

Aaron winced.

"When I put the damper on you," he said slowly, "there was a lot of stored up magic that slammed into me all at once, just to be immediately locked away when I put it on again."

That was putting it mildly. The internal whiplash had left him feeling like he'd been thrown back against a stone wall, just to bounce off and slam into another.

"That was quick thinking," Analia said.

"It was the only thing I could think of. Although, Analia, how am I not burned to a crisp right now?"

Analia ducked under a branch, her expression softening. "I heard your voice," she said simply. "And I knew I couldn't stop the flames. But I couldn't let them hurt you, either."

As Analia continued down the hill, Aaron felt the ice he had cocooned himself in the past three weeks begin to thaw. *I couldn't let them hurt you.*

Aaron and Analia paused behind the wall of foliage between the woods and the garden. It was remarkably recovered from the last time Aaron had crashed through it, one of the Devourist's amputated bones flying after him to smack him on the temple.

He was too slow without his magic, but with his magic flowing, it was only a matter of time before it sucked him dry. But after tonight...

Analia said, "It's going to hunt me down the moment it senses my magic in the garden."

"Good thing it will be too distracted to do so."

Aaron expected Analia to argue, but she only pocketed her sunstone and nodded.

"Don't take this off," she said, touching his damper chain and sending a tiny thrill down his spine. "I'm not going to pretend like I know every secret that comes attached to it, but I know they're not worth risking just to maybe take down one demon."

Aaron didn't have words for the emotion that clogged his throat. He nodded, and Analia let her hand drop, repositioning herself at the bracken wall.

"You know," he said, stepping up beside her, "the last time we were here, I told you to be careful."

Analia snorted. "Perhaps this time you should tell me to be heart-stoppingly reckless."

Aaron tapped her nose. "Smartass."

Analia flashed a smile, as if they weren't about to face a demon, some unknown magic, the impending wrath of an entire kingdom. As if she weren't wrestling with a magic far more powerful than she had the ability to control.

Aaron shifted closer, feeling the heat from that power roiling just beneath the surface. "I'll be right behind you," he promised in her ear.

Then, not giving her time to respond, Aaron pushed through the foliage. Just to find the Devourist already waiting for him at the boundary.

Analia watched from the shadows as Aaron strolled toward the Devourist, hands in his cloak pockets, the picture of casual. He stopped at the border and rocked back on his heels, the two taking a moment to observe one another. Then, undoubtedly with a wicked grin, Aaron darted into the garden, the Devourist snarling as it flashed after him.

"Be careful," Analia whispered, her fingers tightening around Pryanth's pendant in her pocket. Then, not wasting time, she took off, over Othin's shield and through the glamor. There was no point in trying to hide. Not with the magic she could feel screaming inside her, demanding to burn—not just Pryanth, but everything.

Analia vaulted over the wall, Sun magic slamming into her. But she didn't flinch away. Instead, she let it wash away the flames, the rage, the devastation of what she'd done to Pryanth—what he'd done to her.

There was no time for that now. Not as Analia marched up the three white stone steps to the temple's door. A temple that, she realized, was carved out of one massive sunstone.

Hand on the glittering knob, Analia gave herself three seconds. Three seconds to grieve, to adjust, to turn the knob and step inside.

Ember sat beside Cadmus at Ronun's interrogation table, the cook—who she had learned was named Wae—seated across from them, unshackled.

"But I already told Ronun all of this," Wae said, finishing his recount of the night.

"I know," Cadmus said, "but I have questions that he hadn't gotten to."

"Of—of course, Your Highness."

Cadmus placed his hands on the desk. "My uncle. He never requested wine?"

"Never," Wae said quickly. "Well, at least not in the past thirty years."

Ember and Cadmus swapped a look.

Cadmus asked, "What did he drink instead?"

"Tea. Every meal, he wanted tea."

Ember asked, "And what type of tea did he request?"

"For lunch and dinner, it always changed. It's impossible to say—"

Wae cut off as he caught sight of the flame winding around Cadmus's knuckles. Ember pinched his leg under the table, but it wasn't fury like before. This was desperation.

"What about breakfast?" Cadmus asked.

Wae shifted in his seat. "I don't know," he mumbled.

"How do you not know?" Cadmus demanded.

"He only requested boiling water."

Ember couldn't stifle her sound of surprise.

"He never asked for tea," Wae said, wiping the sweat from his brow. "He always rejected it when we offered."

"When did that start?" Ember asked after a beat, realizing Cadmus was slowly turning to stone.

"Thirty years ago."

Which was when he started taking xenol. And seeing as though he stopped drinking wine at the same time...

"He knew," Ember breathed.

Wae's face was a mask of confusion, quickly melting into fear as that trailing flame flared. Ember gripped the sides of her chair as Cadmus turned back to Wae.

"The night Sun came," he said, "did King Accalon request wine be added to his tea?"

"Well, no." Wae's eyes bounced between Ember and Cadmus, who wore identical looks of triumph. "But His Majesty was not the one who ordered drinks that night."

The temple wasn't large. The walls, floors, and ceiling were shifting shades of gold, carved with swirling runes. To the left was a staircase, leading up to the second-floor balcony that curved like a ring high above. Various catwalks stretched across the open gap, acting as shortcuts from one area of the ring to another.

Analia took two steps into the temple, the door slamming shut behind her. And before she could so much as blink, the sunstone flared a brilliant gold.

Tendrils of light arced from the stone, converging around her, forming a cage of shimmering sunlight. Trapped.

And standing in the center of the room, as if waiting for her, was Deardryn.

# Chapter 58

Dimitri struggled to breathe as he sprawled across Pryanth's bed. He told himself he didn't care that Othin would be on him in a matter of minutes. But he couldn't deny how his hands shook on the poetry collection he'd taken to carrying around in his cloak.

He could do this. He could do this, he could do this, he could do—

Dimitri's heart jolted at the sound of pounding footsteps racing down the hall. He forced his body to remain relaxed as a moment later, Othin, followed by a unit of guards, stormed through Pryanth's door.

Othin's eyes swept the flame-scorched room, eventually landing on Dimitri, who still hadn't looked up from his book. "Dimitri—"

"Were you really about to storm in on your son and daughter-in-law consummating their marriage?" Dimitri turned a page. "That's disgusting, even for you."

Othin's face burned scarlet. Dimitri smiled faintly, all too aware of the six sword tips aiming at every spot that would kill him in an instant. That would certainly take care of the king's bastard.

"Leave us," Othin said quietly to the guards.

Dimitri sat up straight. The guards exchanged uncertain looks.

"You have your orders," Othin snapped, and they quickly retreated.

As the door shut behind them, Dimitri suddenly missed the swords as his father glared down at him with eyes identical to his own. Except Othin's shone with a resolve that Dimitri knew would have his head on a spike.

Analia slammed her hands against the golden bars of her cage, somehow tangible despite being forged from light. Immediately, she felt a zap and a tug, as if something were being sucked out of her. Analia gasped.

"I would not advise doing that," Deardryn said from where she stood in the center of the temple. She still wore her dress from earlier that night, but now Analia spotted the slits in the skirt that would enable greater mobility. "Those bars are forged by Sun magic. I presume Aaron already explained to you the duality of my magic."

Replenishing and healing minds, souls, and magic networks. But also, taking them away.

Analia struggled to yank her hands back, stumbling as she tried to avoid the bars at her back. Plan, she needed a plan.

"I was wondering when you would arrive," the Dragoness went on. "Tell me, where's my son?"

"In his chambers," said Analia coolly.

Deardryn fingered her golden bracelets. "I suppose you did what you had to do?"

Analia didn't reply. She still didn't know if Deardryn knew of her magic, and if she did...

Analia forced her leaping flames back down. She had to be patient.

"I'm surprised it took you this long to enter my private study," said Deardryn conversationally.

"I didn't want it to be you."

"Oh?"

Analia didn't have to fake the emotion in her voice as she said, "You were my mentor. You defended me, protected me. You... You cared about me."

Analia shook her head, her eyes flicking over her surroundings.

"None of that was a lie, Analia."

"But you're not going to deny it? Everything you've done?"

The only way to reach the second floor was the staircase to Analia's left. Shelves and drawers filled with neatly arranged objects lined the walls, separated by carved marble altars.

Deardryn shrugged a slim hand. "Why should I?"

"Because you preach peace! You're the one Royal who has wanted to reunite the kingdoms, and yet you've been slaughtering them behind their backs!"

Porcelain horns, glittering jewelry, ancient books. All magical, judging by the headache arcing across Analia's forehead. She raised her shield high, thickening it from stone, to iron, to steel.

"Tell me why I might do that," Deardryn prompted.

Analia's head jerked up. Was this just another test? As if nothing had changed between them? As if Deardryn's betrayal hadn't sent a dagger carved from ice through Analia's heart the moment she'd figured it out in Pryanth's chambers.

"Was it a way to deflect suspicion?" Analia asked. "One big lie—"

Analia reared back as the bars condensed. Magic slammed into her, sucking her energy, burning claws of light slicing through her mind.

She tried to jerk away, only to fall against another bar, zapping down her spine.

"Analia," Deardryn chided, "you of all people should know the bigger the lie, the faster it crumbles." She flicked her hand, and the bars flashed back to their original position. "Try again."

Analia's entire body trembled. "You wanted to create chaos," she said. "Create turmoil, spark a war, and fight your way back to unity—"

Analia was ready for the slam this time, but bracing herself was pointless. The light converged on her, chipping away at her mind, her magic, reducing her down to every single shard she'd been slowly smoothing out the past four months.

"Don't insult me, Analia," Deardryn said, stepping closer. Once again, the bars retracted, and Analia fell to her knees. "Try again."

She had to get out of this cage. But then what?

"It doesn't make sense," Analia said desperately. "Why attack the people you want to unite? All it does is frighten them, put them on guard with blades at each other's throats..."

Analia's words trailed off. It wasn't the other kingdoms the Royals were suspicious of.

Deardryn smiled faintly. "What better thing to unite around than a common enemy."

"So, they were all you," Analia said faintly.

"Indeed." Deardryn stepped up to the bars. "It started with my own brother, twenty years ago. The utter thorn in my side. Insisting Rosala had chosen me, I should be a healer, not a queen. Saying that our sister couldn't rule, she spent too much time on bedrest."

Deardryn's lip curled. "He never cared about Saura. He only coveted the throne for himself. And he denied it at every turn, claiming he was providing a new perspective when blocking my decrees. I suppose that 'new perspective' also included his attempted coup."

"So, you killed your own brother."

Analia closed her eyes, trying to steady herself.

"He would have killed me. At least with his death, he proved my magic-sealing theory."

"But I thought you said you didn't know how Gavare made his rings."

"I do not," said Deardryn. "I found my own way.

"Currently, there is no research on how to trap Royal magic outside the body. It's simply too powerful. But there are countless stories of demons, spirits, ghosts, and the like being locked away in various inanimate objects."

"Like armor," Analia supplied.

Deardryn nodded. "Consequently, while I couldn't trap the magic itself inside a ring, I could trap a creature that had absorbed it. A conduit, of sorts. As long as each object had a Devourist that had absorbed a Royal's magic inside, that magic could be pulled forth."

Analia's mind flashed to the silver collar attached to the Devourist's cloak. But Marcos had said demon tamers were rare—incredibly rare—due to the amount of power they required.

At least that confirmed one thing: Analia hadn't been training with Gavare's rings. Deardryn never had them in the first place.

"But that was twenty years ago," she said, slowly lowering her mental shield. "Why now?"

"I grew tired of waiting," Deardryn said simply. Her hand drifted to the collection of bracelets on her wrist, then quickly jerked away. "I had been arguing for reunification for decades, and there comes a point where you must take matters into your own hands."

"And you started with Wind," Analia said.

"Very good," said Deardryn. "I suppose you're tracking through the rings?"

"And the necklace you were wearing the day we found the dead Mist Princess that suddenly contains Mist magic."

Located in the damper box Analia found on the right-hand side of the second floor. The one spot of yawning magical emptiness.

"Astute indeed, little dragoness."

Deardryn reached through the bars, smoothing a hand down Analia's hair. Analia's insides yanked apart as she simultaneously wanted to lean into that touch and smack it away.

"The first ring was my brother's magic, as we have already discussed."

"Then why kill Cabir?" Analia demanded.

Deardryn flinched, almost imperceptibly. "He... He was not supposed to die. I knew you'd made it into the garden—you did a poor job of leaving no evidence behind. You were poking around, and I had to bat you off my trail. I only intended for the demon to leave a mark on his neck."

Deardryn composed herself quickly. "But there is nothing I can do about that now."

Analia didn't try to hide her revulsion.

"Wind being my next target was happenstance," Deardryn continued. "I had been on the border, using the abundance of collected magic there to open the Hell Realm. I was only intending on summoning the Devourist at that point, but the prince must have sensed the power. He raced over, alone, and I found myself in the perfect position to strike.

"For Baylen, it was a matter of waiting to see if news of the Wind Prince's death spread and allowing enough time to pass that the deaths weren't immediately connected."

"And you killed Sand during that week you were gone," Analia said, bracing her hands on the carved floor.

"Correct again, little dragoness."

The bars flickered. Analia tensed. Deardryn let the magic relax.

"But why steal their magic?" Analia pressed. "Why wasn't killing them enough?"

"Analia, you don't honestly believe I would tell you parts of the story you couldn't figure out on your own?"

A thin ribbon of Sun magic trailed down Analia's spine. Analia shuddered so hard her teeth ached.

Deardryn retracted the magic as she continued, "The Solstice was rapidly approaching at that point, and I was running out of time. I knew that the way the numbers stood, it would be near impossible to take advantage of all six kingdoms being together, easy to strike, but concurrently evade suspicion."

"So, you poisoned Patryclas in order to heal him and deflect attention."

"And I have you to thank for that very scheme."

"Me?"

"Lev discovered your herbology books. One book open, and he had told me of your discussion of xenol with Chia—"

"But Lev is Othin's guard," Analia interrupted.

"Yes, and it's remarkable how loyal a person becomes once you've saved their life."

Lev's stab wound. His argument with Dannel. All orchestrated by Deardryn, with Othin as her shield.

Analia's flames crackled faintly.

"My husband might have married me," Deardryn said, "but he has never loved me. He has never done anything but attempt to get in my way."

"So, you won his closest weapon over to your own side," Analia said.

Deardryn's eyes flashed with an approval that had Analia's heart breaking.

"As for xenol," she said, "it took me centuries to locate it, simply for research's sake. Then, when I did, I sent an oblivious Othin to retrieve it."

"Is that why you smudged out the page?" Analia asked. Her mind locked in on a thrum of power, directly across from her and up.

"That wasn't me," said Deardryn. "That was done centuries ago, from what I can tell. I was the one who was slowly removing the ink.

"Regardless, I realized it would be the perfect way to stage an attack, especially with my ability to heal magic networks. All I had to do was grind some leaves into a powder, secure the vial to my arm—hidden beneath my sleeve—and slip it in while passing the goblet along. Patryclas was poisoned, I healed him before the wine could enable the xenol to attack his life force, the Mist Princess was killed, I tried to heal her, and suddenly, no one kingdom was under suspicion. Although I must ask why you were looking into xenol."

Analia's head jerked up. "Because you used it to kill my uncle!"

"Me?" Deardryn asked. "I didn't poison Accalon."

"Yes, you did!"

"Analia, he was the last person I wanted to target. He was just compassionate enough to consider my way."

"But then who…"

"Think, Analia." Deardryn leaned in close, not reacting as the bars of light brushed her cheeks. "Who stands to gain the most from a king's death?"

Analia's stomach dropped, straight into starving flames.

"I will say, however," Deardryn said, "I am sorry his death worked out for me."

And Analia let those flames erupt.

# Chapter 59

Dimitri eyed his father, still standing in the center of the room with arms folded expectantly.

So, it was to be a silent stare down? Well, Dimitri wouldn't kid himself into thinking he could ever win one of those.

"Oh no," he said, slipping his book back in his cloak. "Are you trying to play parent, now?"

Othin's face grew stern. "Where is she, Dimitri?"

"I understand not wanting to deal with the whole infant stage, they're always sticky and secreting something—although it's half your fault there even was an infant in the first place—"

"Dimitri, where is Analia? Where is Pryanth?"

"Dead of embarrassment," said Dimitri. He vaguely waved toward his lap, his voice conversational as he continued, "I hear demons can help with that, though."

"Dammit, Dimitri!" Othin slammed his fists down on Pryanth's desk, Dimitri's stomach doing a flip. "This isn't a game! Do you have any idea what you've gotten yourself tangled in by being here—"

"Aw, you *are* playing parent," Dimitri whined. "The obnoxious, protective parent that comes around twenty years too late."

"I'm not playing—I am your father, Dimitri, and I am also your king—"

"Kill any innocent 'mothers' lately, Your Majesty?"

Othin's magic flashed across his skin in a network of brilliant blue.

Yes, there was certainly a reason Dimitri had decided to stay behind. It wasn't his innately abrasive nature. Not his ability to stall, not the fact that Aaron would be far more helpful getting Analia into the temple.

It was for this moment. Feeling the burn in his veins, the thrum of the sunstones behind him, all pounding to the furious rhythm of his pulse as he stared up at the man who gave him nothing but suffering.

Othin took a step toward Dimitri. "You don't get to throw that in my face," he hissed. "Not when I was protecting you."

*"Protecting me?"* Dimitri exclaimed, shoving to his feet. "Was that what you were doing when you didn't stop your hag of a wife from putting me to work at three? When your spoiled brat of a son chased me around the castle and used me as magical target practice? When every single gods-damned person in this castle turned their backs on me because they couldn't do so to you, their king, who threatened to destroy their kingdom's reputation because you wouldn't toss me on the street with every other bastard of Elefthia?"

There were so many more words, all having ached for years to be loosed like a volley of arrows, but Dimitri clamped his mouth shut. Not because of the devastated look on Othin's face, but because of the splintering in his own chest.

"I did my best," Othin said. He extended a hand toward Dimitri. "Dima—"

"You don't get to call me that," Dimitri snarled, smacking his hand away. "Not when you only did the bare fucking minimum."

"I tried!"

"You gave up!"

Dimitri's entire body trembled.

Othin searched for words. "Deardryn and Pryanth are my duty," he said. "I tried to love them, and I succeeded in destroying them. I couldn't do that again, even though you are my—"

"Don't," Dimitri said, raising a hand and cringing away. "Don't call me your family when we both know where that falls on your list."

Othin flinched as if struck. Dimitri sat back on Pryanth's bed, grabbing his book and hiding his face in the pages.

"Dimitri," Othin said, taking a few hesitant steps toward him, "I have done nothing but put you first. All these months Analia has been here? It wasn't Deardryn or Pryanth I feared for, it was you.

"Watching that mouse grow more and more powerful. The countless things she could do to you. It terrified me."

Dimitri didn't look up as Othin's voice broke.

"Seeing how she lit up that sundial, knowing the type of power she has? Knowing she could use you to try and hurt me? Dimitri, I tried to tell you to be careful! I've tried to help you throughout your life—"

"Don't start with that," Dimitri said, finally throwing the book aside. "Don't try to blame this on me pushing you away. You weren't respecting my wishes by avoiding me. You were appeasing your wife."

Othin flinched. Bull's-fucking-eye.

"I love your mother," Othin said quietly. He made it to the bed, his gaze dropping to his feet. "I have always loved you, Dimitri. I just wish you would let me..."

Dread curdled Dimitri's insides as Othin's face changed. He knelt, Dimitri knowing he was powerless to stop him as he reached under the bed and pulled out a piece of bone, his eyes wide with fear? Desperation?

Crystal spare him.

Analia's cage was consumed by midnight flames.

Deardryn launched herself back, heat blasting across the temple. Analia scrambled to her feet, still unsteady from Deardryn's magic, and darted for the stairs.

"So," Deardryn said, "your magic has finally made an appearance."

Light erupted from the floor around Analia, sending jabs of pain up her legs. But she sprinted up the stairs, two at a time, her fire wavering behind her.

She just had to make it to the second floor, which was composed of wood, not the sunstone. As long as she didn't make contact with the stone, she would be fine.

Five more steps. Four. Three.

Analia strained to keep her fire going, the one barrier she had between herself and Deardryn.

Two. One.

An explosion of gold blasted apart her flames. She launched herself onto the second floor, rolling behind the first marble altar.

"There's no point in hiding, Analia," Deardryn called.

At her words, the walls flashed a blinding gold. Analia pressed herself against the marble, waiting for the magic to slam into her. But curiously, she remained unscathed.

Analia cautiously lowered her mental shield. Deardryn's magic was spread in a thin film across every wall, curling around the ceiling and floor, causing the stone to glow. But the magic didn't project out.

Did Deardryn not have enough power to fill the entire temple? If that were true, she wouldn't be able to strike Analia wherever she hid. She had to find Analia first, then concentrate her magic around Analia to trap her.

"I sensed that magic in your uncle the morning he died."

Analia stiffened. Deardryn's voice was coming up the stairs. Keeping low, she darted out from behind the altar, Deardryn's voice gliding behind her.

"So much power. More than I'd ever felt before."

Analia had detected the scroll directly across from the door. The fastest route would be to take one of the catwalks, but it provided no cover. But if she could just make it to the next altar, twenty paces away, she would be covered again.

"Roiling inside him."

A spear of light shot down from the ceiling. Crystal spare her.

Analia hurled herself to the left, just in time. Then, she rose—no point hiding now—and vaulted over the second altar. Two more.

"I tried to absorb his magic myself, not wanting to waste an opportunity. But it utterly disobeyed me."

The mark on Accalon's neck. It had been so faint. Not from the Devourist, but from Deardryn trying to extract his magic herself.

Deardryn reached the first altar. She sent another spear of magic streaking toward Analia as she ran for the third altar. Analia tried to dive out of the way, but the spear grazed her shoulder.

Pain raced along her muscles, sending her crashing to her knees. Gritting her teeth, Analia crawled toward the third altar, the sound of Deardryn's unhurried footsteps coming closer.

"All that magic," Deardryn said. "And it went straight into you."

Analia's heart lurched. She barely managed to drag herself away from the next set of flying spears. But she reached the third altar.

"The reason you couldn't summon your magic before?" Deardryn said. "It's because you had none. You were empty. A leaky cup. But now?"

No, that was impossible. Magic had never been passed down like that before. Never.

But Analia's mind flashed back to Accalon's chambers, how she had felt something stir inside her. Something too hot to be her temper. And Analia felt her heart shatter.

She'd been right on her turret: it wasn't worth it. Not at all.

A spear of magic sliced down from the ceiling. Analia rolled, but that was exactly what Deardryn wanted.

A second spear blasted from Deardryn's hand, angling over the altar and down. Analia scrambled back. Right into the column of magic that had been waiting for her. And as the magic engulfed her, Analia didn't try to fight back her scream.

Aaron caught the demon's swinging bone on his dagger, a metallic thrum echoing in the garden. The Devourist had once again resorted to using its own rib as a weapon, moving almost too fast to track.

Aaron ducked another swinging blow, dancing back toward the border. He couldn't get too close, though. The Devourist would lose interest, and then it would charge after Analia. But it was taking every ounce of skill Aaron had to dodge the attacks without his magic.

Aaron caught another swinging blow, trying to step in close enough to stab its core. The Devourist slammed its foot into Aaron's knee.

Aaron dropped, catching its foot as it kicked toward his head. He yanked, toppling the demon, but it slashed at him with taloned fingertips.

Aaron rolled out of the way. He couldn't fight a creature whose whole body was a weapon; he couldn't get close.

Aaron's hand inched toward his damper chain. Could he risk it?

The Devourist charged. Aaron tried to twist out of the way, but he was too slow.

The rib slammed into his chest, sending him flying backward. He landed with a painful thud, rolling with the impact and coming up on his feet.

His mission, his people, his home. That was what mattered. And Analia was heading for that temple to get the scroll for them. For him.

The demon slashed at his face.

Aaron ripped off his damper, an explosion of silver light illuminating the garden and slamming into him as he dropped his damper in his pocket. Time to end this.

"What have you done?" Othin breathed, still kneeling on the floor. Dimitri's mouth went dry.

"Dimitri," Othin said sharply, rising to tower over him. "What is this?"

Dimitri dragged his gaze to the handful of ash and bone in Othin's palm. "Fine, I never actually cleaned his chambers."

"Did she kill him?" asked Othin quietly.

"Who?"

"Don't play dumb, Dimitri. My son is gone, there is a pile of ash under his bed, and a scorch mark in the middle of the floor."

Othin kicked aside the chest Dimitri had dragged over, revealing the damaged stone that had sat in the heart of Analia's flames—plenty of evidence elsewhere in the room. "Where is she, Dimitri?"

"You think Analia did this?"

"She's an Ash Royal!"

"With a shit's worth of magic."

"Until now, it seems."

Othin fell back to his knees, collecting what he could of Pryanth's ashes, tears glimmering in his eyes. Dimitri couldn't help but wonder if Othin would have cared as much if those were his ashes. Despite all of Othin's protests to the contrary, he doubted it.

Ignoring the kick to his gut, Dimitri rose from the bed, casually sitting on the desk beneath the entrance. Sunstones flickered behind him as Othin twisted to look at him.

"You know," Othin said. "You know she escaped through the passageways. You know what she did, and you were left behind to stall me."

Dimitri didn't respond. Othin's face clenched in anguish.

"I can't protect you from this, Dimitri," he said, ash sifting between his fingers as he brought his hands to his face. "You are an accessory to a Royal murder. I can't spare you from that punishment, from Pryanth's justice. Not if you don't tell me."

He took a step closer, and Dimitri leaned away. "Tell me where she went."

Dimitri dropped his gaze to his hands. They were calloused from years of servitude, of loneliness, of having to survive on his own. He'd done it for twenty years; he could do it longer. It would be preferable to the fate that would befall him if he didn't move aside, point his thumb over his shoulder and send Othin on his way. It wasn't like he was escaping either way.

Othin rested a hand on Dimitri's arm. Panic blasted through his insides. The panic that came from years of never being touched, comforted. Never learning those touches were comfort. Touches Analia and Aaron had learned to keep to themselves.

Dimitri drawled, "No idea."

Analia was encased in a cocoon of Sun magic, the light rapidly sucking her dry. She desperately tried to blast it apart with her lingering flames, but they refused to come. She needed far, far more training in order to wield them properly. As a result, she was trapped, helpless, as Deardryn advanced on her.

"The moment I sensed the magic go into you, Analia, I knew I needed you. You were the key I've been searching for."

Key to what? The magic snatched the thought away with sunshine claws.

"I had brought up the marriage pact the night before, completely cognizant that it would be shrugged off as ridiculous, but it would nevertheless redirect attention from Baylen. But then, it became the perfect idea."

She reached Analia, dismissing the magic with a wave of her hand. Analia fell to the ground in a crumpled heap, shaking so hard she couldn't move. She could still feel the traces of Deardryn's magic clawing through her insides, snatching with greedy hands until barely a spark remained. Accalon's spark.

Analia didn't try to fight her tears, dampening the polished wood beneath her cheek. She didn't try to escape as Deardryn knelt before her and lifted her head.

The queen's face was remorseless, disappointed if anything, but there wasn't enough of her left to care.

"Lev's attack didn't just win him to my side," Deardryn said. "It also established firm enough grounds for the marriage pact to be considered once more. And you did that negotiating for me. All that was left was Pryanth."

Deardryn briskly wiped the tears from Analia's face. And Analia realized she still didn't know.

Analia started to laugh. A furious, heartbroken laugh.

Deardryn's calm mask slipped. "What's so amusing?" she asked.

"Was it worth it?" Analia asked, still laughing. "Was your own son's life an acceptable price for your war?"

Deardryn's expression faltered. Analia reveled in it.

"You killed him?" Deardryn whispered.

"How's that for a trade?"

She couldn't feel the guilt or grief anymore. Only rage. Flames roaring their justice as Deardryn's face crumpled. She wanted her to hurt, to feel every stab of heartbreak that Analia had endured the past four months.

For a moment, Analia thought the Dragoness would break right there. Instead, her anguish twisted into wrath.

"You," she snarled. She shoved Analia away, her body slamming into the altar behind her. Analia forced herself into a sitting position, knowing what would come next.

Deardryn slammed her glowing hand against Analia's heart. Analia's back arched, a scream ripping from her throat as pain like she'd never known before blasted through her veins, her mind, slicing her awareness to ribbons.

But she didn't try to fight. She let the pain destroy her, piece by piece. Because this pain was nothing compared to the loss of her uncle, the realization that it was his magic flowing through her veins.

She didn't fight as Deardryn's magic found her spine, pressure building, building, building. It was almost over.

The door to the temple burst open. Deardryn whipped around. Analia crumpled as a new power stormed through the temple, carried on a mass of silver shadows.

"Impossible," Deardryn breathed.

Analia's entire body screamed as she lifted her head at the sound of slow, unhurried footsteps. And out of the haze of magic stepped the only remaining Star Royal in Elefthia.

# Chapter 60

A aron's heart stopped as he entered the temple. His magic snarled around him, responding to his absolute terror as he caught sight of Analia.

She lay crumpled before Deardryn, her skin so drained of color he could see the dark network of her veins. Motionless.

No. Not her, too. Gods, not her—

Analia struggled to lift her head. Her eyes searched through his magic, passing over his face, stained with the obsidian remains of the Devourist, finally finding his eyes.

Something clicked in Aaron at that moment. His knees threatened to give out, but he shoved all emotions aside, stepping out of his silvery veil with his cold, apathetic mask in place.

"Well," he said, rocking back on his heels, eyes doing a lazy flick around the temple, "this is cozy."

Where was the scroll?

"You." Deardryn's tone raised the hair on his arms. "You're supposed to be dead."

"I suppose you should have double-counted when you were slaughtering children."

Deardryn's face twitched. She stepped up to the railing that encircled the second floor, eyes flashing across his face. "A third," she breathed.

"Bravo." Aaron gave a smattering of sarcastic applause.

Deardryn's hands tightened on the railing. Behind her, Analia stirred.

"But that's impossible," Deardryn said.

"Were you expecting Queen Elspeth to joyously announce a pregnancy in the middle of a war?"

Deardryn ignored his sarcasm, her expression growing thoughtful. "Elspeth," she murmured. "I thought there was something vaguely familiar about your face. But you have the oddest mix of their coloring."

"Add a damper, and I'm practically unrecognizable."

Aaron winked, sending a blast of magic over her head toward one of the shelves behind her. Deardryn's eyes widened. She hurriedly raised her hand, knocking his magic aside with her own. Interesting.

She returned her attention to him, her gaze almost greedy as she leaned slightly over the railing. "This changes everything."

"You must have had quite the thrill," Aaron said. "Managing to completely erase that from history. Painting us as the villains after the Free Fall Wood, when you're the one who started that war."

Aaron's magic raked icy fingers across his skin. Magic he had used to strangle lungs, decay hearts, obliterate lives. But he wouldn't take another step in Deardryn's direction.

"And you believe two lives are worth an entire legion?" Deardryn asked.

"They were soldiers, not children," Aaron spat. "They chose to fight in that war. My siblings didn't choose to be kidnapped in the middle of the night."

Aaron sent a blast of magic behind him, not glancing at the golden spear Deardryn had tried to stab through his back. How fucking typical of her.

Deardryn said, "They had a chance to survive—"

Aaron's patience snapped. He sent a direct wave of magic slamming into her, Deardryn throwing up a golden shield just in time.

"You stuck my eight-year-old sister's head in a cage above the square's fountain," Aaron snarled. "Filling it with rocks, one by one until it dragged her head under. You tied a noose around my brother's neck and told him he could save her if he could reach the dagger to cut himself free. Just out of his reach."

Aaron's magic flared once more, this time to the side of Deardryn, backing her toward the steps. Analia rose to her feet, leaning on the altar beside her.

"You put a shield around them," Aaron said, his voice frozen with fury. "No one could get through."

Images flashed through his mind. All events he'd never seen, but nevertheless plagued his nightmares.

Deardryn. The new Queen of the Sun. Her idea.

Aaron could have sworn he caught Deardryn's composure crack. Yet, when he looked again, her expression was smooth, unreadable.

"And you're still holding this grudge," she said as she reached the stairs. "A century later. That's war, Aaron. It is on too grand a scale to be personal or indifferent. There's only victory and defeat."

"If that were true, you would have slit their throats." Just as he'd imagined doing to her, every gods-damned minute he'd been in this kingdom.

Deardryn said, "But would your mother's rage have been so acute? Would she have killed that legion and created the final push the rest of the kingdoms needed?"

Aaron slowly shook his head, almost in awe. But he didn't unleash his magic.

Deardryn's eyes narrowed. She spun around, just in time to see Analia step through the silver magic behind her, dagger plunging toward Deardryn's throat.

The next few seconds were a blur. Deardryn shoved Analia aside. Analia slammed into the railing. Aaron's magic blasted Deardryn down the stairs, but a column of golden light shot from the temple wall beside her, slowing her descent.

Aaron swore under his breath, drawing a dagger. He'd originally been trying to draw Deardryn away from Analia, allowing her to escape. But then Analia had flashed the dagger.

Aaron spared Analia a single glance, but she'd grabbed the railing, managing not to get flipped over. And below—

Aaron faded into the shadows as a wave of gold blasted toward him. He staggered out a few feet to the side, trying not to wince.

He'd been pushing it with his magic, the lasting effects of the damper still tugging on his network. But he only needed to last a bit longer. Just enough for Analia to make it down the stairs and out the temple—where was she going?

Dimitri counted the seconds before Othin called in the guards. Six swords. Dimitri cornered against the wall. Even if he managed to escape into the passageways, it would only be a matter of time before—

"Run," Othin whispered, tears in his eyes.

Dimitri gaped. "What?"

"Through the passageways. Go."

"But—"

"Guards!" Othin called.

Dimitri didn't stop to think. He whirled, slamming his palm on the stone, sliding it aside.

The door burst open behind him. The six guards poured into the chamber, but Dimitri didn't look back. He sealed the entrance shut behind him and took off down the passageway, ignoring the grief bubbling in his stomach. No time to think about that now.

Dimitri barely made it around the first bend when he heard the entrance open once more. The hunt was on.

The ground level exploded with silver and gold. The temple was filled with a deep vibration that Analia felt in her bones as she stumbled toward the scroll.

She didn't think of the bruises blossoming across her back in the shape of the railing. She ignored how Deardryn's magic still left her exhausted, trembling, and every inch screaming. Because Analia had heard the agony in Aaron's voice as he stalled for her. He'd removed his damper, revealing himself, putting everything he loved at risk. She couldn't fail him in return.

Analia stumbled past the second, then the third altar. Golden light blasted up from below, slicing through her path. She stumbled back, not bothering to summon her own magic. She'd made it this far without it. She didn't need it now.

Analia dragged herself across the final altar, tumbling to the ground on the other side. She was so close. Just a few more steps. But when Analia tried to push herself up, her arms buckled beneath her. She sagged back to the ground, choking on a sob.

She was so tired. Tired of the pain, tired of fighting, tired of holding herself together. But she'd stared at an unlit candle wick for twenty-two years. She'd risen again for fifteen. Her uncle had deemed her the strongest phoenix of all. And she couldn't give up now.

Analia's body protested with every movement, but she dragged herself to her feet. Then, a few excruciating steps later, Analia made it to the shelf. She stretched on her toes, reaching for the scroll—

"Analia!"

Aaron only had a moment to think as the shelf tipped toward Analia. He twisted, taking a blast of magic to the flank as he sent his own wave toward the shelf, slamming it back and sending the scroll and everything else flying.

Deardryn screamed in outrage. Aaron turned, just as a wave of magic blasted him across the temple.

Aaron's head cracked against the wall, something skittering away from him across the floor. He tried to fade into the shadows, but he could feel his magic burn to ash inside him. He was trapped within Deardryn's magic; pinned under the agony of her slicing through his organs, smashing his bones to splinters, healing and destroying him, over and over again.

There was a part of him that wanted to submit to the power, the promise that this pain would end.

But Aaron had been trained in the Underground. He'd learned to fight through darkness, pain, even against death itself.

Aaron slid the rest of the way to the floor. He rolled onto his stomach, barely evading the next wave of magic that slammed into the wall where he'd been a moment before. Choking back a groan, he dragged himself into the shadows once more, Deardryn's cry of vexation plunging after him.

Gods, she was too quick, sending blast after blast, not having to work with a half-functioning network. But Aaron had seen how she carefully kept her distance. He just had to find an opening to get in close with his dagger.

Analia clutched the scroll to her chest, having just managed to catch it as Aaron's magic sent it flying. She ran her fingers along the aged parchment, clasped shut with seven rings that thrummed with magic. Royal magic.

Analia didn't have time to contemplate. She staggered to her feet, ready to bolt, ribs screaming with every shallow breath. She dared a glance down, and her heart froze.

Deardryn stood across from Analia on the first level. She had backed herself up against the wall, her eyes scanning back and forth, Aaron nowhere to be seen. Not until he stumbled out of the shadows on Deardryn's left.

Deardryn spun to face him. Right as Aaron slid his dagger beneath her arm and between her ribs, her movement just enough for Aaron to miss her heart. He quickly withdrew his blade, a blossom of scarlet spreading across the white of Deardryn's gown. He tried to back away, but Deardryn slammed her palm against his chest. Magic erupted from her hand, sending Aaron flying backward, crashing into the door.

"No!" Analia screamed, her voice drowned out by the raging vibration of Deardryn's magic as wave after wave slammed into Aaron.

She waited for him to try and shadowjump, roll away, do something. But Aaron remained slumped, unmoving, blood trickling from his nose.

Analia's hands tightened around the scroll. There was only one reason he would remain so still. He had no magic left to help him do otherwise.

He had known it was a risky move; it was the risk of wielding a dagger. Aim for the vitals, but that meant exposing your own. But he had done it anyway. For her.

Analia tore her gaze from Aaron, her tear-blurred vision landing on the damper box. She still didn't know why Deardryn had collected the magic. But Deardryn didn't act without reason. And Analia wouldn't let that reason come to fruition.

Analia tucked the scroll in her belt beside Aaron's dagger. Then, she stepped onto the catwalk. She'd managed to make it to the central conjunction point when another blast of gold struck beneath her feet.

Analia gasped, half jumping, half falling toward the nearest catwalk as the ground gave way beneath her. Her hands slammed into the catwalk's railing with jarring impact. But without its proper support, the narrow walkway snapped beneath her weight, sending her tumbling.

Analia had a momentary feeling of freefall. She knew there would be no surviving impact, not with the speed at which she was moving. She would smash on the ground below. Her final mark on the world, the same it had always been: close, but not close enough.

Finally dead, right alongside Aaron. Dimitri, too, if she had to guess. Both dead or dying, all because of her—no, not because of her. *For* her.

Analia closed her eyes. She reached for that well inside her, finally filled. Then, screaming between gritted teeth, Analia sent a blast of magic crashing downward.

The force of her black flames slamming into the ground was nowhere near the impact of Aaron's or Deardryn's magic, but it was enough to throw her upward. Analia reached out as far as she could. Her hands slammed into the second-floor railing with bone-cracking force, but Analia hauled herself up and over, shuddering at the crash of the catwalks hitting the ground.

Analia rolled to her feet, reaching for the damper box on the nearby shelf and flinging open the lid. She tore through the contents, finding the Ash ring.

Yanking it out, Analia squeezed the ring in her palm. She didn't think. She simply focused all her lingering magic into the ring, feeling it burn hotter, hotter, hotter.

The ring cracked.

Fire erupted outward from her palm, the vivid red of Baylen's magic. It flashed across the wooden shelves and floor, devouring them in seconds, sending Analia crashing to the level below. And this time, there was no magic to save her.

Analia hit the ground with a thud, the wind whooshing out of her lungs as several cracks radiated throughout her body. No time for pain. No time to recover. Not as the Devourist, trapped inside the ring, stepped out of the flames before her. Impervious to the last flickers of midnight flame she managed to summon, it charged through, tackling Analia back down and clamping its mouth down on her neck.

# Chapter 61

Dimitri's heart pounded in his ears as he skidded around corners, his pursuers close behind. He would've been dead by now if he had to so much as hesitate before taking turn after turn, slamming into walls, sending a throbbing ache across his nose, his forehead, his shoulder. He just had to make it down two floors and then a few turns and he would be at the exit, and he could lose them outside.

"There's nowhere you can go, Dimitri!" one of them boomed behind him. "You might as well surrender."

Dimitri's breath raked through his lungs. He grabbed one of the hidden ladders on his right, sliding down the side bar and immediately taking off once more. If he was lucky, he had been far enough ahead that they hadn't seen him go down the ladder—

Dimitri cursed as he heard the thud of landing boots behind him. He zigzagged through corridors: left, right, right again. No.

Dimitri skidded to a stop, face-to-face with a dead end. How had he gotten turned around? It was supposed to be a ladder here, unless—he'd missed the third left. Crystal spare him.

The bootsteps drew nearer. Dimitri had ten seconds at most. There was no time to turn around. There was only an alcove to his right, a closed entrance to his left.

Eight, seven.

A wild idea entered Dimitri's mind. So unbelievably stupid it would definitely get him killed if it failed, but it might just work.

Footsteps rounded the final bend. Dimitri slammed his palm on the entrance.

Five seconds.

He felt the click beneath his palm.

Three, two.

Dimitri slid the entrance open. Then, he dove back into the alcove, just as the first guard came into view.

Dimitri flattened himself against the wall, praying he was hidden in the shadows. He held his breath as the first guard charged down the hall, then paused. It was fifty-fifty which way he looked first. Left or right.

Dimitri's nails dug into the stone. The guard's eyes landed on the entrance. "He's out there!" he called back, shoving through the entrance.

Dimitri didn't dare move as the rest of the squad hurried into view. One, two, three of them followed their leader out. Four was halfway through the entrance, the last about to follow him, when he suddenly glanced back. And his eyes met Dimitri's.

"Sir!" the guard bellowed. "It's a—"

Dimitri darted forward. He rammed the guard with his shoulder, sending him toppling into the fourth soldier still in the entrance. They staggered, falling through the entrance. Dimitri grabbed the stone and slammed it shut. And before the first guard could so much as hammer on the wall, Dimitri was running once more. Finding the right turn. Falling down the final ladder. Bolting out of the castle side door.

Dimitri burst into the night-coated Sun Kingdom, his skin sticky with sweat. He darted through the shadows, one eye on the distant darkness where he knew soldiers patrolled. But he made it to the tree line.

Dimitri doubled over, gasping for breath. What in the name of the Crystal had he gotten himself into? What in the name of the five gods was he supposed to do now?

Dimitri slumped back against a tree, his feet sliding on the leaf-strewn ground until he was seated on the roots. There was no going back to the castle. Not when he was a known suspect in Pryanth's murder. Gods, all of this for one little princess?

But it was that little princess, and later her obnoxious guard, who'd shown him that while he had thought he could never miss something he'd never had, that didn't mean he didn't yearn for it. They showed him there were people willing to stick around, even when he was too afraid to let them.

And it was those people Dimitri headed for as he hauled himself to his feet and stumbled off into the woods.

Analia was back outside Accalon's chambers. She watched as Brenn fumed, as Accalon deteriorated.

*Dying,* the Devourist whispered in her mind. *All alone. Because you walked away. Duckling.*

Analia didn't try to fight this time. Instead, she let the grief tear through her insides, smashing her to pieces, grinding them to dust, to ash, floating on the wind. And Analia reveled in it.

She could feel the Devourist's confusion. It froze the memory, stretching out Accalon's collapse. *How did you not notice? How did you not hear it in his voice?*

Because that voice's last words to her had not been to keep his pin safe. *Love you, little fledgling.*

The Devourist snarled. And Analia shoved right back.

Images flashed across her awareness, almost too fast to register. Rois when he told her he had chosen the guard. Ember grinning as she played her harp. Cadmus, always glancing away. Aaron holding her together as she sobbed on her turret.

She felt it all. The grief, the joy, the heartache, the affection, the loneliness—every emotion she'd locked away for the past fifteen years roiling to the surface in a chaotic wave.

But Analia didn't try to stay afloat. She was tired of running from the inevitable. Instead, she turned and opened her arms as the agony took her under.

The Devourist screeched, trying to clutch her tighter. But there was no fear to paralyze her as she tumbled through the currents. No despair to force her into submission.

The temple began to materialize around her. But the demon had one last card to play.

Analia's heart froze as the Ash Castle entryway formed around her. Brenn stood talking with the Crystal Guard, his red hair slightly longer, sporting a long, dark gray jacket that was in style fifteen years before.

*Remember this?* The demon's icy whisper skittered down Analia's spine as she watched herself and Cadmus, seven and four respectively, tumble into the entryway. Cadmus managed to skid to a stop, but Analia bounced off of Kuno's armor-clad leg.

He steadied her, amused as he bowed and playfully tugged one of her braids. Behind him, Brenn scowled.

"You two must look where you're going," he said.

"Apologies, Father," Cadmus said, unbothered as Brenn beckoned them to his side and placed a hand on each of their shoulders. Young Analia went completely still.

"Well," Brenn said, "if you insist on stealing our attention, you might as well put it to good use. Cadmus, show the guards the technique you just learned."

Cadmus squirmed as the guards looked to him expectantly. He raised his hands, forming a ball of golden flame between his palms. The guards applauded politely, and Cadmus blushed. Analia's younger self paled.

"And you, Analia?" Brenn said. "Would you like to show them your magic?"

Analia whipped her head back to look at him, but he only gestured for her to begin. She frantically looked for help, but the guards only waited, Cadmus's gaze fixed to the ground.

"Well?" Brenn asked. "What are you waiting for?"

Analia tried to look away, but the Devourist cackled.

Seconds bled into minutes. The guards shared puzzled looks.

"Summon your magic!" Brenn finally demanded, his hand tightening around Analia's shoulder.

"I..." Her younger self blinked back tears.

"Why won't you do it?"

"I... I can't."

Shock.

Analia's lack of magic had been kept quiet until then. No one had known. And judging by the red creeping across Brenn's cheeks, the conjured look of embarrassment, he, too, pretended to have no idea.

"What do you mean, 'you can't'?" he asked slowly.

Analia's tears spilled free. "I don't have any magic," she whispered. "I can't do it. I'm... I'm sorry."

"Sorry?" Brenn asked softly.

Terror flashed across Analia's face. She tried to jerk away from Brenn's grip, but he held her so tight that a hand-shaped bruise later appeared on her shoulder.

He turned to the guards, all of whom looked utterly uncomfortable. "She has no magic," he repeated, as if in disbelief.

Analia could repeat his following speech verbatim. How he was shocked. How it was a complete embarrassment. How he had no idea what to do now. His heir, magicless? How could she keep this from him until now? How could she disappoint him like this?

Analia was forced to watch as the guards' expressions morphed. Pity for Analia. Sympathy for Brenn. Disgust for the situation Analia created. Disgust that would later transform into jeers and open disdain under Brenn's careful prodding because that was what he had wanted all along.

A way to twist Analia's defect into sympathy for himself, not something that could be blamed on him. The unwitting victim of a secret that would inevitably get out. Saving his own reputation before it could at his own child's expense.

By the time Brenn had finished, both versions of Analia were sobbing, wrapping their arms around themselves to create what little shield they could against his words. But nothing could withstand the blow of his final seven words: "You're the worst decision I ever made."

The memory froze, locking onto Analia's anguished expression. Analia could see her younger self shut down, reaching a level of pain that couldn't be processed. And Analia finally shattered completely.

Pain—there was no other word for it—tore through her insides, released after fifteen years, leaving nothing but devastation in its wake. Utterly rejected by the one person she thought was supposed to love her. But that had never been Brenn.

It took everything Analia had to sink into that pain, to not fight back. Somehow, she let the memory play on.

Analia finally wrenched out of Brenn's grip. She flew up the stairs, not looking where she was going, just having to move, faster and faster until she stumbled onto the roof. But that wasn't good enough.

Analia hurtled toward the nearest turret, digging her nails into the stone. At first, she immediately slid back down, unable to get a proper hold, but she couldn't stop. She had to be high. High as she could. Above everything that happened below.

Analia finally made it to the top. She curled into a ball, feeling herself shudder apart at the seams as she sobbed. She didn't know how much time had passed when she heard someone climbing up the turret.

No, no, she couldn't do this again. She couldn't see the contempt in Brenn's eyes, the disappointment on the guards' faces.

Accalon pulled himself up a moment later. She had never seen him so close to losing control before. Blue flames licked across his shoulders, lighting the fury in his eyes.

Before Analia could speak, he sat beside her, pulling her into his lap, holding her so tight she could barely breathe.

"I'm sorry," he whispered, rocking her as she cried into his shoulder. "I'm so, so sorry."

Accalon held her for a long, long time. Even when Analia's tears trickled out, he did not let go. Even when she plucked up the courage to ask, "Do you hate me, too?"

Accalon flinched. He took her chin in his hand, forcing her to look at him. "Never," he said fiercely.

The memory shattered. The Devourist fought for control, but memory after memory of Accalon flooded her awareness. The day he presented her with her gilded harp. The times they had snuck off to the forges to hide from angry councilmen. The countless hours they had spent on the turret, the stars sparkling above their heads.

Shard after shard sliced through her heart, but they also began to smooth. Finally, she landed on a memory she didn't immediately recognize. She couldn't have been older than four, standing beside Accalon at the Phoenix Gate.

"A piece of me," he said.

Her younger self studied the gate. "Where?"

"Right in its chest," Accalon said. He lifted her in his arms, high enough that she was almost level with the massive phoenix. "Can you reach?"

Analia stretched, just managing to touch her fingertips to the phoenix's heart. "I can!"

"Excellent!"

Analia beamed. She snuggled back against Accalon's chest, and he kissed the top of her head.

"And you, too, will always have a piece of me," he told her.

"Like a finger?"

Accalon laughed. "No," he said, touching her chest. "A piece in here. A tiny flame. When I'm here, and when I'm gone."

Analia looked up at him in alarm. "But I don't want you to go."

"I'm delighted to hear it," Accalon laughed.

He knelt to the ground, remaining at eye level as he set Analia back on her feet. "Just remember, little fledgling. If you hold the flame too tight, too close, it will burn. But that warmth is why we keep it alive: to drive away the chill of when it's gone."

He pulled her close. "I love you, Analia. And I will always keep you warm."

The Devourist howled. The temple fuzzed back into existence, the Devourist still on top of her, trying to latch back on.

But Analia was no longer burning, no longer numb. She was warm.

Analia whipped Aaron's dagger from her belt, plunging it through the Devourist's rib cage, straight into the shining core in its chest. The demon reared back, but Analia moved with it, sending every last spark of her magic, Accalon's magic, into its core. The Devourist wanted her magic? It could have it.

The core glowed, brighter, brighter, brighter. The Devourist screamed.

Finally, the core erupted in an explosive flare of light. The demon shattered apart in a cloud of obsidian that coated her skin. Analia coughed, her ribs screaming.

But there was no time for injuries or pain. No time for the exhaustion that had her wishing she could collapse right there.

She was still in the temple. Deardryn was still here. Aaron—oh gods.

Analia whipped her head from side to side, blood pumping through her veins. All she could see was scarlet flames. Deardryn must have used her magic to dim the stone. She was coming. Coming from anywhere. She had to be ready.

Analia planted her shaking hands on the ground. She'd barely struggled to her feet when her knees gave out, a sob of panic building in her throat as the floor rushed toward her. She couldn't go down. It wasn't safe. This wasn't over yet.

But her knees never made contact. Arms wrapped around her middle from behind. And before Analia could so much as flinch, there was a voice in her ear.

"It's all right, Anna, you're safe. It's just me."

Analia's relief was overwhelming. It washed over her like the tide, leaving nothing in its wake. Not even the strength in her muscles as she breathed Aaron's name.

"It's all right," he said, catching her as she sagged in his grip. In one fluid movement, he shifted her up into his arms. "You're safe. I promise."

Analia brought shaking hands to her face, faintly surprised when her fingertips came away damp.

"Just hold on tight, Anna," Aaron murmured.

Analia did. Not just to Aaron as she pressed her face to his shoulder. But also to the tiny flame she found in her chest. Her uncle's flame. One she now knew she could take out in the darkest and the coldest moments.

"I've got you," Aaron whispered.

And Analia believed him as they faded into the shadows.

# Chapter 62

Cool night air kissed Analia's sweaty skin. She peeked over Aaron's shoulder, recognizing the moonlit clearing she had found after their first visit to the garden. But Aaron didn't pause.

He took two steps back, sinking down on a fallen tree trunk. Settling Analia sideways on his lap, his eyes darted over every bruised, obsidian-stained inch of her.

"Are you all right?" he asked.

It took Analia a moment to force out the words. "Broken wrist. Magically drained. Fractured ribs. Definitely hit my head when I fell, but alive."

Aaron gingerly pulled her close once more, pressing his face into her hair.

"I saw it," he breathed. "Those flames distracted Deardryn long enough for me to dive clear. But Analia, I saw it grab you. It latched onto your neck, and you went completely limp, and then its core glowed brighter and brighter."

Aaron shuddered. "I tried to get to you, but Deardryn got in my way. And she somehow put out the light and managed to escape. And by the time I reached you—"

"I'd already killed it," Analia said, voice muffled against his chest.

"And before that, I thought it killed you. And before that, I thought Deardryn killed you." Aaron let out a shaky laugh. "You keep it up, Analia, and you won't have to push me off the roof to off me."

"I thought she killed you, too," Analia whispered.

"She almost did. Turns out, fighting with a near-depleted network wasn't a good idea. Who would have thought."

"But you're all right?"

"Alive, at least."

Analia sagged against him. She could feel his heart pound beneath her ear, keeping time with her own. But she could also feel his network, power thrumming around her in a smooth, sliding rhythm.

"You took off your damper," she said, her uninjured hand brushing Aaron's neck. "I told you not to, it wasn't worth it. Why did you do it?"

Aaron hesitated. "Let's just say I saw what was important."

Analia opened her mouth, but no words came out. Ignoring the pain in her wrist, she tightened her arms around his neck. "You idiot."

Aaron laughed once. He touched her hair as if to say he understood, then reached for his tattered cloak.

"The damper's gone if it makes you feel better." He returned his arm around her. "It must have fallen out of my pocket at some point."

"Well, there's no getting it back now."

"Doesn't matter," Aaron sighed, turning his head so his cheek rested against her hair. "There's no getting the scroll, either."

"What do you mean?"

"The scroll. It was on the shelf I blasted away from you. It's gone."

"Aaron, no, I got it."

Aaron pulled back to stare at her. "You what?"

"I got the scroll."

Analia moved to sit on the trunk beside him, every exhausted inch of her whining in protest. She pulled the scroll from her belt and handed it to him.

In the stunned silence that followed, Analia finally got her first good look at him in the moonlight. His leathers were falling apart, revealing the dark shirt and pants he wore underneath. Blood crusted around his nose and chin. But his eyes...

The silver had already been startling with the damper on. But now removed, his magic had them sparkling like actual starlight.

Those eyes looked up, locking on hers with something far deeper than gratitude. Just for a moment, they dipped down. Then, he pulled her into a quick hug, careful of her ribs as he whispered, "Thank you."

Aaron released her, his attention back on the rings. He was definitely puzzled as he fingered the rings, but there was something else. Something that had her heart squeezing.

"I didn't know about your family," she said quietly.

Gods, she couldn't even fathom how excruciating it must be. Not just losing his family in that way, but then to have it completely erased. Never able to get justice, only left to be the undisputed monsters.

"There's nothing we can do about that now," he said, looking away as he tucked the scroll in his belt.

"I'm still sorry."

Aaron looked up at her. Just as there came the sound of approaching footsteps.

Aaron could have sobbed with exhaustion as his decades of training kicked in. He reached for Analia, every thought on escape. Just as Dimitri stumbled into the clearing, looking thoroughly annoyed.

"Finally!" he exclaimed, plopping down in front of them. "I've been looking for you two forever. Have you any idea how hard it is to wander through these woods, in the dark, without a magic magnet? The least you could have done is sent up a flare—"

"Dima!" Analia slid off the trunk as if to hug him, but her hand flew to her ribs.

Aaron followed her to the ground, slumping back against the trunk. They needed to find a healer—they needed to get out of the Sun Kingdom. But where would they go?

Not wanting to take a single step down that road, he focused on Analia as she asked Dimitri what happened.

"Othin found the remains," he said. "I had to escape through the passageways."

Aaron asked, "Does he suspect?"

"Uh, yes. Flashfire here isn't exactly the most ambiguous of killers. You should probably work on that."

Analia flinched, her hand going to the lump in her pocket. Before Aaron could inquire, he felt Dimitri's eyes land on him.

Aaron's nails dug into the rotting trunk behind him. Every instinct screamed for him to slam the lid on his magic shut, hide, protect his secret.

But Analia knew. Deardryn knew, for that matter. There was no point in hiding. More importantly, he didn't want to hide. Not from Dimitri. So, heart pounding, Aaron let his power thrum.

Dimitri sat back on his heels. "So," he finally said. "Star Royal?"

Aaron nodded.

"You're what, master of death or something?"

"I suppose."

Dimitri considered. "Well, all right then."

Aaron's jaw dropped. "That's it?"

Dimitri turned to Analia. "I told you he's too pretty to be a guard."

Analia snorted. Aaron felt oddly lightheaded.

He'd spent so much time fretting about not just Analia's and Dimitri's reactions, but anyone's reaction. He'd known for so long that he was the undisputed monster that he'd given up on hoping for any other type of reception.

Yet, Dimitri didn't care, didn't even seem fazed. And Analia...

With a jolt, Aaron realized that the look on her face on the turret hadn't been fear. She had been startled. Betrayed. But never afraid. But that hadn't stopped him from shoving her away. And that hadn't stopped her from coming back.

"Let me guess," Dimitri went on. "Flashfire found out first, you got all moody about it, and neither of you were able to pull your heads out of your asses until earlier tonight."

"Something like that," Aaron said.

"Typical."

Analia blushed and dropped her gaze. Aaron nudged her, quietly reminding her they were good. Even though he knew a piece of her would always regret what happened on that turret. Just as a piece of him would regret it, too.

Aaron turned back to Dimitri, unable to help himself. "You know, I must say, I'm a bit disappointed with your reaction, Dima. I had all this buildup for months now, and all I get is an 'all right, then'? Not even a particularly sharp joke about my family history?"

Aaron spread his leaden arms wide, waiting for Dimitri to take the free jab. To his surprise, Dimitri only picked at the grass.

"I will judge you on everything else, Bordello," he said, "but a fucked-up family is off the list."

Aaron slowly lowered his arms, exchanging a look with Analia.

"Speaking of fucked-up families," Dimitri went on, "what happened in the temple?"

That was a fantastic question. Aaron turned to Analia, who rubbed her eyes.

"Well," she said, "that story is not completely finished yet."

"What do you mean?" Aaron asked.

"We have one last stop to make tonight," she said, offering him her uninjured hand.

Aaron took it without hesitation, acutely aware of how her fingers slid between his. Crystal spare him. He extended his free hand toward Dimitri, who leaned away.

"We're only shadowjumping, Dima," Aaron said. "I promise, I'm not looking for anything serious right now."

Dimitri wrinkled his nose, reluctantly taking Aaron's hand. "Where are we going?" he asked.

"To the Ash Kingdom," Analia said. "There are a few more people who need to hear this story, and I don't want to tell it twice."

Aaron lightly squeezed her hand. Then, having a feeling of just who she was talking about, Aaron mustered the last of his magic and pulled his friends into the shadows.

# Chapter 63

The sky was just lightening to dawn as Analia climbed the Ash Castle steps. Her injuries were mostly healed, but she still had to fight back her exhaustion. With every step, however, she could feel herself slipping into a state of preternatural calm, solidifying as she entered the Throne Room.

Shadows collected around the edges of the dark stone chamber. The walls were carved with ancient lava flow lines, highlighted by the flickering Everflame light. Accalon had always spent as little time in the room as possible, finding it horribly gloomy. Yet, Cadmus had informed her that Brenn spent every free moment in the chamber, seated upon the slick obsidian throne placed in the center of the room.

Indeed, he sat there now, head bowed, dressed in a dark gray jacket, the orange-gold buttons shaped like soaring phoenixes. He didn't look up at the sound of Analia's footsteps, his right hand absently rubbing his left wrist as he muttered to himself.

Analia paused at the foot of the throne. She watched her father in silence, that familiar tangle of emotions rising to the surface. But she nudged them back down with a gentle hand as she cleared her throat.

Brenn looked up. His hands quickly dropped to his sides, something odd in his eyes. "Duckling? Who let you in?"

"I've come to give you my final report," she said.

Brenn gave an exaggerated eye roll. "Analia, I already told you, Accalon wasn't murdered. He killed himself."

"I'm aware."

"So, you've returned to tell me I was right?" Brenn snorted. "More likely you've returned because Deardryn sniffed you out. Is that it? You failed to solve Accalon's case, and you failed to stay where I put you. Honestly, Analia, can you do anything right?"

Analia remained silent, hands clasped behind her back.

"I don't suppose you managed to wriggle free without exposing why you were there," Brenn went on, filling the silence. "Should I be expecting a war on my doorstep? You've made a mess, and are now running home with your tail between your legs, hoping I'll fight for you?"

Brenn stretched, shoving his crown back into place. "You're lucky it's me on this throne, duckling, not my brother. That man refused to fight, even when it was necessary."

"Yes," Analia said. "You said that when we discovered Baylen's body."

"And then look what happened! I swear, if Accalon had just attacked Sun, we wouldn't be in this mess." Brenn huffed. "Sometimes, the best form of compromise comes with a sword tip."

"Or a serving of wine," Analia suggested.

Brenn went perfectly still. "What are you talking about, duckling?"

Analia met her father's eyes. "I'm talking about how you poisoned my uncle."

Brenn stared. And stared. Then, he laughed.

Analia kept her face smooth, but she couldn't stop her hands from squeezing tighter behind her back. She could feel the years of resentment boiling in her stomach, heated by the fury that had been ignited back in Deardryn's temple.

Who stands to gain the most from a king's death? His successor.

The man who had tormented Analia for years, that had taken her people's respect from her, her confidence, her worth. And now, he'd taken her uncle. The one thing she thought he could never snatch away from her.

Betrayal wasn't a strong enough word for her own blood slicing her so deep. But Analia didn't explode. Instead, she watched, waiting.

"Duckling," he finally said, wiping a tear, "I knew you were magicless, but I didn't think you were completely stupid."

"You were the one who told me Accalon was using xenol," Analia said. "Cadmus can attest to that."

"Yes, yes, I told you. He was my brother. We didn't keep secrets."

"Which is also why you were overheard speaking about Accalon's clandestine monthly meetings. Procuring xenol?"

"Who overheard that?"

"You admit there was something to overhear?"

"I already told you I knew about the xenol," said Brenn. "Good luck trying to survive the leap between knowing and killing."

"You knew he was using xenol," Analia said, forcing her voice to remain steady. "You knew why he was using it and what it did. You were his confidant, and yet you conveniently forgot to tell Ronun any of this."

"Because I wanted to keep you in Sun," Brenn said, shifting restlessly. "Analia, this is nothing new. Go to your chambers, I'll deal with you later."

"You know what you also told me?" Analia said, taking a step closer. "You told me you knew I would never succeed in Sun. You were waiting for me to fail. And with my inevitable failure, there would come a war. The very thing you were advocating for when we found Baylen's body. Proving to everyone that you had made the right call, the inevitable call, that day on the border."

"Are you trying to vilify me for wanting justice?" Brenn demanded, his temper starting to crackle.

"You're saying this is all true?" Analia verified.

"Of course it is! But Accalon said no, and he was my king, so we didn't."

"Forcing you back into the shadows," Analia said. "Not getting your way, once again. Did that sting, Father? Feeling powerless? Feeling like you didn't matter?"

"Don't mock me, duckling," Brenn warned, shoving himself to his feet and taking a step toward her.

A midnight spark flashed up between them. It quickly winked back out, a sharp pain lancing across Analia's neck. Brenn took a step back, eyes widening.

"I'm not mocking you," Analia said softly. "I'm empathizing. I know exactly how that feels. You shoved me down to the pathetic level you felt Accalon had pushed you into, just so you could try and claw your way back up."

She took a step closer, her voice whisper soft. "But that didn't work. You were still in the shadows. You were still unseen. And Accalon dismissing you in front of the guard was your breaking point.

"You poisoned him with his own plant and pinned it on the Sun Kingdom, getting you your war, your justice, and the vindication you felt you deserved."

She was so close she could feel Brenn's ragged breaths on her cheek.

"I didn't realize the Sun Kingdom was full of storytellers," he said.

"And I didn't realize the Ash Kingdom was full of backstabbers."

"You have no proof that it is," Brenn said, pushing her away from him. "You have no one who will believe you and your tall tale."

"You ordered the drinks," Analia said, not flinching away from the heat that pulsed off Brenn. "You ordered the wine in Accalon's mug—"

"To ease his nerves—"

"To react with the xenol and to force it into lethality—"

"That plant isn't lethal."

"Not on its own, maybe," Analia said. "But Accalon stopped drinking wine as soon as he started taking xenol because he knew the wine would increase its potency. He knew that when xenol runs out of magic to absorb, it attacks the life force. And if he told you about everything else, like you claim, he would have told you this, too."

"Why are you so convinced I would kill him?" Brenn asked. "He was my brother!"

"And he was my uncle!"

"Well, maybe it's about gods-damned time you joined him, then."

Brenn's hand shot out, grabbing Analia by the throat. He squeezed, fingers burning, his temper flaring hotter than Analia expected.

"He was my brother! My brother! And you're going to stand here condemning me? Like I enjoyed what I did? He was endangering our kingdom! I had no choice!

"It was his own gods-damned fault. My brother focused too much on being a beloved king. He didn't realize love doesn't stop someone from stabbing you in the back. I did what was best for the kingdom—"

"For yourself," Analia mouthed.

Brenn's voice boomed off the walls, "I had to kill him!"

The doors burst open. Brenn shoved Analia away, the shape of his fingers burned into her throat. Analia coughed, gratefully sucking down air as Aaron and the soldiers she had instructed to wait outside marched forward.

"What's this?" Brenn demanded.

"Your confession," Analia rasped. She put a hand to her burning throat as the Ash Crystal Guard converged on her father.

Cadmus stepped up beside her, the orange threads in his gray tunic catching the light from his flickering flames. He took Analia's hand, and her fingers hesitated to curl.

After Aaron had jumped them to Ember's apothecary, it had been a disaster. Aaron had promptly gone unconscious, having far surpassed his magical limits on top of his extensive list of injuries from Deardryn. Analia and Dimitri couldn't hide who he was at that point from Ember and Cadmus—who had just returned from their interrogations of Wae.

But after that chaos had been sorted out, Cadmus hadn't left her side as Ember healed her and Aaron. Not perfectly—Ember didn't have all the required rings to do so—but enough Analia that could tell that night's story. Enough that she felt mostly steady on her feet as she confronted her father.

Before she'd left, Cadmus had pulled her aside. And tears in his eyes, he apologized for the past fifteen years.

"After seeing how far Father could bury his own child," he said, "I was terrified he would do that to me, too. I... I was a coward, at your expense. And I know it doesn't change anything, but I'm truly sorry."

Fifteen years of resentment churned in Analia's stomach. A part of her wanted to tell him it was too little too late; that if he was truly so distraught, he would've done something sooner.

But then, a still-exhausted Aaron came up behind her and poked her in her ribs. "Come on, grudgy, you know you want to forgive him."

Analia squeezed her brother's hand. She could have sworn his shoulders slumped slightly. Then, he straightened once more, his eyes the cold ice of their mother as he looked to the guards struggling to restrain Brenn.

"Enough!" Brenn boomed.

Orange flames flashed around him, and the guards lurched back. Brenn lunged forward, reaching for Analia. Aaron grabbed him by the throat and yanked him back.

"You will never touch her again," he said in Brenn's ear, his voice terrifyingly cold.

He spun Brenn around and stomped hard on his foot, Brenn wailing as his bones snapped.

"Take him," Aaron said, shoving Brenn at the guards. Then, not sparing them a glance, he crossed to Analia and gently lifted her chin.

"Gods, Analia," he breathed. His fingertips whispered over the burns on her throat, Analia barely noticing.

She watched as Brenn was dragged out of the chamber, the doors slamming behind him. Somehow, despite everything they'd been through, that tie to him in her gut remained. A part of her thought it always would. Especially now.

She distantly felt Cadmus release her hand, saying he would go with the guards. Analia thought she nodded, but she wasn't sure. All she knew was the thoughts that repeated over and over in her mind.

It was him. He did it. He killed Accalon. His brother, his king. Her everything.

He'd sat at that council table, silent, as Accalon drank to his demise. And then he had the audacity to wail over his corpse.

"Analia?" Aaron said uneasily. "What's that look on your face?"

It was all his fault. The past four and a half months of fear, manipulation, and the hot, relentless agony in her chest she had tried to suppress for so long.

Accalon was dead. Her father had done it. Her eyes shifted over Aaron's shoulder, landing on the empty obsidian throne. And it was all for that.

"Anna," Aaron said.

Analia marched around him. She climbed the dais steps, pressure building behind her ribs.

It was all for the throne. And Analia sent a vicious kick into its side, letting out something between a scream and a sob.

"How could he?" she choked out, sending another kick into the throne. "How could he, how could he, how could he, how could he."

A crack appeared in the base of the throne. Arms wrapped around her from behind, pulling her off the dais. Analia struggled, but Aaron only drew her close.

"I know," he soothed, resting his cheek against hers. "I know destroying that throne feels like the only thing you can do right now, and I would let you if it weren't for the scandal. But if you want to break something, we'll have to find you something else."

Analia blinked hard. She knew he was right. But it still took her several moments to catch her breath, even more to fall still.

Finally, she eased back against Aaron's chest, focusing on the throne in front of her. She could still feel that pain thundering through her chest. But she forced herself to take a slow, deep breath, letting that pain be until it faded into something heavier than exhaustion.

"He's dead," she said, her voice breaking over each word.

Aaron sighed, his hand running down her arm. "He's dead."

For the longest time those words had rattled through her chest like a loose pebble. But now, she finally felt it settle inside her. Accalon was dead.

"Aaron," she said, not looking back at him.

"Yes?"

"I think... I think I'm ready to wallow now."

"Good news," he said. "You've already started."

Aaron gently turned her to face him. And a tremor of relief moved down her body as he drew her close once more, his arms mercifully tight around her. Analia wrapped her arms around his neck, pressing her cheek to his chest.

She could feel the silent rush of tears behind her eyes. Yet, there was no urge to suppress them. No fear of losing control as the first one slipped free. This wasn't grief and agony. It was a release. And Aaron gave her something to hold on to all the same.

For a long, long time, they remained before the empty throne, Aaron's embrace melting into something tender. Something Analia couldn't bring herself to pull away from. Because it was there, his steady heartbeat beneath her ear, that for the first time since her uncle's death, Analia felt completely safe.

# Chapter 64

T he following days were a storm of meetings, confusion, and councilmen with heads dangerously close to exploding.

After Brenn had been escorted from the Throne Room, he'd been promptly locked away in the castle dungeon. Even though Analia had gotten a confession out of him, there would still be a long road of trials ahead. One that, regardless of the outcome, left the Ash Kingdom without a ruler in the meantime.

In the scramble, Analia, Cadmus, and Aeley were all granted temporary authority. Consequently, it took a week for Analia, Aaron, Dimitri, and Ember to gather in the apothecary back room. Cadmus would have joined as well, but he was busy filling in for Analia in the Ash Castle's political chaos.

"I still think I should be the one to go to Moon," Ember said. She'd shrugged off her healer robes, now dressed in a pale blue shirt and black pants, her light brown hair loose around her shoulders.

"Em, we've been over this," Analia said, seated on the edge of her desk. "I know you can explain the complexities of xenol, but accusing Deardryn is a complete violation of your healer oath."

"I haven't technically sworn it yet."

"But you're only one ring away," Analia said.

Ember made a face, scratching the latest white ring that had been inked around her eye. Her medical mystery marking.

"It's not an accusation if the Old Hag admitted it," Dimitri pointed out. He stood behind the desk, unabashedly poking through Ember's drawers—she'd given up yelling at him to stop after the fifth time.

"An admission only I heard," Analia said. "Besides, Em, the main thing we need to warn them about is her hunting with the Devourist, which lies outside your jurisdiction."

"But they still deserve to know about Patryclas," Aaron murmured from where he leaned against a shelf, dressed in a simple black tunic and pants.

Analia ran a hand through her hair. They'd been going round and round for so long. Everyone agreed they had to warn the Moon Kingdom—it was the one form of magic Deardryn didn't have in ring form. Well, that and Ash, although Analia had already made sure her kingdom was on guard. And Aaron—she had no idea how Deardryn would go about getting Star magic. Gods, she didn't know why Deardryn wanted the magic in the first place.

"We could write a letter," Ember suggested half-heartedly.

"Too risky," Aaron said. "There's no way to make sure it gets into the right hands."

"And there's no telling what might happen if the wrong hands get it," said Analia.

"Fine, I'll go," Dimitri sighed.

Analia's eyebrows shot up. "Since when were we trying to convince you?"

"You weren't," Dimitri said, closing a drawer and coming to perch on the other side of the desk. "But I figured it was inevitable and I was getting bored."

"Dimitri, you don't have to do this," Analia said. "Our bargain is fulfilled."

"I know, I know. But now that I'm out, what else do I have going on?"

For a moment, their eyes locked. A lump rose in Analia's throat. She let her hand hover over Dimitri's on the desk, quietly telling him she understood, he didn't have to say it.

Dimitri's face twitched, and he quickly looked away.

"It's not going to be a quick stroll to Moon and back," Aaron warned him. "Sylas won't be inclined to listen to you. He still thinks Deardryn saved Patryclas, and he has no reason to believe you."

"Let alone talk to you," Ember muttered. She shoved Dimitri's feet off her chair.

"I can handle a grumpy old man," he said, immediately kicking her chair instead. "Bordello can jump me to their castle, we can bicker for a few days, and it will be fine."

"Well."

Dimitri's eyes narrowed. "Well, what, Bordello?"

"I can't exactly jump you to the Moon Castle," Aaron admitted. "I've never stepped foot in Moon territory, so the closest I can get you is the Star Castle."

"You're joking!" Dimitri exclaimed.

"There's still time to back out," Analia said.

Dimitri grumbled under his breath but didn't retract his offer.

"Well," Ember said, "if you're going to be talking about both the demon and xenol, we are going to have to study."

"Study!" Dimitri sounded like Ember had just requested half the blood in his body.

"Yes, study," Ember said. "You are going to be representing me and all my work. So, you are going to study and make sure I come off as the brilliant, fabulous healer that I am."

"I'm not allowed to name you."

"But it's still my work! And it's Anna's mission, so I'm not going to let you muck it up by sending you off to ramble to the Moon King about things you hardly understand."

"Oh, bite me, scratchy."

"Kiss my ass, shorty."

"Oh gods," Analia muttered.

"I'm not going," Dimitri said, folding his arms.

"Oh yes you are," Ember said, rising from her seat.

"You can't make me—ow!"

Ember grabbed Dimitri by the ear, yanking him off the desk and marching him away. The two bickered back and forth, their voices cut off by the closing door.

Analia sighed. Aaron wore the dawning look of a child who just received a gift he never would have expected.

"Usually," he said, "I would be placing bets right now. But I don't think either of them are walking away at the end of this."

Analia muttered, "I'm just waiting to be informed that they had to be separated in the streets by a passing guard."

She hadn't been expecting the two to clash so thoroughly. But Dimitri's utter lack of caring who he offended, combined with Ember's propensity for forming incredibly fast—and long-lasting—opinions? Well, Analia was just glad Ember was sworn to healing, and Dimitri was too lazy to go through with most of his threats.

Aaron laughed. He pushed himself off the shelf and came to join her on the desk.

"How's your mark?" he asked, eyes drifting to the raised collar of her embroidered gray jacket. She'd taken to wearing it the past week, not because of the light chill in the air, but rather to hide the slowly fading black circle on her neck.

"Alive and thriving," she sighed.

She knew from experience it would take a while for her magic to completely return to her. A part of her had hoped that after killing the Devourist, her magic would return to her network, similar to removing a damper. Yet, a week later, not only could Analia barely sense any magic—Ember's in particular—but she could barely produce a spark. Not that she was trying.

Aaron leaned toward her. "Is this the part where I kiss it better?"

Analia shoved him back. "Knock it off."

Aaron gave her a wicked grin. Analia tried, but she couldn't maintain a straight face.

"Do you think warning Moon will be enough?" she asked, leaning against the wall.

Aaron's grin faded. "It's better than doing nothing."

"I just wish I knew what she was doing."

"We just have to take it one step at a time."

"But she's so many steps ahead."

"And we will catch up."

How was he so sure? How was he so calm when Analia could feel the anticipation slicing through her insides? Anticipation and—

"Analia," Aaron said in a singsong voice, "you've got the look again."

Analia tore her gaze from Ember's devinroot box, the lid left flagrantly open. "No, I don't."

"Yes, you do. And now it's mixed with your 'Aaron's being annoying' look."

Analia rolled her eyes. Aaron lightly nudged her with his knee. "Come on, what's wrong?"

Analia hung her head. "Deardryn had an Ash ring," she said. "I thought by destroying it, I was setting her back a step, I was giving Baylen... justice? I don't know. But if she still needs an Ash ring, did I just reattach a target to my family's back? Did I just make Baylen's sacrifice meaningless?"

Aaron let out a long sigh. "That," he said, "I don't know."

Analia swallowed hard. Just the thought of Deardryn returning to her kingdom, hunting down Cadmus when things were finally starting to mend between them. Or gods, sweet, innocent Lucilla.

Aaron put a hand on her cheek, turning her face to his. "What I do know," he went on, "is that even if all of that is true, at least you're now prepared. You know to be careful, to watch your backs. And because of that, Deardryn is going to have a far harder time regaining what you took from her."

Analia squeezed her eyes shut, wanting to believe him. But she couldn't shake the unease prickling along the back of her neck.

For a few moments, she allowed herself to sit with that fear. Then, she let it settle back into the background.

"You're right," she said, opening her eyes and leaning out of Aaron's grip.

"Of course I am," he replied, settling back against the wall, pride in his eyes.

Analia let the quiet settle for a few moments.

"Have you figured out what the scroll says?" she asked.

Aaron made a face. "Well, that would require opening the scroll, and it doesn't seem inclined to do that any time soon."

"Why would it?"

Aaron laughed, unperturbed. "Oh, Analia," he said, playfully tugging her hair, "there's never a dull moment when you're around."

"Don't remind me," Analia grumbled, swatting his hand away.

Aaron caught her hand, suddenly serious once more. "You know what's coming, don't you?"

Analia's lips pursed. Yes, she certainly did. And she was not prepared in the slightest.

# Chapter 65

Analia was starting to hate council meetings.

The Council Chamber had been abuzz with the six councilmen's droning voices for two hours now, discussing everything from taxes, to clan squabbles, to, well, Analia stopped paying attention at that point. Instead, she studied the paintings on the walls of King Hester and Queen Elspeth.

Aaron truly did have the oddest muddling of those two. His father's eyes, but several shades darker. His mother's messy dark hair, although hers was black, whereas Aaron's was brown, hints of lighter browns and golds coming out in the sunlight. Definitely not the sandy brown of his father's. But he did stand like them.

"And your say, Princess?"

Analia's gaze snapped back to the table. Councilman Ganze stared at her expectantly, his tiny eyes trying hard not to look down his thin, pointed nose.

"My say?" she asked.

Ganze let out a pointed sigh. "To your ascension."

Analia's stomach dropped. She had been waiting for this moment. Her temporary joint power was just that, temporary. She knew they would want an official—what? Interim queen? Regent? Regardless of the title, she was next in line.

"Is that what you wish?" she asked, eyes moving from face to face, taking in the anticipated disgruntled expressions. Part of her expected one to pipe up about some nonsense legal clause so they could wriggle their way out.

"I agree," Cadmus said to her left. "I don't know why we're even discussing this."

The councilmen shifted. While Cadmus still remained his solemn, quiet self outside the Council Chamber walls, something seemed to pass over him once he stepped through the door. Something that had his always straight back relaxing, not having to fake his confidence anymore. And the councilmen were seemingly struggling to adjust.

But though they awkwardly shuffled their papers, it wasn't solely out of resignation.

"Are you sure you want a magicless ruler?" Analia asked, leaning back in her seat.

"You're not magicless," Ganze said, surprised.

"And you're next in line," added Councilman Laird begrudgingly.

"And you brought our king's killer to justice," said Councilwoman Marie.

"It's obvious," Cadmus finished. "You are our next queen. At least for now."

Analia waited for the burst of joy; the giddiness at finally, finally earning back the respect that had reluctantly settled in the councilmen's eyes. Instead, she pushed back her chair and rose to her feet.

"I'll consider it."

Analia strode toward the door, her footsteps echoing in the silent chamber. She pushed it open, and voices exploded behind her. But she let the door close behind her with a thud.

Analia wandered through the castle. She spotted the stairs that would lead to the roof, but she didn't pause as she walked past. Instead, she descended into the entryway, passing out the castle doors and heading down the winding path toward the Phoenix Gate.

Summer was coming to a close around the Ash Kingdom. A cool breeze ruffled Analia's hair as she reached the Phoenix Gate, her head tipped back to examine the phoenix at its top. *A piece of me.*

Analia removed her pin from her gray-and-black jacket. She popped off the top of the phoenix, looking down at the tiny pinch of ash she'd stored inside one last time. Then, she tilted the pin, letting the ash gently fall before getting swept up by the breeze.

"Rise again, Uncle," she whispered.

The breeze was cold against the two tears that trailed down her cheeks, but Analia didn't wipe them away. She'd expected this moment to hurt, and it did. But it was more of an ache, one of built-up pressure being alleviated, leaving her feeling lighter than she had in months.

Analia peered down at the small black stone in her pin, pulsing with a faint magic field. Puzzled, she tried to pry the stone free, but it remained locked in place.

Analia glanced up at the Phoenix Gate and shook her head. "I never could quite understand you, Uncle," she murmured, reassembling the pin and attaching it to her jacket.

"So, when are you going to tell them 'I'll consider it' means yes?"

Analia didn't glance back. "What makes you say that?"

Aaron stepped up beside her. "Because I know you. And because you're down at your uncle's gate and not on the roof."

Analia smiled faintly.

"How are you?" Aaron asked, sliding his arm around her shoulders.

Analia leaned her head on his shoulder. "Heartbroken. Grieving. Drained. But otherwise all right. And you?"

Aaron grimaced. He'd been staying out of sight as much as possible the past few days—which clearly hadn't stopped him from eavesdropping on their meeting. But Analia could still feel his tension from having to maintain such a tight control over his magic.

"Surviving," he sighed. Glancing around to make sure none of the sentinels were too close, he carefully let his hold on his magic slacken.

Analia slid her arm across his back. For a long time, they stood like that, neither quite sure who was holding who up.

"They're only willing to accept me as their queen because I now have magic," Analia said. "They say it's because I'm next in line, because I solved Accalon's murder, whatever else.

"But I've been gone for four months. They have no idea who I am anymore, how I may or may not have become someone worthy of that respect. They just know that now, I have magic."

"A magic you wouldn't have if your uncle hadn't died," Aaron said, his hand curling around her shoulder to play with her pin.

Analia breathed through the stab of grief. "It's not worth it," she whispered.

Aaron sighed. "I know."

Analia brought her hand to her phoenix pin, her fingers brushing Aaron's. "The point," she said after a moment, "is nothing has changed. They respect my magic, not me, and honestly, I'm too tired to care."

"Does that mean you're not going to take the crown?" Aaron asked, stepping back to look at her fully.

Analia looked up at the Phoenix Gate, at the distant sentinels, trying to covertly watch her. Through the bars, out to the kingdom beyond.

"This kingdom meant everything to my uncle," she said. "These are his people. He gave everything he had to this kingdom, and in four months alone, Brenn nearly burned it to the ground. But even if he hadn't, this is my birthright."

"And no one is going to stop you from taking it."

Analia nodded, feeling for Accalon's tiny spark in her chest.

"They're stuck with me," she said. "Whether they want me or not. Especially since this is the best position for me to deal with Deardryn."

"This game certainly isn't over, is it?" Aaron said, eyes lost in thought.

"No," Analia said. "It certainly is not."

Analia loosely gripped the curving metal rods of the gate, watching the kingdom life beyond. She knew Deardryn would be coming for her. Not just because of Pryanth, but because of the comment she'd made, something about Analia being the key.

Key to what, though? Did it have to do with her sensing abilities? Why was she able to still sense the different magics? And how could she find out before Deardryn could strike? She had too many questions, but at least there was one she could answer.

"So," she said, turning to face Aaron once more, "when are you leaving?"

Aaron's head jerked in surprise. "What makes you say I'm leaving?"

"Because I know you, too."

Aaron chuckled. "The funny thing is," he said, stepping closer and lowering his voice, "the longer I stay, the less I want to leave."

Analia shoved him. "Don't be an idiot! You haven't seen your family in months. You can see me any time, Aaron, go to them."

Analia expected Aaron to make some retort, at least flash his usual smirk. What she wasn't expecting was his flicker of—was that disappointment? Before Analia could be sure that's what she saw, his expression cleared.

"I know," he said, "you're right. I should actually be leaving right about now."

"Oh."

She'd meant it when she told him to go be with his family. But now that it was real...

"Hey."

Analia looked up. Aaron pushed up the sleeve of his thin black jacket, revealing a bracelet woven from enka flowers.

"Take this," he said, sliding the bracelet off his wrist and offering it to her. "If you need me, just call out. If you're wearing the bracelet, I'll know."

"How?" Analia asked, sliding the bracelet on her own wrist.

"Magic, Analia."

"That's helpful."

Aaron laughed. "Tell you what. You use it, and then I'll let you know. Although, I will warn you, this magic might be a little finicky. I had to split it in half so I could give one to Dima. Knowing him, he'll probably toss it in a sewer grate just to spite me."

Analia's mouth twitched. Aaron had shadowjumped Dimitri to the Star Castle earlier that day. He'd allowed her to give him a quick hug in farewell, the only thing more shocking being what her returning senses told her in that brief moment. Then, he clambered up on his horse that Analia prayed he actually knew how to ride, and they were gone, Analia's heart aching.

"Dima won't throw it away," she said. "He might refuse to wear it, but he'll keep it."

Aaron snorted. Then, there was a pause. A quiet. And in the same moment, they reached for each other.

"I hate goodbyes," Analia said into his chest, breathing in metal and spice.

"Oh, Analia darling," Aaron said, smile audible in his voice, "I'm offended you think you can get rid of me so easily."

"What is this, then?"

"How about... see you later. Until next time? 'Til we meet again? Analia, I'm not going to stop until I see you smile, and it's all downhill from here—there you go."

Aaron leaned away, just enough to touch his fingertips to the corners of her mouth. "Five hundred and three."

"You were actually counting?" Analia asked.

"Of course I was." Aaron gave her a smile of his own, although it was far softer than Analia had ever seen before. Then, he pulled away, and Analia had to fight the lump rising in her throat. He glanced over his shoulder, checking the sentinels weren't watching.

"Rise again, Your Majesty," he said quietly, sketching a genuine bow. Then, with a final wink, he faded into the shadow of the Phoenix Gate.

Analia watched the spot where he disappeared, knowing she would see him again, his absence nevertheless leaving a dull ache in her chest. Just one of many aches and pains that had been dragging down her insides ever since fleeing the temple. But Analia would have plenty of time to start putting herself back together again.

Analia straightened. She would give the council their answer. But first, she had more pressing matters, including an incredibly disorganized healer and a harp.

Smiling at the sentinels—"No, you must have missed him as he left"—Analia passed through the gate. As she headed off into the kingdom, the dying rays of the sun struck the Phoenix Gate, setting the gold ablaze as its shadow stretched out behind her like a pair of wings.

Rise again.

# Ready for More?

Want to read Aaron's reaction to learning what Pryanth did in chapter 39, plus his recount of the moment he first saw Analia in the Ash Kingdom?

Download your free bonus chapter by subscribing to my newsletter at www.abigaile hrhardt.com.

# Author's Note

I've written out several drafts of this author's note at this point, with each version being perfectly acceptable. Yet, none of them feel right. I think it's because there are so many things I want to say, so the idea of condensing it all into a single statement seems... daunting? Impossible? But at least I have one straightforward thing to say: thank you.

Thank you for picking up this book. Thank you for taking a chance on me. Thank you for reading far enough to reach this point. I hope you enjoyed the ride as much as I enjoyed writing it—and wow has it been a long time.

While the version of KOMAM you have in your hands didn't come about until around June 2021, many of its quintessential pieces have been floating around in my mind for much longer. I think the first time they truly started to fit together was in 2017 during my junior year of high school—more specifically during precalc when I started creating character profiles instead of filling out my worksheets... Oops. But that's when I first started to get to know Analia, Aaron, Dimitri, and so many of the characters you've either met or will be meeting soon.

Even some of the key elements of this world were born in that class, including the once seven, now six kingdoms, Aaron's identity, and some secrets that you've yet to discover. But the one thing that always evaded me was the story itself.

Part of the problem was I didn't know how to construct a plot in the first place. The other problem was I was looking at this story solely from a fantasy perspective.

So, I tucked all of these ideas away until February 2021, when I read A Court of Thorns and Roses by Sarah J. Maas for the first time—yes, I know, I was late to the game. But that series is what made me realize my two major missing pieces: the magic system, and the romance. And about four months later, this series finally started taking shape.

By the time I started writing, it was the busiest part of my junior year of college. Yet, the timing just felt right. I think it wasn't until that point that I not only had the skill and perspective to write this book, but the readiness to do so—in more ways than one. These characters and I had a lot of growing up to do to reach this point.

But now, we're here. And speaking of these characters: Analia and Aaron. Those two didn't end up where you were expecting, huh?

Don't worry, their story is far from over. Same with Dimitri, Ember, and everyone else. We still have five books to go in this treacherous, secretive world, which means we're only just getting started.

So, if you enjoyed this first part of the journey, it would mean the world to me if you'd consider leaving a review on Goodreads or Amazon. You have no idea how much even a star rating, a single sentence, helps us authors. If you're also interested in being the first to know about book news, releases, new art, and all other kinds of fun stuff, consider joining my newsletter at abigailehrhardt.com.

For now, I'd just like to say thank you one more time, and I can't wait to see you in book two: Kingdom of Smoke and Starlight, coming soon.

# Glossary

**The Ancient Ones:** three dark, malevolent beings that ruled over Elefthia during ancient times.

**Ash Kingdom:** founded by Azar Valarus, this kingdom is ruled over by the Ash Royals and is known for its forges, creativity, and volcanoes, specifically Mt. Vasolus.

**Ash Royal:** descendants of Azar Valarus—one of the Defiants and rulers of the Ash Kingdom. All are Blessed with fire magic, which can range in a variety of colors.

**The Belt:** a string of volcanoes located in the Ash Kingdom.

**The Bend:** a network of drug dens, brothels, and other nefarious businesses on the outskirts of the Sun Kingdom.

**Bless:** the act of bestowing Blessings.

**Blessed:** the humans—and their descendants—whom the Crystal gifted magic to. All Blessed are guaranteed to have an extended life span, faster healing, and heightened strength and reflexes, as well as the same magic as their parents. It's a fifty-fifty chance for either magic if both parents have magic.

**Blessing:** a word that has become synonymous with a person's magic, extended life span, faster healing, and heightened strength and reflexes.

**Copper fleck:** the smallest unit of currency.

**The Crystal:** the Ancient Ones' most powerful weapon. Translucent and palm-sized, the Crystal is responsible for magic flooding Elefthia, bestowing Blessings, and sealing away the Ancient Ones. At some point during Talitha's reign, it disappeared.

**Crystal Guard:** existing in all kingdoms, the Crystal guard is made up of the seven strongest warriors in each kingdom, charged with protecting the Royals.

**Damper:** created from onyx, after various carvings and charms, a damper can act like a magical plug, drawing all of a person's magic to itself and not releasing it until removed. The longer the damper is worn, the longer it takes for the magic to return.

**Darmanten:** one of the five major gods, he is the god of day and night.

**The Defiants:** seven humans that stepped up during the war against the Ancient Ones, ultimately sealing the Ancient Ones away, enabling the Crystal to release magic into Elefthia, and founding the seven kingdoms.

**Demiblessed:** those with one Blessed, one human parent.

**Devinroot:** a plant that grows off of magic and is a highly addictive stimulant.

**Devourist:** the demons that made up the majority of the Ancient Ones' army.

**Elefthia:** the name of the continent the once seven, now six kingdoms are found on.

**Elladine:** one of the five gods, she is the goddess of death and younger sister of Rosala and Kierra.

**Enka flowers:** a flower whose magic can create communication pathways between people.

**Everflame:** a flame created by Azar, which cannot be extinguished and provides the majority of the Ash Kingdom's magically powered light.

**Ferrin:** one of the five gods, he is the god of time and prophecy.

**Gold piece:** the highest unit of currency.

**Gritta's:** a drug den in the Sun Kingdom.

**Healers:** Blessed, Demiblessed, and, in extremely rare cases, humans, that have been chosen by Rosala to receive healer magic from the Crystal. Healers swear vows of celibacy and political neutrality.

**Healer markings (sometimes referred to as "markings" or "rings"):** the rings inked around a healer's eyes, which depict their level of training. There are four rings: herbology, internal, external, and mystery, which are marked in white as apprentices, but turn the healer's kingdom's colors upon completion of their apprenticeship.

**Human:** while Royals, Blessed, Demiblessed, and healers are all human, the term has predominantly come to refer to magicless humans, or to the race as a collective.

**Kierra:** one of the five gods, she is the goddess of life, and older sister of Rosala and Elladine.

**Magic network:** the internal network that a Blessed's or Demiblessed's magic runs through.

**Mist Kingdom:** founded by Noelani Sai, the Mist Kingdom is ruled by the Mist Royals and is considered to be the most devout of the kingdoms.

**Mist Royal:** descendants of Noelani Sai—one of the Defiants—Mist Royals rule over the Mist Kingdom. All are Blessed with water magic.

**Moon Kingdom:** founded by Mahina Ruanega, the Moon Kingdom is ruled by the Moon Royals and is known for its bogs, tattoos, and secretive people.

**Moon Royal:** descendants of Mahina Ruanega—one of the Defiants—Moon Royals rule over the Moon Kingdom. They possess Blessings that allow them to manipulate darkness—although they are intentionally vague about what that specifically entails.

**Mt. Lanula:** one of the three major mountains of Elefthia, located in the Wild Lands.

**Mt. Raegyr:** one of the three major mountains of Elefthia, located in the center of the Star Kingdom.

**Mt. Vasolus:** one of the three major mountains of Elefthia, Vasolus is a volcano located in the Ash Kingdom.

**Nymphs:** appearing incredibly human-like outside of their slit pupils and pointed ears, nymphs derive their life source from a specific plant—although they have a general affinity for all plants.

**The Phoenix Gate:** the gate in the center of the wall surrounding the Ash Castle, created by King Accalon Valarus during the early years of his kingship.

**Rosala:** one of the five gods, she is the goddess of healing, and older sister of Elladine, and younger sister of Kierra.

**Royal:** the descendants of the seven Defiants and rulers of the once seven, now six kingdoms of Elefthia.

**Sand Kingdom:** founded by Theistan Rubarena, the Sand Kingdom is ruled over by the Sand Royals, and is known for its red deserts, and general practice of not using animals for work or food.

**Sand Royal:** descendants of Theistan Rubarena—one of the Defiants—Sand Royals rule the Sand Kingdom. They are Blessed with earth manipulation.

**The Serpent's Tail:** one of the three major rivers of Elefthia, which runs from the Wind Kingdom at the northeast, down to the Sun Kingdom, southeast to the Mist Kingdom, and then southwest to the Moon Kingdom.

**The Shattering:** the climax of the seven-year war between the Star Kingdom and the six kingdoms. The Star Royal line was completely eradicated after Royals from all six kingdoms sent a deadly blast of magic through the Star Castle, so powerful that King Hester's bone fragments were all that survived. This effectively ended the Star Kingdom's rule over the other kingdoms.

**Silver chip:** the unit of currency valued higher than a copper fleck, and lower than a gold piece.

**Solemnai:** a celebration that happens every three months in the Sun Kingdom. The tradition was started by Queen Deardryn Oshar to help bridge the gap between the commoners and Royals.

**The Solstice Ceremony:** occurring once a year, the Solstice Ceremony takes place at the foot of Mt. Raegyr. Here, the reigning Royal from each kingdom releases a blast of magic into the ground to maintain the magic flow across Elefthia.

**Soul gate:** the Soul Gate can only be opened on the Summer Solstice and the days following and preceding. Each gate can only be opened by the magic of the reigning Royal, and permits direct access to the Star Kingdom where the Solstice Ceremony takes place.

**Star Kingdom:** founded by Talitha Stelingente, the Star Kingdom was once ruled by the Star Royals. After the Shattering, it became the one piece of neutral ground the six kingdoms could gather on.

**Star Royal:** descendants of Talitha Stelingente—leader of the Defiants—and rulers of the Star Kingdom. Star Royals are given the Blessing of death.

**Sun dragon:** dragons that are exclusively found in the Sun Kingdom. Their bodies are long and serpentine, covered in scales in varying shades of gold that are as strong as steel. They have small, white wings, short, stubby legs, and large, golden eyes.

**Sun Kingdom:** founded by Helia Oshar, the Sun Kingdom is ruled by the Sun Royals, and is known for its research, scholars, and library full of forbidden texts.

**Sun Royal:** descendants of Helia Oshar—one of the Defiants—Sun Royals rule over the Sun Kingdom. Their Blessings revolve around the life force, enabling them to heal the minds, souls, life forces, and magic networks that healer magic cannot reach.

**Sunstone:** golden fist-sized stones that can sense Sun magic and glow in response. They provide most of the magic-based light in the Sun Kingdom.

**The Unleashing:** the moment that the Defiants procured the Crystal and used it to release magic into Elefthia for the first time.

**The Wild Lands:** the southernmost section of Elefthia, where the Crystal dumped all of the Ancient Ones' dark, malevolent power. It is wisely left alone as a result.

**Wind Kingdom:** founded by Raiden Cruchendai, the Wind Kingdom is ruled by Wind Royals, and is known for its mountains and cold temperatures.

**Wind Royal:** descendants of Raiden Cruchendai—one of the Defiants—Wind Royals rule over the Wind Kingdom. Their Blessings revolve around air manipulation.

**Xenol:** a mysterious plant that has seemingly been lost to time... or perhaps purposefully erased.

# Acknowledgments

Sitting down to write these words might be the most surreal, unnerving moment in my entire book journey thus far. For the past two-and-a-half years, I've written, revised, deleted, rewritten, and overthought this book so many times that at some point, it became a comforting routine. But now, this is the last thing I have to do. KOMAM is... done?

So, thank you, dear reader, for picking up this book. And an enormous thank you to everyone who has made it possible for you to do so.

First and foremost, I need to thank Kylee. Not only were you the first person to read KOMAM's questionable first draft, but you have also become my hype woman who has done so much for me that I have nowhere near enough room to thank you. You'll never know how much it meant to me every time you complained about how much work you had to do because you just wanted to keep reading.

I also have to give massive thanks to my unbelievably talented beta readers. KJ, my logic/spelling/grammar/punctuation/sanity checker, a fountain of "How the fuck do you know that?" knowledge, and the incredible human that patiently listened to me as I overthought paragraphs... and sentences... and individual words. Marlena, my master of lore, integration, and character arcs, president of the Aaron fan club, and provider of the most entertaining reader reactions. Vikki—Auntie Vikki, what didn't you do? Not only did you also read a questionable early draft, but you helped proofread, became my art consultant, and never failed to ask what my thoughts were first before giving your own.

Finally, Brian, the catcher of minute details, and the person who not only reminded me that I do, in fact, have a well-thought-out story, but also called me "Kingslayer" for an entire day after reading chapter 5 (an absolute honor).

I'd also like to give an overwhelming thank you to my editor, Noah. We had a bit of an adventure with this one, what with my delivery schedule and refusal to have consistent capitalization. Thank you for being absolutely wonderful to work with. I'd promise to do better with book 2, but I think we'd both know I'd be lying.

I also want to thank my incredible proofreaders, Sarah and Clara. Sarah, you're officially the Crowned Queen of Punctuation, made even more impressive by everything you had going on while paying such careful attention to these pages. Clara,  thank you for being absolutely lovely to work with. Someday I'll understand semicolons.

Moving along to my designers, thank you so so much to Liz from Raven Pages Design for the dust jacket, paperback, and eBook covers, as well as the interior art. This definitely turned into a labor of love, and I had an absolute blast going back-and-forth with you. And just look at the final results! Massive thanks to Maria Spada as well for the stunning under jacket design. I still have no idea how you managed to get so much symbolism in one design.

I also have to thank Kenna, who, for some reason, hasn't gotten sick of me in the past eleven years and has done some truly random things to help with KOMAM. In addition to Kenna, thank you Christi, Cynthia, and all of my friends who have been so invested in KOMAM that sometimes, I think you all are more excited about it than I am. I appreciate you all tremendously.

To wrap this up, I want to thank my immediate family. I feel like the moment you decide to be a writer, you're bracing yourself for someone to tell you all the reasons why that's a bad idea. Instead, all of your reactions ranged from excitement to "Well duh." Jake, you told me in the middle of me secretly drafting KOMAM that you always thought I was going to be a fantasy author and knew I had drafts hidden away somewhere, and brother dearest, it felt like you electrocuted me (I say with love). Bonus thanks to Oompa for all of the little signs and well-timed encouragements (even though it always took me a hot second to put them together).

Finally, thank you, Mom, for doing everything in your power and then some to make sure I could reach this point (including literally putting a ruler to a computer screen during design and formatting consultations). I hope this book made you proud.

# About the Author

Abigail Ehrhardt has been writing absurdly elaborate stories since she was nine years old, to the point her teachers had to confine her plots to forty-five minute time frames. It still didn't help. Now, her stories are just as fantastical, just as intricate, but (hopefully) a lot easier to follow.

As a baby, Abigail was diagnosed with bilateral retinoblastoma, a rare cancer of the retinas. After having one eye removed and the other severely damaged, she quickly realized books were her key to unlocking a world that was no longer designed for her. Now, she writes stories of her own, featuring a healthy dose of magic, romance, and wounded dreamers.

You can find her in Connecticut, where she's probably hoarding nail polish, adopting far too many plants, and becoming more emotionally attached to the side characters than protagonists of whatever book she's reading.

instagram.com/abigailehrhardt.author/

facebook.com/profile.php?id=61553660026246

tiktok.com/abigailehrhardt.author